Critical Approaches to Children's Literature

Series Editors: **Kerry Mallan** and **Clare Bradford**

Critical Approaches to Children's Literature is an innovative series concerned with the best contemporary scholarship and criticism on children's and young adult literature, film, and media texts. The series addresses new and developing areas of children's literature research as well as bringing contemporary perspectives to historical texts. The series has a distinctive take on scholarship, delivering quality works of criticism written in an accessible style for a range of readers, both academic and professional. The series is invaluable for undergraduate students in children's literature as well as advanced students and established scholars.

Published titles include:

Cherie Allan
PLAYING WITH PICTUREBOOKS
Postmodernism and the Postmodernesque

Clare Bradford, Kerry Mallan, John Stephens & Robyn McCallum
NEW WORLD ORDERS IN CONTEMPORARY CHILDREN'S LITERATURE
Utopian Transformations

Alice Curry
ENVIRONMENTAL CRISIS IN YOUNG ADULT FICTION
A Poetics of Earth

Margaret Mackey
NARRATIVE PLEASURES IN YOUNG ADULT NOVELS, FILMS AND VIDEO GAMES
Critical Approaches to Children's Literature

Kerry Mallan
SECRETS, LIES AND CHILDREN'S FICTION

Andrew O'Malley
CHILDREN'S LITERATURE, POPULAR CULTURE, AND *ROBINSON CRUSOE*

Christopher Parkes
CHILDREN'S LITERATURE AND CAPITALISM
Fictions of Social Mobility in Britain, 1850–1914

Michelle Smith
EMPIRE IN BRITISH GIRLS' LITERATURE AND CULTURE
Imperial Girls, 1880–1915

Forthcoming titles:

Elizabeth Bullen
CLASS IN CONTEMPORARY CHILDREN'S LITERATURE

Pamela Knights
READING BALLET AND PERFORMANCE NARRATIVES FOR CHILDREN

Susan Napier
MIYAZAKI HAYO AND THE USES OF ENCHANTMENT

Critical Approaches to Children's Literature
Series Standing Order ISBN 978–0–230–22786–6 (hardback)
978–0–230–22787–3 (paperback)
(outside North America only)

You can receive future titles in this series as they are published by placing a standing order. Please contact your bookseller or, in case of difficulty, write to us at the address below with your name and address, the title of the series and one of the ISBNs quoted above.

Customer Services Department, Macmillan Distribution Ltd, Houndmills, Basingstoke, Hampshire RG21 6XS, England

Secrets, Lies and Children's Fiction

Kerry Mallan

First published 2013 by
PALGRAVE MACMILLAN

Palgrave Macmillan in the UK is an imprint of Macmillan Publishers Limited, registered in England, company number 785998, of Houndmills, Basingstoke, Hampshire RG21 6XS.

Palgrave Macmillan in the US is a division of St Martin's Press LLC, 175 Fifth Avenue, New York, NY 10010.

Palgrave Macmillan is the global academic imprint of the above companies and has companies and representatives throughout the world.

Palgrave® and Macmillan® are registered trademarks in the United States, the United Kingdom, Europe and other countries.

ISBN: 978-1-137-27465-6

This book is printed on paper suitable for recycling and made from fully managed and sustained forest sources. Logging, pulping and manufacturing processes are expected to conform to the environmental regulations of the country of origin.

A catalogue record for this book is available from the British Library.

A catalog record for this book is available from the Library of Congress.

For Sue

Contents

List of Illustrations

Series Preface

The Critical Approaches to Children's Literature series was initiated in 2008 by Kerry Mallan and Clare Bradford. The aim of the series is to identify and publish the best contemporary scholarship and criticism on children's and young adult literature, film and media texts. The series is open to theoretically informed scholarship covering a wide range of critical perspectives on historical and contemporary texts from diverse national and cultural settings. Critical Approaches aims to make a significant contribution to the expanding field of children's literature research by publishing quality books that promote informed discussion and debate about the production and reception of children's literature and its criticism.

Kerry Mallan and Clare Bradford

Acknowledgements

This book began as a small idea when I was attending the International Research Society in Children's Literature Congress in Frankfurt in 2009. Sitting alone one night in the hotel courtyard, I decided to look occupied and so started to map out an idea for a book about secrets and lies. Along the way from that initial private musing in a country far from home to the publication of this book I have been the recipient of much generosity, encouragement and helpful criticisms. The difficulty in writing acknowledgements is that given the vagaries of memory the list will undoubtedly be incomplete.

I should begin by thanking the many colleagues who directly and indirectly offered comment, showed interest or suggested texts to read. These include the Critical Dialogues group at Queensland University of Technology; the conference delegates at the Girls, Texts and Cultures symposium at the University of Winnipeg, the Australasian Children's Literature Association for Research (Canberra), the International Research Society for Children's Literature (QUT, Brisbane) and the ChLA Congress (Simmons College, Boston); the colleagues and students from Beijing Normal University and Tianjin University; and teachers and early childhood professionals from The Gowrie state conference (Brisbane).

I have also benefited in countless ways from the counsel, suggestions and perspectives of colleagues and friends. I single out a few names to thank for especially valuable help and support: Rod McGillis for his initial review of the proposal and subsequent critique of the manuscript which helped to sharpen my focus and clarify my ideas; Michelle Dicinoski for her helpful suggestions and insights; and Clare Bradford, my friend and colleague, for her unfailing support of my work. I also express my gratitude to Geraldine Massey, Cherie Allan, Amy Cross, Erica Hateley, Ingrid Johnston and Annette Patterson for their support in various ways: offering sustained interest in the project, recommending texts and assisting with locating elusive sources. I also very much appreciate the support and professionalism of the Palgrave team, especially Paula Kennedy and Sacha Lake. Many thanks to Monica Kendall for her thorough editorial support in seeing this book through to press.

And as always, I have benefited in more ways than I can acknowledge from the loving support of my family: Kimberley, Christopher, Helen and Steve who showed prolonged interest in this project, and especially to Mick for being a most judicious reader and constant helpmate.

Thank you to the following for permission to reproduce illustrations:

From (page 5) *PERSEPOLIS: THE STORY OF A CHILDHOOD* by Marjane Satrapi, translated by Mattias Ripa and Blake Ferris, translation copyright © 2003 by L'Association, Paris, France. Used by permission of Pantheon Books a division of Random House, Inc. Any third party use of this material, outside of this publication, is prohibited. Interested parties must apply directly to Random House, Inc. for permission.

From (page 151) *PERSEPOLIS 2: THE STORY OF A RETURN* by Marjane Satrapi, translated by Anjali Singh, translation copyright © 2004 by Anjali Singh. Used by permission of Pantheon Books, a division of Random House, Inc. Any third party use of this material, outside of this publication, is prohibited. Interested parties must apply directly to Random House, Inc. for permission.

Illustration from *THE INVENTION OF HUGO CABRET* by Brian Selznick. Copyright © 2007 by Brian Selznick. Reprinted by permission of Scholastic Inc.

From the book *DANCING THE BOOM CHA CHA BOOGIE* by Narelle Oliver. Text and illustrations copyright © Narelle Oliver 2005. First published by Omnibus Books, a division of Scholastic Australia Pty Limited, 2005. Reproduced by permission of Scholastic Australia Pty Limited.

Illustration from *MY DOG* by John Heffernan and Andrew McLean. Text copyright ©2001, John Heffernan. Illustrations copyright © 2001, Andrew McLean. Reproduced by permission of Andrew McLean.

Illustration from *KOJURO AND THE BEARS*. Illustrated by Junko Morimoto. Based on a story by Kenji Miyazawa. Copyright © 1986. Reproduced by permission of Junko Morimoto.

Illustration from *FOWL PLAY* by Jonathan Allen, Orion Children's Books, London. Copyright © Jonathan Allen 1996. Reproduced with permission of Orion Children's Books.

Illustration from *SKIM* written by Mariko Tamaki and illustrated by Jillian Tamaki. Illustrations Copyright © 2008 Jillian Tamaki. Reproduced by permission of Walker Books Ltd, London SE11 5HJ www.walker.co.uk

From *SUNDAY CHUTNEY* by Aaron Blabey. Copyright © 2008 Aaron Blabey. Reprinted by permission of Penguin Books Australia. Copyright

© 2009 Aaron Blabey. Published by Front Street, an imprint of Boyds Mills Press. Reprinted by permission.

From *FOX* written by Margaret Wild and illustrated by Ron Brooks. Copyright © text Margaret Wild 2000. Copyright © illustrations Ron Brooks 2000. First published in 2000 by Allen & Unwin 9 Atchison St, St Leonards, Australia. Reprinted by permission of Allen & Unwin: www.allen-unwin.com.au.

From the book *WOMBAT STEW* by Marcia Vaughan and Pamela Lofts. Text copyright © Marcia Vaughan 1984. Illustrations copyright © Pamela Lofts 1984. First published by Scholastic Press, a division of Scholastic Australia Pty Limited 1984. Reproduced by permission of Scholastic Australia Pty Limited.

Illustration from the cover of *TOAD HEAVEN*. Copyright © 2001. Text copyright © Morris Gleitzman, 2001. Illustration copyright © Rod Clements, 2001. Reprinted by permission of Penguin Group Australia.

From *LIES, FLIES AND STRANGE BIG FISH: TALES FROM THE BUSH* chosen by Bill Scott and illustrated by Craig Smith. Copyright © illustrations Craig Smith 2000. First published in 2000 by Allen & Unwin 9 Atchison St, St Leonards, Australia. Reprinted by permission of Allen & Unwin: www.allen-unwin.com.au.

From the book *UNCLE DAVID* by Libby Gleeson and Armin Greder. Text copyright © Libby Gleeson 1992. Illustrations copyright © Armin Greder. First published by Scholastic Press, a division of Scholastic Australia Pty Limited, 1992. Reproduced by permission of Scholastic Australia Pty Limited and Armin Greder.

Illustration from *THE COCKY WHO CRIED DINGO* by Yvonne Morrison and Heath McKenzie. Text © Yvonne Morrison 2010. Illustrations © Heath McKenzie 2010. Published by Little Hare an imprint of Hardie Grant Egmont. Reprinted by permission.

Introduction: The Burden of Truth

Liar, liar, pants on fire.
Hangin' on a telephone wire!

(Children's rhyme)

Deceiver, dissembler
Your trousers are alight
From what pole or gallows
Do they dangle in the night?

('The Liar' by William Blake, 1810)[1]

Many children learn from an early age that telling the truth is something they must always do to live a good life. Others learn that telling lies is something they must do to survive in life. These lessons may also be learned by one and the same child regardless of whether he/she is living the good life or not. The notion of the 'good' life versus the 'necessary' life implies that one kind of existence must give way to another, less desirable, but essential one. However, these two kinds of existence are not necessarily separate. The varied lessons about how to live are part of life's paradoxes and are the concern of this book, which explores the contradictions, choices, dilemmas and problems that arise when we choose between truth and its alternatives, between openness and concealment, between public and private. Secrets or lies are the shared theme or topic that links the chapters. However, survival explains the why of the secrets and lies, and enables readers to see secrets, lies and deception as key survival strategies, which may be necessary adaptive or transformative behaviour. Hence, survival is the overarching issue that connects the key concerns of this book. This book is about how fiction for young people handles situations where secrets are chosen

1

over openness, where lies and deception are chosen over truth. These choices are often viewed as moral ones. It is also about how we can read these texts to uncover other secrets, paradoxes and silences.

Children learn that not everyone tells the truth, at least not all of the time. They also learn that people lie, deceive and trick others and themselves into believing something that is not true. Children also learn to live with paradoxes. While telling the truth carries a heavy moral burden, so too does telling lies. Tellers of the truth are often held up as moral icons with stories of their truth-telling enshrined in the public psyche and used as models for children to emulate. Liars, on the other hand, are taunted when found out, and as the opening epigraphs show, their visibility is made all the more apparent by the metaphorical flames that will fly from their pants: an unsubtle reminder that they are on their way to the gates of hell. While Pinocchio, a famous liar known to many children, did not burn or swing from the gallows, he nevertheless suffered the indignity, and inconvenience, of having his nose grow every time he told a lie. Glory awaits the truth-teller, the gallows or worse await the liar. But is this absolutely true? Separating the wholesome from the wicked (or foolish) elides the moral complexity of truth-telling and deception.

As well as delivering some hard lessons about truths, children's literature also engages with paradoxes concerning truth and lies, offering readers incongruous ideas, tendering unorthodox insight or exposing contradictions. Literary scholars too delight in examining texts to uncover their paradoxes and contradictions, so they can explain how these literary or rhetorical devices serve the text. A story that has been told for many years about the virtue of telling the truth is of a young George Washington who admitted to destroying his father's prized cherry tree. However, the story, which was first described in *The Life of George Washington* by Parson Mason Locke Weems (1833), is a lie. Not only did this incident never happen to young George, but the tale is plagiarised from a poem, 'The Minstrel', by moral philosopher Dr James Beattie, which was published in London seven years prior to Weems's account (cited in Nyberg 1993: 155). By the time either story was published, George Washington had already been dead for a number of years and so was not available for comment on its truthfulness. There is a lovely irony as a story that is not true has been told for more than two hundred years by parents and teachers as a lesson on the virtues of telling the truth.

Children's literature galvanises in a particular way the multiple contacts between children, texts and contexts (social, moral and political).

My aim is to show how children's literature illuminates obscured philosophical or moral perspectives and exposes cultural connections that would otherwise remain unseen. The work of literary scholars is to anchor their investigations with a focused practice of close reading. The connections between text and context are not always obvious, nor are they always there to be made. However, close textual analysis can often yield how texts carry significant hermeneutic and heuristic potential.

This study is the result of my investigations of narratives for children and young adults that are about secrets; some of these texts are openly about secrets, while others conceal secrets within themselves. Uncovering these secrets and the changing fortunes that often arise from such discoveries reveals the powerful and often overlooked engagements between children's literature and the study of truth. While most people want to tell the truth, and be told the truth, we all by necessity cover, distort or misrepresent the truth on an almost daily basis. With deception and lying being such a part of social practice can any of us – and specifically children – know what truth is?

What is truth?

The difficulty in pinning down the truth is something J. L. Austin notes when he says that 'truth' is itself 'an abstract noun, a camel, that is, of a logical construction, which cannot get past the eye of a grammarian' (1999: 149). Austin asks whether truth is a substance, a quality, a relationship or a property of beliefs. The easy answer is that truth is all of these things, but not necessarily all at the same time. Throughout this book I attempt to show how truth is something that is not easily grasped, yet despite the difficulties that scholars have entertained about truth for many years, we expect children to have a clear and uncomplicated understanding of the truth. Children are taught to tell the truth but they learn from adults how to lie. There are many reasons why we all lie – fear, embarrassment, playfulness, competitiveness, to save face or to do harm. We also lie to protect the feelings of others: this is a lesson children learn from life about the etiquette of lying, or the necessity of lying. But telling the truth is not always easy. We often ask children: 'Are you telling the truth?' This may seem a straightforward question that would require a yes or no answer, and implies that there is no choice, there is only one truth. But this is not always the case.

Philosophers like Austin have argued persuasively that the illocutionary force of speech acts is built on expectations about what words do, as well as what they mean. When these speech acts are performed in an institutional setting then the expectation is reinforced. In a law court we are bound to tell the whole truth and nothing but the truth and the expectation is that unless the truth is told then punishment for not telling the truth will be forthcoming. The promise to tell the truth is not then just a statement, but an expression of intentionality of the speaker. However, Sissela Bok contends that 'the whole truth *is* out of reach' (1999: 4, emphasis original). The reason has as much to do with the limits of our memory as it has with our ability to convey our experiences with faultless accuracy. Bok suggests that discussions of truth need to distinguish between two domains: 'the *moral* domain of intended truthfulness and deception, and the much broader domain of truth and falsity in general' (6, emphasis original). She admits that the two domains are not isolated from each other, but overlap, and each is often indispensable to the other. If we move away from a 'real' world context and consider a fictional world, we can also see how these ideas apply. For example, when Chicken Licken calls 'The sky is falling' after an acorn falls on her head, she is not telling the truth, but believes that the world is coming to an end. Therefore, the statement is true (and untrue) and there is no intention to deceive on the part of Chicken Licken. This example shows that the distinction between truthfulness and deceit refers to the intentions of the speaker, and not to the actual state of the world; it also shows that fiction also circumscribes truth, and lying is not simply the opposite of telling the truth. David Nyberg (1993) notes that essential cognitive skills for tactical deception emerge within the ages of four to six years, even though much younger children are capable of deceptive behaviour. This age range is the time when most children enter formal education where they begin to interact with peers and the wider social community. It is quite possible that these cognitive skills may serve an important function in a child gaining an understanding of self, and learning adaptive behaviour. Whether children, or Chicken Licken, know they are being deceptive depends on their intention, their understanding of reality, their imagination and creative response to the world.

When Jerry Siegel created Superman and his mandate to fight for 'Truth, Justice and the American Way', he was playing on readers' psychological need for truth as something that is certain, something that matters. Many children may want to believe in Superman as much as they may want to believe in Santa Claus, but their reasons for believing in him may not necessarily be because he defends Truth. Nyberg posits a reasonable explanation for our desire to believe in something that is good (like Superman and Santa Claus): 'Generally speaking, we have a tendency to think that if something makes us feel very good, if something brings about a highly desirable and satisfying feeling of harmony and well-being, then perhaps that something, because it is so highly valued, is what we mean by the goodness of truth' (1993: 31). No doubt there is an important psychological need to believe in truth and all that we associate with truth, such as trust, goodness and a sense of well-being. However, knowing the truth can sometimes be psychologically harmful and emotionally distressing. It can break one's trust in another. It can even result in violence. Lies are similarly problematic.

Lies are classified in terms of the intention of the liar. Lies are often referred to as 'white', social or altruistic if the liar's intention is to avoid harming another or to achieve a good outcome, such as complimenting someone on their hair when it is clearly an unflattering style (the etiquette of lying). Lies can be serious, cruel, blatant or dangerous if the liar intends harm: for example, spreading gossip about someone when there is no basis of truth to the story. There are also protective lies that parents may tell their children in order to allay their fears, and conversely lies children tell to protect their parents. Another kind is Plato's 'noble lie', a lie that is told for the sake of the public good. However, we also need to consider the impact of the lie on the one who is lied to. It is often the case that we think of the one who is lied to as the dupe, the victim, the innocent. However, literature and life abound with examples of the targeted 'dupe' being someone who is astute, not easily conned and capable of seeing through the deception.

The pedagogical function of much children's fiction draws on examples of innocent young people who are conned by less scrupulous older children or adults: in this book, *The Other Side of Truth* (Chapter 2) and *Web of Lies* (Chapter 3) by Beverley Naidoo are examples. In other examples, such as Andersen's *The Emperor's New Clothes* (discussed below), the child sees through the deception of others. While lying and deception are often discussed in terms of their evil or harmful effects, there are other arguments which consider that the ability to lie is 'an invaluable tool developed to avoid early extinction, either of the individual or of the species' (Jay 2010: 21). In examining the mendacious capacities of animals (Chapter 7), I consider how animals, like humans, employ deception as a strategy of survival, as well as for individual or social gain. Similarly, deception may also prove to be a useful tool for social manipulation by governments as discussed in *The Hunger Games* by Suzanne Collins, *Little Brother* by Cory Doctorow, and *Article 5* by Kristen Simmons (Chapter 4). *Sunday Chutney* by Aaron Blabey (Chapter 6) shows how self-deception may also be a helpful adaptive skill. The argument that the ability to lie or deceive can have functional advantage if used skilfully is one that sociobiologist David Livingstone Smith has recently made, naming the area in the unconscious that teaches us to lie, 'the Machiavellian module' (qtd in Jay 2010: 21). Machiavelli made a virtue of mendacity in the public sphere. However, there is another side of mendacity when it is viewed as harmless deception. Children often deceive or fib to be playful. Playful deception can be exciting and fun; it can provoke laughter and gain attention. As noted above, children learn at an early age much about the subtleties of deception, such as what forms and degrees are acceptable in which circumstances, through the games they play and through other cooperative activities in which they participate at school or away from school. Children's literature also entertains and instructs its readers about the consequences of keeping secrets, telling lies, and the virtues of truth-telling.

Children's literature and literary truth

Historically, critics, writers and teachers have seen children's literature as serving a moral purpose, instructing the young on how to be good. In her Preface to *The Governess; or, Little Female Academy* (1749), Sara Fielding makes her position clear as to literature's true function:

> Before you begin the following sheets, I beg you will stop a Moment at this 'Preface' to consider with me, what is the true Use of reading: and if you can once fix this Truth in your Minds, namely that the true Use of Books is to make you wiser and better, you will then have both Profit and Pleasure from what you read. (Qtd in Sarland 1999: 40)

Fielding was not alone with her sentiments about literature, but as Charles Sarland notes (40–1), the debate about the moral purpose of children's literature which was lively in the eighteenth and nineteenth centuries, and re-emerged in the late 1970s, shifted its emphasis from moral instruction and moral truths to the influence of ideology which promotes its own form of didacticism.

The belief that literature in general is truthful as opposed to being political is one that is often attributed to a humanist standpoint. But as Sarland says, the influence of ideology on texts is one that has been taken up by many scholars in children's literature.[2] Outside of children's literature the postmodernist scholar Slavoj Žižek makes the distinction between (factual) truth and truthfulness. He explains that what renders any narrative of trauma, for instance, truthful is 'its factual unreliability, its confusion, its inconsistency' (2009: 3). When a victim of trauma narrates the story with consistency and clarity Žižek suggests this very quality makes us suspicious of its truth. *The Adoration of Jenna Fox* by Mary E. Pearson (Chapter 6) provides another side of the trauma narrative when the truth is disguised from the victim of the trauma through omission, and unreliable, confusing accounts of the past.

The position espoused by some liberal humanists is that good literature contains 'objective truth' just waiting to be uncovered by the reader or critic. This unvarnished truth is not only profound, but free of ideological bias. This stance has been firmly criticised by postmodern theorists such as Foucault and other critics, who argue that truth is tied up with ideological struggles (Foucault). A further feature of humanist thinking is that the text (realism, romance, comedy or other generic type) imitates or mirrors some objective feature of life. While there is arguably a case for mimetic value in literature, this value is not tied to a mimesis of truth. Others seek the individual author behind the text and attempt to uncover the intentions of authors through examination of the texts, and depending on the form of humanism one subscribes to, the text may hold social intent, an anti-authoritarian vision or simply an individual authorial outlook on life. These differing perspectives are important for children's literature, which has a strong humanist tradition.

Many adults hold the opinion that books written for children are a genuine source of knowledge or wisdom and that the authors of these texts have important truths to share about society and all aspects of life. The interest in author blogs, websites, book talks, school visits and conference presentations is an indication of this fascination with the author. The perceived epistemological function of fiction emphasises the use value of fiction; in other words, we can learn from fiction. The knowledge that one can undoubtedly gain from literature 'might or might not be propositional, in the sense of involving the grasp of truths' (Lamarque and Olsen 1994: 13). This claim to literature's truth value is quite a different argument from the mimetic view that sees a work of fiction 'ringing true' or 'true to life', meaning that it is sincere, or has verisimilitude, or is lifelike. To argue about whether literature is true or not is a different argument from the one here, which is concerned with truth. Resemblance and lifelike relations between literature and life do play a part in readers' understanding or connection with a text, but they are not the same as truth. In addition to the notion of literature containing a truth there is a strong humanist insistence that texts have a shared public meaning.

The line of argument promoted by E. D. Hirsch Jr (and many practitioners) is that meaning is a 'constant, unchanging pole' or 'relationship' binding the text and the reader (1967: 129). For Hirsch, meaning is in the text and it is what the author meant (willed) and intended the reader to grasp (8). However, Hirsch does not suggest that there is only one possible interpretation of a text. Rather, his point is that there may be a number of different, valid interpretations, but all of them must be within a system of expectations which the author's meaning permits. For Hirsch, this is a matter of a text's significance rather than its meaning. Readers assign significances to a text, and therefore significances may vary, but authors assign meaning, which remains constant. While Hirsch regards meaning as being the rightful property of the author, public consensus requires that there is an agreed true account of a text. Hirsch later came to revise his ideas on the fixity of meaning by conceding that 'we must take a more generous and capacious view of what remains the same' (1984: 210). The relationship between meaning and significance needs to take account that readers read in their own way, that readers and critics have their own techniques of understanding and interpretation, and that the context in which reading is undertaken can govern understanding of a text and its meaning. The most readily available example of institutional context is the classroom and the role teachers play in contributing to students' understanding of a text (cf. Stanley Fish's [1980] notion that texts are constructions of interpretive communities). However, a text's meaning is not value-free or neutral. Meaning has political import. As McGillis reminds us: 'every children's book participates in some way in political maneuvering' (1996: 107).

Children's literature has variously been viewed as apolitical, neutral or innocent, as well as political, subversive and dangerous. Kimberley Reynolds makes this point by explaining that children's literature occupies a 'paradoxical cultural space' that is 'simultaneously highly regulated and overlooked, orthodox and radical, didactic and subversive' (2007: 3). Reynolds is right in her view about the regulatory controls on children's literature, more so than on adult fiction. Children's literature is a highly mediated field whereby rules, relationships and conventions from various sectors, including the marketplace, shape both artistic production and reception. In terms of the subject of this book, my position follows the line of argument that Fredric Jameson (1971) offers, namely, that while texts do not contain any objective truths, they nevertheless may have social significance between text and society (context) that is speculative and hypothetical, as opposed to real or a mirror to an independent, external world. Children's literature is part of the world and it continues to be valued, produced, sold, read, reviewed and cited, and for this reason alone deserves our attention. However, to propose that children's literature gives us a privileged access to a pure and essential truth or reality is foolhardy, and is not the course set for this book. I am well aware that the literary text is a product of culture and is inseparable from the historical and material contexts from which it emerges and in which it continues to exist. However, my attention to close reading is to not dwell on the obvious moments of secrets, lies and truths that sit on the surface of story, but to ask what might be not readily visible or what allusive links might exist between text and context that would enable us to understand better the text's social, philosophical and moral resonances. While this book is framed within wider theoretical and social debates, my approach nevertheless hinges on giving primacy to the fictional text before speculating on its possible social, political or philosophical significances. In other words, I am as much interested in what could be called theory-inflected interpretation as I am with examining how literature works, taking account of the texts themselves and discovering what Umberto Eco calls an 'excess of wonder' (cited in Culler 2007: 182).

All interpretations of literature can only ever offer partial understandings of what a text means; similarly, we can only ever have partial understanding of what theory means. Interpreting a narrative is a way of creating another narrative, one that we may try to convince readers is a correct and true account. Kermode regards interpretation as an 'indispensable instrument of survival in the world, and it works there as it works on literary texts' (1979: xi). Interpretation invites a lifting of veils of one kind or another. As a metaphor of concealment or disguise, a veil invites the idea of revelation. But what happens when the veil is merely an elaborate surface concealing nothing?

Veiling and unveiling the truth

The veil and truth share an interrelationship that stretches back to classical times. While the 'veiled goddess' and other veiled women feature in many cultural myths and stories, as well as art and sculpture, not all claim an association with truth.[3] One that makes the connection clear is the story of Phryne, a beautiful fourth-century Greek courtesan. Although the accounts of her story vary, one that is relevant here concerns her participation in the Eleusinian Mysteries. Participants in these annual initiation ceremonies had to undertake a vow of secrecy. Phryne is said to have bathed naked in the sea before the people at the ceremony and was subsequently tried for profanity. In a desperate attempt to save Phryne, Hyperides, who was defending her at trial, pulled off her garment[4] and asked the court how a body so beautiful could possibly be guilty of such a crime. The judges agreed, and Phryne was acquitted. The judges' decision was not because the beauty of Phryne's naked body overcame them, but because her beauty was seen as a facet of divinity, a divine truth. This story serves as a useful example of how the veil can be interpreted as concealing a hidden truth, which can only be known when the veil is removed. In covering the truth, the veil reveals a mystery. Chapter 1 explores this idea of unveiling the truth and, among its examples, *When You Reach Me* by Rebecca Stead demonstrates that unlike beauty being the divine truth, the grotesque and the mad may also have truths that need to be apprehended. Truth in this sense is mystery itself, a paradox central to the humanist approach to literature.[5] This brings us back to Hirsch and others and how we understand literature. If interpretation seeks to unveil a text, then what it does is to demonstrate that the text is inextricably mysterious.

Jacques Derrida uses Hans Christian Andersen's story of *The Emperor's New Clothes* to explain how stories veil a nakedness (1975: 37). The fairy tale tells how two imposters pretend to weave an expensive garment for the Emperor which they claim will be visible only to the good and loyal subjects. When the Emperor parades in the streets before his subjects, all the spectators fear being seen as disloyal and thereby fail to notice the Emperor's nakedness. At least, the text leads us to believe that they fail to see: this is what Frank Kermode (1979) would regard as a secret of the text. Only a child appears to speak the truth and exclaims: 'The emperor has nothing on!' (Andersen 1993: unpaged). (However, the imposters too speak the truth which is verified by the adults' reactions.) While *The Emperor's New Clothes* may parade the naked Emperor, it is the nakedness that enables the child to utter the truth. Thus the story, Derrida suggests, is a 'staging of the truth itself – the possibility of truth as a process of baring' (1975: 38). While not taking the humanist line that literature contains Truths, Derrida offers a more equivocal position suggesting that literature can 'produce, stage and advance something *like* truth. Its power thus extends itself beyond the truth of which it is capable' (1975: 38–9, my emphasis). Here is the mystery of the text. Derrida suggests that literature is in the service of truth, and that this truth can be taught. He acknowledges that this is typical of a philosophical form of literary criticism, such as Hirsch's belief that the text stands naked before the reader, and this nakedness is its meaning. But Derrida's point is that literature can be an accessible and engaging form of pedagogical illustration and is often used by psychoanalysts such as Freud and Lacan (and we can add philosophers, educators, politicians and business leaders – almost all sectors of society) 'to make clear the meaning of a law or a truth' (1975: 45) in an exemplary way. Interestingly, it is often children's literature that is called upon as an exemplar of truth.

In contrast to Hirsch, we could also put the argument that a text is never naked. Kenneth Clark (1956) makes the distinction between the naked and the nude; his point is that the nude is the body 'clothed' in art. In much the same way, a story is always clothed in language, convention and context, which ensure that its nakedness will continue to be shrouded in mystery. Language is always slippery (following Derrida) and it is difficult to know what it could be for a text to have 'a "pure" intention or express a "pure" meaning' (Eagleton 1983: 69). Due to the metaphorical nature of language there will always be a surplus of meaning. *The Name of this Book is Secret* by Pseudonymous Bosch (Chapter 8) cleverly attempts a metafictive game of concealing and revealing by playing with narrative conventions and literary devices. But for all its trickery, its art of deception, the text remains clothed with only flashes of lightly veiled nakedness to tease the reader's curiosity.

As its title suggests, this book focuses on the intersection of secrets, lies and fiction and how these not only present a staging of truth, to use Derrida's term, but are valuable survival strategies. Despite my persistent use of 'literature' in this Introduction, I make no special distinction between literature and fiction. I acknowledge that what makes a work fictional is not the same as what makes it literary or not. My interest is more with how fictionality can be used in works of 'literature' for children and young adults. By children's fiction, I mean here contemporary novels, picture books, fables and fantasies, and I have tried to include a wide range of texts published in English and targeting a wide demographic of readers. I have also included film. The unifying point is the texts' treatment of how the key concepts – secrets, lies and deception – that underpin this study are linked by a notion of survival. However, I also concede that there are other instances when these same strategies work against survival, or justice for the traumatised subject, but support the survival and freedom of the perpetrator. The scapegoat is one example (Chapter 3); another not discussed in this book is in cases of sexual abuse of children (see Lampert 2012). The purpose of this Introduction is to set the scene for some of the key ideas and theoretical perspectives that follow.

The book has three parts. Part I: 'Truth, Lies and Survival' examines the problematic nature of trying to unveil the truth as if there is a naked truth that can be revealed. It also considers how secrets and other forms of concealment such as lies, deception and half-truths may be necessary for survival. It questions notions of the truth-teller and whether those who live outside the limits of the 'normal' world have truths to tell or are ignored, their words discounted as nonsense. Finally, it discusses the idea of the scapegoat as a necessary sacrificial mechanism for ensuring that order can be returned to a community after an upheaval. The scapegoat is cast as the guilty party and exiled, and lies become the truths that the community wants to hear and accept. Part II: 'Secrets and Secrecy' continues to illustrate the necessity of secrets for survival. The chapters use the idea primarily offered by Georg Simmel that the secret is a central means for information control in contemporary society. As society has become more mobile and networked there is increased interaction between strangers as well as friends. Ironically, there is more control over information, more 'disinformation', and more ways to track and keep information than ever before. Additional forms of secrets and secrecy examined in this section include secret societies and crime families, and the ways in which group dynamics, exclusivity and loyalty affect the keeping of secrets. A final chapter concerns our secret selves, the lies we tell ourselves and others and the private and public impact of lies and (self) deception. Part III: 'Tangled Webs' examines how deception and mendacity, rather than solving problems, can lead to even more complex webs of deceit. It considers the virtues and vices of mendacity, especially in animals, and considers how a different understanding of animality emerges when we accept a non-human perspective. The final chapter explores how fiction is a game of deception between readers and text: a game which is exploited most openly in metafiction which playfully traverses the boundaries of text and world. By examining fiction's aesthetic role in comic deceit such as tall tales, the discussion considers how fiction supports characters who play on others' vulnerabilities, biases, imaginations and confused states of mind to achieve their deception. How one goes about deceiving is complicated and often relies on cunning, and an ability to distort, deflect, deny, exaggerate and amuse. The chapter also returns us to the question of truth, leaving open the matter of whether the truth sets one free.

Part I
Truth, Lies and Survival

1
Unveiling the Truth

As an item of clothing, the veil is inscribed with various historical and cultural meanings. Muslim women and girls who wear 'veils' or head-scarves[1] in accordance with hijab follow the dictates of their religion regarding modesty in dress and behaviour. From a Western perspective with its economic investment in fashion, the veil would seem to inhibit emulous display among women. Veils cover the hair, ears and throat or, in the case of the burqa, the entire body, with only a grille or netting over the eyes to allow the wearer to see. The concealment of the woman's body is to ensure sexual modesty.[2] In another religious context, when a woman 'takes the veil' she becomes 'a bride of Christ' giving up all worldly goods, taking vows of chastity and poverty, and often living within a religious order. A very different kind of veil comes into play with the dance of the seven veils by Salome, a performance that has been copied by other *femmes fatales* in many films. This dance of seduction is a striptease, a spectacle which Barthes (1957: 84) notes is 'based on fear', or 'the pretence of fear', 'a delicious terror' with the veils, or other adornments (furs, fans, gloves, feathers, fishnet stockings), tantalising and evoking the idea of nakedness and sexual fantasy. We have a collection of veil wearers – striptease performers, dancers of the seven veils, *femmes fatales*, nuns, Muslim women and girls (and there are more) – and while in each case the veil serves a different purpose, the eye of the beholder will respond sometimes with fear, sometimes with excitement, sometimes with shock or surprise, sometimes with respect. These varied instances of the veil and of veiling assign cultural, material, spatial, communicative and religious meanings (El Guindi 1999: 6). The veil, therefore, is a material object as well as a trope that evokes multiple interpretations. It hides a mystery, and signifies a host of oppositional binaries: difference or recognition, exotic or traditional, freedom or oppression. Thus, a seemingly innocent piece of clothing is capable of provoking diverse reactions. More significant for this chapter is how the veil, as both a noun and a verb, can reveal or conceal truth.

To consider the implications of the veil, of veiling and unveiling, this chapter narrows the possibilities that beckon by first considering the veil in memoir and fiction about Muslim girls, namely, *Persepolis: The Story of a Childhood* (2003) and *Persepolis 2: The Story of a Return* (2004) by Marjane Satrapi, and *Does My Head Look Big in This?* (2005) by Randa Abdel-Fattah. In the second part of the chapter, my attention turns to 'un/veiling' in a metaphorical sense, examining how both the clothed (animal) body and the naked (human) body can serve as a metonym for truth. The discussion throughout this chapter complicates the rather simplistic idea of concealment as deception, and unveiling as truth, by taking into account how subjects transform themselves in their quest to find the truth.

Seeing through the veil

If all fiction veils a nakedness, as Derrida suggests, then one of the most potentially exposing forms of writing would be the story of the self, or the life narrative. However, as I mention in the Introduction to this book, it is doubtful that any text is ever 'naked' as the metaphoric nature of language always offers a 'veil of words' (Krajewski 1992: 124). Therefore, to consider a genre such as life writing as an example of the 'author stripped bare' is naïve, but, nevertheless, life narratives offer spaces of exposure within the inevitable covering of words and their metaphorical associations. Life narratives are part of a larger body of literature that comprises autobiography, diary, memoir, confessional writing and literature of trauma. Whitlock suggests that 'contemporary life narrative touches the secret life of us; indeed, it is part of how we come to imagine "us"' (2007: 10). Life writing carries a burden of truthfulness, if not some truths, and a claim to authenticity. But like literature, these stories mediate accounts of personal life experiences into the public domain, often bringing with them 'a socio-cultural history', and always a temporality (Douglas 2006: 44). In children's literature, life narratives often take the form of fictionalised autobiographies or diaries. Chapters 2 and 6 examine fictional/ised diaries but my interest here is in the graphic memoirs *Persepolis: The Story of a Childhood* (2003) and its sequel *Persepolis 2: The Story of a Return* (2004). Whitlock notes that Satrapi uses the graphic memoir as an alternative form of autobiography, conveying the story of her childhood and young adulthood (2007: 188).

In *Persepolis: The Story of a Childhood*, Marjane Satrapi tells a story of her life in Tehran from ages six to 14, a period which sees the overthrow of the Shah's regime, the Islamic Revolution of 1979 and the Islamic theocracy that followed. It also tells of the effects of war with Iraq. In *Persepolis 2: The Story of a Return* she tells of her life as an adolescent in Vienna and her return to Iran as a young woman. My purpose is to explore how these narratives of survival and adaptive behaviour unveil the author's life experiences, weaving together fragments of truths drawn from autobiography, family biography, history and culture. The discussion considers how these fragments come to express a truth of lived experience, as well as construct extra-textual truths. The third text, *Does My Head Look Big in This?* by Randa Abdel-Fattah (2005), is not a life narrative, but a fiction. However, the story emerges from the author's political and cultural beliefs as an Australian Muslim woman.[3]

In all these texts, the narratives creatively reconstruct and redescribe the veiled experience. Paul Ricoeur (1985) uses the term 'redescription' to explain how narrative (or specifically metaphor) cannot directly reference the world outside the text but it can permit us to see it in a new way. For Ricoeur, art cannot simply imitate life, in the Aristotelian sense of mimesis, but it can borrow from life and transform it. In writing about a life, the representation may appear as mimesis, mirroring the author's real life. Ricoeur considers the concept of poiesis in the Platonic-Aristotelian interpretation as a form of mimesis to be not so much about the production – the finished 'poem' – but the act of poetic creation. This concept of poiesis as artistic production is useful in considering how the idea of truthful revelation, which memoir (or life narrative) seeks to disclose, is always framed by notions of reliability, authority and authenticity, which readers come to expect when they encounter a text that asserts its autobiographical status: the cover blurb of *Persepolis: The Story of a Childhood* describes Satrapi's book as a 'wise, funny and heartbreaking memoir'. However, to consider life writing to be more 'truthful' than fiction, ignores the function of poiesis as an artistic process with the ability to both reveal and transform: '*poiesis* reveals structures which would have remained unrecognized without art, *and* that it transforms life, elevating it to another level' (Ricoeur, cited in Wood 1991: 182, emphasis original). Furthermore, life writing and fictionalised accounts that interweave 'fragments of the real' intersect at a point which draws attention to how creative production can assist readers to understand human actions and socio-political history by reconstructing them in the world of the text: a world which is arguably an imaginary universe, but one that reveals and transforms as it symbolically renders the past under the sign of memory or redescription. The Persepolis stories are not mimesis, copies of Satrapi's life, but poiesis: a creation and a construction of her past. Satrapi reconstructs and creatively redescribes the thoughts and experiences of her childhood and youth through words and comic-strip illustration. Whitlock sees the comic format performing a dual function: on the one hand, the illustrations are 'elemental', evoking a naïve, childlike quality, but they are also sophisticated, which forces readers 'to pause and speculate about the extraordinary connotative force of cartoon drawing, which both amplifies and simplifies' (2007: 188). As the dominant mode of storytelling in this text, the illustrations convey the physical, emotional and political transformations that the represented subject (Satrapi) undergoes as she not only moves through childhood to adulthood but also moves away from her home and her life in Iran.

Self-representation is the element that defines all forms of life writing. How one reveals or conceals details about oneself is a necessary strategy, or deception. Self-representation also requires an account of others, and how we actively assimilate and transform ourselves and others contributes to our subjectivity and intersubjective relations. Foucault's (1978, 1980) accounts of social and historical existence and the often perilous conflict or dialogue of forces one encounters provide an important lens for my reading of the Persepolis texts. These texts illustrate how 'Satrapi' or her narrated self 'Marji' is affected and transformed by external forces. However, she is not simply passive, yielding to outside influences. Rather, she is a subject with agency who is capable of interpreting and acting upon the world. Satrapi draws on a range of techniques in her poetic reconstruction of a life that once was. Both Persepolis texts use humour (irony and satire), exaggeration and caricature to mediate harsh realities providing avenues for comic relief.

Persepolis: The Story of a Childhood begins in 1979 in Iran at the time of what was to be known as the 'Islamic Revolution', and the fundamentalist Islamic regime that followed. By 1980 it had become obligatory for girls to wear the veil. Writing in the first person, the narrator, Marji, explains how the significance of the veil eluded her and other children: 'we didn't really like to wear the veil, especially since we didn't understand why we had to' (2003: 3). In describing girls' attitudes to the veil the text uses an idiomatic discourse with accompanying subversive illustrated incidents within the one scene showing the children using the veil as a toy thing, pretending that it is a skipping rope ('Give me my veil back!'), a rein for a horse ('Giddyap!'), a disguise ('Ooh! I'm the

Figure 1.1   Illustration from *Persepolis: The Story of a Childhood* by Marjane Satrapi

monster of darkness'), mocking the ruling regime ('Execution in the name of freedom') and complaining ('It's too hot out'). This scene carries a generational significance that goes beyond cultural limits as the young girls place play above compliance. Their reactions also separate the world of adults with their ideological allegiances from the world of children who live within that world but create a carnivalesque space that does not permit authoritarianism and seriousness (Stephens 1992: 121). The sign–referent relationship is playfully disrupted, showing the relativity of the 'truths' and ideologies inscribed by the dominant discourse of the Islamic rule with the physical reality and 'truths' of the children. The tensions and differences of ideological viewpoints are carried through to the ways the Iranian women represented in the text see the veil as either an object of oppression or a sign of religious observance: 'Everywhere in the streets there were demonstrations for and against the veil' with the illustration showing women dressed in chadors chanting 'The veil, the veil', and women in modern dress countering with 'Freedom! Freedom!' This internal polarity is one that is familiar in the extra-literary world, especially with respect to contrasting ideological discourses (the West and Islam) to veiling. As the ideological divide between fundamentalist and modernist Islam widens, clothing becomes a complex signifier within the cultural discourses of beliefs (Figure 1.1).

Words and images contrast fundamentalist and modern dress, emphasising the ideological imperative and minor reactionary stances:

In no time, the way people dressed became an ideological sign. There were two kinds of women. The fundamentalist woman. The modern woman. You showed your opposition to the regime by letting a few strands of hair show. (2003: 75)

Iranian men are contrasted as 'fundamentalist' or 'progressive', and as a mark of resistance a 'progressive' man is depicted as having shaved, with the comment that 'Islam is more or less against shaving' (75). In addition to these small acts of rebellion, Marji reveals that the oppressive regime provokes other deceptions as people attempt to avoid being exposed as being not a true Muslim. This attempt to deceive is conveyed through her parents' sighting of their neighbours as they walk through the streets dressed in fundamentalist dress:

[Mother]:   'Look at her! Last year she was wearing a miniskirt, showing off her beefy thighs to the whole neighbourhood. And now Madame is wearing a chador. It suits her better, I guess.'

[Father]:   'As for her fundamentalist husband who drank himself into a stupor every night, now he uses mouthwash every time he utters the word "alcohol".' (75)

Ironically, while the parents scorn what they see as the couple's hyprocrisy and deceit, Marji's mother perpetuates a similar hypocrisy when she tells Marji that she must lie: 'If anyone ever asks you what you do during the day, say you pray, you understand?' Marji finds lying comes easily as she competes with other children in a lying contest of sorts. When one of her friends piously claims: 'I pray five times a day,' Marji replies 'Me? Ten or eleven times ... sometimes twelve' (75). It would seem that Marji and her mother regard lying for a good reason as different from other forms of deception, such as those in which her neighbours engage.

Lying is a form of concealment (veiling), a concealment or veiling of truth. While the traditional moral distinction separates lying and concealment, this text shows how the line of demarcation is often blurred. This blurring is most obvious in public and private spaces. In public, Marji, her mother and grandmother cover their heads with scarves, and the older women wear modest black dresses. Their public displays of truthful allegiance to the law conceal their opposition, which they are not free to display openly. However, at times, Marji openly flaunts her anarchic spirit, creating her own personal dress style by wearing a new denim jacket with a Michael Jackson badge, jeans and a new pair of Nikes in public. She also trades in the black market to pay for two music tapes by Western pop stars. However, these visible signs of rebellion and freedom almost cause her to be taken to 'HQ' when two women, 'guardians of the revolution', attempt to arrest her for being improperly veiled. Marjane narrowly avoids being arrested by telling a pack of lies:

> 'Ma'am my mother's dead. My stepmother is really cruel and if I don't go home right away, she'll kill me [...] She'll burn me with the clothes iron. **She'll make my father put me in an orphanage**.' (134: emphasis original)

Marji's necessary lying for survival illustrates how the binarism of truth and falsehood is far from uncomplicated, especially when individual freedom is at stake. Truth-telling is not elevated beyond other rhetorical accounts as it becomes part of her storytelling repertoire and serves a purpose that lies outside a moral or ethical dimension. The contradictory self-representations and dress concealment – as a veiled girl, a revolutionary activist, a subject of abuse – demonstrate the complex relations between concealment and lies, between veiling and unveiling.

The interplay that the veil evokes between sight and body draws attention to layers of concealment. By modestly concealing parts of the body, the veil (or burqa in concealing the full body) effectively replaces individual differentiation by cultural differentiation. In wearing the veil, chador or burqa Muslim women appear to erase their individuality: the implication is that agency is also erased, and culture is symbolically rendered. We will return to this point about erasure of individuality in the discussion of *Persepolis 2*, but for now my point is to highlight the hierarchy of dominance and submission, as well as homogeneity, that the veil evokes when viewed through a Western lens. Whitlock puts it this way: 'The image of the veiled woman in particular is a powerful trope of the passive "third world" subject, and it sustains the discursive self-presentation of Western women as a [*sic*] secular, liberated, and individual agents' (2007: 49). Marji disrupts this projected image of passivity. After the death of her friend, she becomes rebellious, wearing jewellery and jeans with the mandatory long black dress and headscarf to school. After she argues with and assaults her Principal, Marji is expelled. Her aunt manages to get her accepted into another school, but Marji argues with the religion teacher, accusing her of telling lies about the Islamic Republic. After this second act of rebellion, her parents decide it would be safer to send her to Austria to live with their friends, and enroll her in a French school. They fear that Marji (now 14) could be executed if she stays in Tehran and continues to be dissident.

Persepolis 2: The Story of a Return takes up the story on Marji's arrival in Vienna. It marks a transitional period during which Marji takes on a more serious self-transformation than her former more playful anarchic gestures. It is also a time when she encounters the dilemma regarding truth and deception: both are necessary for survival. The seriousness of the strictures and controls that characterise life in Iran is given clarity when her mother's friend Zozo and her daughter Shirin meet her at the airport. The initial conversation between Marji and Shirin opens up the ideological divide. Marji expresses to Shirin her relief and excitement about not having to wear the veil to school or 'to beat myself every day for the war martyrs' (2004: 2). However, Shirin fails to respond to Marji's experience and instead boasts about her 'really fashionable' ear-muffs, her raspberry, strawberry and blackberry-scented pens, and her 'pearly pink lipstick'. Marji's unspoken thoughts about her friend's conversation condemn her as 'a traitor': 'While people were dying in our country, she was talking to me about trivial things' (2). Her time with the family is short-lived as Zozo takes her to a boarding house run by nuns. There is an irony in that escaping one form of religious dogmatism she finds herself living a cloistered existence with nuns. She soon is forced to leave the boarding house as she fails to conform to its rules. The Mother Superior lies to her parents saying that she stole food and decided to leave on her own volition.

Life in Vienna becomes a lonely and conflicted time for Marji. It is a time when she lives unveiled but struggles with knowing what truths she should be seeking in order to live her life, and she recalls her grandmother's advice to 'be true to yourself' (41). However, self-realisation eludes her so she experiments with clothes, hairstyles, interpersonal relationships and different social practices, all the time seeking new modes of self-presentation and identity, but she confides: 'The harder I tried to assimilate the more I had the feeling that I was distancing myself from my culture, betraying my parents and my origins, that I was playing a game by somebody else's rules' (39). In Foucault's (1976) terms Marji is undertaking practices of self-transformation in forming and shaping herself as a certain kind of subject. Unable to understand the different culture in which she lives, Marji can only comprehend the Other that she encounters in terms of her own rules, which means that 'their' reality eludes her unless she wholly abandons her entire way of thinking, and becomes one with them, entering into their form of life. When she speaks to her parents on the telephone she knows that the lies she tells them are the truths they want to hear: 'If only they knew … if they knew that their daughter was made up like a punk, that she smoked joints to make a good impression, that she had seen men in their underwear while they [her parents] were being bombed every day, they wouldn't call me their dream child' (39).

Marji's transformation of the self is a form of solipsism that goes beyond 'normal' adolescent identity angst and desire to fit in with the peer group. It goes beyond because of the additional layer of cultural and ideological difference that characterises the individuals and groups with whom she mixes. This point of disjuncture is made vivid when Marji accompanies a friend to a revolutionary anarchists' party; the invitation excites her and reminds her of her former political beliefs and actions of her childhood in Iran. However, when they arrive at the secluded location in the forest she finds a group of adults playing hide and seek amongst the trees (57–8). Marji also participates in her own game of hide and seek. Her liberal-minded home-life was a stark contrast to the religious fundamentalism that she came to experience while growing up in Tehran. In order to live outside the home, she had to hide her true beliefs and attitudes, something which she found difficult to do. However, the imposed totalised, enclosed thinking that existed beyond the home was incapable of recognising points of view other than its own, and was another form of solipsism that did not allow for alternative truths. The fundamentalist rules and standards, especially in relation to dress codes, education and male–female relationships, were taken as set in stone, to have a timeless truth. In Vienna, Marji openly participates in the solipsistic world of youthful Western decadence while also feeling guilty about not adhering to her family's cultural beliefs and practices regarding drinking alcohol, and other forms of socialisation between males and females.

When she returns to Iran as a young woman (four years later) she continues to feel trapped by her family, her country and herself. Each enclosure limits Marjane in terms of recognising alternatives, as she cannot think beyond these boundaries. She becomes depressed, sees psychiatrists, takes anti-depressants and smokes excessively. The insularity of her condition and inability to think beyond the limits resemble the Islamic Republic's enforced fundamentalist, rigid, closed system of thought. Her break out of this pathological state comes when she fails in her suicide attempt, despite having swallowed enough pills, which her doctor tells her 'should have been enough to finish off an elephant!' (119). Marjane makes the conscious decision to change: 'From now on I'm taking myself in hand' (119). Taking her self in hand leads her to participate in the wider world, not the world outside Tehran, but the world beyond her home and family. She embarks on a new transformation of the self and finds that her new life is full of paradoxes: joyful yet unsettling, often dangerous, but stimulating and revitalising. As the bubble of solipsism that enclosed her life bursts she finds that in encountering new friends and relationships she moves beyond herself to a renewed sense of self: one that is eager to learn, to socialise and to revive her political beliefs. Marji's actions represent Foucault's (1976) point that even in situations where the social order is repressive there will also be resistance, revolt and struggle against imposed constraints. Despite the enforced wearing of the veil in public, Marjane does not adhere to the Islamic law of chastity. She also reveals how the hijab is variously used to indicate differences within what is often seen as homogeneity, as noted above. Marjane demonstrates the science of wearing the veil, explaining that despite the strict rules about how no hair should be shown, women nevertheless 'were winning an eighth of an inch of hair and losing an eighth of an inch of veil' (139). Furthermore, she confides 'even though they were covered from head to foot, you got to the point where you could guess their shape, the way they wore their hair, and even their political opinions. Obviously, the more a woman showed, the more progressive and modern she was' (140). Marjane's reading of the Muslim woman's body draws attention to seeing as something that goes beyond notions of invisibility and anonymity. Clearly, the women recognise one another, learning to read hidden signs (how hair is styled under the hijab for example), as well as reading more visible signs such as stature, mannerisms and so on.

Through her own efforts of self-transformation and rebellion, Marjane finds ways to subvert the power imbalance and social injustice that characterise her life in Tehran. She also comes to understand her own truths through the choices she makes within her specific cultural and historical setting, and by questioning some of her own certainties. At university, where Marji studies Art, she continues to question the rules that must be followed. One rule concerning modesty provides a further impetus to rebellion when students are expected to study anatomy, yet the life model is always clad in a full chador. Marji explains the folly of the law: 'Not a single part of her body was visible. We nevertheless learned to draw drapes' (145). However, Whitlock notes how this experience undoubtedly contributed to Satrapi's individual artistic style: the 'iconography of Satrapi's cartoons derives from a tactical response to censorship and to the particular artistic constraints that followed from enforced veiling after the Islamic revolution in Iran' (2007: 192). As the external world closes in more on her, Marjane finds freedom with a group of like-minded friends. They gather at one another's houses to do life drawing, and in the privacy of their homes the women are unveiled, often dressing in revealing modern clothes, wearing make-up and having their hair styled according to Western fashion. The private/public distinction enables Marjane and her friends to enjoy a secretive pleasure in exercising personal choice in clothing behind closed doors, and while their public dressing conforms to Islamic law they nevertheless carry with them the satisfying knowledge of private subversion, which Figure 1.2 captures with subtlety.

They party every night, but are always on the look out for guardians of the revolution. Marji acknowledges that the excesses of her lifestyle need to be tempered in order to live safely. However, the restrictions on male–female relationships force her to decide to marry; a decision which she comes to regret almost immediately as she realises that she has compromised her own set of truths by which she wants to live her life: 'I had conformed to society, while I had always wanted to remain on the margins. In my mind "a married woman" wasn't like me. It required too many compromises. I couldn't accept it, but it was too late' (163). Marjane soon finds the only path open to her is to divorce and leave Iran for good.

The Persepolis books deal with veiling and unveiling, bringing a candid perspective to what is a complex issue. In terms of unveiling the truth, these texts reveal that while for some truth is monolithic and static, for others it is always multiple and variable. The texts also characterise the differences between Western and non-Western ideas of truth and the relations between truth and power. While fundamentalism demands adoption of a specific monolithic truth, equally other forms of dissenting behaviour or ideological persuasion are also monolithic in their refusal to entertain points of view other than their own. Marjane encounters both forms – in Tehran and in Vienna – and finds that she is caught between 'regimes of truth', to borrow from Foucault.[4] Marjane flirts with and enjoys Western ideas of truth shaped by economic consumption, the media, educational institutions and forms of political debate and issues of social struggle. However, she also feels the pull towards her family's liberal political beliefs, as well as their religious commitment to Islam. She explores the truth in terms of her desire to know her family's history and its relationship to the current political regime. Similarly, she desires to know the Other when she encounters different cultural and political beliefs when living in Vienna. All these contexts have different forms of knowledge and systems of rules in relation to the acquisition of truth. When Marjane goes through a process of self-transformation she seeks to acquire truth which she

Figure 1.2　Illustration from *Persepolis 2: The Story of a Return* by Marjane Satrapi

believes lies in her 'new destiny' (121); part of this destiny lies in study-ing Art. Art (poiesis) in turn becomes the means by which these books are created and thereby fulfil her 'destiny' to be a successful artist (and filmmaker).[5] The comic-strip format of the Persepolis texts juxtaposes a graphic tradition of fantasy or untruth with a memoir that carries a tradition of truth-telling. Whereas photographs are often part of the truth-telling that memoirs or autobiographies attempt, the black-and-white comic strip of these graphic novels shows how truth-telling need not rely on conventional styles of illustration, but can create its own poiesis. The image, whether drawn or photographic, supports the narrative by revealing and disclosing further details.

Whitlock comments that it is impossible to read the veil from a 'neutral space' (2007: 48). The veil carries different meanings for both Islamic and non-Islamic cultures and societies: 'The veil, then, is a shifting signifier, open to various and strategic uses and frequently invoked as an intractable symbol of cultural difference' (2007: 51). *Does My Head Look Big in This?*, by Randa Abdel-Fattah, draws readers into considering veiling and how it marks cultural difference, especially in a secular, Western country such as Australia.

Amal Mohamed Nasrullah Abdel-Hakim is an 'Australian-Muslim-Palestinian' who lives with her liberal Muslim parents in 'Camberwell, one of Melbourne's trendy suburbs' (2005: 5). Both her parents are professionals, and while her mother wears the veil, they are concerned when 16-year-old Amal tells them that she has decided to wear hijab. That her parents do not actively encourage her to wear the veil is an attempt in the text to redress the misperception that all Muslim parents are extreme fundamentalists. Amal, like Marjane, is similarly interested in Western forms of consumption. When Amal prepares for wearing the veil, she tries on all her clothes, mixing and matching them with an assortment of coloured scarves as she dances to Western pop music. Each sartorial gesture seeks a pleasing aesthetic: 'I try different styles with the scarves and attempt to figure out which shape makes my face look slimmest' (16). However, she is committed to wearing the veil as part of her Muslim identity and as a sign of her faith. When her mother tries to prepare her for the negative reaction she will meet, Amal replies defiantly:

'What's the big deal? It's a piece of material.'
[...]
'So what? I can deal with all the crap [...] I want to try [...] and I want that identity. You know, that symbol of my faith. I want to know what it means to be strong enough to walk around with it on and stick up for my right to wear it.' (22)

The materiality of the veil and its religious significance become clear to Amal when she ventures into public for the first time wearing hijab and is acknowledged by three Muslim girls who offer the Islamic greeting 'Assalamu Alaykom' (Peace be upon you). This gesture of recognition and unity is focalised through Amal's thoughts: 'These girls are strangers to me but I know that we all felt an amazing connection, a sense that this cloth binds us in some kind of universal sisterhood' (25). Later when she prepares for her first day at school, Amal considers both the textual and aesthetic properties of the veil: 'I've chosen a plain white scarf, made of a soft chiffon [...] I want a perfect shape, a symmetrical arch to frame my face. That means no creases, no flops, no thread pulls' (29). It is worth noting at this point, how the aesthetic offered in this scene is carried through in the cover of the Pan Macmillan (2005) edition. Although this novel is unillustrated, the cover image shows an attractive, smiling Muslim girl in the foreground wearing a maroon-patterned hijab, a white headband and make-up, with two other girls seated in the background wearing jeans and T-shirts. This image and the description of the aesthetics of the veil in the extract are in contrast to the stark, elemental, black-and-white cartoon style of Satrapi's text. Both, however, create their own poiesis: Abdel-Fattah's book cover offers a deliberately non-confronting, pleasing aesthetic designed to appeal to a Western young adult readership. Satrapi's book cover offers a non-Western aesthetic. The photographic simplicity of *Does My Head Look Big in This?* is in stark contrast to the intricate, stylised Persian motifs cover design of the Persepolis books.

Throughout *Does My Head Look Big in This?* the veil is treated as an aesthetic and cultural signifier. One scene where Amal tries on different scarves as she prepares for her first day at school 'veiled' gives a sense of this mix. After 45 minutes of trying on clothes, Amal has the shape she wants. Looking at her image in the mirror she utters: 'Don't I just look like a *Ralph* magazine cutout. Grr' (29).[6] This scene, with its mixture of aesthetic and cultural codes, is repeated in similar ways throughout the text. Amal's ironic juxtaposition of concealing and revealing (Islamic morality and Western sexual display) ties the different cultural perspectives to notions of respectability, sexuality, eroticism and privacy. The scene also recalls the contrasting Western/Muslim-style dress that Marjane and her friends wore in private/public spaces. More importantly, the scene underscores the point that Amal, like Marjane, is an embodied subject who exists in the world and is conditioned, influenced and affected by that world and its competing views of how to live in the world. Whereas Marjane and her friends achieved some resistance to the strictures imposed on them through acts of resistance (often in private, but sometimes openly in voicing an opposing point of view), Amal undertakes a more public risk in seeking to unsettle dominant Western views and prejudices about Islam and specifically veiled Muslim girls. While the two contexts in which these texts are set are shaped by different political conditions, the prejudice that is evoked by mainstream Australian society in seeing a veiled girl calls for a different encounter with the Other which impacts both Amal and the non-Muslim beholder of the gaze.

In relation to how these texts unveil the truth, Foucault's account of 'practices of the self' is helpful as it provides a way of understanding how the activity of forming and shaping oneself as a certain kind of subject carries with it certain principles and truths. In general, Foucault's practices of the self involve:

> techniques that permit individuals to effect, by their own means, a certain number of operations on their own bodies, their own souls, their own conduct, and this in a manner so as to transform themselves, modify themselves, and attain a certain state of perfection, happiness, purity, spiritual power. (1982: 10)

Marjane transformed herself by changing her body shape and appearance through exercise, make-up and clothing, and by changing her lifestyle, living a life of freedom and decadence in Vienna, and by her illicit behaviour in Iran. Her attempts at self-transformation were in opposition to the fundamentalist culture of her country and the religious tenets of Islam. Consequently, her efforts were against the normative principles of her culture and religion as she refused to become a subordinated subject. Amal chooses to wear the veil and also attempts self-transformation by not only dressing in hijab but by trying to observe the religious principles of Islam in an attempt to form herself into a moral subject (for example, she decides not to have a sexual relationship with Adam, as sex before marriage is forbidden by Islam).

Further contrasts between Marjane and Amal concern how they open up a space for the Other. For Marjane it is a turn to history – the history of her family as well as the history of her country. By turning to history she comes to comprehend herself, the principles that her parents hold, and the ones by which she must live her life in order to be true to herself. For Foucault, a turn to history and the process of reflection – which he initially calls 'genealogy' and, later, the 'historical ontology of ourselves'[7] – opens up a space for the Other in one's world. Through her involvement with individuals who had a very different history, culture and religion in Vienna, Marjane is able to go beyond the enclosures that she initially experiences to create a new life for herself. For Amal, her decision to wear the veil does not prevent her from opening up a space for the Other. In fact, she credits a list of 'others' for helping her come to realise who she is, deliberately mixing cultural stereotypes and epithets to demonstrate the impact of cultural differences on her world and on her own embodied subjectivity:

> It's been the 'wogs', the 'nappy heads', the 'foreigners,' the 'persons of Middle Eastern appearance,' the Asians, the 'oppressed' women, the Greek Orthodox pensioner chain-smoker, the 'salami eaters,' the 'ethnics,' the pom-turned-curry-munchers, the narrow-minded and the educated, the fair-dinkum wannabes, the principal with hairy ears who showed me that I am a colourful adjective [...] their stories and confrontations and pains and joys have empowered me to know myself, challenged me to embrace my identity as a young Australian-Palestinian-Muslim girl (Abdel-Fattah 2005: 339–40)

Amal and Marjane create their 'selves' through their interactions with other people. While they do not discover their 'true' selves, they are able to gain knowledge about themselves, the world in which they live and the principles by which they wish to continue to live their lives. Before Marjane departs from Tehran for the last time, she wanders around the surrounding mountains memorising every corner, visiting the Caspian Sea with her grandmother, making pilgrimages to her grandfather's tomb and her uncle's grave, and spending time with her family (Satrapi 2004: 186). This dual process of memorialising and memorising is a necessary 'genealogy' or the making of her personal ontology as she embarks on a new life in France. For Amal, the year ends with a renewed self-knowledge. She comes to realise that wearing hijab is not enough for her to internalise and live by the knowledge that Islam offers. At a moment of self-reflection she says: 'But what's the good of being true to your religion on the outside, if you don't change on the inside, where it really counts?' (Abdel-Fattah 2005: 314). The hijab conceals the body but does not reveal a person's true beliefs. For most of the story, Amal is focused on how she *looks* in the hijab (the title alludes to physical appearance), mixing and matching colours, experimenting with make-up, frustrated with her wardrobe and what clothes she can wear to coordinate with her headscarves and hijab. This performance attempts to strategically position readers to *see* Amal as a 'normal' (Western) teenage girl. By the close of the narrative, she claims she is 'through with identity', but her declaration that she is 'going traditional now', paradoxically reinforces her commitment to an Islamic identity. Whereas Marjane chooses to live life unveiled, Amal's choice is to live with the veil. These contrasting approaches reflect the ongoing debates about Muslim women's wearing of the veil or hijab. However, the texts give readers a non-Western perspective on the veil: a perspective that disrupts the 'fantasy of the illicit penetration of the hidden and gendered spaces of "the Islamic World"' that Whitlock notes (2007: 58).

The naked truth

The previous section discussed the veil in its literal, material sense, but it also spoke of it in metaphorical and ideological terms. In the introduction to this chapter, I used the analogy of the dance of the veils as a way of explaining how fiction exposes and conceals through its 'veil of words', a phrase used by Bruce Krajewski. Krajewski draws our attention to how allegory protects readers as it mediates the impact of the truth: 'The truth cannot be viewed directly, so allegory or "the veil of words," mediates the truth' (1992: 124). Just as the Western gaze seeks to penetrate the Muslim veil, readers also seek to penetrate the veil of words to discover what is hidden, to read allegory for its veiled meaning. However, our efforts to discover the truth through our interpretation of a text can only ever be our own constructed version of it. Fiction is not scientific in its approach, nor does it endeavour to offer proofs. It does propose, however, 'a way of being in the world' (Krajewski 1992: 9), offering speculations and probabilities, a staging of the truth.

In exploring the so-called 'naked truth', I consider the idea of nakedness and why it is often linked with truth. The truth 'clothed' in words or symbol invites a comparison with Kenneth Clark's argument that the nude is a body 'clothed' in art. Clark makes the distinction between the naked and the nude, elevating the nude to a higher level of aesthetic appreciation as he considers it to show the body transformed: 'the nude remains the most complete example of the transformation of matter into form' (1956: 23). This transformation from the naked to the nude moves from the actual corporeal matter in its unformed, unruly, unbounded state, to the ideal form which is balanced and 'pure' (in a Kantian sense). Here the body stripped of artifice conceals nothing and is therefore the embodiment of Truth. The nude Phryne is able to stand as an allegory of Truth because her beauty is not only beyond compare, but it makes her seemingly beyond reproach. While there are a number of points in Clark's book that invite challenge, the one that is pertinent to this section is the paradox that resides within his discussion regarding representation. Clark's dualistic construction of the nude and the naked is problematic not only because of his hierarchical valuing of one form over the other, but also because of his formulating of the nude body as a body outside representation. Lynda Neal draws attention to Clark's flawed distinction and theory of representation: 'there can be no "naked" other to the nude, for the body is always already in representation [...] there is no semiotically innocent and unmediated body' (1992: 16). Further comment on Clark's distinction between naked and nude is taken up by Rob Cover, who says that by rendering the naked as nude 'ignores how it [the naked body] is always already represented and constrained by codes of behaviour, contexts, differentiation from the clothed body, loose significations and cultural rituals' (2003: 53). Cover notes that in film, nakedness often connotes 'vulnerability, humiliation or comic transgression', and singles out teen comedies in which he says there is invariably 'a scene of male nudity in a public space for comic purposes' (54).

Cover's refocusing on the naked male body as a comic sight recalls *The Emperor's New Clothes*, an allegorical tale in which nakedness invokes 'a staging of truth' (Derrida 1975: 38). Elsewhere I have discussed this story as a text that opens up ways of reading the exposed male body as a spectacle (Mallan 2002). Picture-book versions of this story have variously shown the Emperor in a bare torso view, completely naked, or in the case of David Mackintosh's illustrated version (Andersen 1993), the Emperor strides confidently out on to the streets, with his chin jutting forward, while wearing only his Y-front underpants (and socks and shoes). This partially naked/clothed body draws attention to what it attempts to conceal. When the Emperor's nakedness is announced by the child, the Emperor's boldness, arrogance and theatricality evaporate and he becomes self-conscious of his exposure, reduced to a defenceless, embarrassed subject, whose title no longer distinguishes him as being superior to the people over whom he rules. Unlike Michelangelo's *David*, or the statue of Apollo, famous 'nudes' that Clark speaks of, the Emperor does not offer a purity of form, nor does he arouse some erotic impulse for the viewer, something which Clark believes is mandatory for the nude to evoke: 'it is necessary to labour the obvious and say that no nude, however abstract, should fail to arouse in the spectator some vestige of erotic feeling, even though it be only the faintest shadow' (Clark 1956: 8). Clark would no doubt see the representation of the unclothed Emperor as an example of the naked body, not the nude, and one which supports his claim that 'naked' pertains to life (the actual) and 'nude' pertains to life transformed by art (the ideal):

> To be naked is to be deprived of our clothes, and the word implies some of the embarrassment most of us feel in that condition. The word 'nude,' on the other hand, carries, in educated usage, no uncomfortable overtone. The vague image it projects into the mind is not of a huddled and defenceless body, but of a balanced, prosperous, and confident body: the body re-formed. (3)

Clark's contention that the nude body is re-formed by art denies the ways in which context shapes representation. Cover makes a similar point in noting that context plays a key part in how nakedness is received. When nakedness is performed without company it invites the gaze of the self, only this gaze is one that scrutinises as it seeks and finds imperfection, or sometimes pleasure or beauty. To return to Mackintosh's text, prior to the parade the Emperor stands before a mirror admiring his reflection, while the rogue tailors fit his naked body with the invisible clothes. In this mirror scene, the Emperor sees himself, as the Emperor, and fails to see the naked man that is reflected in the mirror. It is only when he moves out into the streets that this privileged imperial viewing is destroyed by a child's vocal declaration of his nakedness: 'No longer protected by the veil of invisibility, as was the Emperor's privilege, the now marked and visible man masquerading as an arrogant, vain ruler is the object of the derisive spectacle' (Mallan 2002: 33–4). This text shows that the truth lies in exposure. But as a fiction, the text offers a double exposure of the truth. The first comes as the veil of words is lifted to reveal to readers the truth about the Emperor: that he is not a leader of integrity or intelligence, but a vain man who cares only for his appearance and costly attire. The second exposure is for the subjects within the fiction when the truth is exposed through the Emperor's folly when he parades under the veil of illusion that he is dressed resplendently as befitting an Emperor.

When *The Emperor's New Clothes* is read as a picture book (or viewed as a film) it invites a different kind of reception compared with an oral or written account devoid of illustration. Representation of the naked body in fiction for children (especially in picture books or illustrated texts) relies on both artistic procedure or technique (aesthetic treatment) and a 'proper' viewing from the prospective reader. Some texts invite a 'blind' reading of the body, whereby the reader like the Emperor does not *see* the naked body before him/her. Other texts rely on a viewer's sharp eye to detect something that is beyond the artifice of a semioti-cally innocent and unmediated body, a point noted by Neal above as a counter to Clark's nude/naked distinction. To explain these different ways of seeing (after Berger), the first part of the discussion below con-siders how stories for children of 'naked' animals often rely on a reader's 'blindness' not to simply not *see* nakedness, but to not see the truth that clothing veils. The discussion then moves on to consider how truth exists but how we are often blind to its manifestation or unable to see how it waits to be discovered through a play of signs in a 'queer time and place' (Halberstam 2005).

In the picture book *Wanted: The Perfect Pet* by Fiona Robertson (2009),[8] a boy and a duck come to form the perfect match, but not before the duck undergoes a masquerade. Henry believes that all he wants is a dog, and while he has 27 varieties of frog, he is not happy: 'they are boring' (unpaged). What Henry wants is a pet with a personality, and he con-structs the image of the perfect dog pointing out its physical features (floppy ears, waggy tail, soft wet nose, warm furry tongue) and skills (catch balls, fly through flaming hoops, balance on a unicycle while holding a ball on its nose). A lonely duck that lives a reclusive life 'at the top of a cold and windy hill' sees Henry's advertisement and decides to apply, after transforming itself with the 'perfect disguise' (a pair of old socks for long floppy ears and a tail, and an egg box and some string for a snout). When Henry sees the 'dog' he is excited and happy. However, his dog soon proves totally inept at performing the tricks and games Henry wants to play with it. Bit by bit, items of clothing drop off the dog until its true duck body emerges. Henry quickly accepts the duck for what it is and discovers its natural talents.

This simple story offers an equally simple truth: *To thine own self be true.* Initially, Henry sees what he wants to see, and his desire to have a dog casts a veil over his powers of discrimination. The duck is already an out-sider (ducks don't live alone on cold windy hills in an egg-shaped house) but it is prepared to become other than itself in order to have a compan-ion. The duck's resort to human clothing and materials is a common device of many anthropomorphic stories. The human disguise works to conceal the animal's true nature and serves as a 'civilising' strategy.[9]

In *The Tale of Peter Rabbit* (Potter 1902), like many other books by Beatrix Potter, animals wear human clothing, and, as Carole Scott points out, these clothes often 'represent the various classes and levels of sophis-tication found in human societies' (1994: 70). More significantly, how-ever, Scott notes that although the clothes were necessary items of accoutrement for the animal characters, they were also a nuisance and often restricted natural mobility and stability, and were totally imprac-tical for the purposes of daily animal life: 'Mrs. Tiggy-Winkle's volu-minous clothes – cap, print gown, petticoat, and apron – cannot cover her hedgehog prickles, which stick right through' (1994: 77). Another example is when Peter Rabbit needs to cast off his shoes as he tries to escape Mr McGregor's garden, as they impede his natural speed. His clothes not only impede his speed, but they also trap him when the brass buttons on his blue coat get caught on a gooseberry net. When Peter finally sheds his clothes and runs on all fours instead of just his hind legs he is able to get away from danger, but his mother punishes him for disobeying her and losing his clothes. Scott suggests that there is an allegorical significance behind these stories which points to the restrictions of clothing (especially for women at the time of Potter's writing) and how these impact on both animal/human freedom. More significantly for this discussion, Scott sees the clothes as a form of con-cealment of the true being: '[clothes] mar and hide the real, natural self, rather than provide a means to express it' (1994: 79).

In another instance, Perry Nodelman reports on his university stu-dents' responses to an exercise where the gender of Peter Rabbit was changed to female – renaming the story as *The Tale of Honeysweet Rabbit*. While the students felt that the gender switch did not make any major changes to the antics of the main protagonist, they did find Honeysweet's nakedness held a different meaning for them, which Nodelman theorises in terms of gendered sexuality:

> A naked girl is a sex object, even a naked girl rabbit. She makes us uncomfortable because the revelation of her nakedness implies, not physical aggression and competence, but availability, lack of control or restraint, a dangerously or deliciously unbridled revelation of pas-sion and instinct. (Nodelman 2002: 6)

Consequently, the students were evidently 'blind', or turned a blind eye, to Peter Rabbit's nakedness but saw in their minds the unaccept-ability of a naked Honeysweet. Nodelman's observation harks back to Kenneth Clark's point that the (female) nude offers 'some vestige of erotic feeling', but unlike Michelangelo's *David*, the students did not appear to admit to or attribute any erotic significance to Peter Rabbit. While this classroom exercise lacked any scientific process it neverthe-less highlights the point that the naked/nude distinction is not a simple one to make, especially in terms of attributing an erotic significance regardless of gender.

No matter how we read the naked (human) body it is never liberated from cultural and historical convention. For the early Greeks, the naked body of Phryne may have caused the judges to reconsider their verdict as they saw before them the Ideal, the same ideal of structure, geometry, harmony of which Clark gives a detailed account in his book. However, when the body is not ideal, then, from Clark's position, the viewer is no longer held in quiet rapture or meditation, nor enjoys a hastened heartbeat. Rather, the viewer is profaned, desecrated or violated (1956: 320). Neal explains that profane means literally 'outside the temple'. The grotesque or mad have bodies that are 'outside the temple', but in themselves may carry a 'truth' worth contemplating. In the following text I consider how those we consider to be mad or crazy can offer a truth that is invisible to normative ways of being.

The title of *When You Reach Me* (2009), a novel by Rebecca Stead, gives an indication to the two central ideas in the text – time and space. The first clue to this organising thematic can be found on the cover of the book (Australian edition), with its simple street map with a dotted line, the cityscape depicted in silhouette on the horizon, the random items (key, shoe, book, green jacket, mailbox and three buildings) and the personal pronouns (you, me); all these combine to suggest a spatio-temporal logic of location, movement and identification.[10] However, time and space in this story take on a different logic from the more compressed notion of time-space that we have come to associate with contemporary globalisation (see Harvey 1990). For one, the story is set in 1978–79, a time which had not yet experienced the explosion of mass communication technologies and rampant globalisation that impacted the late twentieth century and which has continued to shape everyday life in the West, and many other parts of the world. The story's location is in a small part of Manhattan and, as the cover visually encodes, movement of the characters is tracked along a restricted path as they go about their day-to-day lives. The restricted traversing from one point to the next is due to the age of the main characters – Miranda, Sal, Colin, Julia, Annemarie and Marcus, who are 12 years old – and the concern of the adults, especially parents and teachers, that children are not safe out on the streets on their own. The daily schedule of normal activity provides a regular beat of time passing, spaces travelled and experienced, but normativity is also disrupted in this text, producing a non-normative construction of time and space, as well as of location, movement and identification.

A key factor in this disruption is a character – 'the laughing man' – who appears mad or crazy. He lives on the street, sleeps with his head under a US mailbox, laughs, mutters, and does high kicks for no apparent reason. Drawing on Foucault's study of madness in *Madness and Civilization*, Clare O'Farrell notes that because of the transformation of medical science over the course of time, madness has been 'tamed and stripped of its capacity to point to another world, and to extreme experience and to truth' (2005: 38). *When You Reach Me* recovers this potential, and the mad, laughing man does indeed point to another world, which is not so much a place as a temporal dimension which sees future and present not as a linear march from one point to the next, but as a travelling back and forth through space. The mad man also speaks the truth, but this is not realised until after his death. Foucault regarded death as 'the lyrical core of man: his invisible truth, his visible secret' (*The Birth of the Clinic*, qtd in O'Farrell 2005: 38), and in this story both Miranda and readers come to know the laughing man's secret and the visibility of his truth. These revelations are explained in the following discussion where I use time and space as frameworks for considerations of life and truth, as they are understood within this fiction.

The story is focalised through the perspective of Miranda, who lives with her mother in a small apartment in Manhattan. Miranda loves Madeleine L'Engle's *A Wrinkle in Time* (1962) which offers a clue as to how time is treated in *When You Reach Me*; it also mediates the idea of time travel that underpins the plot and intrigues Miranda.[11] Her friend Marcus tries to explain the concept of time: '"Think of it like this," said Marcus [...] "Time isn't a line stretching out in front of us, going in one direction. It's – well, time is just a construct, actually –"' (Stead 2009: 118). Julia elaborates, demonstrating with her ring that is studded with diamonds: 'Look. It's like every moment in time is a diamond sitting on this ring. Pretend the ring is really big, with diamonds all around, and each diamond is one moment. Got it?' (119).

Miranda's mother's boyfriend, Richard, is a constant visitor but Miranda's mother is not convinced that he should be given a key to their apartment as this suggests a future to which she is not ready to commit. Family time is spent at home, and largely devoted to preparing Miranda's mother for her appearance as a contestant on *The $20,000 Pyramid*, a television show hosted by (the timeless) Dick Clark. Within the apartment there is a normative progression and scheduling of daily life, and on one occasion when Miranda slips out early but fails to let her mother know where she is, the normative routine is severely disrupted and her mother becomes frantic over Miranda's safety. Other normative schedules follow in the school Miranda and her friends attend, the shop she visits after school which is owned by her mother's friend Bella, and

Jimmy's pizza place where Miranda, Colin and Annemarie work during their lunch break. Outside the regulated time-schedules of these enclosed spaces, the laughing man moves and lives according to a non-normative logic and activity within time and space.

Halberstam's notion of 'queer time' comes closest to describing how we could conceive of the laughing man's non-normative behaviour. For Halberstam, the concept of queer time and space opens 'new ways of understanding nonnormative behaviors that have clear *but not essential* relations to gay and lesbian subjects' (2005: 6, my emphasis). The laughing man is a queer subject in that he experiences a way of life that is a 'wilfully eccentric mode of being', a description Halberstam uses with regard to how some, not all, gay, lesbian, transgender people live their lives (1). Miranda explains how the eccentricity of the 'crazy guy' frightens her, and that walking alone past him is in the top half of her 'list of bad things':

> A few kids called him Quack, short for Quackers, or they called him Kicker because he used to do these sudden kicks into the street, like he was trying to punt one of the cars speeding up Amsterdam Avenue. Sometimes he shook his fist at the sky and yelled crazy stuff like 'What's the burn scale? Where's the dome?' and then he threw his head back and laughed these loud, crazy laughs, so everyone could see that he had about thirty fillings in his teeth. And he was always on our corner, sometimes sleeping with his head under the mailbox. (18–19)

The laughing man's veil over his words covers their meaning and leaves his listeners convinced that he is crazy. In a related way, the explanations of time that Marcus and Julia offer are similarly met with confusion from Miranda. The opacity of the characters' spoken words and their elusive allegorical meanings form part of the text's dance of veils. Further confusion from word games follows when Miranda receives mysterious notes that only come to make sense for her after the laughing man dies. Readers too can retrace their way back through the story and realise the significances of veiled references in the notes: 'I have been practicing and my preparations go well. I'm coming to save your friend's life, and my own' (first note: 68); 'Your letter must tell a story – a true story. You cannot begin now, as most of it has not yet taken place [...] The trip is a difficult one [...]' (second note: 78); 'You will want proof. 3pm today: Colin's knapsack. Christmas Day: Tesser well. April 27th: Studio TV-15' (third note: 114). The notes refer to things that have not yet occurred in narrative time. But Miranda is writing the story that the second note asks of her, and therefore she is recounting (using past tense) how at the time of receiving the notes their meanings were cryptic: 'I had absolutely no idea what this could mean, or how you knew Colin' (114). She also uses second-person address when she reveals the notes. The address to 'you' is not the 'implied reader', but to the person who wrote the notes: a secret not revealed to readers until the end of the story.

The story is written *after* the events that we read, but the chapters map a linear movement in narrative time and space, with plot events unfolding with Miranda as the focalising narrator. The notes and Miranda's switch to second-person address appear within the folds of the narrative, becoming a wrinkle in time: on the one hand, they speak of things to come; on the other, the use of past tense implies a knowledge of things that have passed. The narrative structure conforms to Ricoeur's interpretation of narrative time as involving memory and anticipation – as readers we move back and forth in our thinking about the story, perhaps rereading parts to check that our memory of events serves us correctly, always anticipating a conclusion, an end point, which will provide a position to review, revise and recount. Ricoeur sees the conclusion in narrative as enabling readers a backward glance at the actions that led up to it (1981: 170). The text cleverly installs Miranda as the storyteller who recounts a 'true story', one she recalls from memory and evidence (the notes, and other pieces of information). But she participates in her story as a part of the unfolding action, while intermittently stepping out of this role, to speak directly to the note writer, whereby it is clear that the two share a secret of which the readers become progressively aware.

The secret reveals a truth about an alternative temporality. Halberstam argues that queer subcultures produce alternative temporalities that enable them to imagine a future according to 'logics that lie outside of those paradigmatic markers of life experience – namely, birth, marriage, reproduction, and death' (2005: 2). The laughing man lives according to an alternative temporality in that he knows that he lives his future in the other characters' present, while the other characters live their present time in an expectation of moving towards their imagined futures. When Miranda and Marcus talk about the time travel in *A Wrinkle in Time*, Miranda is adamant that 'the end can't happen before the middle' (Stead 2009: 57), a belief shaped by the logics of time that see conventional linear narrative time and the paradigmatic passing of time from birth to death.

We discover that the laughing man is also the naked man who has been seen in the neighbourhood, a nakedness that children are forbidden to see: 'The Monday after Thanksgiving we were stuck in the school cafeteria for lunch. The naked guy was back, running down Broadway, and they wouldn't let any kids out of the building' (101). His nakedness poses a threat, and hints of danger, because it disrupts the normal way of being. He covers his nakedness after he steals clothes from Miranda's place: clothes that belonged to Richard, her mother's boyfriend. The laughing man's non-normative lifestyle has a different temporal rhythm to the rest of the characters whose days follow what Halberstam terms a 'schedule of normativity' (2005: 7) – family time, school time, after school time. He lives on the edges in a time/space that is limned by risks, vulnerable to both the weather and mischievous people. Miranda is aware of the dangers: 'The laughing man was still asleep with his head under the mailbox. He had found some cardboard to put underneath him. Still, he must have been freezing. Some mornings, I'd seen kids banging on the mailbox and yelling, "Wake up, Kicker!" I hope no one would do that today' (Stead 2009: 113). However, the laughing man's liminality, his queer temporality, offers a viewing point that is not part of the naturalised spatial practices that occur around him. In other words, he sees what goes on around him, and speaks to Miranda when he chooses, but only becomes involved when he must save Marcus from being hit by a truck. Miranda documents the truck incident in numbered steps, each describing the temporal moment:

29. Suddenly, the laughing man was in the street, his right leg flying out in a mighty kick.
30. The laughing man's foot hit Sal's body.
31. Sal flew backwards and hit the ground, hard.
32. The truck hit the laughing man. (186–7)

Saving Sal is the purpose behind the laughing man's presence in the children's lives – the *difficult trip* he had to make. After this incident, Miranda is able to see the truth of what has happened and why it needed to happen. She remembers her mother telling her that people need to lift the veil that prevents us from seeing the world as it really is. The veils are convenient as they stop us from seeing truths, but when they are lifted for just a moment – 'We see all the beauty, and cruelty, and sadness, and love' (82). The veil makes the world 'kind of blurry, and we like it that way' (81). Miranda's moment when the veil lifts provides her with insight into the events of the past weeks with the note writer, the laughing man, her friends and time travel. This may not be a revelation of the naked truth, but Miranda has knowledge about the past that had previously eluded her.

In exploring the idea of unveiling the truth, this chapter has highlighted the ways that truth is often regarded as something that can be discovered, revealed or hidden. This suggestion implies that truth has a tangible quality, a core essence, which is both problematic and impossible. My selection draws on a range of texts that spans different historical periods and cultural contexts, as well as different genres. What connects these varied texts is the idea that truth is not monolithic, and that the connection between unveiling and the truth is a tenuous one. Additionally, I have shown how the veil has multiple significances within both non-Western and Western cultures. When the veil (or veiling) is used metaphorically, the suggestion that it conceals a truth is both true and not true, and is subject to motivation and interpretation. For some, veiling or concealing the truth is a means to survive in a dangerous or unfamiliar environment; for others, it is a way to adapt to become Other to oneself in a quest to find acceptance or a means to assert one's true identity. In other instances, the truth is concealed in a veil of words that invites deciphering.

The idea that fiction contains hidden truths which are waiting to be discovered by readers has persisted over time. Unlike the child who sees through the veil of deceit and vanity in Andersen's fairy tale, the access to the truth in memoirs or diaries is never guaranteed. What the texts in this selection have shown is that there is no distinct line separating truth and lies. For some, the need to conceal one's true beliefs is a necessary strategy for maintaining a sense of self, or becoming a certain kind of subject. In these instances, characters such as Marjane and her friends attempt self-transformation, which is dangerous but necessary. For Amal the veil is given a significance that is part of her developing subjectivity as a Muslim. In other instances, characters use disguise in an effort to achieve a different kind of self-transformation but find that their 'true' self, the unveiled one, is the only means to self-realisation. Finally, the naked man reminds readers that there are those who 'live outside the temple', the mad, the grotesque who may have truths to tell but their utterances are often ignored or dismissed as nonsense.

2
Lies of Necessity

The moral philosopher Immanuel Kant condemned all lying without exception.[1] Kant's view is not only extreme but fails to take account of situations where lies are necessary. This chapter examines some of these necessary situations. While Sophocles believed that 'to tell lies is not honourable', he nevertheless conceded that in some circumstances where 'the truth entails tremendous ruin' then 'to speak dishonourably is pardonable' (2007: 318). Others might dismiss the idea of honour all together and take a more self-serving view that lying is necessary to achieve one's goals, ambitions or desires. Like most of the questions this book poses, the answers are never easy or straightforward. These different perspectives on the role of lies and deception describe the contrast between moral imperative on the one hand, and survival instinct on the other. Literature conveys lessons about honour, an admirable quality that requires us to handle the 'slings and arrows of outrageous fortune' with integrity, truthfulness and fearlessness. But our instinct for survival tells us that lies, camouflage, guile and trickery are very useful (and successful) strategies when we find ourselves in a desperate situation. There is no doubt that the desire to survive, to live, is a strong natural instinct. However, people will sacrifice their lives for the sake of a belief, to avoid breaking a trust or as an act of martyrdom. I argue that in children's fiction, lying may be justified as a survival strategy when a character is faced with extreme circumstances of life or death, but telling the truth will always be valorised as the moral, and therefore superior, course of action. The implied readership of the texts is no doubt a factor in ensuring that there is a win-win outcome: lies can be told and justified but in the end truth will win out.

The violence or marginalisation that is characteristically directed against the figure of the liar also finds its counterpart in the truth-teller who might similarly be subjected to acts of violence or psychological maltreatment for telling the truth or aspects of the truth. I discuss how this occurs in the fictions in this chapter. The texts also show that in order to avoid being the subject of violence or marginalisation one often resorts to not telling the truth. A key feature of not telling the truth is the art of concealment. Concealment of the truth or simply not telling (or showing) the truth is common to both social practice and fiction. Sometimes secrets are a way of concealing the truth. A secret may not be a lie, and a lie is not necessarily a secret. A secret withholds information, whereas a lie alters or invents information. These terms are central to the discussion of the characters' survival. Nietzsche makes the point that human existence depends on necessary fictions, or what he terms 'the art of simulation' (1954: 43). Sometimes the process of concealing or revealing may be tied to the experience of fear, mourning, anxiety or forbidden love. When faced with death or trauma one may quickly learn that to lie may be the means to survive even if the consequences may make life paradoxically unlivable. Similarly, keeping a secret may be a necessary means for short-term survival but its long-term concealment may paradoxically result in death.

Bok suggests that knowledge of the facts or the truth gives power, and lies affect the distribution of power: '[lies] add to that of the liar, and diminish [the power] of the deceived, alternating his choices at different levels' (1999: 19). Such shifting power balances emerge in the following sections as I examine how children are often positioned to have limited power or are indeed powerless in circumstances that are controlled by adults, or by older children, especially when they (children) are the targets of violence. Foucault was interested in power and knowledge, sometimes writing the two words as a compound 'power-knowledge', to illustrate how he considered them to have equal status, and to be mutually generative. For Foucault, knowledge emerges from networks of power and the exercise of power produces certain types of knowledge (1980). He is also not so much concerned with the problem of truth, but with the problem of the truth-teller or truth-telling. For Foucault, truth-telling revolves around four questions: Who is able to tell the truth? About what? With what consequences? With what relation to power? He asks: 'What is the importance for the individual and for the society of telling the truth, of knowing the truth, of having people who tell the truth, as well as knowing how to recognize them?' (2001: 170). Foucault's questions about truth-telling are considered in terms of this chapter's focus on fiction's treatment of survival as being contingent on secrets and lies. The discussion begins by considering how texts for young people deal with the consequences of violence and how children may be forced into keeping secrets for fear of their lives.

Lying to protect

Lies protect and expose, just as truth can harm and bind: these are the paradoxes that infuse *Secrets* by Jacqueline Wilson (2002), *Number the Stars* by Lois Lowry (1989) and *The Other Side of Truth* by Beverley Naidoo (2000). The connecting thread in these texts is how children learn to survive life-threatening conditions through lies and deception. Survival in *Secrets* and *Number the Stars* depends on a friendship between two girls where one provides a refuge for the other and thereby assumes the role of protector. In *Secrets*, India hides her friend, Treasure, in the attic of her family home to avoid her being returned to an abusive home environment. In *Number the Stars* Annemarie's family provides a safe refuge for a Jewish family which includes Annemarie's friend Ellen; Annemarie, like India, takes on a protecting role. In hiding Treasure, India's fascination with Anne Frank's story is revivified as she hides her friend in the attic of her own home: the persecution of Jews (which also is the heart of the unspeakable trauma in *Number the Stars*) becomes a phantom presence in *Secrets*. In *The Other Side of Truth* soldiers under General Abacha's regime in Nigeria (1993–98) murder an innocent woman, the mother of Sade and Femi, who need to assume false identities and travel with an unscrupulous people-smuggler to England to also avoid being murdered. The children's father is a journalist who refuses to write anything but the truth about the corrupt regime and thereby puts his own life and his family in danger. *Nasreen's Secret School* by Jeanette Winter (2009) and *The Invention of Hugo Cabret* by Brian Selznick (2007) each tell a story told from a point of view shaped by context, history and 'truth'. These stories also highlight the mechanisms for survival when life is threatened or under surveillance.

As noted above, Nietzsche asserts that human existence is founded on necessary fictions – such as 'deception, flattery, lying and deceiving, talking behind the back, posing' – indeed, that survival is contingent upon such 'simulations' (1954: 43). In this section, the fictional texts illustrate the circumstances whereby survival is contingent upon lies. Whereas Nietzsche held the radical view that truth is an invention, 'a mobile army of metaphors [...] truths are illusions' (46–7), it is the covering up of the truth, and the invention or *rendition* of truth, that drive these narratives. The novels reach closure but do not close down the subject of truth and deception. The lingering tacit knowledge that readers may take away with them when the final pages are read is that renditions of truth will continue to shape human interaction, and the violence that we perpetrate upon one another will necessitate acts of deception in order to silence, and to survive.

Secrecy, like storytelling, has a relationship to power. Bok says that secrecy imposes both a power and a burden (1989: 36). This paradox emerges in *Secrets* by Jacqueline Wilson. The story is told from alternating diary entries from the two main characters – Treasure and India. Readers are positioned to accept the 'truths' presented from the point of view of these fictional diarists as there is no corroborating or contradictory viewpoint. The diary mode in *Secrets* is a means to bring together the stories of two girls living in difficult, yet very different, family circumstances; diary writing is the common element they share. The diary entries are polished and extended text and there is no attempt to mimic the diary writing of adolescent girls.

The peritext is also complicit in the deception. For instance, the cover illustration of the two diaries and two small keys dangling from the words in the title further connote the message of secrecy. The background split of reverse colour writing encodes the two diarists, and the partially visible, fragmented text serves to frustrate a reader's attempts to read and make sense of what it says. There is a double-play at work in the book's title with the cover designed to lure readers to open the book and discover the secrets that lie within. The preface by the author Jacqueline Wilson underscores her role as author and the text's status as fiction: 'I'm the author. I have power over the plot! So of course I made the girls meet and get to know each other properly. They tell their stories in alternate chapters' (unpaged). Wilson's unnecessary reminder that she is the author and as such has power over the storytelling also undermines the text's mimetic value.

The disclosure of the fictionality of the text is at odds with its purpose to deceive, which the cover image of two diaries and the subsequent diary entries attempt. Treasure's diary is a notebook, which, she explains on the first page, is the 'Official Terry Torture Manual'. Terry is her stepfather who makes her life a misery. From the outset we are positioned to see Terry as aggressive and violent. When he discovers the notebook he rips out the pages and strikes Treasure with his belt: the buckle causes a long and deep cut on her forehead and the force of the attack breaks her glasses. We can also assume from the title of her journal that this was not the first act of violence by Terry, a point which is confirmed near the end of the novel when India reveals that Treasure had told her 'several real stories about Terry and what he had done to her [...] they were far more scary than my imaginary melodramas' (185).

Treasure does not address her diary in the manner of 'Dear Diary', but India begins each entry with 'Dear Kitty' – borrowing from Anne Frank, who created an imaginary friend to whom she confided her thoughts and situation. India's mode of address exceeds the more impersonal and conventional address that Treasure adopts, and as the novel progresses India's obsession with Anne Frank runs deeper. Wilson too reveals a similar obsession: 'I was obsessed by Anne Frank like India, reading her very moving diary again and again. I had a photo of Anne by my bedside for years' (unpaged). This invocation of Anne Frank in the preface and in the author's life as a young girl becomes a truth claim to verify the truthfulness of the author in revealing the influence of Anne Frank and her diary on her own girlhood. We can read this piece of truth-telling as imposing a kind of self-perpetuation: like Jacqueline Wilson and Anne Frank, the implied girl readers may themselves become famous writers. Additionally, when Treasure reads India's copy of *Anne Frank* she begins to draw parallels with her own situation, comparing Terry to the Gestapo: 'It's like he's all Anne Frank's Gestapo rolled up into one monstrous man' (144). She also considers her solitary situation to be worse than Anne's: 'At least Anne had her sister and her parents and Peter and his family [...] I just want someone to talk to. Anyone' (145). She even makes a 'Clothes Person' she calls 'Kitty': 'just like Anne Frank's imaginary friend' (145). Given Wilson's fascination with Anne Frank as a child, and the comparisons drawn between Treasure's situation and that of Anne Frank, and the simulated 'Kitty', it would seem that the trauma of the Holocaust and the unspeakable violence perpetrated against the Jews haunts this fictional story of a child hiding in fear of her life.

As a work of fiction, *Secrets* could be seen as not making claims to literal truth, except possibly to the in-text references to Anne Frank and her life as recorded in her diary, but even the authenticity of that text as having been written by a teenage girl has been the subject of legal deliberations and ongoing public debate. Wilson discloses her girlhood fascination with Anne Frank in the preface, and apart from these truth-claims, secrets and lies permeate the text. Treasure and India have secrets which they reveal to the reader, and which place the reader in the position of confidante. The first secret revealed by Treasure is that her stepfather Terry cut her forehead with his belt buckle in an act of physical aggression. However, her mother covers up this fact or truth as she fears the repercussions if doctors or social workers hear of it: 'They'll come down on Terry like a ton of bricks' (11). The mother subsequently lies to hide the act of violence; she also lies to herself – 'No, no, it was an accident, his belt –' (10), and despite the fact that the cut required stitches she insists 'It's just a nasty nick' (11). Treasure's mother's inability to let the truth be known for fear of what the system (doctors, social workers, police) might do to Terry recalls Foucault's questions: Who is able to tell the truth? About what? With what consequences? With what relation to power? Later Treasure's beloved Nan reluctantly becomes part of the deception when she confirms Treasure's lie to the hospital staff that the cut was caused from playing a cowboy game with her siblings and she ended up being lassoed. While Nan backs Treasure's story, her motives for doing so are more about protecting her own status as someone who will not be seen as collaborating with the police: '"Though why we should protect that pig I don't know," she muttered, lighting up a ciggie. "Still, I'm not having anyone call *me* a grass"' (15). Her decision not to reveal the truth to the authorities confirms her daughter's fears about the consequences of truth-telling.

The two girls forge a friendship and when Treasure has to flee the safety of her grandmother's home to avoid being taken back by her mother and Terry, India decides secretly to hide Treasure in the attic of her family home. India is bound by this secret because to disclose the whereabouts of Treasure could result in Treasure being returned to her mother and Terry. Treasure hides in the attic of India's home, and this is the ideal setting for the two girls to simulate to some extent Anne Frank's life of hiding in a secret annex. Such 'simulation' in Nietzsche's terms necessitates secrecy, deception and lying. Thus, readers become knowers of the secret which is not only part of the plot, but an intrinsic feature of the fiction which gradually converts a state of unknowing (which we experience at the beginning of any fiction) to a state of knowing or thinking about the secret, and is what Frank Kermode (1979) terms the literary 'genesis of secrecy' that aims at converting 'unknowing' itself into a secret form of knowledge. This point is given expression in the conclusion of the preface when Wilson invites readers into the fictional world as truth by asking: 'Do you think Treasure and India will stay best friends forever? I do hope so' (unpaged). The direct address to the reader is what Kermode (1980) would regard as a veiled 'invitation to interpretation' rather than an appeal 'to a consensus' (93). Wilson's comment foreshadows the uncertainty that the girls express at the end of their own diaries wondering if their friendship will continue forever. It also recovers Wilson's initial dismissal of mimesis and denies readers any epistemological certitude. We only come to recognise her comment as a metafictional conceit once we have finished reading the story, and discover the text's literary secret.

In refusing to break her friend's confidence and reveal where Treasure is hidden, India is trapped in a moral dilemma. Ironically, the need to hide is reasoned by both girls as a necessary step to ensure Treasure's survival, just as it was a necessary survival means for Anne Frank. Hiding serves a double purpose: in hiding Treasure in the attic, India conceals Treasure's location, as well as the truth behind her reason to hide. Metaphorically, the girls are 'truth' in so much as the nature of truth is to conceal itself (as discussed in Chapter 1). Literally, the girls learn the art of survival: India takes on a caretaker's role, skilfully creating a comfortable space for Treasure, tending to her needs, and deceiving her parents and the au pair through lies, cunning and creativity. Treasure too learns a different art of survival by finding ways to entertain herself and learning how to be quiet and brave. However, the secret is tested when media coverage of Treasure's disappearance mounts and her mother and Terry appear tearful and grief-stricken on television news. The situation escalates further when Treasure's asthma becomes a risk to her physical health, causing India to be faced with a further dimension to her dilemma: one where life literally hangs in the balance. Paradoxically, but necessarily, survival which first depended on secrecy and concealment now requires unveiling and openness in order for Treasure to live. Revealing or unveiling is what secrets seek.

Lois Lowry's *Number the Stars* serves as a bridging text between *Secrets* and *The Other Side of Truth* by showing how the discourses of survival and persecution often inscribe texts that deal with secrets and lies. Life in Copenhagen changes dramatically for its citizens under the German occupation in 1943 and *Number the Stars* focuses on how the war and the persecution of the Jews by the Nazis impact the lives of two friends – Annemarie Johansen and Ellen Rosen, who is Jewish. Whereas the friendship between India and Treasure had been formed through serendipitous circumstances, Annemarie and Ellen are already firm friends, neighbours and school mates from the outset of the story. Because of this friendship Annemarie becomes Ellen's protector when she and her family need to avoid being taken away by the Nazis.

It is important to link the hidden drama that plays out in the lives of Annemarie, Ellen and their families with the larger societal context of anti-Semitism and persecution discourses. The persecution of the Jews from pre-Holocaust to the Jewish Holocaust during World War II follows what René Girard detects as well-established patterns of persecution discourse in modern Western society. The patterns include targeting marginalised figures or outcasts, people living on the fringes of society who are for that reason often vulnerable to the kinds of violence that is perpetrated upon the surrogate victim: 'Ethnic and religious minorities tend to polarize the majorities against themselves' (Girard 1986: 17–18/31). One of the most apposite persecution examples is the Nazi depiction of the Jews as being responsible for Germany's defeat in World War I, known as the 'Stab in the Back' legend or *Dolchstosslegende* when Field Marshal Paul von Hindenburg asserted that traitors – Jews, Socialists and Communists – had engineered Germany's defeat in the war and stabbed her in the back. During the years between the First and Second World Wars, the Jews were also held responsible for the failed policies of the Weimar government and the collapse of the German economy during the Great Depression (Alvarez 2010: 69). As Alvarez notes, by scapegoating the Jews, the Nazis were able to rally the national community against a common scapegoat. I will explore scapegoating in more detail in the next chapter.

The Jews, like the fictional Jewish characters in *Number the Stars*, found themselves marginalised within their own community by virtue of their religious distinctiveness. In *Number the Stars* local Jewish citizens – like Mrs Hirsch, who owns a little shop that sells thread and buttons – suddenly disappear, their shops closed and their homes vacated. When Annemarie finds Mrs Hirsch's shop closed, with a new padlock on the door and a sign written in German, she is puzzled as to what has happened: 'I wonder if Mrs. Hirsch is sick' (20). When it becomes unsafe for Ellen and her family to stay in their apartment, Annemarie's parents take Ellen into their home where she has to pretend to be Annemarie's deceased sister Lise who died at the beginning of the war. Her death in a 'car accident' proves later to be only a half-truth; the full truth is that Nazi soldiers 'ran her down' (131) after she and other Resistance fighters tried to flee when Nazis raided their secret meeting. During this period of social turmoil and trauma, secrets, secrecy and lies were a necessary part of survival for many people, especially for Jews and those who tried to protect them and help them to escape from Denmark to safe countries such as Sweden.

On the first night that Ellen stays with the Johansen family, soldiers search the apartment looking for the missing Rosen family. Before they storm into the bedroom where the girls are sleeping, Annemarie breaks off the gold chain bearing the Star of David from Ellen's neck. After the soldiers leave, she unclenches her hand which holds Ellen's necklace, and 'saw that she had imprinted the Star of David into her palm' (49).

The imprinting of the Star of David is emblematic of the secret that she now bears and the necessary lies and deceit she must perform in order for Ellen to survive. It also serves as a symbol of religious identification, which was also used perversely to 'mark' Jews, who were required to wear the black armband with the yellow Star of David. The gold chain identifies a subject (Ellen) who is deemed by some as worthy of expulsion, extinction or what Girard terms 'surrogate victimage' (Fleming 2004: 49). The gold chain is also a recurring motif in the story and appears on the cover of the 1989 edition.

In his discussion of *Number the Stars*, Don Latham makes the point that because of the environment that characterises the time period of the story, there is a blurring of 'the distinctions between children and adults, showing that both groups, in spite of being victimized, can prove to be resourceful, capable and courageous' (2002: 5). Resourcefulness includes knowing when to keep silent, when to pretend and when to recognise the necessity for lying. Annemarie proves to be adept in all these abilities. When stopped by soldiers on the way home from school, she knows instinctively to not talk too much and reminds herself to: 'Just answer them, that's all' (3). Later when she volunteers to take a secret message to her Uncle Henrik she is intercepted again by soldiers and heeds the advice of her mother to pretend to be 'a silly, empty headed little girl' (105), and as she carries her basket of food and the secret handkerchief she tells herself the story of Little Red Riding Hood, thereby using storytelling to perform the role she must play. On the night that her uncle and Peter plan to take Ellen, her family and other Jews out of the country to Sweden, Annemarie realises the lie that her mother and uncle must tell in order to save the lives of these people. The lie is that the body of (a non-existent) great-aunt Birte lies in a coffin in the living room of her uncle's cottage by the sea, whereas in fact it contains warm clothing for the cold journey ahead. When soldiers become suspicious of the number of people who are at the home, the lie of the wake is almost exposed when the soldiers decide to open the closed coffin. Annemarie's mother tells a further lie to conceal the truth, she does so by pretending to agree with the soldier's command:

> Mama worked quickly across the room, directly to the casket, directly to the officer. 'You're right,' she said. 'The doctor said it should be closed, because Aunt Birte died of typhus, and he said that there was a chance the germs would still be there, would still be dangerous. But what does he know – only a country doctor, an old man at that? Surely typhus germs wouldn't linger in a dead person! And dear Aunt

Birte; I have been longing to see her face, to kiss her goodbye. Of *course* we will open the casket! I am glad you suggested –' (85)

Her ruse works and while she suffers a slap across the face by the officer, the coffin remains closed. Annemarie and her family are depicted as resourceful and brave, yet Ellen and her parents are denied any of these traits.

The Jews remain the silent reason for the Danish people's courage and integrity. They are depicted as powerless and needing to rely on others to save them. In the 'Author's Note', Lois Lowry says that after hearing of the stories told by her friend, Annelise Platt, about her life in Copenhagen during the years of the German occupation, she 'had always been fascinated and moved by Annelise's descriptions not only of the personal deprivation that her family and their neighbors suffered during those years, and the sacrifices they made, but even more by the greater picture she drew for me of the courage and integrity of the Danish people' (133). Later, Lowry mentions that on the New Year of the Jewish High Holidays in 1943, the Rabbi told his people that the Germans were to relocate the Jews: 'And so the Jews, all but a few who didn't believe the warning, fled the first raids. They fled into the arms of the Danes, who took them in, fed them, clothed them, hid them, and helped them along to safety in Sweden' (135). In telling of the bravery and kindness of the Danes, Lowry also unwittingly paints the Jews as naïve and powerless. The authorial comments carry the note of surrogate victimage of which Girard speaks. The Jews are depicted as fleeing into the arms of the Danes who take on the role of protector. Were these Jews not also Danes? The mark of religious distinction ensures that they are not only victims but responsible for their own downfall – if only those who remained behind had fled from Denmark instead of fleeing into the arms of the Danes, then the Danes would not have been put in the position of having to feed, hide, clothe, help them. A similar hidden note of victimage and sacrifice underpins the fiction which can be seen as participating in its own form of unintentional persecution.

As the previous texts have shown, there are times when lies need to be told or truth not revealed when circumstances call for such tactics. As its title suggests, Naidoo's *The Other Side of Truth* is not about a one-sided Kantian notion of truth. In this story, telling lies is necessary for survival, but lying is rarely a singular occurrence: lies require further lies. When soldiers murder an innocent woman, the mother of Sade and Femi, the children must leave Lagos, Nigeria for fear that they too will be murdered. To leave the country they must conceal the truth of their identities and say nothing of their plans to go to London. The plan is for the children and their father to travel separately to London with false passports, while the children are to be taken by a woman named Mrs Bankole. As their uncle explains to them, she 'has a British passport with a girl and a boy on it – just the right ages for you both – but they aren't travelling with her. She has agreed to say you are her children – and also to take you to your Uncle Dele [who lives in London]' (2000: 11–12). The children are unbelieving that their uncle expects them to 'go along with a lie!' (12). That there is another side of truth comes as a surprise for the children whose father, a journalist, who has been critical of the Abacha regime, has always said: '*The truth is the truth. How can I write what's untrue?*' (6, emphasis original).

Leaving Nigeria is the beginning of a long journey for the children, not just in their travels to another country, but in terms of realising that truth is not as absolute as they were once led to believe. The children's father (Papa) also has to realise that there are times when telling lies is necessary for survival. While he is uncompromising with the truth of his journalism, he finds that compromise is necessary if his children are to live. Lying becomes a secret code between the children and their father and a necessary means for negotiating the boundaries of the unspeakable. Papa tells the children that they must use their new surname 'Bankole' and the names that are in the passport ('Yemi' and 'Ade'), and emphasises the necessity for lying: 'You know how much I hate lying, but right now we have no choice' (16).

While lying may seem the only alternative if the children are to survive, lying leads to further complications. The children find themselves alone in London after Mrs Bankole abandons them soon after they arrive. The children feel powerless and without agency, in that they are in a strange land, cold, lost and with very little money (80 pence). A change of circumstances comes when they are innocently caught up in a video-shop vandalism and taken to the police station for questioning. When the police officer, who Sade silently calls 'Miss Police Business', asks for their names, their parents' names and where they live, the children are frightened to tell the truth as they fear that the English police may contact the police in Nigeria. This fear can be understood in terms of rendition as surrender and the political implications that would hold for the children. The children refuse to speak and are taken to a safe house as a temporary measure, before being declared refugees. When pressed by two friendly social workers to tell them their names, Sade does not speak but writes their real first names – Sade and Femi – and the surname of their mother, Adewale, and Ibadan as the name of their home village, when in fact it is a city close to their village. By being caught up in the dilemma of truth-telling or lies, Sade chooses to tell truths but not the real truths. And it is this rendition of the truth that causes further problems.

Truth and truth-telling are rendered unspeakable in this story in much the same way as we saw in *Secrets* and *Number the Stars*. Sade fears that to speak the truth about the horror of what happened to her mother, the reason for the lies on her passport, and the name of the woman who brought them to London, will lead to further horrors: 'Mrs Bankole's words rang in Sade's ears. *"If you tell anyone my name, my friend in Lagos will never help your father"'* (88, emphasis in original). Each lie enacts another lie. By being in the position of one who cannot tell the truth, the children are temporarily powerless to seek justice for their situation.

The story is also about a different kind of power: the power of fiction, and, specifically, the power of storytelling. The moral dilemmas that Sade struggles with over truth-telling or keeping silent about her background and circumstances are presented textually with her own internal wrestling with what she should do, and the consequences she fears could happen if she reveals her true situation. These internal struggles are counterpointed by the remembered advice of her mother which comes unbidden in the form of aphoristic sayings, which, in the context of the dilemma that confronts Sade, creates a hermeneutical tension between truth and the other side of truth. Mother's words are always on the side of truth, and textually they are written in italics: '*A lie has seven winding paths, the truth one straight road*' (135).

A further device that the fiction employs to tell truths is allegory or imaginative rendition. For example, while Papa is imprisoned in London awaiting an outcome on his appeal for asylum status, he relays to the children in a letter the story of 'Leopard and Tortoise'. The story tells of a hungry leopard who comes across a tortoise, but before he devours him the tortoise begs for a few minutes' grace. In this time, leopard watches curiously as tortoise scratches furiously at the grass under his feet, working in ever-increasing circles. When the time is up, leopard asks: 'Why have you done this?', to which the tortoise replies: 'From now on, anyone who comes to this place will see that some creature put up a great struggle for life here. You may eat me, but it is my struggle that shall be remembered!' (193). Papa uses this story as a way of explaining to his children why the struggle against injustice is important: 'I believe in the power of stories we tell. If we keep quiet about injustice, then injustice wins. We must dare to tell. Across the oceans of time, words are mightier than swords' (193). Throughout the text, truth must adopt the disguise of storytelling – fable, allegory and aphoristic story – in order to steer a moral course. Yet, these fictions (or 'lies' in Nietzsche's thinking) also reveal the power of lies or imaginative rendition as an alternative mode for truth-telling. For Sade, the ambiguity and protection of lies are juxtaposed by the straight and narrow truth, which like the lies she tells or silences she adopts is similarly about ambiguity and protection: both become rhetorical devices for interpreting human behaviour.

The 'Author's Note' that comes at the end of the story provides information on the context of the story. Naidoo addresses the reader: 'The characters in this story are all fictional' (225) but three political figures mentioned in the text were real people. The fiction is a 'lie' of necessity because to write of the atrocities that people like Papa and his family suffered in Nigeria would mean that the book would probably have never been published for children. Truth therefore needs to be embellished and disguised in order for it to be told, especially for child readers. Naidoo replicates the Nigerian situation with the inceptive moment of the killing of the children's mother. This killing is emblematic to a degree of the killing of the real Nigerian journalist Ken Saro-Wiwa, who was hanged by the military government in November 1995 after reporting on the injustices of the Abacha regime. As Naidoo notes, 'The novel is set immediately after this event' (225). While the hanging of a journalist in Nigeria may not have an impact on children in the West, reading of a murder of a mother and the threat to murder a father from the point of view of the children carries enormous emotional weight. Thus, through this moment that impacts on a fictional family, readers may enter more willingly into the larger story of corruption, injustice and persecution.

Dangerous secrets

The previous texts have shown how keeping secrets can be dangerous, especially when refusal to disclose could have fatal consequences. The picture book *Nasreen's Secret School*, by Jeanette Winter (2009), illustrates how some secrets themselves are dangerous but necessary for survival. In examining how truth is rendered in this text, my discussion includes the way illustrations enhance the account, providing additional metaphorical significance to the story.

Nasreen's Secret School takes a 'pro-truth' position. The various adherences to 'pro-truth' include: mimetic (fiction imitates or mirrors the world); epistemological (fiction imparts knowledge and belief); moral (fiction offers moral truths or knowledge); integrity (the sincerity of an author is the mark of 'truthfulness' or authenticity of the fiction); and affective (the effects – emotional, cognitive, psychological – that fiction induces) (Lamarque and Olsen 1994: 11–14). The picture book's subtitle, *A True Story from Afghanistan*, posits the truth of this text. To verify its claim as 'a true story' an 'Author's Note', as a prefatory statement, explains how the author, Jeanette Winter, was contacted by the Global Fund for Children 'about basing a book on a true story from one of the groups they support' (2009: unpaged). Winter further explains that she was drawn to an organisation in Afghanistan that founded and sup- ported secret schools for girls during the 1996–2001 Taliban regime.[2] Further evidence that this story is based on a truth and the need for secrecy of its primary source is supplied: 'The founder of these schools, who requested anonymity, shared the story of Nasreen and her grand- mother with me. Nasreen's name has been changed.' This information frames the story as containing a truth that corresponds to a specific historical period (similar to *Persepolis*). However, the story is already mediated, coming to Winter from a source who heard it from someone else. Winter then reframes the story as a picture book forming a bridge between the historical and the fictional worlds.

The text is a boundary crosser in that it attempts to shift context from a 'reality' in the real world to a fictional reality. The reader is required to understand the narrative within its 'real' world context – the suppres- sion of human rights under the Taliban, which the Preface explicitly frames. The central motifs of freedom and female rights are set against the text's claims to 'truth': 'A true story from Afghanistan'. *Nasreen's Secret School* tells a story about how a grandmother was able to help her granddaughter overcome the insular life of living under the Taliban regime in Afghanistan by assisting her in attending a secret school for girls. To understand how it achieves this portrayal we need to look closely at how the story is structured and for what purpose. However, direct reference is not possible as fiction inevitably distorts what it por- trays through its aesthetic processes (poiesis). For example, rather than simply 'mirroring' the facts of the Taliban rule, the narrative filters facts through layers of linguistic and artistic artifice.

As the author-illustrator of the text, Jeanette Winter shapes the nar- rative from a specific point of view and consideration of her implied readership. By choosing a picture book for children certain conven- tions (genre and publishing) already limit what can be said and the for- mat of its storytelling. Consequently, Winter has made decisions about what to tell, what is important, what can be left unsaid, and how the narration will be temporally and causally structured. In addressing a particular kind of reader, authors and illustrators make decisions about language (vocabulary, imagery, complexity), and the illustrative style will produce by necessity narrative distortion. In *Nasreen's Secret School* there are facts that exist independently of this narrative, and Winter was commissioned to write this story by the Global Fund for Children. Also, the aesthetic processes will inevitably distort the events. I now look more closely at how these considerations impact on the truth status of the text.

History, as Robert Scholes notes, is 'a narrative discourse with different rules than those that govern fiction' (1981: 207). *Nasreen's Secret School* is not a historical text, but a fictional one that refers to a specific historical period and attempts to bring extra-textual information to bear on the events of the narrative. The narrator of the story is Nasreen's grandmother, a figure whose familial and cultural status carries narratorial weight. As the omniscient narrator, she speaks for her granddaughter, and has intuitive access to Nasreen's thoughts and feelings. As someone who lived in Herat, Afghanistan, before the Taliban she imparts information about that time: 'Art and music and learning once flourished here.' The past tense indicates that this is no longer the case, and the cause for their disappearance is the Taliban. The appearance of the Taliban soldiers is metaphorically expressed and the tense shifts from past to present: 'Dark clouds hang over the city.' This association with the Dark Ages is extended: 'girls are forbidden to attend school' and 'learn about the world'. Through reference, verisimilitude and aesthetic language, the text is both empirical and fictional. The language that describes the Taliban is prosaic, and filtered through the narrator who speaks of them in terms of their actions: 'the soldiers came to our house and took my son away'; 'I heard of a soldier who pounded on the gate [of the secret school] demanding to enter.' Nasreen is described as passive and silent: 'Poor Nasreen sat at home all day'; 'Nasreen never spoke a word. She never smiled. She just sat, waiting for her mama and papa to return'; 'Nasreen stayed inside herself.' The moment of change for Nasreen comes when she returns to the secret school after the winter and speaks to another student, Mina, for the first time. Language breaks the silence and precipitates a renewed contentment, learning and imagining: 'Windows opened for Nasreen in that little schoolroom.'

The illustrations similarly encode the change of state and the contrasting characterisations of the Taliban and the children. Literally presented as a series of coloured frames, the illustrations imaginatively construct individual windows onto the fictional world of the text where readers glimpse the characters that are placed in specific contexts – home, school, the street. How the illustrations represent the various scenes is similar to how the words use metaphor or metonymy. Dark clouds or shadows consistently accompany images of the Taliban soldiers, metonymically linking the two to convey menace and a threatening presence.

Once Nasreen immerses herself in books her learning and knowledge of the world are communicated to readers through a metonymic chain of imagined worlds – the schoolroom becomes a series of windows opening up vistas of other worlds (Egypt, the ocean, a city with skyscrapers); the city of Herat is shown full of colour, occupied by artists, writers, scholars and mystics; fairytale characters emerge from books. While the Taliban remain in the temporal space of the narrative, their control and determination to eliminate all that preceded them are conveyed in the image whereby the reader is placed from behind Nasreen who looks out to a mountain range above her city. Dark clouds cross the sky but from behind one of them appear the figures of presumably Nasreen's parents who have disappeared. Holding hands they look back at Nasreen. Culturally coded metaphors of peace and paradise are conveyed in this illustration through the images of the white dove and the pomegranates.[3]

This metonymic sequence and the metaphoric associations illustrate how these visual and verbal signs reference a general humanist concern for peace and harmony, a utopian paradise. The final illustration in the book comprises a small inset frame of the grandmother (who looks out at the reader) and the partially represented face of Nasreen (who looks up at her grandmother). The larger frame depicts a starry black night above lavender-coloured mountains. Below the illustration, the grandmother's narration conveys the belief that once the windows on to a wider world have been opened, the 'soldiers can never close' them. This optimism is however tempered by the final words 'Insha'Allah' (God willing).

This text explicitly constructs 'an alternative world' to carry its motifs of freedom and human rights. The secret schools, which continue to exist in parts of Afghanistan, are literally an alternative world for girls. The imagined alternative worlds projected through the final illustrations and words shift between the past (how Herat once was) and a desired future (what it will become). This shift from a remembered past that only the grandmother has access to in this fictional world moves to one that she imagines is what Nasreen now possesses as part of her embodied knowledge of the world – beyond Herat and beyond the textual boundaries of the fiction. In this way, the text appeals to a number of truths: it mimetically seeks to mirror the world through embodying what are perceived as universal truths – the desire for peace, freedom, love, and through verisimilitude (similarity of events that happened to girls in the real-world context of Afghanistan); it reiterates a firm epistemological belief that we can learn from books and from this particular fiction; it offers a 'truthfulness' of artistic presentation in that illustrations and events are authentically rendered; and it appeals to a reader's sensitivity or heightened awareness of the circumstances that other children experience in the world.

The graphic novel *The Invention of Hugo Cabret* by Brian Selznick (2007) and the film *Hugo* (2011), on which it is based, are texts that, like *Nasreen's Secret School*, illustrate the necessity of lies and secrets for survival.[4] Survival in both texts is both physical and psychological. Survival of the spirit characterises the character Hugo who has to adapt to extreme circumstances of physical and emotional impoverishment in order to live, and to achieve his goals. Unlike *Nasreen's Secret School*, however, the title of Selznick's original text does not signal its truth status. The title – *The Invention of Hugo Cabret* – could be forewarning readers that Hugo Cabret is an invention, not a 'real' name or maybe not a 'real' person. It could be referring to something – an invention – that this character Hugo Cabret makes. It could also be calling Hugo Cabret into being, naming him into existence. All three explanations are true within this text, and the multiple meanings are symptomatic of the story that unfolds. It is not until the end of the book that readers discover that the book's narrator, Professor Alcofrisbas, is the name that is given to Hugo Cabret, who learns to become a magician and a master automaton maker. Rod McGillis (2008: 8) sees a network of associations in these names, which link to the filmmaker Georges Méliès, the secret character in this text:

> Professor Alcofrisbas [is] a character who appears in many of Georges Méliès's films. Alcofrisbas is an anagram of François Rabelais; Alcofrisbas Nasier is the pseudonymous name of the writer of *Gargantua and Pantagruel*. Invoking Rabelais in *The Invention of Hugo Cabret* suggests the sort of magic associated with carnival [...] His last name suggests 'cabaret', the site of a mixture of performances. Selznick's achievement is to foreground form, but also to manipulate form in the service of carnival.[5]

This is a story told in two parts. The first part aligns well with the purpose of this section – a story about dangerous secrets that are necessary for survival. The second part tells a version of the true story of the film-maker Georges Méliès whose secret past is gradually revealed. There are several veiled references to Méliès and his films in part one, but part two provides a full revelation about the history, films and achievements of this almost forgotten filmmaker.[6] *The Invention of Hugo Cabret* is a homage to Méliès, whose most famous film, *A Trip to the Moon* (1902), features in this book along with many other stills from early films by Méliès and other filmmakers of that time such as René Clair.[7] There are other pieces of information that readers will discover as they read this text that can be verified as being true. This text is neither a biography nor a history of filmmaking, even though it contains copies of film stills and illustration from real films. The text is a fiction which draws on, and draws in, facts to create its own reality. Finding the facts and comparing them to the real world is what the correspondence theory of truth seeks: facts to prove the truth of something; in other words, if something is true then it must correspond to the facts.[8] However, this reductionist view of the truth works against fiction which may draw on facts but does not need to prove the truth of its claims.

The Invention of Hugo Cabret creates the illusion of verisimilitude, even of biography or film history, by introducing real people, events and film references from the past through both words and illustration. As McGillis notes above, Selznick's achievement is to foreground form. An extensive appendix, 'Credits', gives sources for illustrations, film stills, film citations, directors named in the text, as well as films that Selznick read as part of his research for the book. (In the companion text to the film, *The Hugo Movie Companion* (Selznick 2011), additional informa-tion is provided about the research that went into making the film, and other facts about Méliès.) Selznick adds a further touch of verisimilitude by drawing his subject in a way that bears a striking resemblance to the available photographs of the real Georges Méliès.[9] The text's bound-ary crossing moves not only across empiricism and fiction, but across format – picture book, graphic novel, illustrated text – a synchronicity of cinematic still, illustration and word. The generous series of charcoal illustrations carries the narrative as much as the words, and the film stills alter readers' understanding of context, shifting what might have been fiction into the realm of reality.[10]

Hugo Cabret is called a thief and it is true that he steals. He steals milk and croissants from the shops in a Paris railway station and he steals toy parts from the toy booth owned by Papa Georges. On one occasion, Hugo attempts to steal a wind-up toy but he is caught in the act by Papa Georges: '"Thief! Thief!" the old man yelled down the empty hallway.

"Someone call the Station Inspector!"' (Selznick 2007: 50). The old man forces Hugo to hand over all the objects he has stolen: 'screws, and nails and bits of metal, gears and crumpled playing cards, tiny pieces of clock-works, cogs, and wheels' (51). Despite Papa Georges's repeated calls for the Station Inspector, the dreaded Inspector, who locks criminals – even boys – in his cage in his office, fails to appear. If the Station Inspector arrives, 'Hugo knew everything would be over' (51). The Station Inspector is a threat to Hugo's survival, and his cage in the office is a reminder of what will happen to Hugo if he is discovered. In the book, this charac-ter is a threatening presence (similar to the Taliban in Nasreen's story) whereas in the film the character is a buffoon (played by Sacha Baron Cohen), whose attempts at wooing his romantic interest are comical. His dog, Maximilian, like his owner, is another source of both terror (for the other characters) and amusement (for the viewing audience) as it wreaks havoc when unleashed.

Hugo lives a secret life, but this was not always so. Once he lived hap-pily with his father, a clockmaker, who taught him how to fix things. His father had a night-time job at the museum and on one fateful night he was burned to death in a fire that destroyed part of the museum. Hugo's Uncle Claude claims him after the death and takes him to live with him at the Paris railway station where he is the Timekeeper. They live in the rooms hidden in the walls of the station: 'a cluster of secret apartments that had been built for the people who ran the train station years ago' (76). Hugo learns how to keep the many clocks running to time. However, when his uncle disappears, and presumably dies, Hugo is forced to keep his presence and location secret for fear that he will be handed over to the Inspector and put in an orphanage. In order to keep his existence a secret, Hugo has to ensure that the clocks are always showing the right time, and he must 'take his uncle's paychecks from the office when no one was looking (although he didn't know how to cash them)' (132). Hugo has another secret, an automaton, which threatens to be revealed when Papa Georges takes his notebook and refuses to return it to him. Mysteriously, the notebook contains another secret that only Papa Georges knows. When he opens the notebook, the old man pauses on the page that contains the drawing of an automaton, and mutters enigmatically, '"Ghosts … […] I knew they would find me here eventually"' (60). Hugo's father's notebook contains his detailed drawings for reconstructing the automaton that he found in a state of disrepair in one of the storage rooms in the museum (Figure 2.1).

The automaton 'was built entirely out of clockworks and fine machin-ery' (115) and Hugo's father surmises that it can write, as it appears

Figure 2.1 Illustration from *The Invention of Hugo Cabret* by Brian Selznick

poised as if to hold a pen. The automaton is a marvel of technology with its 'dozens of wheels that have edges cut with notches and grooves' (115). But it is rusty and broken and needs the skill of a clockmaker to fix it. Hugo's father explains that early magicians were clockmakers who used their knowledge of machines to build automata which dazzled their audiences. No matter what these machines did – whether they danced, wrote or sang – 'the secret was always in the clockworks' (115). The automaton, which is colloquially called the mechanical man, has its own internal secrets and Hugo is determined to repair it back to working order to discover the message it will write. Hugo gives a life-saving significance to this note, which exceeds its potential. He believes the note will answer 'all his questions and tell him what to do now that he was alone. The note was going to save his life' (132).[11] Hugo guards the secrecy of the automaton, but Isabelle (Papa Georges's godchild) discovers this secret when she follows Hugo back to his room.

The story entertains the idea of ghosts – ghosts from the past, and a ghostly presence, which are tied to repressed memories and death. In his discussion of mechanical instruments and automata, Christopher Faulkner makes the observation that since the early nineteenth century and the Romantic period, artists often registered their fear of certain kinds of automata, 'sensing their affinity with death and/or the uncanny' (2011: 16). After the old man first sees the sketches in the notebook and mutters, 'Ghosts', the idea of a ghostly presence recurs repeatedly in the narrative. The next time is when Hugo is alone with the broken mechanical man in his secret room, and hears a voice that says, 'Fix it.' The command is spoken twice, but no other person is present: 'Hugo didn't know if it was his own thoughts, or if it was a ghost, but he had heard it clearly' (Selznick 2007: 131). A further recurrence happens when the shopkeepers at the railway station learn that the uncle has died. They wonder at first if 'his ghost kept the clocks running' and when the clocks begin to break down they fear 'the station is haunted!' (411).

These ghosts stand in for the living, or, in Freudian terms, effect a return of the repressed. Who are the ghosts that Papa Georges fears have found him? Is it Hugo's father who speaks to him from the dead or is it a voice from inside Hugo that speaks? Has Hugo, as the invisible timekeeper, become the ghostly presence that had kept the clocks working and made everything seem familiar and normal?[12] The mechanical man too doubles for the living, its movements offering an illusion of life, as they appear to cross between the borders of machine and living organism. The psychoanalytic approach known as the 'metapsychology of secrets' (Rashkin 2008: 93) offers a different notion of the phantom from Freud's in that a subject, such as Hugo, does not resist the return of something that has been repressed (which is the case for Papa Georges). Rather, the phantom relates to what someone else conceals. Hugo's father had been obsessed about the mechanical man – filling several notebooks with drawings, determined to fix it, hiding it in the attic of the museum – and he and Hugo had come to think of 'the automaton as an injured animal that they were nursing back to health' (Selznick 2007: 121). In psychoanalytic terms, Rashkin says that the child haunted by the phantom becomes 'a living tomb or repository' (2008: 94) where the secret lies buried. A further comparison can be made between Hugo and Rashkin's explanation of the child who 'stands vigil, intrapsychically, to insure the absolute inviolability of the secret' (95). Hugo guards the secret of the automaton so carefully that he takes on his father's obsession after his death and is bound inextricably to him and their secret. For Hugo, the thought of losing the mechanical man 'was too much to bear. He had grown to love it. He felt responsible for it. Even if it didn't work, at least at the train station he had it nearby' (Selznick 2007: 138–9). When he finally manages to fix the automaton and it draws an image, one that Hugo recognises from the film that his father had told him about, '[s]hivers ran down his spine' (251). In the film, Hugo leads Isabelle to his secret rooms and as they move through the tunnels Isabelle likens the experience to Victor Hugo's nineteenth-century novel *Les Misérables*, saying, 'This is marvellous! [...] I feel like Jean Valjean!' In his reply, Hugo likens himself to another character, but one that is a phantom: 'I used to imagine I was the Phantom of the Opera. Like in the movie.'[13] (However, any historical attention to detail is lost when Isabelle surveys the cramped space with its chaos of tools and machine parts hanging everywhere and announces: 'This is such a boy place.')

There is a further phantom that haunts the story: the passing of an era, an era which this text attempts to memorialise.[14] In the extended chase scene between the Inspector and Hugo, at one point Hugo climbs through the enormous clock face and clings to the outside of the clock just like Harold Lloyd in the silent movie *Safety Last*; Hugo had told Isabelle about this film, which was the one that his father had taken him to see on his last birthday (Selznick 2007: 173). A further citation to an earlier (1895) film, *A Train Arrives in the Station*, is reinterpreted in a scene when Hugo, who is being chased by the Inspector, attempts to retrieve the automaton that has crashed onto the tracks. He is almost hit by the train but saved at a crucial moment by the Inspector (347).

The final chapter is logically entitled 'Winding It Up'. However, there are other possibilities hidden in this title. In an earlier scene, Hugo compares Georges to a broken toy: 'If you lose your purpose ... it's like you're broken' (374). Later, Georges too describes himself in these terms: 'I am nothing! I'm a penniless merchant, a prisoner! A shell! A windup toy!' (298). In one way, the automaton serves as a symbolic embodiment of Papa Georges, a man who has become disillusioned and hardened, a machine without feeling or purpose, and one who has many secrets locked inside himself. Does 'Winding It Up' mean that Papa Georges/ Georges Méliès now has a purpose? Possibly, but if this is the message then it comes as an afterword as the previous chapter revealed that Méliès was received back into the film world, and honoured by a ret-rospective showing of his surviving films to an enthusiastic audience. McGillis notes the ambiguity of the chapter's title: 'a phrase which cap-tures the ambiguity of setting things going and closing things down' (2008: 8).[15]

The fantasy worlds of the old films that *The Invention of Hugo Cabret* recalls were produced during the period in France known as *la belle époque*, a time characterised by optimism, peace, new technology and scientific discoveries. Méliès experimented with new technologies to produce the magic that his films seemed to display. The time in which *The Invention of Hugo Cabret* is set (1931) was a very different period, it was a time of the Great Depression and Hugo represents the many poor, orphaned and street children who struggled to survive those harsh economic and social times. The films that Hugo loved provided escape from the real world and its hardships, offering a temporary distraction. Although set in a different time and place, *Nasreen's Secret School* also shows how the imagination and story can provide children with an alternative world, but a world which is, to borrow from John Fowles, 'as real as, but other than the world that is. Or was' (1969: 86).

The texts discussed in this chapter provide convincing accounts of situations that call for lies and secrets, times when 'truth entails tremendous ruin'. In challenging Kant's absolute view on lying, I have focused on two considerations – survival and fiction's truth-status. As the texts have shown, the need to lie is prompted by the need to survive or to help someone else to survive; such a driving motivation will override the Kantian notion of condemning all lying without exception. *Secrets*, *Number the Stars* and *The Other Side of Truth* reassure their implied child readers of the importance of telling the truth, but they also provide convincing justification for telling lies or not telling the truth when matters of life and death are at stake. However, *Secrets* and *The Other Side of Truth* also provide cautionary tales about the other side of deception. Lying may be necessary, but the truth still holds the upper hand. Ironically, by not telling the truth, the lives of Treasure, Femi, Sade and Papa are put at risk. Finally, *Nasreen's Secret School* and *The Invention of Hugo Cabret* illustrate how many children live with dangerous secrets. The story of secret schools provides young readers with the truth of a situation which requires secrecy and deception. In extreme circumstances, the need to keep silent is essential for survival. *The Invention of Hugo Cabret* shows how the isolating conditions of secrets and lies may be crucial for psychological or physical survival. However, their revelation and disclosure may not be disastrous and may in fact lead to new forms of harmonious co-existence.

3
The Scapegoat

Scapegoating is a process that entails lies about an innocent subject. The reason behind scapegoating is varied but fear is often the most prevalent: fear of the stranger or Other, fear of punishment, fear of change. Many scapegoats are forced to flee their home or community, to live secret lives in order to avoid being persecuted or in extreme cases killed. Scapegoating is an ancient ritual whereby a community transferred all their sins and misdeeds on to an animal or human who was then cast out or killed.[1] This ritual enabled the community to be restored or freed from whatever trouble had plagued it. More recently it has come to mean blaming an individual or a group for the misfortunes befalling a society or community, and scapegoating becomes the 'necessary' means used by the community for restoring social order. One such example of a scapegoat being cast out of a community is Alfred Dreyfus, an innocent Jewish officer in the French army who was convicted on false evidence for a crime of high treason. Émile Zola responded to this injustice by writing an open letter to the President of the French Republic which was published on the front page of the French newspaper *L'Aurore* on 13 January 1898: an excerpt reads: 'Dare to tell the truth, as I have pledged to tell it, in full, since the normal channels of justice have failed to do so.' With the accusation – 'J'accuse' – Zola added his strong condemnation of the scapegoating of Alfred Dreyfus. Dreyfus was stripped of his rank, publicly degraded and exiled to the penal colony of Devil's Island to serve a sentence of life imprisonment, and under inhumane conditions. This event, which became known as the 'Dreyfus Affair', resulted in major uproar and debate across France and other parts of the world, and Zola and other outspoken critics of the government were punished. In September 1899, the President of France pardoned Dreyfus, but he had to wait until 1906 before he was exonerated of the charges, after which he was reinstated to his former military rank (Pagès 1996).[2]

While there is a predominant perception of the scapegoat as an innocent – the 'fall guy', the victim – there are also scapegoats who are guilty of a crime or action. The idea of a guilty scapegoat seems a contradiction, an oxymoron. However, as the texts that follow demonstrate, history of past misdeeds may not be evidence of a suspect's guilt. Furthermore, scapegoats may not necessarily be individuals or groups of people who are blamed because of their ethnic, religious or cultural difference to the mainstream community or society. Governments, political ideologies and movements are also blamed for society's ills and therefore become scapegoats when they may not in fact be fully responsible for current problems that beset a community. In discussing various kinds of scapegoats in children's fiction and the lies and deception that are part of the process of blaming and victimisation, I also examine how the fictions themselves, more often than not, side with the innocent scapegoat and vindicate them of any possible wrongdoing. There are other examples of scapegoats who are 'sacrificed': a process that is concealed rather than made explicit in the narratives, but, as I argue, sacrificing is a necessary move for the fictions to support a pragmatic solution to restore, albeit temporarily, the social imaginary at play in the text.

Sacrifice often entails a scapegoat or a victim on whom a necessary violence of sorts is enacted for the good of the community. This violence can take different forms – expulsion, concealment of the truth, false accusation, stigmatisation and abuse. In all of these actions against the scapegoat, the community engages in deception by concealing the truth or their deep-rooted fears. René Girard speaks of a 'scapegoating mechanism' or a 'sacrificial crisis', which is a necessary 'act of collective expulsion [that] can bring [...] oscillation to a halt and cast violence outside the community' (1978: 26/35). Girard draws on the Bible and classical myths (as well as select literary works) to expound his theory of the scapegoat and sacrificial victims.[3] He argues that human communities are based on the sacrifice of an innocent victim and that it is only by a collective act of projection onto a victimised outsider (a scapegoat) that harmonious co-existence can be restored between competitive or warring humans. The scapegoat is both the evil and the cure (Girard 1978), as well as a form of deception and a means for survival.

As the Dreyfus example demonstrates, the scapegoat occupies the shifting ground between condemnation and exoneration. A similar oscillation occurs in the case of liars. John Vignaux Smyth says that Kant held the sacrificial view that 'liars should be held accountable for murders they did not commit' (qtd in Smyth 2002: 5). Smyth's argument, however, is that liars are 'scapegoated, "sacrificed" on the altar of reason, and indeed threatened with a violence that is far from merely symbolic' (5). This view is congruent with René Girard's point (1977) that all societies are founded upon myths of sacrifice, and that it is only by a collective act of projection that a victimised outsider is targeted as responsible for social upheaval, and thereby justifies being removed. In children's fiction, known liars can easily become scapegoats even in situations when they are telling the truth: a situation that reflects Kant's sacrificial view.

In the following discussion of children's fiction, I draw on Girard's work to show how communities restore harmony to survive. Sometimes communities employ what could be termed the Dreyfus effect: expelling the scapegoat only to later accept him/her back into the community. I also extend the idea of a scapegoat as an individual (person or animal) to include more abstract entities such as an ideology, a nation, a government or an instrument of these collective powers (such as government departments, armed forces) that are charged with the responsibility for carrying out laws, policies or political dictates. In these instances, deception or mendacity produces a particularly virulent form of violence that in some instances demands counter-violence.

The necessary scapegoat

In this section, my attention turns to the scapegoat as stranger or marginalised Other. The scapegoat was briefly mentioned with regard to Lowry's *Number the Stars* (see Chapter 2), which serves to remind us that children's literature includes numerous incidences of scapegoats being ostracised from a community, killed or persecuted. As *Number the Stars* shows, innocent scapegoats are often selected and targeted based on a symbolic, cultural or religious marker. Girard suggests that markers of difference become easily recognised and distinguishable during times of extreme social upheaval or disruption. He contends that 'difference' (ranging from genetic deformities, injuries, disabilities, mental abnormalities) extends to other victimary signs: 'in boarding schools for example, every individual who has difficulty adapting, someone from another country or state, an orphan, an only son, someone who is penniless, or even simply the latest arrival)' (1986: 18/30–1). From this list, it is clear that anyone can be chosen as a scapegoat based on an arbitrary whim of prejudice. In *Number the Stars* the primary targets of anti-Semitism were Danish Jews who occupied the paradoxical position of being both internal to the Danish community and marginal to it. Their marginalisation was by virtue of their cultural and religious distinctiveness.

A direct connection between a real event of victimisation and the sacrificial scapegoating in myths, as Girard argues, is one that is debatable, but as the following discussion of the texts shows, we can detect a basis in real victimisation that corresponds with the fictional plots. Three Australian picture books are the focus of the first part of the discussion: *Dancing the Boom Cha Cha Boogie* (2005) by Narelle Oliver, *My Dog* (2001) by John Heffernan and Andrew McLean, and *Kojuro and the Bears* (1986) by Junko Morimoto. These texts provide examples of how the scapegoating mechanism is necessary for attributing blame and restoring social order.

A significant feature of scapegoating is that it is a sacrificial mechanism that provides communities with a sense of collective identity: an idea that informs the story of *Dancing the Boom Cha Cha Boogie*.[4] This allegorical tale serves as an example of the stranger as scapegoat. The collective identity of a community (the snigs) becomes unsettled with the arrival of the stranger (the murmels). The murmels and the snigs come into contact with each other after the murmels are swept away from their homeland by 'wild whirligig winds' that take them far away to a foreign land – Grand Snigdom. The key source of conflict that arises between the murmels and the snigs is that one group (murmels) has entered the other's homeland 'illegally', or, in terms of the story, they arrive by a force of nature. A second important reason for the hostility of the snigs towards the murmels is that they are of a different 'species', and from the perspective of the snigs, the murmels are an inferior species. The murmels have colourful, rounded shapes with a curved tail, and the snigs have monotone, angular bodies with pointed spikes and arrow-like tails (Figure 3.1).

On waking after being washed up on to the shores of Snigdom, the murmels are insulted and threatened: 'Curly whirly strangers are not permitted in Grand Snigdom. No doubt you have your shifty button eyes on our precious sea slugs' (unpaged). When the oldest murmel tries to explain that they had nowhere to go, the Boss Snig snaps 'Silence!' and tells them that once their boat is fixed, 'Then you must leave.' But before then, they are locked in a prison. The situation in which the murmels find themselves is one that is familiar to many asylum seekers, refugees or illegal immigrants. Snigdom, with its authoritarian Boss Snig, has its counterpart in other similar societies where individual rights are curtailed and a sense of insecurity and fear of the stranger

Figure 3.1 Illustration from *Dancing the Boom Cha Cha Boogie* by Narelle Oliver

pervades the populace. Snigdom is a metonym for ethnic homogeneity. The following picture book treats ethnic homogeneity in a more literal fashion.

My Dog concerns a young boy, Alija, whose life in his quiet village of Liztar is abruptly changed when war breaks out in Bosnia and ethnic cleansing begins. As life in the village changes, the people begin to leave the village in search of a safe place to live. Alija's father assures him that the fighting will 'blow away like the winter wind' and nothing bad would happen to Liztar: 'We all live together here [...] Bosnian,

Serb, Croat, Muslim, Christian. We're all one people.' This sense of community identity based on a utopian vision of harmonious integration is at odds with the converse utopian idea of the perfect nation as an ethnically homogeneous population – a similar society characterised Snigdom before the arrival of the murmels. Signs of split allegiances and ethnic disharmony emerge in *My Dog* when a neighbour of Alija's decides to fly his ethnic flag outside his house. By the close of the story, Alija, now living with his aunt on the coast, sits with his dog 'at the edge of the town, where the road from Liztar comes in' waiting for his family (Figure 3.2). The final image of the boy and his dog is made the more poignant with a reader's knowledge that in the *real* situation there would be no reunion. The boy is the victim of sacrificial violence. Because of the violence he has had to be removed from his village and family and must now wait and hope for a better future. While there is a utopian community formed between the snigs and murmels who eventually assimilate – they eat the same foods whereby they all become colourful – and former hostilities fade, there is no utopian closure for *My Dog*.

These two picture books show that group identity (we could extend this to the identity of the nation state) often attempts to strengthen cohesion by 'benevolent' assimilation (as in *Dancing the Boom Cha Cha Boogie*) or, by contrast, ethnic cleansing (as in *My Dog*). Both stories invite an extra-literary knowledge of the political and historical circumstances that form the context of their stories (see Bradford and Huang 2007; Dudek 2011). For example, *Dancing the Boom Cha Cha Boogie* resonates with Australia's shameful treatment of asylum seekers and refugees who are held for long periods in detention centres. Heffernan's text refers to the ethnic cleansing and other atrocities (the boy's mother is taken by soldiers and we can assume she is raped) that occurred during the Bosnian War (1992–95). Although neither is explicit in drawing attention to these real-world contexts, they are nevertheless illustrative of national scapegoating in that alien others are blamed as responsible for the disruption to an imagined 'utopian' way of life. Initially, the murmels are these alien others. Whereas the murmels are benign, the soldiers who invade Liztar capturing, killing and abducting the villagers are a more dangerous and feared alien Other for the people of Liztar. The two picture books are different in that one foregrounds its fantasy (through its illustrations of fantastic creatures and inventive naming of characters and places), while the other foregrounds its realism (through its realist-style illustrations and identifiable naming of towns and real events). However, both texts can be seen in Girard's terms as fulfilling

Figure 3.2 Illustration from *My Dog* by John Heffernan and Andrew McLean

a realist criterion in that a real event of victimisation is behind the fictional scapegoat (the refugee, the innocent victim). The utopian closure of *Dancing the Boom Cha Cha Boogie* invites young readers to see the possibility of a transformed community, one that is free of prejudice and difference (they all eventually share a sameness of appearance and play happily together). This erasure of difference, however, echoes the nationalistic utopian narrative of ethnic homogeneity. It is also an example of Girard's argument that as rivalry between individuals or groups intensifies, characteristics that had previously distinguished them begin to dissolve, with the antagonists becoming 'doubles' of each other (1977: 164–5).

The utopian society is something that Girard regards as a myth that societies construct and come to believe as true. According to Girard, these myths comprise a social imaginary that operates according to a mechanism of scapegoating often concealed from public consciousness. For Girard, the destruction of an innocent outsider is the price that communities pay to ensure unity and sameness. This social imaginary is vivified in *Kojuro and the Bears* and comprises both human and non-human animals. Kojuro the bear hunter is scorned by the townsfolk who dismiss him and buy his skins for 'a humiliating sum'. His outsider status is visually encoded in the illustration below where Kojuro takes his hot sake alone in the dark and cold while the shopkeeper enjoys his pipe in the warmth of the inside room (Figure 3.3).

The townsfolk's marginalisation of Kojuro can be interpreted in terms of Girard's point that for communities to retain harmonious social co-existence requires a collective act of projection whereby the outsider

Figure 3.3   Illustration from *Kojuro and the Bears*. Illustrated by Junko Morimoto. Based on a story by Kenji Miyazawa

is victimised and carries the burden of their guilt. The townsfolk dismiss Kojuro for being a bear hunter, but they nevertheless purchase the skins and enjoy the livers he brings them.

The bears are an integral part of the Buddhist-inspired social imaginary: 'they were all part of a great wheel' (Morimoto 1986: unpaged). Despite Kojuro's occupation, he and the bears share a mutual respect. On two occasions, he decides not to kill the bears when he hears them speak. The bears are given both human speech and emotion, which positions the reader to see the point of view of the 'other'. In drawing on Donna Haraway's work *When Species Meet* (2008), we can also understand these textual events as examples of species meeting and responding to one another. When Kojuro hears the bear and her cub speak on the first occasion, he responds by not shooting them. On the second occasion, when he is about to kill a huge bear, it asks: 'Why do you hate me, Kojuro?' Kojuro responds by saying: 'I have no hate for you, but I must kill you. Forgive me, but the choice is not mine.' But Kojuro does make a choice and decides not to kill the bear, agreeing to a pact of sacrifice between man and bear. The bear presciently comments: 'In two years I will come to you – but not yet.'

Kojuro sets off from his home for the final time, with the foreboding of his impending death. The death knell rings when Kojuro is killed by a large bear who speaks his own version of Kojuro's earlier confession: 'Forgive me, Kojuro. I do not hate you, but the choice is not mine.' Kojuro's parting thought is: 'The wheel has turned. Forgive me, bears.' The reciprocal offering of forgiveness completes the sacrifice, and restores a balance between human and non-human. The bears form a silent circle and keep a vigil around the dead body of Kojuro. The illustration connotes an atmosphere of respect for Kojuro as the bears bow in silence around his body. Girard notes that when the sacrificial scapegoat (the hunter in this example) is completed then the community forgets their hatred for the scapegoat and often come to revere or deify the victim. In making the decision not to kill the bear, Kojuro accepts his fate and is aware of his guilt as a bear killer.

Guilt is often a condition that justifies or seeks a scapegoat. Guilt from breaking a law is probably the most common, although guilt stemming from other vexatious human interactions is another that can trigger the scapegoating mechanism. From the point of view of the guilty one, the scapegoat can be a way to ease a troubled conscience, especially if one begins to believe that the scapegoat is ultimately responsible for, or the cause of, the problem in question. The context which gives rise to scapegoating is often characterised by mounting tensions leading to violence. Pók reasons that individuals and groups often want 'mono-causal explanations for all events. Therefore, finding a scapegoat is often the easiest solution for the dilemma' (1999: 533). Research on family relations (coming from a psychodynamic Freudian tradition) brings an interesting perspective to how families use the scapegoating mecha-nism as a form of conflict resolution whereby the focus of the conflict or problem is shifted from the parents to the child. The symptomatic child becomes 'the focus for the projection of unacceptable characteris-tics, conflicts and problems and the object onto which aggression may be transferred' (Yahav and Sharlin 2007: 92). The result is that the child often experiences feelings of rejection and blame. *Web of Lies* (2004), a novel by Beverley Naidoo, is an exemplary text for demonstrating the symptomatic child as scapegoat within family relations because it situ-ates lying, concealment and fiction in the context of a (mimetic) sacri-ficial analysis of socio-cultural conflict more generally.

The sacrificial mechanism

Web of Lies continues the story of Sade, Femi and Papa that I discussed in *The Other Side of Truth* (Chapter 2). In this sequel, the focus shifts to Femi. Femi has now commenced high school in London and becomes caught up with a gang of older boys who force him into shoplifting. The internalised and externalised symptoms conspire to make Femi a scape-goat. Still feeling the loss of his mother, Femi is unable to speak about his emotional distress, and conceals his feelings by keeping silent and being a loner. His only friend is Gary, who has his own family secrets, which Femi never asks about as: 'He knew about not prising open a lid that was nailed down' (Naidoo 2004: 7). Femi's father works at two jobs, and after 18 months of living in London the family live with the uncertainty that they may be sent back to Nigeria if their application for permanent residency is rejected. Femi's vulnerability carries physi-cal symptoms – he is troubled by spasms of cramps in his stomach, and he is embarrassed and annoyed by his father's overprotectiveness: he is unable to walk home from school alone but must be accompanied by his sister; he is refused his own house key; and he is restricted in terms of what he can do and where he can go when he is not at school. At home, Femi feels rejected by his father and believes he does not trust him.

These internal tensions find a release when Femi is approached and seemingly befriended by an older boy, James, who is part of a gang whose leader is Errol Richards (aka 'Lizard Eyes'). Femi is flattered, yet fearful of the consequences if his father or Sade finds out. James calls Femi 'Little Brother', and the protective and possessive connotations make him feel special. As he becomes more drawn into the gang, Femi reasons that there are personal benefits by objectifying his own victim status: 'People always played with you when they thought you were weak. If he were in the same gang as James, no one would laugh at him, would they?' (42).

The story signposts the scapegoating mechanism at work between the gang and Femi, cueing the reader to see how Femi becomes a naïve but foolish victim. The stages of the gang's scapegoating mechanism provide insight into the trap that is set for Femi. *The enticement*: James appears to befriend Femi, commiserating with him about how difficult girls can be to understand, what it is like to have a strict father and finding that they follow the same football team. James gives Femi a 20-pound note: 'Get some Arsenal stuff, little brother. A present, right! I'll see you around' (28). *The deal*: James intercepts Femi on his way home and takes him to meet Errol who wants 'to do a little business' (35) with him. While Errol is evasive about what it is he wants Femi to do, he knows that Femi needs money and offers him protection: 'James will take care of you in that Avon School. No one will mess with you, know what I mean?' (36). *The crime*: Femi is told to meet James outside the Leisure Centre on Saturday morning. At the rendezvous, Femi is told to steal CD covers. James tells Femi the plan and Femi reluctantly goes along with it. After the shoplifting is successfully completed, Femi feels quite exhilarated: 'He had to restrain himself from running towards James at the far end of the arcade. But he couldn't stop himself grinning nervously' (50).

As Femi finds himself being drawn deeper into the gang, so too does he find that he needs to lie to his father and Sade so that he can spend the time with the gang that is expected of him. Femi also has to keep secrets about his stolen goods (which he hides in a drawer) and the activities he does with the gang such as smoking marijuana and stealing. Femi's association with the gang affords him a certain amount of status in the eyes of other students; it also estranges him further from his family and his friend Gary. The gang's credo is 'brethren always look out for brethen' (50). This sense of binding brotherhood provides a marginalised group of black youth with a sense of collective identity. However, even within this group, Femi is an outsider as he is new to the school, younger and from Nigeria. Femi also becomes increasingly an outsider in his own home. Sade expresses her fear that Femi's involvement with Lizard Eyes will cause trouble with the Immigration Department who might reject their father's application: 'You're going to make trouble for us. The immigration people won't give Papa his papers because of you!' (61). Sade firmly places the blame on Femi for potentially threatening the future of the family and the gang are using Femi as the scapegoat for their criminal actions. Both Sade and the gang are triggering the scapegoating process. Sade uses a monocausal logic in attributing the possible extradition of the family to Femi's actions. The gang sees Femi as a convenient solution to their problems, a solution which has been carefully orchestrated. These dual actions towards Femi constitute a move towards a sacrificial crisis, which requires a guilty one to be expelled for order to be restored. While Errol (Lizard Eyes) is soon arrested and charged for assaulting Femi, there is another more abstract scapegoating that occurs which requires a different sacrificial crisis.

Girard's point of 'sacrificial crisis' returns us to the idea that the effacement of difference, rather than the idea of difference *per se*, is an explanation of the root cause of social-cultural conflict. Effacement of difference is the gradual erosion of distinctions in which the differences among individuals and within communities are used to establish their identity, for example as British citizens (Girard 1977: 49/77–8). This is a plausible explanation for considering the situation in Nigeria, where Papa was an insider in the community but, because of his contrary views of the Abacha regime, was forced to flee and become estranged from his homeland. In Britain, he is an outsider who is unable to gain insider status despite his political views being more closely aligned with a multicultural Britain than with the ideology of persecution and violation of civil rights in Nigeria at that time. The ideals of multicultural Britain stand in stark opposition to the persecution mechanism (racism) directed at the marginalised Other. Both Sade and Papa blame London and its racial problems as a major cause for the problems. Papa's overprotective behaviour towards his children is fuelled by his fear that they will be subjected to physical violence on the unsafe streets. In her diary, Sade gives voice to her silent concern that at the new high school, 'I won't be surprised if Femi and I are the only African children in the whole school ... probably the only black children' (212). Multiculturalism, especially in terms of problem black youth and asylum seekers from Nigeria, becomes one of the text's tripartite mimetic antagonists; the others are white, Anglo Britain, and the Immigration Department. The text supports positive multiculturalism in the form of Papa, Sade, Femi and their uncle Dele, who is so successfully integrated that Papa teases that he 'has become a real English gentleman' (211); he is also taking up a teaching position at a college and has a permanent work permit. However, Dele is the lucky one: at the close of the book Sade reveals 'that almost every Nigerian who has asked the British Government for asylum in the last three years has been turned down!!!' (211).

Fiction corresponds with the real context when in the 'Author's Note' at the end of the book Naidoo writes: 'By 1997, almost 15,000 Nigerians had come to Britain, asking for asylum. Fewer than 25 had been granted permission to stay' (215). The Immigration Department is an antagonist throughout the story, always the one that holds the power of whether or not the family can stay in Britain. The immigration officers are pitted against the Nigerians in Sade's mind. She accuses them of not understanding Papa's reason for their becoming refugees, but because they 'haven't believed THOUSANDS of other Nigerians, what are our chances??? They claim they are fair, but if you are Nigerian, they don't even care whether your story is true' (211). Modood contends that multi-culturalism 'unpicks the negative treatment of "difference" – stereotypes, racism, Islamophobia and so on' (2008: 17).

As I have shown, the scapegoat as the marginalised Other, the stranger, emerges in *Dancing the Boom Cha Cha Boogie*, *My Dog, Kojuro and the Bears* and *Web of Lies*. While the innocent victim is the most likely scapegoat, the contemporary notion of scapegoating extends the logic of locating a guilty one to more abstract or generalised entities – government, political party, religion, racial or sexual Other – in order to fend off criticism, to cast blame for a society's ills or personal misfortune. The scapegoats are blamed for social upheaval and the 'sacrificial mechanism' is a necessary means for restoring social order. The discussion now considers characters that have a history of committing wrongdoing and therefore are easy targets to blame.

The usual suspects

As noted in the introduction to this chapter, liars can easily become scapegoats especially when a Kantian view is taken that they are always guilty by virtue of their history of lying. The titles of the two picture books discussed in this section – *The True Story of the 3 Little Pigs!* (1989), by Jon Scieszka and Lane Smith, and *Fowl Play* (1996), by Jonathan Allen – make truth-claims. The first asserts a truth that is a lie; the second offers a subtle truth by laying the charge of guilt through its pun. When characters like wolves and foxes have a history of deceiving (even lying) it becomes difficult for readers (and other characters) to accept what they say as true. Thus as liars they are vulnerable to becoming scapegoats.

Alexander T. Wolf or Al (*The True Story of the 3 Little Pigs!*) wants to put his side of the story of the Big Bad Wolf, which he believes is 'all wrong'. In presenting his account of 'the real story' (which readers brought up on this familiar story will dismiss as a pack of lies) Al explains that he had a terrible sneezing cold and was making a birthday cake for his dear old granny when he ran out of sugar. In trying to borrow some sugar he inadvertently blew down the pigs' houses (because of his terrible sneeze). And rather than leave 'a perfectly good ham dinner' go to waste he ate the pigs. He comes to his bad end when the third pig insults his grandmother by saying 'And your old granny can sit on a pin!' after Al asks for some sugar to bake granny's birthday cake. Al then explains he was the subject of a media beat-up which framed him as the Big Bad Wolf.

News media are often accused of creating scapegoats as a way to get good circulation numbers for a story, especially for stories of crimes. Al believes that he is wrongly accused and is the subject of media scapegoating. However, unlike the Dreyfus Affair there is no national figure who can write on his behalf. The media presence outside the third pig's home and the subsequent newspaper article with the banner headline 'BIG BAD WOLF!' actively construct the 'wolf' as an immoral subject and a liar. The media's construction of the wolf is in direct contrast to the innocent, moral subject that Al claims to be. Within the context of contemporary news reporting and consumption practices, the wolf's claim to have been 'framed' is given a literal interpretation in the newspaper article which shows a framed picture of the wolf seemingly caught in the act of huffing and puffing outside the little pig's house, or it could be a case of innocent sneezing. The caption 'A.T. Wolf Big and Bad', linguistically names him into being: into being a big and bad criminal. However, Al's final defence of his innocence rests on being framed: 'That's it. The real story. I was framed.' This statement is both true and not true. Its different truth-claims can be understood by drawing on Judith Butler's argument in *Excitable Speech* (1997) that words are not context or convention bound (as Austin's distinction between illocutionary and perlocutionary speech acts makes out). For Butler, a speech act is the 'condensation' of past, present and even foreseeable meanings; in this sense, they are 'excitable' or beyond the speaker's control (14). In reporting the wolf's guilt and naming him 'Big and Bad' the media report is condensing past stories and actions of the wolf in fairy tales and in this way readers will be forever convinced that he is guilty. So who is telling the truth? Readers are persuaded by the text and the wolf's past history to disbelieve Al's story.

What works against the truth-claims of Al's words and his attempts to convince readers that he is a victim, a scapegoat, are the illustrations which show him to be a liar by including contradictory pictorial clues. For instance, in stating, 'This is the real story,' the words are shown first as letters cut out of a newspaper suggestive of a ransom note, and individual letters contain a pig's body parts – a snout, a curly tail; a wolf's body parts – a tail, ears; and materials from the pigs' homes – straw, bricks and a roof with a chimney. It would appear with the weight of such forensic evidence that Al is not innocent but guilty. The scene showing Al dutifully making a cake for his granny has a framed photograph on the wall of a wolf dressed in Little Red Riding Hood's grandmother's nightcap and glasses, and lying in her bed. Al wears a similar pair of glasses so one suspects this wolf has a history of crime: a subtle clue that is planted to implicate Al or to alert the reader to his lies. Of course, Al does speak the truth when he explains that wolves eat meat and implies that it would be against nature for him to not eat a couple of dead pigs.

The title, *The True Story of the 3 Little Pigs!*, makes a truth-claim or a rhetorical statement which is an ironic inversion of the truth. The cover illustration is designed as a mock newspaper with the dubious title 'Daily Wolf' with a paw print separating the two words. However, unlike the article that appears later in the story that reports that Al is a BIG BAD WOLF, this cover article is penned by A. Wolf himself and writes back to the accusation of his guilt by putting his side of the story. This acknowledgement of the 'Author' supports the first proposition that the story is the truth. But the counterclaim is that 'Authors' are 'linguistic, artistic and cultural inventions' (Waugh 1984: 134) and therefore there is no guarantee that this story contains more truth than any other version. Scapegoat or not, Al fails to win support for his true story of the three pigs and is imprisoned – living his days exiled from society.

The sacrificial mechanism is at work in another humorous picture book, *Fowl Play*, by Jonathan Allen, which plays with readers' prejudices and knowledge about foxes and their appetite for small animals among other creatures. This prejudice against foxes is similar to the prejudice against wolves, and is used to set up Foxy as the scapegoat for a crime he didn't commit.

The charge against Foxy begins when Herbert Hound and his fellow canine assistant named Reg are called to investigate the mysterious disappearance of six prize chickens from Farmer Pugh's henhouse. Evidence – a hole in the chicken wire fence, a trail of paw prints – leads

to Foxy. However, when the sleuths interview Foxy he swears his innocence and claims that he is being framed, offering the truism: 'foxes
aren't popular you know'. But when Herbert finds two dead chickens
hanging upside down in his cupboard, Foxy is quick to explain: 'I know
it looks bad, but I bought them from a door-to-door chicken salesman
at about 10.30 last night.' Further interrogation of other suspects leads
to a similar discovery of two dead chickens inside Badger's cupboard.
It seems the door-to-door chicken salesman had a busy night. Clues
are assembled and eventually the canine detectives, Herbert and Reg,
solve the mystery – Hilda the Rabbit had donned a disguise as a chicken
salesman, making false paw prints in the soil by attaching a fox-like
paw onto a stick to create a pattern leading to and from the henhouse
(Figure 3.4).

The mendacious Hilda Rabbit in this story is reminiscent of another
trickster character, Brer Rabbit. Hilda Rabbit's deception is not simply

Figure 3.4   Illustration from *Fowl Play* by Jonathan Allen

argued as part of the animal's nature and need to survive. Rather, she deliberately deceives the others by telling lies, and carrying out a series of calculated deceptions in order to cast blame on the likely suspect – Foxy. Unlike Al, Foxy is exonerated of guilt and presumably accepted back into the farmyard community.

Ideological scapegoating

The different scapegoats presented to this point in the discussion are perceived by the dominant group to be cunning, dangerous, even powerful, and are targets of discrimination and aggression especially in times of crisis. I have also touched on how the policies and ideologies of governments seek scapegoats and are in turn blamed as scapegoats by others. In this final section, I want to consider more closely how different ideologies are blamed for causing social disharmony or a real social danger. When social order breaks down, Girard (1977) suggests that individuals become the 'double' and rival of each other. In a situation of spiralling violence, where competing groups strike out for what they believe is rightfully theirs, the scapegoat becomes the means to cast blame and restore order. The death of the scapegoat can bring the violence to an end and unanimity among the competing groups.

The final text is one that since its first publication in 1945 persists in its relevance today as a political allegory about 'innocent and necessary revolution turning into dictatorship and betrayal' (Bradbury 1987: xvi). *Animal Farm: A Fairy Story* by George Orwell has been translated into numerous languages. It has been on high-school reading lists for many years, studied at universities and made into at least two films. The first British animated film version was in 1954, a project funded by the Central Intelligence Agency (CIA) as part of American Cold War propaganda.[5] The film script suffered from the financier's demands which resulted in significant changes to the plot and characterisation of the original text (see Leab 2007). The second British version was a made-for-television film first screened in 1999. This film includes real animals and humans as well as digitally manipulated animals. While each of these three texts is worthy of discussion in its own right, the following discussion makes some comparative comments where it is felt necessary for highlighting how the issue of scapegoating is dealt with in Orwell's original text and subsequently interpreted in the film versions.

There has been much written on *Animal Farm* and its parallels between Russian history and the plot of a group of oppressed farm animals staging a revolution against their cruel and neglectful owner Mr Jones.

However, less attention has been given to the issue of scapegoating in the text. The eviction of Jones from the farm by the animals who revolt against his neglect is the impetus for a new order to be established under the leadership of two young boars, Snowball and Napoleon. Together with another small, fat pig named Squealer, the three pigs elaborate the ideas of freedom and rebellion (that the old pig Major announced before he died) into 'a complete system of thought, to which they gave the name of Animalism' (Orwell 1987: 10). Snowball and Napoleon further reduce the principles of Animalism to the Seven Commandments which they write on 'the tarred wall in great white letters that could be read thirty yards away' (15). However, the ideals of Animalism are short-lived and the narrative unfolds the series of events that sees the goals of equality and justice become unrealisable. The Commandments also suffer from self-serving interpretation by the pigs, giving them licence to enjoy a life of excess while the other animals labour and starve.

Schematically, the book tells of the Russian Revolution and the dangers of totalitarianism. However, the story has a wider relevance than to any one country, with Orwell borrowing from history and political figures: Italy (Mussolini), Germany (Hitler) as well as Russia (Lenin, Stalin and Trotsky). As a political allegory or modern fable *Animal Farm* can be read as a sharp criticism of Communism, and indeed Orwell writes in a 'proposed preface' to the book that he believes 'the existing Russian régime [under Stalin] is a mainly evil thing' (1987: 106). He also criticises liberals 'who fear liberty' and intellectuals for 'their timidity and dishonesty' (107). These comments are borne out in the text which can be understood as a criticism of a range of ideologies and ideologues – communism, liberalism, democracy, intellectuals, dictators, as well as party hacks and mindless followers.

With the seemingly benign subtitle, *A Fairy Story*, Orwell is able to raise a number of complex ethical issues. The story has a circular structure: the rise and fall of a new order and a return to origins carry the assumption that nothing really changes. Orwell begins his novel: 'Mr Jones, of the Manor Farm, had locked the hen-houses for the night, but was too drunk to remember to shut the pop-holes' (1987: 1), thus establishing the character of Jones, and the pretentious naming of his farm. However, the 1954 animated film begins like an Edenic tale with the opening scene of springtime in an English countryside accompanied by the sound of a flute. The male narrator says: 'In the world we all know which may or may not be the best world possible, once again springtime has come but all the magic of spring was not enough to conceal the misery of Manor Farm.' The bucolic countryside gives way to a bleak-looking farmhouse down in a valley. A sense of foreboding accompanies the change in the music and images, signifying a dark tale with menacing shadows, and an evil-looking and cruel Jones, who whips his animals mercilessly. The starkness of the animation and soundtrack caused *New York Times* critic Bosley Crowther at the time of its release to observe, 'the shock of straight and raw political satire is made more grotesque in the medium of cartoon'.[6] The universalism of the opening words with their veiled reference to democracy ('which may or may not be the best world possible') is designed to appeal to the prejudice of a Western viewing audience who at the time of the 1950s were repeatedly cautioned by their governments about the evils of Communism, which proved to be an effective scapegoating mechanism.

The 1999 film begins as a tale of retribution, with a female narrator (a new character created by the filmmakers in the form of Jessie the sheep dog) who says with serious authority: 'It was a storm of judgement.' The ominous background music, and scenes of a rain-soaked English countryside and bedraggled animals making their way back to a derelict Animal Farm are intercut with scenes of the rain washing away white-painted lettering on a barn door: this act of erasure by Nature symbolises the erasure of the animal-made Seven Commandments. Jessie explains the reason for the escape and now the return: 'For years we had been hiding from oppression. Hiding from Napoleon's spies. But now nature was washing away the disease.' As the music rises to a triumphant note, Jessie says: 'I always knew as with all things built on the wrong foundations. The farm would crumble [...] The poisonous cement that held Napoleon's dreams together was being washed away.' This introduction ensures that viewers are positioned to see this film as a warning of what can happen when evil takes hold of people's lives.

All three texts rely on an audience that has a shared understanding of certain ethical concepts, namely equality, justice, liberty and the oppressive forces that work to destroy these values. This point is given a heavy-handed treatment in the CIA-sponsored film, where the ending of the novel is changed significantly to reflect the overthrow of Napoleon by a union of animals from the surrounding farms marching on Animal Farm. Leab (2007) draws the analogy between the united animals and the Russian people with the help of free nations overthrowing Stalinist rule.

Animal Farm functions as a persecution text – Girard's (1978) term for any text that tells of sacrificial violence against a victim. As noted previously in this chapter, the aim of a persecution text or sacrificial violence is to attribute responsibility for the social crisis to a culprit/victim and then to restore order by destroying or expelling the alleged culprit. I want to look at the various ways in which the 'culprit' in *Animal Farm* can be viewed as a scapegoat, according to Girard's thinking. While the story has its scapegoats, a new order rather than a 'restored order' results when the culprits are expelled; however, the community of animals is led to believe that order and harmony have been restored, and initially after Jones is expelled there is a new sense of freedom and harmony among the animals. However, once Napoleon takes on the leadership, expelling Snowball, the animals are tricked into a state of false consciousness whereby they are either too stupid or too intimidated to believe anything that contradicts the 'myth' of an evil culprit.

Jones, a cruel, irresponsible drunkard, is responsible for Manor Farm going to wrack and ruin. However, when the animals rebel and expel him from the farm, thereby taking over its ownership and running, he synecdochically stands in for a universal 'Man' and becomes a scapegoat when things begin to go wrong for the animals after he is expelled. Old Major in his final speech to the animals publicly announces the culpability of Man: 'Man is the only real enemy we have. Remove Man from the scene, and the root cause of hunger and overwork is abolished forever' (4). Jones is referred to throughout the story as a reminder of a past regime and no matter how difficult the new order under Snowball or later Napoleon, it is compared favourably against Jones's time. The repeated invocation of Jones as a threat guarantees the tyranny of the pigs. When the animals are told that the pigs are taking the milk and apples, Squealer explains that pigs (as the intellectuals) require brain food to ensure the farm's security against Jones: 'Milk and apples feed the brains and if our brains aren't fed then Jones will come back. Do any of you want to see Jones back?' (1999 film). His words ensure that the animals live with fear of the return of evil.

Despite the ascribed threat of Jones, Snowball is the most explicitly scapegoated character. In Orwell's text Snowball is marked as a 'traitor', 'a criminal' and 'a dangerous character and a bad influence' (39) by Napoleon and Squealer. The twinning of Napoleon and Snowball and other doubles – Napoleon and Whymper (1987), Pilkington and Whymper (1954), Napoleon and Pilkington (1999) – are integral to a persecution text as it enables collusion and reciprocal incitement to violence. The double or 'double mediation', as Girard terms it, also facilitates a process whereby each party blames the other for the conflicts between them (Girard 1965: 101). Napoleon takes control of the farm after setting his pack of dogs on Snowball, chasing him out of the farm. The dogs function like the violent mob that outcasts the scapegoat from the community. In both the 1999 film and the novel, Snowball escapes the dogs but 'was seen no more' (1987: 36). However, he continues to be blamed for everything that goes wrong; he is the culprit. In the 1954 film, the dogs kill Snowball, and in his first speech as leader, Napoleon performs the double mediation (Snowball–Jones) by firmly blaming each for past tyrannies and establishes them as twinned culprits in the minds of the naïve animals: 'Comrades, Snowball is a traitor. What was he really planning? [pause] To bring back Jones.' Just as Stalin made Trotsky a primary scapegoat for the violence that ensued during his purges, so too does Napoleon make Snowball the scapegoat for his treachery.

The stories that Napoleon tells about Snowball are similar to the myths of which Girard speaks, as both are rooted in 'real acts of violence' (Girard 1978: 38). In speaking of the atrocities committed by Snowball, Napoleon seeks out possible co-conspirators such as the naïve hens that are sacrificed for crimes they did not commit, or at least did not know they were crimes. This execution is an instance of atavistic violence and victimisation that follows the initial scapegoating of Snowball. Napoleon and Squealer justify these sacrificial acts in terms of the good of the community. The narrator in Orwell's text explains how the myths of Snowball's culpability spread amongst the animals:

> Whenever anything went wrong it became usual to attribute it to Snowball. If a window was broken or a drain was blocked up, someone was certain to say that Snowball had come in the night and done it, and when the key of the store-shed was lost the whole farm was convinced that Snowball had thrown it down the well. Curiously enough they went on believing this even after the mislaid key was found under a stack of meal. (1987: 52)

The mass deception that pervades the farm is integral to the sacrificial mechanism that scapegoats Snowball, and, at the same time, provides the farm animals with a sense of solidarity united in a common act of persecution. To further ensure that the animals remember only the past according to Napoleon and Squealer, they are indoctrinated into disremembering the heroic actions of Snowball during the Battle of the Cowshed, the point when the animals revolted against Jones and other farmers who sought to regain control of Animal Farm:

> In the late summer yet another of Snowball's machinations was laid bare. The wheat crop was full of weeds, and it was discovered that

on one of his nocturnal visits Snowball had mixed weed seeds with the seed corn [...] The animals now also learned that Snowball had never – as many of them had believed hitherto – received the order of 'Animal Hero, First Class'. This was merely a legend which had been spread some time after the Battle of the Cowshed by Snowball himself. (1987: 65)

A source of unease in Animal Farm is the scarcity of food for the animals, and the excessive consumption by the pigs. Girard (1986) contends that conflict for scarce resources in society is resolved (temporarily) by making common cause against an identifiable enemy. To deflect blame away from the pigs, Snowball again becomes the target, with rumour fuelling the myth of the evil enemy: while the animals (except the pigs) live a miserable existence of meagre food supplies and excessive hard labour, Snowball is living 'in considerable luxury, so it was said – at Foxwood' (1987: 67). Each of these acts of blaming and demonising Snowball as the common enemy is a collective projection on to the social imaginary.

A strength of *Animal Farm* as a persecution text is that the narrator does not side with and vindicate the innocent: a point Girard (1986) claims the Bible does for biblical victims. One could argue that the narrator in Orwell's novel contributes to the scapegoating through its focalisation, which is arguably itself an implicit judgement on Snowball, and does not offer a counter viewpoint. Readers are left to determine whether these reports about Snowball are lies or truths. The narrators in the three texts, however, note the injustices (the cat who shirks work, the overworked but underfed Boxer, the consumption of the milk and apples by the pigs), but like the other instances of scapegoating mentioned above only Jessie offers a dissenting voice. As the motherly narrator, Jessie questions the pigs' domination, and the following interchange between her and Boxer demonstrates the difference between those willing to question and those who are blind followers:

[Jessie]:   'Boxer, the pigs always tell us what to do.'
[Boxer]:   'We must have leaders'.
[Jessie]:   'But what if they're wrong?'
[Boxer]:   'Napoleon's never wrong.' (1999)

Despite Jessie's questioning of the pigs to Boxer, she never confronts them in the film and only speaks her disquiet when narrating the story retrospectively. However, after Boxer is taken away to the knackers,

Jessie reproaches herself for not doing something to help him. Her feeling of guilt spurs her to take the animals away from the farm to find a safer place to live.

The conclusion of *Animal Farm* in all three texts does not end with harmony and the return of the scapegoat. Only Jessie holds on to a memory of Snowball as someone who tried to bring about a change for the good of the animals. In the closing scenes of the film (1999), Jessie observes the new owners approaching the farm (parents and two children: all blond and fair-skinned, Aryan even) – the picture of a happy, middle-class family is in stark contrast to the earlier arrival at Manor Farm at the beginning of the film, which showed a coarse farmer, Pilkington, his flashy wife and their two porcine-looking boys who cruelly shoot pebbles at the animals with their slingshots. The class difference is no guarantee that life will be different with the new owners and Jessie tells the viewing audience that if things don't go well, then the animals will rebel. This warning with its implicit message of class warfare in human and animal relations returns to the underlying principle of Animalism: 'Four legs good, two legs bad' (1987: 21), and reasserts the animals' determination not to allow their lives to return to a state of subjection under tyranny. Such a stance speaks metaphorically against totalitarianism or authoritarianism. As noted previously, the 1954 film advances the rise of the oppressed against the oppressive through the united front of all the farm animals destroying the farmhouse and killing the pigs. The donkey Benjamin leads the march, and, as the new leader, he is heralded by a clash of symbols in the soundtrack after the fall of Napoleon. Benjamin is Snowball's double – friend and now leader. In Orwell's novel, the ending speaks of things returning to their origins: Napoleon had renamed the farm Manor Farm 'which, he believed, was its correct and original name' (1987: 94). At the drinking and card-playing session at the farmhouse between the pigs and the farmers an argument breaks out between Napoleon and Pilkington after 'each played an ace of spades simultaneously' (95). The farm animals watching the scene through the window could no longer distinguish pig from man, man from pig.

While totalitarianism is the ideology that is cast in a bad light in *Animal Farm*, it could also be seen as a scapegoat along with democracy, capitalism and Western liberalism, as these ideologies are variously shown to be the cause of problems that arise on the farm. Old Major and Snowball envisage a utopia, a place where animals would be free and equal. However, it soon becomes evident that the animals need to work together to find ways of ensuring that there is enough food for everyone to survive the long winter. Snowball's plan for a wind-mill is the first step towards the modernisation of Animal Farm. When Napoleon takes charge after expelling Snowball, his personal ambitions and greed replace any desire for the collective good, and his lack of lead-ership spells disaster for the windmill and a self-sustaining community. He develops a liking for alcohol (breaking the fifth commandment: *No animal shall drink alcohol*), and enjoys dressing in men's clothing (third commandment: *No animal shall wear clothes*). Farmer Pilkington and Whymper (the accountant/broker) exploit Napoleon by encouraging and financially benefiting from his increasing capitalist desires. The trade between Napoleon and Pilkington and Whymper marks a radical shift – from the feudal-like economy of the farm under Jones and more socialist economy under Snowball – to capitalism. Greedy excess is the cause for the demise of Napoleon's regime and Animal Farm: particu-larly, Napoleon's desire to trade farm produce for whisky. Squealer keeps a tally of the production outputs of the farm, and disingenuously denies that profits are the goal. In this way, the text shows greed and individu-alism as the cause for a failed social order.

Animalism stands in for Communism in that both ideologies extol a classless and egalitarian society. Animalism can also be seen as syn-onymous with liberal humanism in that both have freedom of the indi-vidual as their basis. However, the idea of freedom and equality for all is a failed promise in *Animal Farm*, as from the beginning there are inequalities among the animals: only the pigs get to make the laws, and some of the clever animals (the dogs, Muriel the goat, Benjamin and to some extent Clover) could read the commandments but 'the stupider animals such as the sheep, hens and ducks, were unable to learn the Seven Commandments by heart' (21). Man was considered the centre of liberal humanism, and so are the pigs similarly produced; however, the 'stupider animals', like marginalised others in any society, have less access to power, economy and freedom of choice. The farmyard is a microcosm of society and ideas of equality are encapsulated in the commandment 'ALL ANIMALS ARE EQUAL.' However, the pigs' sup-plement to the commandment – 'BUT SOME ARE MORE EQUAL THAN OTHERS' (90, emphasis original) – speaks the truth, as equality neces-sitates unequal outcomes. The supplements that eventually change all Seven Commandments serve the interests of the pigs and diminish the rights and freedom of other animals, producing a community that shares fear and desire: fear of violation and desire for retribution.

Scapegoating is part of the larger context of secrets and lies in that it is a process that requires a refusal to see the truth or a cover up of the truth, and lies and deceptions are common to this process. I noted at the beginning of this chapter that fear is often behind scapegoating, a point which is borne out in the texts. Girard considers rivalry to be at the heart of scapegoating: the desire for what the other has, whether it be material goods, power, respect or talent, is most apparent in *Animal Farm*. Girard also goes so far as to see persecution texts (or sacrificial myths) as having their root cause in real events, historical facts. Some of the texts discussed in this chapter can be read as political allegories and readers could draw a comparison with their own communities' need to find scapegoats for social or national political failures and problems, or targets of collective hatred based on religious or cultural affiliation, or simply strangers. No matter the reason for the scapegoat, the need for survival of the community remains paramount.

Animal Farm is a fitting final text for this chapter as it brings to the fore the need for understanding how scapegoats have always been a part of the world, and history is marked by the names of many famous scapegoats such as Leon Trotsky, Alfred Dreyfus, the Salem witches and Jews. Scapegoating continues to have relevance in current societies across the globe where there is a transference of guilt/blame on to an innocent. Whenever tensions mount in a society or community there is also a demand to find a scapegoat often causing mass deception, delusion or misguided belief. Often the media is accused of finding a scapegoat, so too are the police, the justice system, political parties and governments. Children too may blame a scapegoat to avoid carrying the burden of guilt for a wrong act that they committed, no matter how trivial. In some extreme cases, the attitude towards the scapegoat results in violence. The process of scapegoating can therefore be used in a more serious way than simply pointing the finger at an innocent. While some children's books may work to resolve the scapegoating through conciliation, repentance or contrition, others expose the inhumane outcome of such victimisation. Scapegoating is something that affects everyone – adult and child. As Girard says: 'Each one of us is obliged to ask where he stands in relation to scapegoats' (1986: 62). Part II pursues further ethical questions in relation to survival.

Part II
Secrets and Secrecy

4
Secrets of State

Secrecy is often bound to moral choice. Having a secret is one thing, but the consequences of revealing or keeping silent is another. It is difficult to determine whether the effects of the action will be good or bad. Even retrospectively, it can be difficult to know whether it was a good outcome or a bad one. Writer and philosopher Sam Harris says that 'one difficulty we face in determining the moral valence of an event is that it often seems impossible to determine whose well-being should most concern us' (2010: 68). Who benefits and who suffers from a course of action is a crucial point of consideration in the texts that I discuss in this chapter. In making a decision or taking a course of action, the subject may consider that he/she is operating from a moral position. When the subject is the government the consequences of that decision or action affect the welfare of a large population. In terms of the welfare or well-being of a population, what are the moral responsibilities of the government in times of war or when resources are scarce? We can also ask what are the responsibilities of the individual in the face of large-scale human suffering? These questions are at the core of the texts discussed in this chapter: *The Hunger Games* (2008), by Suzanne Collins, *Little Brother* (2008), by Cory Doctorow, and *Article 5* (2012), by Kristen Simmons. The issue of rendition is discussed, with parallels drawn between the practices taken by the governments in the fictions and practices of governments outside the texts.

Harris (2010: 70) makes the point that one of the great tasks of human civilisation is to create mechanisms (laws, institutions, codes of conduct) that protect people, not only by ensuring the welfare of a society, but also by protecting the people from being left to the mercy of individual ethical failure towards one another. Does considering the well-being of society mean that the sacrifice of a few is justified in terms of the greater gains of the many? In such instances, paternalism, propri-etariness and protectiveness, which Daniel Metcalfe (2009: 305) regards as 'secrecy's most basic elements', can be used as arguments for and against the moral conduct of a government or an individual. Deciding between those intentions, decisions and actions that are 'good' and those that are 'bad' is not always easy. In a normative sense, morality refers to what is right or wrong, which may be independent of the val-ues or behaviours held by particular people or cultures.

In looking to a world of the near future, or a world that is contempo-raneous to our own, young adult fiction often slips into a moral argu-ment about those in power and those who are subjected to that power. In this chapter, I want to problematise the moral bifurcation of good and bad. In looking at the survival of the individual or group, fiction often supports lying, deceit and secrecy when it serves those on the side of 'good', but not when used by those on the side of 'evil'. This double standard is often rationalised with the argument that whatever it takes to survive or conquer is justified. However, if lying and secrecy are ubiquitous to human behaviour, then why is there outcry, shock or cynical acceptance when governments are found to be keeping secrets, lying to their constituents, carrying out covert operations or exercis-ing surveillance activities? Should governments (and those who serve them) be above human failing? Moralists might argue that those who have the power to rule should never lie or deceive. Realists might reason that at times it is necessary and justifiable to not tell the truth. Young adult fiction falls on both sides of the moralist/realist positions, but rather than see their alignment with either one or the other position as an end in itself, my point is that as narratives they offer a particular conceptualisation of how the state, or nation state, is part of a rapidly evolving technological world which further complicates matters of sur-vival, freedom and protection.

The ability of new information and communication technologies to pierce previously impenetrable physical, personal and social bounda-ries has particular relevance to contemporary society and young people as there is now more information that can be collected, accessed and distributed about individuals and groups. This ability to *know about* is a consequence of society having become more mobile and networked, enabling increased surveillance, tracking and spreading of disinforma-tion.[1] Secrecy in government and business is directly linked to informa-tion control and as Gary T. Marx and Glenn W. Muschert note: 'secrecy involves efforts to manage information, whether withholding or reveal-ing, and reciprocally discovering or resisting discovery' (2009: 221).

Metcalfe regards government information disclosure and government secrecy as two sides of the same coin. The fiction texts discussed in this chapter open up ways of thinking about secrecy as a form of information control which will have further implications for *knowing about each other*: Who knows? What do they know? What are the consequences of this knowledge? These questions are similar to those posed by Foucault in terms of truth-telling: 'who is able to tell the truth?' 'about what?', 'with what consequences?' and 'with what relations to power?' (2001: 170).[2]

Secrecy envelopes government decision-making processes and outcomes and is often justified in terms of 'the public good' or in 'the interest of the state', yet the steps taken by state officials to ensure state well-being may be deceptive, immoral or inhumane. Bok asserts that the 'esoteric rationale' underpinning control over government secrecy transferred the 'aura of sacredness from the *arcana ecclesiae* of church, ritual, and religious officials to secular leaders' (most notably absolute monarchies of the seventeenth century) (1989: 172, emphasis original). Whereas an individual action might be condemned as unlawful or immoral, the same action by the state is legitimated according to the esoteric rationale. The rationale for such government control is protection of the population; but often protection entails surveillance, tracking, and loss of privacy and freedom. This double-edged sword penetrates the focus texts in this chapter. In some nation states, control and expected compliance do not necessarily ensure harmonious relations between the state and its constituents, but may subdue or overawe them.[3]

A familiar scenario encountered in young adult fiction is the young protagonist (or group) who reacts against the control of the state and seeks to reveal its secrets or overcome its tyrannical hold in order to achieve freedom from oppression. The thematic approach in a typical dystopian narrative is to contrast the benefits of openness with the evils of secrecy and absolute control. However, this bifurcation – good, oppressed, youthful citizens versus evil, controlling, adult governance – does not take into account how knowledge and truth, and associated concepts of secrecy, deception and lies, need to be considered in relation to social, political and economic factors. In the young adult fiction discussed in this chapter, the struggles that the young characters undergo with powerful Others are intricately tied to these macro socio-political-economic factors and are not simply a struggle between the individual and the powerful Other, although an 'us-versus-them' struggle drives the plots. From the protagonists' viewpoint (and the implied reader's), the Other in the focus texts is metonymically expressed as: the Capitol in *The Hunger Games*,

Department of Homeland Security in *Little Brother* and the Federal Bureau of Reformation in *Article 5*. The converse is also true – the protagonists are viewed by the state or its enforcers as Other because of their difference and actions that are contrary to the collective ethics and ideologies of the state.

The Hunger Games, Little Brother and *Article 5*, like many young adult fictions, both reproduce and actively perform the world, or an imagined world, for their readers and therefore have material, pedagogical and ultimately political effects, shaping the ways readers understand and possibly act in their worlds. In each of the focus texts, secrecy is linked to power and moral subjectivity. Foucault's ideas of power relations and ethics provide a useful means for interpreting the relationships between the protagonists, and how they each draw on strategies for compliance and agency in their bid to survive. Foucault considers subjects not in metaphysical terms but as embodied beings who are capable of acting upon the world, and have the ability to influence and transform other forces: a key consideration discussed in Chapter 1. Foucault's view of power at the 'extremities' (1980) is different from Bok's notion of legitimated or sanctioned forms of power and authority held by the state as a central locus that is part of the esoteric rationale. The work of Foucault, and other writers such as Georg Simmel, continues to provide important ways for knowing or apprehending the Other and for understanding how the subject can exist and act in the world.

Simmel was a humanist who wrote from a Kantian, liberal background and was interested in what secrecy could ideally tell us about society and human behaviour. For Simmel, secrecy sets barriers between people but it also offers 'the seductive temptation to break through the barriers by gossip and confession' (1950: 466). His idea of revelation and disclosure as a means to breaking barriers suggests that subjects yield to external influences, but are also capable of acting upon the world, interpreting and shaping it through their words and actions.

Foucault rejects the humanist idea that power is construed as an external force on the human subject. His conceptualisation of power as a productive force similarly sees subjects as active beings, not simply as passive subjects. Whereas the social order in humanist terms requires some superhuman feats to overcome oppressive regimes, Foucault's view would see social order as the outcome of the interplay between various elements of that order; and rather than see domination and compliance as organising society or a microcosm of society in its totality, Foucault would view it as an interplay of power, forces and capabilities. Power is therefore 'power to', that is, the capacity to act. The discussion now turns to how these elements of power, secrecy and the social order are played out in *The Hunger Games*.

Let the games begin!

As its title implies, Suzanne Collins's *The Hunger Games* plays with two key ideas – survival and entertainment. The idea of a group of young people pitted against one another in a fight to survive is one that William Golding delivered in *Lord of the Flies* in 1954: an enduring tale of British schoolboys left to their own devices on a deserted island after their evacuation plane crashes during World War II. Golding's story offers a bleak view on the possibility of humanist governance by children, as the two competing groups kill and plot in their quest for supremacy. Collins's *The Hunger Games* updates Golding's wartime boys' survival story by having a female hero, Katniss, and making the spectacle of killing mandatory televised viewing for the people who comprise the 12 districts of Panem: 'the country that rose up from the ashes of a place that was once called North America' (Collins 2008: 21). Whereas Golding's prepubescent boys were left to play out their future without an adult presence, the adolescents who participate in Collins's 'Games' are subject to the close surveillance, interference and occasional support of various adults – the Gamemakers, groomers, sponsors and coaches.

The Hunger Games bears comparison with the circus games of the Roman Republic which often lasted for weeks and were purely for entertainment, taking place in large amphitheatres. The bread and circuses of Imperial Rome no doubt inspired Walter Benjamin to combine the two antithetical notions 'aesthetics' and 'politics', which he used in reference to twentieth-century fascism and the Third Reich's reliance on ritual, spectacle and symbol (1968: 241). However, the practice of aesthetic politics is not the preserve of totalitarian governments but is pervasive in democratic societies as televised electioneering takes on many of these more superficial features, appearances and performances.

In many respects, *The Hunger Games* performs its own version of bread and circuses, drawing readers into its lurid spectacle: the title announces a perverse form of ludic entertainment; there is an inherent conflict between heroic protagonists and evil rivals; and the story contains alternating moments of humour, crisis, cruelty, change of fortune and tenderness – all of which carry familiar resonances in our world of reality TV and political showbiz.[4] These alternating highs and lows are judged by the viewing audience in the text who vote on whether they will send silver parachutes of food, weapons or medicine to assist their district's contestants. The alternating emotional states also serve the narrative as comic, tragic, melodramatic and romantic emplotments. The text therefore performs for readers, offering a circus analogy that resembles contemporary Western society's appetite for entertainment that may be degrading and embarrassing for the participants, but offers a perverse pleasure for viewers.

Young people become eligible for 'reaping' when they turn 12. As its name suggests, reaping is a time of harvesting the young to participate in the games where they must kill one another until there is only one victor. The agricultural metaphor serves as both an enticement and a reminder. The enticement is that the winner earns bountiful food for the people of their district, as well as personal wealth; the reminder is that the Dark Days of the uprising of the districts against the Capitol must never be repeated. The reaping is punishment for the uprising. The 24 'tributes'[5] are drawn from the lottery pool, and when her sister's name is called, Katniss volunteers to be her replacement. The other tribute from her district is Peeta Mellark. The games are held in an outdoor arena that is under constant video surveillance and players are at the mercy of the Gamemakers who can change conditions in order to ramp up the excitement value for the pleasure of the viewing audience. While the senseless cruelty of the reaping is masked by the market-day celebratory tone, its pretence as a sporting event, the live 'entertainment' telecast by the state, and the dressing-up of the potential tributes in their best clothes, Katniss reveals the truth that no one dares speak: 'the word *tribute* is pretty much synonymous with the word *corpse*' (Collins 2008: 27).

The Capitol's domination and insistence on certain forms of compliance as absolute and universal seek to overcome or dissuade resistance and otherness, and thereby preclude the possibility of different ways of being and acting in Panem. However, despite or because of its totalitarian state control, resistance is inevitable. In setting up a discourse of resistance, *The Hunger Games* raises moral paradoxes and dilemmas, and secrecy both inhibits and supports the moral choices the characters face. Katniss and the others who live in the districts know that secrecy is necessary for survival and to disclose a secret risks not only possible detection by the Capitol but certain death for breaking the law. Consequently, Katniss learns to hunt without detection in the forbidden woods, carefully hiding her weapons the way her father had taught her, and buying and selling on the black market. Even the mayor buys the animals she kills, but always business is conducted in a covert fashion. Although the story is set some time in a future world, the country of Panem exists as a closed world with no apparent outside communications, despite the state-of-the-art technology in the Capitol, the governing city. The technologically sophisticated Capitol with its video surveillance, smart technologies and tracking devices is a marked contrast to the more agrarian-style struggle that many districts endure, with inhabitants surviving by illegally hunting in the woods, or by trading, bartering and stealing. While some districts are better off than others, District 12 is the poorest of them all, and has none of the affluence of the Capitol. The following observation from Katniss explains the inequality:

> They do surgery in the Capitol, to make people appear younger and thinner. In District 12, looking old is something of an achievement since so many people die early. You see an elderly person, you want to congratulate them on their longevity, ask the secret of survival. (150–1)

The Games are a moral paradox. The false love and praise that are heaped on to the tributes during their pre-games preparation are in stark contrast to the purpose of the Games which is to kill. The celebration of the tributes and the pre-games process – preparing them for the combat, meticulous personal grooming so that they attract sponsorship, parading them in a lavish spectacle and conducting interviews with the charismatic host, Caesar, whose job is to draw out the best entertainment value from each tribute – are part of the Games' ludic framework. The framework imposes a double bind of the most intractable kind whereby the young tributes are hailed as celebrities but are also lambs to the slaughter. Tributes are coached like would-be celebrities to charm the audience, but as Katniss notes, this is ultimately a futile exercise. When her coach, Haymitch, tries to find 'an angle' to avoid Katniss's hostility and strong sense of privacy destroying her chances of gaining the approval and sympathy of the sponsors, he suggests she opens up about herself, her life and family – the fodder that feeds celebrity news. But as the following exchange demonstrates, truth is not the issue:

> 'But I don't want them to! They're already taking my future! They can't have the things that mattered to me in the past!' I say.
> 'Then lie! Make something up!' says Haymitch.
> 'I'm not good at lying,' I say. (142)

Despite her reluctance, Katniss finds a compromise by taking the advice of her groomer for the Games (Cinna) who advises her to be

herself and show the audience her fighting spirit. This compromise is
an early lesson that she learns and subsequently performs throughout
the Games. It also demonstrates that Katniss is not simply passive in
her encounters with the Other – the Capitol and those who work for
it – but is able to act upon the world. When Peeta (the baker's son
from District 12) is interviewed he tells the audience of his long-time
romantic feelings for Katniss, which comes as a surprise to her. The
'story' of star-crossed lovers is a huge success with the audience, and
Katniss learns to play up the romance angle in order to win sponsor
support throughout the harrowing days of the Games, especially when
she needs food, weapons and medicine. The pre-games preparations
are a form of acculturation whereby the tributes undergo training and
regulation in order to tame any resistance and to receive instructions
as to how they must perform.

While it is futile to physically resist the Capitol, Katniss has to find
another way whereby she can not only survive, but retain her own
moral position.[6] During the Games, Katniss resists opening up to
Peeta for fear that he is only pretending to be her friend while harbouring the need to kill her for his own survival – 'A warning bell
goes off in my head. *Don't be so stupid. Peeta is planning how to kill you, I
remind myself. He is luring you in to make you easy prey. The more likeable
he is, the more deadly he is'* (88, emphasis original). Nevertheless, her
internal conflict and self-imposed secretive behaviour eventually give
way to an 'ethics of care'[7] for Peeta when he becomes badly injured.
The ethical dilemma which Katniss and Peeta face is to not kill each
other despite the need for personal survival. While the Capitol sees no
moral paradox in the Games, for Katniss and Peeta and some of the
other tributes (such as Rue), loving (or respect for human life) and killing cannot co-exist. However, they do kill otherwise they are killed.
The dilemma is brought to a head and resolved (temporarily at least in
this first novel in the series) when Katniss and Peeta are the remaining tributes. Like the star-crossed lovers that they have performed to
perfection, Katniss decides upon the solution: that they both eat poison berries, thereby leaving no victor. But a double suicide would not
be good for the Games, and would be a rebuke to the Capitol, so the
suicide is quickly averted:

> The frantic voice of Claudius Templesmith shouts above them. 'Stop!
> Stop! Ladies and gentlemen, I am pleased to present the victors of the
> Seventy-fourth Hunger Games, Katniss Everdeen and Peeta Mellark!
> I give you – the tributes of District Twelve!' (419)

The Capitol and its instruments of social regulation and forms of domination are intended to produce a certain kind of citizen, one who is submissive and compliant. Foucault alerts us to a further dimension of such an organising activity, the activity of forming and shaping oneself as a certain kind of subject. I discussed how Marjane in *Persepolis* (Chapter 1) was able to undergo self-regulation, or 'practices of the self', to transform herself to attain a certain state of existence. A similar set of practices of the self is undertaken by Katniss. As noted earlier, prior to the Games Katniss ekes out an existence for her mother and sister, Prim, by hunting in the Meadow at the edge of the Seam, the part of District 12 where she lives, even though hunting is illegal. Rather than become passive and compliant, Katniss has to become an agential subject who takes action in order for her family to survive. She becomes adept in using a bow and arrow, and learns how to behave in public so as not to draw attention to her activities. Her techniques of self-regulation and transformation are disclosed in her account of herself:

> So I learned to hold my tongue and to turn my features into an indifferent *mask* so that no one could ever read my thoughts. Do my work quietly in school. Make only polite talk in the public market. Discuss little more than trades in the Hob, which is the black market where I make most of my money. (7, my emphasis)

By these practices of the self, Katniss locates herself in relation to the normative strictures of the state, but retains herself as a moral subject. Readers are not given any prior knowledge of the history of Panem, other than the mention of revolt during the period known as the Dark Days. During the Games, Katniss draws on prior knowledge and learns new techniques of self-regulation which are necessary for survival: she remembers her mother's instruction about which plants will heal and nourish, and which ones will harm; she uses her hunting skills to kill other tributes and to avoid detection; she learns the power of a good performance and plays up to the video cameras knowing the right emotions to project; she also learns to yield to the other, not as an act of submission but as an encounter that has transformative possibility. This last point needs further elaboration.

Before she became a tribute, Katniss, by her own account above, wore a metaphorical mask that protected her from having to reveal her true thoughts and feelings. Even her hunting companion and friend, Gale, is not her confidante. Katniss reflects on their relationship: 'I can't explain how things are with Gale because I don't know myself' (453). She also breaks the barrier of secrecy that is both self-imposed and imposed by the Gamemasters, when she decides to trust and befriend Rue, a young tribute from another district. Her nascent friendship with Rue is the means for her realising that she is not the author of her own existence, untouched by external influences, and solipsistically isolated from the world in which she lives. She invites Rue to be her ally, saying, 'You know, they're not the only ones who can form alliances' (242). However, the alliance proves to be more than just a strategy of survival as the two girls form a deep friendship and share an ethic of care, similar to the caring that she and Peeta develop for each other. When Rue is dying after being speared by another tribute, Katniss nurses her and sings a lullaby as a way of comforting her during the remaining minutes of her life. The two girls also share personal information which is something that the Gamemakers do not encourage. Given the omnipresent surveillance of all their words and actions they run a risk by speaking openly. Sharing information is dangerous, as Katniss says, 'they don't want people in different districts to know about one another' (246). To inhibit moral action, the Capitol and the Gamemakers mandate secrecy, but in deciding not to have secrets the protagonists are able to support their decisions to act as moral agents.

Katniss's decision to refuse secrecy corresponds with Simmel's valorisation of revelation and disclosure as being an important way for acting upon the world. With their shared intimacies, Rue and Katniss demonstrate that they are not simply 'tributes', but embodied subjects who can be touched and influenced by each other. Later, Katniss discloses her thoughts to Peeta and takes him into what the narrative terms her 'circle of trust'. These moments in the text can be read as fulfilling the humanist tradition whereby individuals rise up against the power exerted by external forces to become fully self-determining, autonomous individuals. An alternative view is to consider Foucault's (1984) notion of human agency which sees human beings as active bodies that exist in the midst of the world of shifting and unstable relations, and as such are wholly and inescapably open to influence and transformation by other forces.

The Hunger Games closes on a note that suggests that Katniss is indeed open to forces that will continue to influence and transform. One threatening force comes from the Capitol. When President Snow lowers the crown on her head in the victory celebration, his smile does not match the look in his eyes, which is 'as unforgiving as a snake's' (442). Katniss knows that as the instigator of the berry-eating act, she is the one who will be punished. The sequels *Catching Fire* (2009) and *Mockingjay* (2010) play out the consequences of her rebellion and whether she is able to retain her moral subject position.

Dare to be free

Simmel's writing on secrecy opens up ways of thinking about secrecy, information and norms from a sociological perspective. Fundamental to Simmel's (1906, 1950) work on secrecy is the role of information in social interactions. Simmel points out that knowledge of the 'other' always exists somewhere between full knowledge (which is impossible) and complete ignorance. When an individual is faced with inadequate knowledge about another, then he/she may compensate by supplying what is imagined to be true. Information technology enables information (true, imagined and false) to be shared across global networks within seconds and this rapid dispersal can work both for and against freedom of speech and the right to know.

The main concern when the information technology revolution first began in the 1960s was that significant amounts of personal information would be stored on large, centralised computers by governments and big corporations. Fiction for young adults emerging from the 1960s onwards has been concerned with this issue of vulnerability and loss of privacy or personal freedom.[8] Many recent texts, such as *Little Brother*, are in step with the changes in technological developments (mobile, wireless, optical and broadband communication infrastructures) and an increasingly regulated environment. We now live in a time of decentralisation of data processing, where the shift is from the computer to the user (Gadzheva 2008). User-control is a key feature of Doctorow's *Little Brother*, which demonstrates an inherent paradox: while savvy users gain control over communication and information systems, many remain clueless as to their loss of privacy in that their personal information can be readily known and used by unknown sources. Gadzheva explains that the shift to the user will make it almost impossible for users to maintain control over data generation, transfer and use, and to remain anonymous and unobservable: 'The Internet, mobile phones, and smart cards all generate personal data and make it possible to track and profile all the activities, movements, and habits of data subjects' (2008: 60).

Little Brother forges the link between secrecy and government, and raises the broader implications of information control, surveillance and privacy. The story begins when high-school senior Marcus Yallow decides to cut school to go downtown to play the Alternate Reality

Game (ARG) Harajuku Fun Madness. Marcus's handle is w1n5t0n, pro-nounced 'Winston', an obvious homage to Winston Smith, the char-acter from Orwell's novel *Nineteen Eighty-Four* (1949). (He changes it to M1k3y when he organises a covert internet resistance force against the Department of Homeland Security.) To leave school undetected, Marcus has to negotiate the school's surveillance system – the gait-recognition cameras which have replaced the face-recognition cameras, which were ruled unconstitutional. As Marcus explains: 'Gait-recognition software takes pictures of your motion, tries to isolate you in the pics as a sil-houette, and then tries to match the silhouette to a database to see if it knows who you are. It's a biometric identifier, like fingerprints or retina-scans' (Doctorow 2008: 10).[9] To change his gait and avoid detec-tion Marcus puts stones in his shoes. He also has to evade physical sur-veillance. A further obstacle is the library book his friend Darryl carries. All library books have an arphid – Radio Frequency ID tag – glued into its binding. The arphid enables library services (checking out of books, reshelving) to be carried out quickly but they also enable the books (and borrowers) to be tracked at all times. But Marcus knows how to deactivate this device and although he carries 'a little Faraday pouch' in his bag – 'these little wallets lined with a mesh of copper wires that effectively block radio energy, silencing arphids' (14), it isn't able to neu-tralise the arphid in the book. However, the microwave in the teachers' lounge performs this function – 'the arphid died in a shower of sparks' (17). The day takes an unexpected turn when terrorists blow up the Bay Bridge causing major death and destruction, and turning the city into chaos: a scene reminiscent of the bombing of the Twin Towers on September 11, 2001. These narrative points also read like excerpts from a technology manual in the detailed information they contain.

Little Brother reflects the new 'ambient intelligence' (AmI)[10] environ-ment that recent advances in microelectronics and wireless communica-tions are making possible. As Gadzheva explains, an AmI environment:

> implies a seamless environment of smart networked devices that is aware of the human presence and together with the ever-enhancing data mining capabilities gives the possibility for personal data to be invisibly captured, analysed, and exchanged among countless sen-sors, processors, databases, and devices to provide personalized and contextualized information services. (2008: 60–1)

These new technologies mean that ways of thinking about privacy, secrecy and publicity are changing, and in *Little Brother* the characters are living with the consequences of these changes. While at the time of writing the phenomenon of AmI does not fully exist, there are technologies available that could facilitate it, such as: Radio Frequency Identification tags (RFID), Global Positioning System (GPS), widespread internet access and increasing computer data-storage capacity. What remains in both the fiction and the extra-textual world is that these issues are inherently social and necessarily imply an Other from whom information (or a secret) is withheld or shared.

With respect to the social relations aspect of secrecy and information, Simmel contends that 'all relationships of people to each other rest, as a matter of course, upon the precondition that they know something about each other' (1906: 441). *Little Brother* provides a chilling account of how society has moved to a point where *knowing about each other* has become both beneficial and dangerous. *Knowing about each other* remains an essential element for developing trust between friends and family. However, as Marx and Muschert note, today 'the conditions and meaning of trust' have been altered as 'we have much less complete knowledge of many of those we encounter in large scale, differentiated, mobile society' (2009: 220). In considering the dangerous side of *knowing about each other* we can ask again: 'Who knows?' 'What do they know?' and 'What are the consequences of this knowledge?' In taking its cue from George Orwell's *Nineteen Eighty-Four*, *Little Brother* illustrates how surveillance technologies can affect individuals' privacy and freedom. It also shows how human beings can succumb to external forces and become passive victims; or, in Foucault's terms, how they can become active bodies who are resistant and struggle against the limits and oppressions imposed on them, and believe in the possibility of reversal (Foucault 1978: 95–6). This capacity to resist, fight back and overcome is the driving motivation behind M1k3y's actions.

While the benefits from technological developments – economic growth, security, individual and social safety – are part of the esoteric rationale, the diegetic and extradigetic narrators of *Little Brother* argue the other side, giving voice to growing concerns such as profiling, surveillance, tracking, identity theft and so on, and urging readers to take action. Integral to taking action is knowing how to circumvent, deactivate and protect user identity. The information supplied by the first-person narrator (Marcus/M1k3y) on hacking, using illegal web-servers, spamming, cryptography and arphid cloning is rationalised in terms of an individual's right to privacy, their right to know and other constitutional rights such as the American Bill of Rights – 'Life, liberty and the pursuit of happiness. The right of people to throw off their oppressors' (Doctorow 2008: 201). The repeated invocation of the Bill of Rights throughout the text can be read as a totalising conception of ideal human existence, and the account of technological sabotage by both the state and M1k3y can shock or surprise readers; it is also intended to abruptly awaken readers from any self-deceptive dreams of self-mastery or an ideal existence in a democratic society (an intention which is made explicit in the 'Afterword').

State control becomes excessive especially when actions known extra-textually as 'extraordinary rendition' are taken. In recent times, 'rendition' has taken on a renewed emphasis with respect to one of its meanings, namely 'surrender'. For example, Zakayo explains that 'in Kenya where extradition is compelled by law, it is known as rendition. Rendition is surrender or handing over of persons or property particularly from one jurisdiction to another' (Zakayo 2011).[11] In response to the terrorist attack, the Department of Homeland Security (DHS) becomes a force to combat terrorism and 'protect' the people of San Francisco. However, in waging its own war on terror with increased homeland security, the DHS takes on the tactics of the terrorists in the protection and security of the citizens. After the attack on the Bay Bridge, Marcus and his friends Van, Jolu and Darryl, along with other people who were on the streets at the time, are taken by force by the DHS to a prison in the Bay – Treasure Island[12] – where they are interrogated as suspected terrorists. In detaining ordinary citizens and subjecting them to torture the DHS performs acts of extraordinary rendition.[13] Marcus's prior history as an internet-savvy user, with an anti-authoritarian attitude, is used as grounds for their suspicion:

[Marcus]: 'You think I'm a terrorist? I'm seventeen years old!'
[DHS officer]: 'Just the right age – Al Qaeda loves recruiting impressionistic, idealistic kids. We googled you, you know. You've posted a lot of very ugly stuff on the public Internet.' (41)

Later, when Marcus is released from detention the DHS officer issues a warning: 'We'll be watching you everywhere you go and everything you do. You've acted like you've got something to hide, and we don't like that' (46). His interrogator insists on Marcus giving her his passwords to his mobile phone, memory sticks and email. However, more sophisticated and pervasive tracking systems are used by the DHS to watch all citizens and to know their whereabouts and actions.

The DHS's threat that they are watching all the time is made possible because of the ubiquitous location-aware technologies they employ. The surveillance systems are extensive – profiling based on embedded RFID (arphids) contained in commuters' transport cards ('FasTrak Pass') and other consumer goods and services, wiretapping of phone and internet, gait monitoring surveillance and spycams. When Marcus goes to a Turkish coffee shop, the owner explains the government's new security measures passed under the guise of the PATRIOT Act II: 'You think it's no big deal maybe? What is the problem with government knowing when you buy coffee? Because it's one way they know where you are, where you been' (82–3). FasTrak readers are installed all over the city logging the time and ID number of motorists, 'building an ever more perfect picture of who went where and when' (114). Tracking and profiling are central to the functioning of AmI. Profiling systems invisibly collect and aggregate data about individuals into their personal profiles, without their consent or control. The DHS uses profiling to identify individuals as part of a group or category of persons (potential threats to homeland security) with the consequence that they lose autonomy and self-determination by being arrested, imprisoned and tortured. Marcus is taken into detention a second time and subjected to 'waterboarding' a 'simulated execution' where the subject is strapped to an inclined bench and water is poured over his/her head, filling the nose and mouth, causing gagging (336).[14] The DHS uses the media to spread disinformation about the Xnet movement and to spread fear. After an internet chat with a BBC journalist who enquired if M1k3y was a leader of the Xnet movement, M1k3y discovers that his candid comments about finding ways around the government's tracking system are misrepresented and reported as 'criminal treason' (233).

Foucault reasons that states of domination emerge when otherness is entirely overcome and relations of power become 'set and congealed' (1978: 93). This idea of entrenched (or 'set and congealed') power is addressed by Darryl after Marcus tells him that he is going to continue to fight the government through the Xnet; Darryl's words carry a note of incredulity that the government could ever be stopped: 'You think you're going to stop them? You're out of your mind. They're the government' (106). However, as noted earlier, power for Foucault is 'power to', corporeal force, the capacity to act, to do certain things. M1k3y mobilises young hackers, 'Xnetters', as a force which manifests their otherness by resisting and transgressing the DHS surveillance and oppressive controls. They do this by beating them at their own game, using illegal, covert communication technologies to circumvent the government's systems. For example, Marcus uses the ParanoidXbox operating system that ensures that documents and communications remain secret within its complicated, detection-proofing system. He also jams the tracking systems for commuters. Marcus explains the *modus operandi*:

> Today as I brushed up against him [a commuter], I triggered my arphid cloner, which was already loaded in the pocket of my leather jacket. The cloner sucked down the numbers off his credit cards and his car keys, his passport and the hundred-dollar bills in his wallet.
>
> Even as it was doing that, it was flashing some of them with new numbers, taken from other people I'd brushed against. It was like switching the license plates on a bunch of cars, but invisible and instantaneous. (122)

By demonstrating this capacity to act, M1k3y and the Xnetters ensure that they are not passive subjects. However, their subversive actions are also condoned in the text as necessary, which aligns with the Realist argument that such deception is justifiable in extreme circumstances.

Simmel's normative ideals of sharing secrets and information remain important for Marcus and his friends, despite the fear that there might be untrustworthy people or spies pretending to befriend them. For a long time Marcus is unable to share the secrets of his ordeal with his parents but he is able to confide in friends. Each time he tells someone of his experiences with the DHS it is likened to a load being lifted from his shoulders. However, Simmel's work could not have anticipated the cyber-world and how this environment makes sharing secrets both an easy and potentially dangerous activity. Marcus talks of the 'web of trust':

> one of those cool crypto things that I'd read about but never tried. It was a nearly foolproof way to make sure that you could talk to the people you trusted, but that no one else could listen in. The problem is that it requires you to physically meet with the people in the Web at least once, just to get started. (141)

In order to make physical contact, Marcus organises a 'keysigning party' whereby everyone signs each other's keys.[15] From this point, others can join the web by virtue of being a trusted friend. Furthermore, the party-goers wear T-shirts with the slogan 'Don't trust anyone over 25' as a sign of revolt against adults and the suspicion to which they feel young people are subjected (158). Marcus and his Xnetters not only challenge the hegemonic domination of the DHS but also what they perceive as domination by adult society. Their challenge through the web of trust and T-shirt statement are attempts to make it possible for their otherness to reassert itself in a form of resistance and transgression. From a Foucauldian perspective, Marcus represents a non-normative idea of freedom, a freedom which he finds can only come with transgression. When the DHS raid the party and spray the young people with a toxic gas, Marcus is concerned about his role in this resistance, and later abandons the strategy of separatism when he confides in his parents and Barbara (the journalist) about his experiences with the DHS.

While acts of resistance are overcome and suppressed by the DHS, the combined efforts of M1k3y and his followers and friends, his parents and Barbara are ultimately able to bring the DHS to the attention of the State Troopers, and renew dialogue between forces within the government, the DHS and the legal system. The agent of change is the resisting human subject, embodied primarily in Marcus/M1k3y. Throughout the story, he affirms his right to be free. In the final scene of the novel, Marcus makes a video documenting his experience with the DHS including his torture. He makes a plea to viewers to 'choose freedom' and concludes: 'My name is Marcus Yallow. I was tortured by my country, but I still love it here. I'm seventeen years old. I want to grow up in a free country. I want to live in a free country' (355). In Foucault's terms, he represents 'a free subject' and 'a subject of action' (1983, 1981). As a subject of action, Marcus does not succumb to be the passive, compliant subject that the DHS demands, but transgresses the existing limits and constraints imposed by them, and imaginatively devises new ways of working within these limits, and of influencing others in turn. His friend Darryl, however, succumbs and is not only passive and compliant, but also psychologically changed after being imprisoned and tortured for months.

Marcus's desire to be free in a free country echoes the Bill of Rights and represents his belief in its tenets of 'Life, liberty and the pursuit of happiness. The right of people to throw off their oppressors'. In the closing events of the novel, Marcus is fined for stealing a mobile phone, a rather minor misdemeanour, but is not sent to trial for the more serious offence of technological sabotage. Marcus welcomes the return to the old world order, the 'system with judges, open trials and lawyers' (341) and the dismantling of the DHS. However, the epilogue reveals that the President and the DHS have come to 'an understanding' (351), and the DHS would hold its own closed, military tribunal to investigate 'possible errors in judgment' (351). This final state of affairs suggests that state secrets will continue to be concealed from the public and the press. The tribunal finds that the actions of the DHS officer who gave the instructions to torture Marcus and others at the detention centre 'do not warrant further discipline' (352). Throughout the course of his detention, Marcus learns of other secrets – the 'disappearance' of people held in detention, the outsourcing of torture of American citizens to Syria, and the disinformation spread by the DHS under the pretext of 'protection' for discrediting individuals, spreading lies and covering up covert actions.

The message that *Little Brother* delivers is that technology is a tool which everyone should know how to use to ensure their privacy and freedom, and that when it is used by a central power such as the state for *knowing about*, for tracking and surveillance, then individuals will be vulnerable. Knowing how to use technology is a source of empowerment for Marcus: 'The best part of all of this is how it made me *feel*: in control. My technology was working for me, serving me, protecting me. It wasn't spying on me. This is why I loved technology: if you used it right, it could give you power and privacy' (80). Furthermore, the closing comment in the 'Afterword' written by Andrew 'bunnie' Huang, Xbox Hacker, exhorts readers to find their inner 'M1k3y' (the hacker-protagonist of *Little Brother*), and resist attempts of the state to take away freedom:

> M1k3y is in you and in me – *Little Brother* is a reminder that no matter how unpredictable the future may be, we don't win freedom through security systems, cryptography, interrogations and spot searches. We win freedom by having the courage and the conviction to live every day freely and to act as a free society, no matter how great the threats are on the horizon.
>
> Be like M1k3y: step out the door and dare to be free. (365)

Both *Little Brother* and *The Hunger Games* provide perspectives on Foucault's 'subject of action', even when the actions are a risk to personal safety. In *Little Brother*, technology and know-how of the AmI environment are the means for staging the transgression and resistance against state domination. However, the final text to be discussed, *Article 5* takes its readers to a time in the future, a time when war has destroyed most of America. Technology has now come full circle, moving from the kind of ubiquitous computing and mass consumerism that typically are experienced by countries such as the USA (and represented in *Little Brother*) to an almost pre-technological and war-ravaged state.

One big happy family

Like *Little Brother*, Kristen Simmons's *Article 5* takes up the discourse of vulnerability that has slipped into American consciousness since the attacks of 9/11 and resulted in increased security precautions and anxieties. Even *The Hunger Games* speaks of North America as having been reduced to ashes. As a former superpower, the idea of the USA being vulnerable to an external attack of such magnitude and resultant devastation once seemed highly unlikely. But this story of America under threat is one of a long line of narratives – fiction and film – that foreshadowed the devastating 9/11 attacks or at least some kind of external attack well before the event.[16]

In the extended state of emergency that is enforced throughout the United States in Simmons's *Article 5*, the American government has the power and authority to enforce mandatory compliance to its Moral Statutes. Extra-textually, Article 5 of the US Constitution describes the process whereby the Constitution can be altered, a fact that lends an air of assumed realism or mimetic possibility to the fictive world of the text. Disobedience results in fines, rehabilitation, torture or death. In this post-apocalyptic world there is no space for dialogue or compromise, and transgression is dealt with severely. It is a world where war (with an unnamed enemy) has destroyed the way of life and infrastructure that American citizens once enjoyed. Homes are no longer filled with the spoils of a consumer culture – television, computers, smart products and services – and 'new' technologies are now 'old' things of the past. The focalising character, Ember Miller, reflects on the difference that this change had made:

> Without a car or a television, we'd been isolated in our neighbourhood. The FBR had shut down the local newspaper on account of the scarcity of resources, and had blocked the Internet to stifle rebellion, so we couldn't even see pictures of how our town [Louisville] had changed. (Simmons 2012: 27)

While concerns and hopes in the extra-textual world of today are often about the kind of world we are creating, or wish to create, with new technologies and the associated social practices they engender, *Article 5* considers not the ubiquity of the world of information technology, but the diminished access by the populace, with almost total control in the hands of the state. Most citizens live in extreme poverty, with many sheltering in abandoned cars, or foraging for food in the wastelands on the outskirts of what were once flourishing towns. In light of the previous discussion, *Article 5* offers a scenario whereby the vision of an AmI environment has been destroyed along with other basic human rights and necessities for living. President Scarboro rules this totalitarian state, and his branch of the military, known as the Federal Bureau of Reformation (euphemistically called the Moral Militia or MM), has the responsibility 'to enforce compliance with the Moral Statutes, to halt the chaos that had reigned during the five years that America had been mercilessly attacked' (12).

Benjamin's aestheticisation of politics discussed in relation to *The Hunger Games* also emerges in this text with the Moral Militia whose uniforms combine a tripartite symbolic representation of Nazi uniform aesthetic, American patriotism and religious icon:

> They were in full uniform: navy blue flak jackets with large wooden buttons, and matching pants that bloused into shiny boots. The most recognized insignia in the country, the American flag flying over a cross, was painted on their breast pockets, just above the initials FBR. Each of them had a standard-issue black baton, a radio, and a gun on his belt. (15)

Accompanying the aesthetics of appearance is the domination of the rhetorical or figural over literal and genuine modes of communication. Ember realises that there is something seriously wrong when she notices two cars parked outside her home – a blue van and an old police cruiser – each displaying the FBR emblem, sunrise logos and the false rhetoric of unity: *One Whole Country, One Whole Family.* The MM soldiers take her mother away for violating Article 5 (in this text it refers to children conceived out of wedlock), but Ember's struggles of resistance result in her also being removed from her home and taken to a 'Girls' Reformatory and Rehabilitation Center' in a remote location.

The antagonistic world of the novel is characterised by a struggle for domination and survival, with the allies and enemies, winners and losers, clearly delineated by the level of power they exert. The general notion of democracy that the state attempts through its motto is one that matches Ernst-Wolfgang Böckenförde's description of a 'pacified unity' (qtd in Jay 2010: 87). As Jay elaborates, 'homogeneity rather than adversarial relations or even pluralist ones are assumed to exist', except in the case of civil war (87). The price of homogeneity in this text is the eradication of difference, especially ideological difference. In this context of extremism, the state operates through intimidation and force, seeking subordination and compliance. The totalising thought and action by the state disavows any dissidence.[17] Ostensibly this closed system of rule is intended to provide a sense of security and stability after the war. By using the metaphor of 'wholeness' and 'family' the state constructs an image of itself as a unified (not fragmented) body politic that controls and regulates its citizens' bodies, while maintaining the apparent unity through incorporation, thereby not acknowledging difference. In other words, the state through its internal force, the FBR, speaks with *one* voice, of only *one* body and *one modus operandi*. However, despite its force and power there are individuals and groups (such as the Resistance) who are not passive, impotent and completely at the mercy of the FBR. Similarities can be drawn between the resistance in this text and Katniss's covert violation of the dictates of the Capitol in *The Hunger Games* and Marcus/M1k3y's subversive internet actions against the DHS in *Little Brother*.

When 17-year-old Ember arrives at the Girls' Reformatory and Rehabilitation Center, she still believes that reason will prevail: 'I looked around anxiously, wondering, *hoping* that there was a separate building for my mother. That maybe they had brought her here to rehabilitation, too. At least that way we'd be close and could straighten out this mess together' (37). The Center is run by Brock, a cruel and domineering woman who is one of the *Sisters of Salvation*: an arm of the MM intended to counteract any feminist thinking by enforcing the FBR's Moral Statute on archaic gender roles: 'Section 2, Article 7 mandates that you become ladies, and until your eighteenth birthday you will be groomed to be nothing less than the very finest models of morality and chastity' (43). Ms Brock is herself a paradox: despite her instruction on the gender codes and the submissive role of women, she governs the Center and has absolute power to control and order those that live and work there, including the male FBR soldiers. When Ember stumbles upon an illicit romance between her roommate, Rebecca, and an FBR soldier, Sean, she is able to exploit this secret to negotiate her escape. However, the escape is thwarted and, before she is tortured, she is rescued by the former love of her life, Chase.

In Foucault's terms, Chase represents an active being (like Marcus and Katniss), who is not simply a shadowy figure of submission, but an embodied, corporeal being who has the power and capacity to act upon the world. As an FBR soldier who was drafted into the force, he suffered brutality and humiliation. However, his love for and loyalty to Ember were the impetus for him to devise her escape, putting his own life at risk. Chase's time with the FBR changed him, demonstrating that, as a human being, he is inescapably open to influence and transformation by other forces. Ember notices this change in him: 'He looked like the old Chase, even if he didn't act like him' (115). And she soon comes to realise that the change went deeper than surface actions when she prevents him from killing an attacker on their route to a safe house: 'Whatever part of him was still *him*, the greater part, the more dangerous part, was always lurking' (153). Unlike the wholeness metaphor used by the state, Ember sees Chase in terms of parts, but wishing that he were whole (and wholesome). What Ember fails to see is that there is no pure, authentic 'Chase' that can be separated from Chase 'the soldier'. In other words, there is no essential Chase who can be separated from his FBR experiences and others before them.

In a related way, other people that Chase and Ember encounter on their journey – the Loftons, a seemingly friendly couple who offer them refuge, but plan to profit from their capture by the FBR; the profiteers who sell them a car with petrol; the members of the underground resistance; Rebecca, Sean, Tucker and other FBR soldiers – all have formed and shaped themselves into certain kinds of subjects, in much the same way that Ember and Chase have done. In each situation, the practices of the self involve their own regulatory practices on their own bodies, conduct and manner, so that they can survive. For some, such as Ember and Chase, the self-transformation means that they are able to resist and struggle against the FBR and those that are intent on harming them but at the same time remain a moral subject: a similar outcome was achieved in *The Hunger Games* with Katniss and Peeta's decision to not kill one another. Survival remains the common reason for how the various characters respond to the oppressions and opportunities that characterise their worlds.

The different encounters with others illustrate Foucault's (1980: 96) idea of 'capillary' power. By not being purely located in the state but extending itself beyond the centre, power invests in institutions such as the Reformatory Centers, and relies on the cooperation of a whole network of individualised techniques. Apart from the FBR soldiers, individuals such as Brock, the Loftons, Sean, Tucker, the homeless and the resistance participate in practices and techniques that contribute to reproducing oppression and domination of other people and themselves. By informing on wanted people such as Ember and Chase, people like the Loftons remain subject to the oppressive regime of the state. Tucker's unrelenting bullying and cruelty towards Chase are practices that he adopts not only to ensure that he is promoted in the FBR but also to fulfil a desire to exercise power and experience the pleasure that comes with domination. Brock's heavy-handed discipline and enforced learning of the Statutes are further instances of capillary power where power reaches into the very bodies of individuals, shaping their actions, attitudes and learning processes (Foucault 1980: 39). Chase and Ember are not simply victims subject to the power of others, as they are also their own agents. While Chase is an agential subject who takes control and directs the course of their escape and journey to the safe house, Ember is frustrated in her inability to take control and tells Chase: 'I never asked you to protect me' (178). Ember's attempts at independence fail and put her life and Chase's in danger. However, when she learns of her mother's death by a FBR officer she slips into a state of depression and emotional detachment and wanders the streets only to be taken by the FBR to a prison. It is through her experience at the prison that she becomes a subject of action, an agential subject who is able not only to secure her own escape, but also to assist a badly injured Chase. Her techniques include allowing Tucker to kiss and fondle her so that she can gain information about the whereabouts of Rebecca, using physical force to tie up the elderly female prison cleaner so that she can steal the prison keys, and finally confronting Tucker with a gun. Ultimately, she makes the decision to act as a moral subject, choosing not to shoot Tucker despite the fact that he was the one who killed her mother.

In reflecting on her decision to not shoot Tucker who was blocking their last hope of surviving when Ember and Chase attempt to escape from a prison, Ember asks: 'Should I have killed Tucker? Should Chase have? Tucker could hurt so many others now. There was no right answer' (357). This choice results in an ambiguous outcome that highlights the point made at the beginning of this chapter: that even retrospectively one cannot always be clear about the net result. This uncertainty also raises the issue of transformation. At the beginning of the novel Ember was certain that she would never kill anyone, no matter what the circumstance, but by the close of the novel, she realises that like Chase she, too, has changed: 'My mother had gone, and with her, the child I had been. She'd been taken with violence, as had my youth, and in their place a new me had awakened, a girl I didn't yet know. I felt achingly unfamiliar' (361).

The three novels discussed in this chapter deal with the idea of personal freedom and how that freedom is put at risk when governments are no longer working for the benefit of the people. As the texts have shown, the governing bodies – the Capitol, the Department of Homeland Security and the Federal Bureau of Reformation – apply the esoteric rationale for government secrecy that sees 'reason of state' as legitimating actions on behalf of the state, actions that would be immoral for private individuals (Bok 1989: 173). Their unrestrained actions and rules arise from a state of emergency: in all three texts North America has wholly or partially been reduced to ashes (*The Hunger Games*), bombed by terrorists (*Little Brother*) or devastated by war (*Article 5*). The post-apocalyptic worlds of these texts are characterised by mistrust, fear and oppression, leaving no space for irenic solutions or compromises, except in the case of *Little Brother*, where there is a gesturing towards peaceful conciliation. The irony that underpins these texts is that, in trying to protect their citizens, the governments use techniques of domination and terrorism to ensure compliance. As noted at the beginning of this chapter, Metcalfe's three elements basic to secrecy, 'paternalism, proprietariness and protectiveness', are particularly inherent in both human nature and governments. Secrecy is maintained in various ways in these texts as a means to avoid detection, maintain illegal activity, forge alliances, control information and maintain covert surveillance. These secret activities are undertaken by both the 'good' and the 'bad'. The Games that the Capitol stages each year are a public relations tool used to entertain the people of the 12 districts, a highlight of their mundane lives, but more significantly it is an evil means for ensuring injustice and control. Through the hyper-publicity during the Games – the parade of the tributes, the televised coverage, the crowning ceremony, and the rewards for the victors and their district – the Capitol conceals its more sinister agenda under the aesthetic cover of extravagant ritual, spectacle and symbol. Katniss learns to survive by stealth and secrecy, and equally learns to open up and disclose her secrets to maintain herself as a moral subject.

The surveillance techniques that are used in *The Hunger Games* are taken to a further level of invasiveness in *Little Brother*, where the DHS uses technology to assist in its coercive regime especially after a major attack, that resonates with a post-9/11 world. Bok makes the point that for coercive governments, 'secrecy is essential to every aspect of the exercise of power' (1989: 176). But she concedes that secrecy is also 'the central means of resistance and survival for those who oppose such regimes' (176). Marcus/M1k3y uses his knowledge of cryptography to navigate the controls on privacy that exist on the internet. He draws on similar strategies of surveillance, tracking and identity theft to reveal the covert practices of the DHS. The text's polemic insists that these measures are justified if one's freedom and privacy are at stake. Secrecy invites prying, as well as imitation and retaliation. As secrecy and covert or mendacious practices spread from both inside and outside the government, individuals and groups can use secrecy to commit crimes, prompting the need for ever greater protection (Bok 1989: 177).

Both *Little Brother* and *The Hunger Games* attempt to show in different ways a world in which technology is being used to sustain a surveillance society. *Article 5* offers a vision of the post-apocalyptic state in which technology is now limited and controlled by the government, whose power is employed and exercised through capillary-like networks. But as this discussion has argued, there is still a space within these oppressive state-controlled regimes for individuals to share information, to trust, and to resist and transform themselves into agential subjects. Simmel's idea that secrecy could tell us about society and individual behaviour continues to have value, despite the change in the evolution of technology from the time he was writing. The conditions of trust, however, have changed. Whilst the protagonists – Katniss, Rue, Peeta, Marcus, Chase and Ember – learn to trust, taking people into their 'circle of trust' (*The Hunger Games*) or 'web of trust' (*Little Brother*), or forging a Simmel-styled trust through social relations (*Article 5*), there is a more complex and pervasive level of encryption that paradoxically works to both enhance and reveal secrets – a central element of *Little Brother*. Finally, these texts update Orwell's idea of Big Brother by asking us to consider not so much who is watching but: *Who knows? What do they know? What are the consequences of this knowledge?*

5
Secret Societies

Secret societies are predominantly the province of adults, but children too have their own secret gatherings. It would be fair to speculate that many are attracted to secret societies because of their allure and dangerous possibilities. Bok makes a similar point: 'Few human activities convey the allure and the dangers of secrecy as vividly as do the secret societies that have sprung up in so many parts of the world' (Bok 1989: 45). Despite the different kinds of secret societies that have existed throughout time, Bok suggests that the one unifying element that they all share is secrecy itself: 'secrecy of purpose, belief, methods, often membership' (46). Ironically, the existence of many secret societies is known to outsiders, but only insiders know the rituals, codes and practices, and even then, knowledge of the internal secrecy of the society may be only gradually revealed. There are other societies, however, which remain a complete secret. To be a member of a secret society holds attraction because of the status it offers: its separatism from the outside world, and the feeling of privilege or exclusiveness of membership.

Children's literature is a rich source for stories about secret clubs, secret societies, cults, subcultures and other kinds of select social networks. In the previous chapter, the Xnetters in *Little Brother* form a secret society that shares computer codes and information through its membership. Other kinds of secret societies are also discussed in Chapter 2 – the secret school for girls in *Nasreen's Secret School*, and the Resistance in Denmark during World War II in *Number the Stars*; another resistance group appeared in *Article 5* (Chapter 4). These various examples demonstrate that 'secret society' is an umbrella term which gathers many different kinds of groups under its nomenclature. Some – such as the Xnetters, the secret school for girls and the resistance groups – are formed under risk, usually arising from living under a repressive regime. Other secret societies not discussed, but familiar to many readers of children's literature, offer safe, often pleasurable, association with low levels of risk. The most popular of this kind for many years was Enid Blyton's Secret Seven series. In recent years, there has been a proliferation of novels for children and young adults which include secret societies of one form or another. No doubt these books are intended to capitalise on the 'allure and danger' of secret societies for the child and youth market. These books are often produced in series format to ensure that the secret society can repeat again and again its practices of heroic activities, overcoming evil, and saving lost and victimised others.[1]

Some secret societies have the goal of establishing a new order achieved through social or political revolution, and are therefore similar to transformative utopian communities. As Bradford et al. explain, 'A transformative utopian vision will challenge hegemonic structures of political power and totalizing ideologies by revealing the ways in which human needs and agency are restrained by existing institutional, social, and cultural arrangements' (2008: 16). The matriarchal societies in Jean Ure's *Come Lucky April* (1992) and Jackie French's *The Book of Unicorns* (1997) attempt with varying degrees of success to produce a new (feminist) social order. Although these communities are not secret, they nevertheless enforce closed membership by gender (including castrated males in Ure's text) and their members live an existence that is separatist, exclusive and homophilic.

Secret societies can be based on fundamentalist beliefs or formed in opposition to a fundamentalist regime. Fundamentalism can exert a powerful influence on all spheres of life – religion, politics, economics, family and education. Fundamentalism does not come in a single form, but is characterised by different types. For example, religious fundamentalists differ from each other though each may lay claim to 'the Truth', a truth that is revealed by their own prophet, and no other (Sim 2004). The Persepolis texts (discussed in Chapter 1) and *Nasreen's Secret School* (Chapter 2) privilege a way of seeing from outside a fundamentalist standpoint through the characters who are opposed to the Islamic fundamentalism that governs their lives. These texts illustrate the dangers to which those living under strict religious rule are exposed, especially if they try to criticise or disobey the laws and way of life set down by fundamentalist Islamic or Taliban rulers. However, the texts also demonstrate that despite oppression, groups and individuals will always form secret associations to provide an alternative form of co-existence which can be lived out temporarily in private spaces. In the secret school for girls that Nasreen attends, she learns about the world beyond her village, and beyond Taliban rule. This learning beyond one's world is a form of *ijtihad*, meaning 'to exert the utmost effort, to struggle, to do one's best to know something', which is different from *taqlid*, 'blind and unquestioning following and obedience' (Ziauddin Sardar qtd in Sim 2004: 62). In a similar way, Marjane and her friends (*Persepolis*) form a secret society where they exercise their freedom of dress, lifestyle and speech within the closed walls of their meeting place.

Religious fundamentalism and intolerance are also part of Western cultures, past and present. Eva Wiseman's *The Last Song* (2012) and *Prisoner of the Inquisition* by Theresa Breslin (2010) deal with the cruelty and oppression of the Spanish Inquisition. The former text illustrates how anti-Semitism reaches back to (at least) fifteenth-century Europe. Through the perspective of a young Jewish girl, readers are provided with an insight into religious intolerance and persecution as a result of the Edict of Expulsion (1492) when the Catholic monarchs of Spain (Ferdinand II and Isabella I) ordered the expulsion of Jews from the kingdoms of Castille and Aragon. The witch trials of early modern Europe (fifteenth and sixteenth centuries) peaked in the seventeenth century with witch hysteria also occurring in North America at that time. The notorious Salem Witch trials were a series of hearings and persecutions against people accused of witchcraft in colonial Massachusetts. Elizabeth George Speare's *The Witch of Blackbird Pond* (1958) and Celia Rees's *Witch Child* (2000) are both set at that time when witch-hunts were at their height and each offers a view into how hysteria, paranoia and fear can result in persecution and victimisation of the worst kind. The Salem witch-hunts also demonstrate 'the way power is politically manipulated in times of crisis' (Awan 2007: 2). These texts and incidents are further examples of scapegoating and demonstrate the ways in which the persecution mechanism operates (see Chapter 3). *Little Brother* and *Article 5* (see Chapter 4) also work with the ideas of power and scapegoating by showing the way a particular form of fundamentalism had taken hold in the United States after a major attack from outside forces. The parallel with the aftermath of 9/11 attacks is easily made. The fundamentalist governments in these fictions exhibit the general desire of fundamentalism for 'order, conformity, and the absence of opposition' (Sim 2004: 29).

The above texts, with their diverse historical and cultural references to religious and political fundamentalism, demonstrate the power of ideological conviction and the importance of human rights. They also show how the two can work with and against each other. All texts note the extreme tendency towards moral absolutism. Furthermore, they illustrate the fact that many secret societies or groups arise in response to a political or religious state of need or oppression. By contrast to the secret societies that are forged through political and religious turmoil, there are also other examples in children's fiction that are non-political, relying on the allure of ritual and symbolic elements. This attraction is particularly apparent in texts that deal with medieval themes, or the occult, such as Philippa Gregory's *Changeling* (2012), where the secret society (and series) named Order of Darkness is based on the Order of the Dragon, a medieval secret society whose purpose was to defend Christendom against its enemies, particularly the Ottaman Turks. Such texts often borrow from ancient rituals and doctrines.

Within the context of secret societies, fundamentalism and moral absolutism, this chapter discusses three kinds of secret societies: a separatist quasi-religious sect in *Sister Wife* by Shelley Hrdlitschka (2008); a high-school vigilante group in *The Mockingbirds* by Daisy Whitney (2010), and a high-school extortion group in *The Chocolate War* by Robert Cormier (1974); and a crime family in *The Robber Baron's Daughter* by Jamila Gavin (2008). These texts have been selected to illustrate the diversity of purpose behind secret societies and how they are treated in stories for young people. *Sister Wife* provides a means for understanding how some rigidly disciplined, fundamentalist communities offer individuals an identity and a sense of belonging that may have eluded them in the outside world. It also shows how the leaders of such groups demand total obedience and submission in order for the society's darker side to be accepted without question. Schools and colleges offer sites for young people to form secret societies, subcultures, networks and other hierarchical groups whereby individuals can claim allegiance and achieve recognition, which in turn may garner respect, fear or disdain for its members and others. There is also the pleasure that comes for the leaders of these groups as the hierarchical structure brings a degree of power and status. Similarly, members can enjoy the benefits that come with being accepted into a select group. Some of these groups work to right wrongs (*The Mockingbirds*); others incite fear among the student body to fulfil their own sadistic desires (*The Chocolate War*). Some of these groups are 'secret societies' in the sense that they demand closed or select membership, and initiates often must undertake a rite of passage as part of the initiation process. Both *The Mockingbirds* and *The Chocolate War* offer perspectives on the effects of secrecy on moral choice and how secret societies that operate within institutions such as schools can become powerful forces to support, exploit or harm students.

The final secret society in this discussion is the group that operates as a crime family, often involving members of a blood family, but also others without any blood ties to the family organisation. This group is different from legitimate, family-owned-and-run businesses in that its goal of economic gain is achieved largely through crime, often employing force, corrupt dealings, and secret or covert activities. *The Robber Baron's Daughter* is an example of this kind of family where secrecy runs so deep that even some family members are not aware of the organisation and its activities. All these examples of secret societies have different internal structures and unlike some of the examples cited in other chapters, none operates under extreme, politically repressive regimes. By contrast, the secret societies in the focus texts in this chapter illustrate how coercion – physical, emotional or psychological – is a means for ensuring that goals are achieved and members remain loyal and obedient.

The Prophet and The Movement: a man's world

One of the main characteristics and functions of a secret society is 'protection of concealment' (Simmel 1906: 472). In *Secrets* by Jacqueline Wilson (see Chapter 2), Treasure and India form a secret society of two, and India's attempt to hide Treasure in order to protect her from her abusive stepfather becomes the secret that ties them together. In a related way, many religious movements have had to carry out their worship and whole existence away from public view to avoid persecution. Simmel argues that corresponding with this 'protective character of the secret society' is 'the inner quality of reciprocal confidence between members' (1906: 472). Specifically, this confidence relies on members preserving silence about the secret society. Members who break the silence break a binding moral imperative of the society. In other sacred contexts that Simmel does not include, others outside the group may know of the religious activities by a select group (for example, based on gender), but the rites and practices of the group may remain secret to only those who are members or initiates.[2]

In his discussion of religious fraternity, George Weckham (1970: 91) draws comparison between secret societies and monastic communities in classical and modern religions, noting both the structural relationship and the religious function within the fraternity. In religious communities, a prophet or priest 'serves as an individual servant of the deity, his cult, or the needs of his devotees' (91). An important visible marker in religious fraternities is clothing (habits, veils or masks) which distinguishes the members. These characteristics of a religious fraternity are evident in the fictional community named Unity in *Sister Wife*. A further point of comparison is the patriarchal hierarchy within Unity. The leader of Unity is the Prophet, the self-appointed head of The Movement who claims to have a direct line of communication to God. Under the Prophet are the Elders – all older men in the community – who carry out the Prophet's commands. Women and girls have no status other than as wives, or 'sister wives' in waiting. They cover their bodies in plain, full-length dresses and keep their hair long.

The normative familial structure of parents and children is not the way of Unity; a fact which Daddy explains to Celeste (one of the many children he has fathered): 'And as you know too, Celeste, daughters do not belong to their mothers or fathers. A daughter is only in her parents' keeping until the Elders have determined who she will be assigned to in marriage. Then you will belong to your husband for all eternity' (Hrdlitschka 2008: 21). However, the Elders have little power in determining the marriage match as it is the Prophet who receives Divine guidance about this arrangement and informs the Elders of his decision. When girls turn 15 they are eligible to marry, not a person of their choice, but an older man that the Prophet has decreed is the one. The Prophet benefits from this arrangement too as he has 'twenty-six wives and more than ninety children' (33). When Celeste ponders the practicalities of so many wives and children living under the one house with a single 'Daddy' she wants to question this requirement of The Movement, but then corrects herself, calling on the doctrine that has been inculcated into the members of Unity:

> Do any of the men of The Movement ever wish they had fewer wives and children? I shake my head and push the thought away. That would be against the principles that the Prophet has laid out. Our men know they need at least three wives before they can enter the Kingdom of Heaven. More is preferred. (104)

Women in Unity are men's stairway to heaven, and with the banning of contraception and the expectation that wives will bear multiple children, women pay a heavy toll – one young woman dies after a difficult childbirth with outside medical help called too late. Celeste's mother, too, almost dies when having her eighth child, and she goes against The Movement's principles by seeking outside medical assistance when she becomes ill: an action which incites the fury of her husband who cruelly removes her from the hospital after the birth, and puts her life at risk by refusing any medication to treat her. He also insists that she is isolated from others in the household, even from her other children. Unity's treatment of women is repressive and oppressive. Not only are young women denied choice in terms of a marriage partner (or indeed of even not marrying), but there is also an expectation that women will bear many children, whether they want children or not. This in itself indicates that heterosexuality is the sanctioned norm and that non-heteronormative sexuality would not be tolerated. *Sister Wife* is silent on this point. There is, however, a double standard about sexuality. While girls are given to much older men in marriage they are not permitted to even talk to boys of their own age, unless they are siblings. In her discussion of religious cults in young adult apocalyptic fiction, Susan Louise Stewart's (2011: 319) point that 'women's weakness remains inscribed in and the central tension of the narratives' applies to the generally submissive and unquestioning nature of the women in *Sister Wife*. While the texts that Stewart examines predominantly depict women as 'troubled, misguided, wrongheaded, and easily influenced by the charismatic leaders' (319–20), the central characters in *Sister Wife* do not necessarily share these same characteristics. Nanette, however, comes close to fulfilling Stewart's description.

Hrdlitschka's strategy of focalising events through alternating chapters in the name of one of the three main female characters – Celeste, her younger sister Nanette, and outsider Taviana – provides differing perspectives on the religious and sexual tensions that exist in Unity. While Celeste and Nanette have only ever known life in Unity and therefore have lived their lives according to the doctrine of The Movement, Taviana has come to Unity as a troubled and lost soul in search of a place of belonging. As Celeste explains: 'She wasn't born and raised here like the rest of us but was found on the outside, living on the streets, and doing unspeakable things' (1). Some of these 'unspeakable' things include prostitution and drug use. Celeste craves the stories that Taviana tells her but knows that she should only hear the ones that will keep her mind pure, ones contained in 'the sacred book' (1). Taviana recognises that Celeste has a strong desire to ask questions and to question, a tendency which gets her into trouble as she refuses to be totally compliant to the dictates of Unity. Nanette, on the other hand, is a true and loyal member of the community. As Celeste says of her sister: 'Nanette is pure. She has internalized the rules. She finds joy in being obedient,' but asks of herself: 'Was I ever like that?' (7). When Nanette suspects Celeste is secretly seeing a boy, Jon, she tells Daddy of this breach of the rules.

One of the greatest means for ensuring conformity in fundamentalist communities such as Unity is the concept of apostasy. Members of Unity hold to the belief that once you are born into a faith (such as The Movement) you cannot renounce it. When Taviana and Nanette are out walking in the community they come across three boys who are apostates, and Nanette issues Taviana a warning: 'Don't go near them' (12). These boys are considered 'tools of the devil' (13). Taviana, however, decides that these boys could not possibly be as sinful as she had been before she joined Unity so decides to talk to them, craving the opportunity to talk to boys of her own age. For Taviana, Unity provides a safe community, with a routine of chores and companionship that she relishes, given her unstable and chaotic life before coming there. However, she admits to missing the opportunity to watch TV and videos, having an email account and going to a library. Taviana's momentary lapse into the pleasures of consumer society implicitly provides readers with a moment to consider the severity of life in Unity. While people outside know about Unity and stories circulate about its polygamous lifestyle and marrying of young girls to older men, the people of Unity avoid as much as possible contact with the residents of the nearby town of Springdale. When Taviana wonders how 'they [Unity] got away with the plural wife thing', Kelvin explains to her that while the laws of the country are in conflict with the laws of their faith, they are nevertheless also 'protected by [American] laws that entitle us to religious freedom, to practice our faith' (59). Consequently, the people in Unity are legally able to pursue their faith but the internal organisation and religious dogma must remain secret from outsiders.

The people of Springdale treat the rare visits made by the people of Unity to their town with a mixture of curiosity, disgust, derision and gossip. Bok notes that while secrecy protects secret societies it 'inevitably sets in motion gossip and rumors concerning what the societies do and speculation about excesses in their midst' (1989: 55). Equally, the people of Unity are intolerant and suspicious of the people of Springdale. One of the paradoxes of secret societies and fundamentalist communities such as Unity is that the desire for total control of members ('the chosen people') is coupled with the inevitability that control can never be fully achieved. Purity of belief, as embodied in Nanette, is always in danger of being stained. Hence, when Daddy finds out about Celeste's secret meetings with Jon, he blames Taviana as a bad influence and she is told to leave Unity. Her eviction comes from a fear that she will encourage others to question the faith. Apostasy is a possibility at any time and must be rigorously circumvented.

A perverted form of punishment for Celeste's indiscretion in seeing Jon, with whom she falls in love, is that the Prophet decrees that she must marry his father. Celeste struggles with the desire to leave Unity with Jon, but in the end decides that she must stay out of concern for her family: a point which is ironic given Unity's view about family belonging and responsibility. Celeste is subjected to a protracted initiation into being a sister wife. She endures nightly visits by her husband until she falls pregnant, after which he leaves her alone and sleeps with his other wives. Her child, optimistically named Hope, is the impetus for Celeste to leave Unity, and begin a new life in Springdale with her daughter. An outcome which suggests that despite her previous hesitations about leaving, her new family responsibilities and the prospect of a different way of living are sufficient reasons for her leaving Unity, and as she says, to be 'finally free to think for myself' (269).

Sister Wife illustrates how a secret society must create what Simmel terms 'a species of life-totality' (1906: 481). Though referring specifically to the military and the religious career, Simmel nevertheless offers an observation that uncannily applies to Unity: 'each [career] composes a variety of energies and interests from a particular point of view, into a correlated unity' (481). Simmel argues that the secret society tries to achieve the same kind of unity as these organisations ('careers'), by claiming the 'whole man' (*sic*). A similar expectation is evident in *Sister Wife* and metaphorically expressed in the name of the community – Unity. Unity's practice of polygyny sets it apart from mainstream American society and the law, since it is illegal to have more than one spouse.[3] Unity constructs its own norms and rejects outside norms. It is through this antithesis that the secret society such as Unity can enact its 'spirit of exclusion' (Simmel 1906: 484). As the following discussion demonstrates, a similar kind of spirit of exclusion occurs in secret societies that operate within school communities.

Vigils and vigilantes: power to give and to take

As *Sister Wife* demonstrates, fundamentalism, whatever its form, is essentially about power. In previous chapters, I discussed how the political fundamentalist regimes and theocracies in the symptomatic texts were anti-libertarian in both their laws and their enforcement of those laws. A common narrative strategy in children's literature about religious or political fundamentalist communities that aligns with secret societies is the contrasting points of view between insiders and outsiders. In order to maintain the exclusivity of a community based on secrecy, these narratives employ strategies of exclusion and surveillance: both are essential to the societies for safeguarding their secrecy and for keeping control over their members. The texts also offer the outsider perspective as a contrast, showing ways of being that are based on freedom of choice, and the power or agency to choose one's future path in life. More often than not, the outsider's perspective shows up the repressive nature of the closed community, and the dilemmas of desire with which insiders invariably grapple. The two texts that the discussion now turns to – *The Mockingbirds* and *The Chocolate War* – provide different ways of looking at the power and control that secret societies can exert, and possible reasons why young people form and join these groups. It also considers how desire lies at the heart of the tripartite notion of: **belonging**; ~~belonging~~; and be~~longing~~.

The Mockingbirds secret society was formed by a young female student (Casey) who saw it as a way to redress injustice perpetrated upon another female student who committed suicide after being the victim of bullying. It also takes its name from Harper Lee's novel, *To Kill a Mockingbird*. The Mockingbirds is not so much a *secret* society as it publicly and privately recruits members (both male and female). Nevertheless, it is selective about who will be admitted into its inner sanctum, and unlike many secret societies it is not male dominated. Among the many flyers posted on the school bulletin board at the prestigious Themis Academy is one that advertises The Mockingbirds in veiled code:

> **Join the Mockingbirds! Stand up, sing out! We're scouting new singers, so run, run, run on your way to our New Nine, where you can learn a simple trick** [...] (Whitney 2010: 13, emphasis original)

When Alex sees this notice she is trying to piece together her memory of the previous night when she believes she was date-raped by another student while she was in a drunken sleep.[4] She recognises that the message is in code and that The Mockingbirds is 'not an a cappella singing group' but 'the law' (14). This knowledge suggests that the existence of The Mockingbirds is widespread and that they carry a high degree of power. The Mockingbirds' mission is 'to make things right' and to 'investigate crimes committed by students against their fellow students' (92). This mission is one that is shared among many secret societies where a group is formed with the desire to overthrow an unjust or corrupt regime. While Themis Academy is not an unjust or corrupt institution, The Mockingbirds believe that the school's idealised view of its already select student body puts a veil over its ability to see its students as capable of perpetrating violent crimes or immoral acts, and thereby its power is rendered ineffectual. As a Mockingbird member explains to Alex:

> The administration thinks because Themis is this liberal, progressive school, nothing bad could happen here. There's no hate speech, no bullying here. How could there be? It's Themis. We're too good for that [...] They think being *enlightened* is enough, that we'd never do anything wrong because we're here and because they had Diversity Day for us. (93)

In a different way, Trinity, the Catholic boys' high school in *The Chocolate War*, is also remiss in its duty of care for its students. The self-serving Brother Leon is a corrupting influence who knows when to call upon the student society named The Vigils for support to further his own ambitions. Unlike The Mockingbirds, who are well known among the student population, but not known to the staff of Themis Academy, The Vigils officially 'did not exist' (Cormier 1974: 25) but on some occasions are nevertheless called upon when help is needed or mutual benefits can be negotiated. Archie, the assignment taskmaster of The Vigils, muses on the knowing/not knowing game between the teachers at Trinity and The Vigils:

> How could a school condone an organization like The Vigils? The school allowed it to function by ignoring it completely, pretending it wasn't there. But it was there alright [...] It was there because it served a purpose. The Vigils kept things under control. Without The Vigils, Trinity might have been torn apart like other schools had been, by demonstrations, protests, all that crap. (25)

How these two groups exercise their power illustrates how secret societies tread a fine line between delivering on their idealistic aims and becoming governing elites with their own authoritarian structures and coercive strategies.

Alex remembers the night of the rape in snatches like short film clips – playing the Circle of Death game with Carter and others at the club; drinking vodka; waking naked in Carter's bed; Carter's crusty white mouth, his sharp nose; 'Ode to Joy' playing in Carter's room; two empty condom wrappers on top of his garbage. When Alex confides in her sister Casey and friend T.S. that she does not know whether or not she consented to having sex with Carter, the girls suggest that she had probably passed out and was raped by Carter who took advantage of her inebriated state. While Alex tries to deal with the guilt and shame of the rape by avoiding Carter at school and hiding out in her dorm, she is eventually persuaded to take her grievance to The Mockingbirds who agree that there is sufficient cause to hold a trial. Alex fears the possibility that Carter may be in a similar situation to Harper Lee's character, Tom Robinson, who is unjustly accused of rape in *To Kill a Mockingbird*. However, this fear is dispelled when she revisits Carter's dorm and recalls the night in his room.

The Mockingbirds operates as a democratic group, but a hierarchical one nevertheless. It has its own board of student governors, and a council of nine students appointed each term to run a mock trial to decide the guilt or innocence of an accused student. When a person is found guilty, the punishment is taking away the thing they love the most, such as giving up a position on an elite sporting squad or stepping down from the Honor Society. This is 'the code' and it is intended as a means to ensure protection and justice for all. They also operate a highly organised system of student 'runners' who manage to ensure that Alex and Carter do not encounter each other at school, and manipulate the school timetable in a way that ensures Carter is disadvantaged. Being a runner is the 'proving ground' (149) before becoming 'a full-fledged Mockingbird' (148). Before the trial proceeds, The Mockingbirds organise a secret ballot of the whole student body on whether they think date rape is a crime worthy of being deemed a violation of the code. When the votes are returned with a majority in the affirmative the trial of Carter begins.

The Mockingbirds' goal of righting wrong is similar to the personal or social transformation that many secret societies produce. As Bok notes, such transformational agendas may be 'in opposition to the larger society or as a tool of the regime in power' (1989: 47). The Mockingbirds deem Themis ineffectual and therefore incapable of supporting a transformational agenda outside of academic and sporting excellence. Ironically, the college's namesake is the goddess of good counsel: Themis means 'Divine law'. Trinity, on the other hand, seeks a different kind of transformation among its students, one that is ostensibly both spiritual and institutional, but ultimately the transformation comes closest to Bok's second option – 'as a tool of the regime in power' – but which regime – Trinity or The Vigils?

The Vigils in *The Chocolate War* are the antithesis of The Mockingbirds in that they do not have idealistic aims that are intended to protect and support their fellow students. Rather, The Vigils operate on the line of a small-time mafia, using intimidation, coercion and exploitation as a means of ensuring the loyalty of their members, and as a way of remaining a powerful force within the student body. Bok contends that the attraction for adolescents to join secret societies is tied up with identity work and social relationships: 'in trying to sort out what belongs to the world of the self and to that of others, and in probing their own identities, they are especially open to the allure of the secret societies' (1989: 48). Furthermore, she suggests that individuals may also long for the hierarchical structure of these societies and their clear lines of authority, and the opportunity to prove themselves as worthy members. This longing and desire for belonging is one that Taviana harbours and is her reason for joining Unity; it is also the expression of Nanette's impatience in becoming a wife to Martin Neilsson before she turns 15 (*Sister Wife*). However, many of the initiates to The Vigils do not share this desire; in fact, for many the call to meet The Vigils is received with a heavy heart. When Goubert (who is mockingly called Goober) is summoned to appear at a Vigils meeting, he reluctantly accepts his impossible assignment 'like a sentence of doom, the way all the others did, knowing there was no way out, no reprieve, no appeal. The law of The Vigils was final, everyone at Trinity knew that' (Cormier 1974: 32). Like The Movement (*Sister Wife*) and The Mockingbirds, The Vigils' law is absolute.

Another level of desire that is closely tied to power, rather than to belonging, is realised in *The Chocolate War*'s Brother Leon and Archie Costello, characters whose actions prompted Sheila Egoff to comment that in this text 'the Devil is in control rather than God' (1981: 44). Despite their different purposes and *modi operandi*, The Mockingbirds and The Vigils emerge from within a larger and potentially more powerful institution – the school. As a religious faith school, Trinity also has a structural relationship with the Catholic Church. The Mockingbirds' formation arises from a need to protect and support students who have been subjected to unfair or criminal behaviour by other students. In taking the law into their own hands, they too subject accused students to unfair treatment. However, there is another implicit reason behind The Mockingbirds' formation: the group is an answer to the political and governing needs of a less powerful group (the students) and is therefore the means for that limited group to achieve political power, at least within its sphere of governance. The Vigils similarly emerge from a minor power base, but they come close to usurping the institutional power. When Brother Leon approaches

Archie and asks for his help as he is taking over the role of Headmaster at a time when the school is in dire financial straits, Archie realises that he (and synecdochically The Vigils) holds the power, even though it may be a tenuous hold:

> Their eyes met, held. A showdown now? At this moment? Would that be the smart thing to do? Archie believed in always doing the smart thing. Not the thing you ached to do, not the impulsive act, but the thing that would pay off later. That's why he was The Assigner. That's why The Vigils depended on him. Hell, The Vigils *were* the school. And he, Archie Costello, was The Vigils. That's why Leon had called him here, that's why Leon was practically begging for his help. Archie suddenly had a terrific craving for a Hershey. (26)

Hershey is a metonym for the transactional deal between Leon and Archie. Leon needs The Vigils to get behind the selling of chocolates – two boxes for each boy – in order to not only balance the books but to provide a healthy profit for the ailing school finances. The idea of a chocolate sale in an economically depressed community is in itself a vexed one. However, it also provides an opportunity for some boys to achieve a level of recognition, even belonging, that would otherwise be impossible; for others it offers a means for self-awareness. Mike Cadden captures this varying response:

> the chocolate sale provides John Sulkey with the opportunity to be recognised for his 'Service To The School' in a way he is never recognised for academic performance (85); the chocolate sale reveals the corruption of teachers to David Caroni, that 'life was rotten, that there were no heroes, really, and that you couldn't trust anybody, not even yourself' (109); the chocolate sale and Jerry's resistance to it inspire Kevin Chartier to do what he'd never thought to do before – resist (133). (2000: 151)

Jerry Renault's refusal to sell the chocolates begins as an 'assignment' issued by The Vigils, but even after the assignment is reversed, he continues to refuse to sell the chocolates. His action is not one of designed rebellion or resistance. Rather, he simply chooses to continue in his refusal to participate in the sale. After a period of being beaten and harassed, Jerry is ostracised by the other students and comes to enjoy his 'absence of identity' (163). However, The Vigils risk losing face and therefore their power if Jerry continues to get away with not being part of the chocolate sale. Archie devises the solution: a boxing match between Jerry and the violent and much stronger Janza. The boxing match is organised as a raffle in which everyone who buys a ticket has a chance to give a direction to one of the boxers in the fight:

> *Janza*
> *Right To Jaw*
> *Jimmy Demers* (173, emphasis original)

The rules are read to the baying crowd: 'and the kid whose written blow is the one that ends the fight, either by knock-out or surrender receives the prize' (178). But the fight goes out of control as Janza pummels Jerry, spurred on by his own uncontrolled violence and the chanting rhythm of the crowd shouting '*kill him, kill him*' (183). After Brother Jacques brings an end to the fight and possibly saves Jerry's life, Brother Leon cautions Archie, telling him that he really didn't use his best judgement in staging the fight (187), before acquiescing: 'But I realize you did it for the school. For Trinity' (188). And as Jacques walks away the narrator offers an insight into Archie's point of view: 'Archie smiled inside. But he masked his feelings. Leon was on his side. Beautiful. Leon and The Vigils and Archie. What a great year it was going to be' (188). This final double victory confirms that The Vigils is a tool of the regime in power.

While power and control remain integral elements in the secret societies discussed to this point, another element that emerges is the importance of identity, or of being identified with a certain organisation or secret society. A desire for belonging, of being identified as a leader or member of a select group, is a strong motivation for characters' decisions to form or join a society. Giorgio Agamben argues that belonging is always circumscribed by limits, the limits of 'being-called' (1993: 10). In each of the texts this notion of 'being-called' is both performative and perlocutionary in its function as characters are being-called – Prophet, Daddy, sister wife, rapist, rape survivor, Assigner, rebel, Mockingbird, Vigil. However, being-called also inscribes difference which in this chapter sets apart the insiders from the outsiders. The next text, *The Robber Baron's Daughter*, examines further this notion of 'being-called' especially when it concerns how one is known or not known within and outside a crime family. From the outset, the title of *The Robber Baron's Daughter*[5] dares to engage in the performative and perlocutionary act of being-called; elsewhere in the text it remains secret.

Secret family business

The opening chapter of Jamila Gavin's *The Robber Baron's Daughter* is entitled 'Memories and Secrets', and begins with a possible ghost, a figure that 'comes out of darkness' (2008: 1). Ghosts, memories and secrets are the recurring elements in the text, lending overtones of *Hamlet*. Both are tragedies that explore the effects of deceit on family trust and the consequences of corruption and evil-doing. However, unlike Hamlet, Nettie (Antoinetta Roberts) is not bent on seeking revenge and pursuing a path of evil. Rather, she seeks answers to questions, so that she can discover the truth; however, she does not forgive and forget.

Nettie lives an indulged life in a London mansion with her adoring parents, Vlad and Peachy, along with her much-loved tutor Miss Kovachev, her Nanny and a number of bodyguards – the most prominent of whom she nicknames 'Swivel Eyes' for his ability to watch and observe with the uncanny ability of a camera, 'panning smoothly and silently, all the way through ninety degrees then back again' (7).[6] However, the book begins after Miss Kovachev has left without a word to Nettie, and the new tutor named Don is trying to coax Nettie to remember the last time she saw Miss Kovachev, ostensibly as an exercise in essay writing. But Nettie does not want to share her memories with Don. Her memories of her time in the company of the beloved Miss Kovachev bring an aching joy and longing. Miss Kovachev's disappearance is the first ripple of discontent that appears in Nettie's otherwise smooth-flowing world. However, her world is one of surfaces: superficially, her parents appear highly cultured, and the family appears to be happy and loving. While this is true in many ways, it also conceals some darker truths.

The Regent Mansion has a Round Tower, which contains a small, bare room that makes Nettie 'quiver with strange excitement' (13), a room which her parents won't let her have as her own, but instead give to Miss Kovachev. A ghost plays games with all who live and work in the house. The ghost is Nettie's secret friend, 'the Boy', who later is revealed as Benny the commissionaire's son who lives with his father in the basement of Nettie's home. Nettie likes playing spying games and Miss Kovachev had given her the code name 'Star Spy .007'. The spying game takes on a different, more serious function when Nettie is out riding with her mother one day and sees Miss Kovachev. Her mother's denial that it is Miss Kovachev makes Nettie realise that her mother is not telling her the truth:

> *She's lying!* Thought Nettie in disbelief. Mothers don't lie, surely? She felt a strange and sudden void open up inside her. If she had

lied about that, what else would she lie about? At a stroke, the world seemed a different place. (73)

The night after the first sighting of Miss Kovachev, Nettie has a dream where her former tutor calls to her with outstretched arms – 'Save me, save me!' (79). The dream prompts her to explore Miss Kovachev's old room, where she finds her notebook hidden away in a drawer under her bed. While most of the pages are written in a strange script, Nettie discovers six letters addressed to her which have occasional sentences in English. These letters are Miss Kovachev's way of telling Nettie the truth about her past and how she came to England: a story of human trafficking, which Nettie later discovers is the source of her father's wealth. The notebook gives voice to the unspeakable drama of Miss Kovachev's life, charting her journey before her arrival at Nettie's home; it does not tell the full story at once, but reveals the story in progressive installments that interrupt the main narrative.

Miss Kovachev's story is one of exploitation, deceit, abuse and evil, acts that were carried out within a network of secrecy and broken trust. The notebook narrates her story through memory and renders her past experiences singular, despite the commonality of its features with other 'real' stories of human trafficking. However, Nettie is not a privileged audience to the story the notebook tells; this is left for the reader who develops advanced knowledge of the tutor's story – the trouble in Bulgaria that saw her father and brother murdered, her forced exile from her home, her illegal journey to England, falling in love with a violent people smuggler who betrays her, and finally her undercover work to help trap 'Mr Big' (Nettie's father) who was responsible for the death of her sister.

Gradually, Nettie's past life collapses into her present, as she begins to realise that the past she knew was lived under the lie that her family were good and upright citizens. Being-Nettie, the child of wealthy parents, comes under erasure as Nettie learns that her life is a tangled discursive web of lies and secrets. Nevertheless, being-Nettie – both past and present – entails a singular kind of subject, shaped by her difference. Her lifestyle of bodyguards, nannies, tutors and luxury sets her apart from many other children, such as her friend Benny who shares her home but is the (ghostly) witness to her day-to-day life. As Nettie begins to unravel the mysteries and secrets of her family she becomes more introspective. When she is given a present of a Russian doll with nine identical but smaller dolls inside a large one, she makes the comparison with her own multiple selves: '*Funny. I feel like that sometimes, as if there are lots of me inside my body – only not all exactly the same me, but different'* (203, emphasis original). Her sense of difference comes to a head when she argues with her parents about wanting to go to a school instead of being taught at home by a tutor. Her parents point out that she is different from 'the rabble' who go to school, travel by Tube and risk their lives in the 'big bad world' (207). However, when her parents relent and send her to an elite school for rich and talented girls, Nettie finds that her difference is not simply based on social and economic class. Unable to find acceptance amongst the other girls, Nettie engages in a doubly self-reflective moment acknowledging her difference, not as multiple selves this time, but as a singular state based on empirical observation and experience at the school: 'She stepped closer to her mirror image. "Am I different?" The question became a statement of fact. "I am different"' (249). However, this epiphany is also a turning point as Nettie finds a friend and eventually discovers the truth that has been hidden from her.

Nettie's quest to find Miss Kovachev and to understand what has happened to her is a journey to discover the truth – a concept that she finds both puzzling and unreliable. Her parents lied to her about Miss Kovachev, her Nanny tells her a lie in saying that she never lies, Benny lies when he tells her a white lie about her father, and Netty struggles to understand the difference between white lies and black lies. Nanny assures her that sometimes it is better to 'tell a little lie' if the truth is painful or cruel and 'you have to weigh up the hurt you can cause by telling the truth on the one hand, with the lie which protects on the other' (181).

Nettie remains naïve yet curious and when Benny tries to tell her about her father's 'business' and his associates, he introduces new words to her vocabulary, words that have little meaning to her – *'the racket'*, *'legit'*, *'rats'*. He also tells her of her father's nickname – Vlad the Impaler – and the vampiric origin of that name, and other nicknames of people who work for her father – Pistol Paddy, Hot Shots, Bernie the Hand, Dopey the knuckle-crusher. He also tells her that the Chief of Police and Father Gabriel are 'not legit' and also work for her father. Nettie's inability to fully understand the gangster association of these names and the true nature of her father's business is partly due to her unwillingness to believe that her father could do anything wrong and her unfailing belief that he is the kindest person that she knows (134). Benny points out that she doesn't know many people, a comment said in jest but one that carries a truth. At 13, Nettie knows little of the world outside her own protected world which is itself a microcosm of a secret society, which like the Russian nesting-doll analogy sits inside a larger secret society, which sits within the wider society.

For Vlad's crime empire to be successful it must have both secrecy and trust. Simmel considers that psychological factors are a significant element of secret societies, while Erickson argues that for secret societies under risk 'the crucial motive is a desire to maximize security' (1981: 188). In *The Robber Baron's Daughter*, both physiological and security reasons play a part in ensuring that Vlad's empire is not exposed for its extensive criminal dealings. Vlad's employees, even the 'legit' ones such as Benny's father, know the importance of keeping secret the affairs of the business. As Benny's father cautions: 'See no evil, speak no evil, hear no evil' (177). And Don expresses his fear that if Miss Kovachev isn't found soon 'someone's going to get impaled for this, most likely me' (129).

Secrecy is therefore the necessary condition of this organisation and it stems from a need to reduce risk of exposure. In such situations, Erickson argues that trust becomes 'a vital matter and hence preexisting networks set the limits of a secret society' (1981: 195). Trust is also used as a tool to prise open the racket that Vlad runs. Nina (Miss Kovachev) seeks to avenge the death of her sister by Vlad and so willingly accepts Mike's invitation to work undercover as a language student and later as a tutor to Nettie. She not only places her trust in Mike and the side of the law but plays on Vlad's need to employ someone he can trust to be a tutor for his much adored daughter. When Nina is later tracked down after her disappearance from Vlad's home, Don warns her: 'He trusted you. Vlad doesn't forgive treachery, especially when it involves his little girl' (302).

Further information is provided about how Vlad built his business: 'started small, as a gangmaster, providing a kind of slave labour throughout Europe with illegals, but that wasn't enough for him; through terror, extortion and murder even, he's become a robber baron – a Mr Big' (281).[7] We are also presented with some knowledge of the extent of his network and of those on his payroll – 'Chief inspectors of police, immigration officers, solicitors, priests, judges, even teachers like Don' (307). The element of trust that binds the organisation is based on fear: '*the penalties for betrayal were terrible. It wasn't for nothing that they called him Vlad the Impaler*' (307, emphasis original). It is up to the reader to speculate if Peachy keeps the family secret or refuses to break the trust out of fear or loyalty. Erickson's research reveals that kinship is the strongest kind of relationship in 'crime families' and the main means for recruitment. Kinship too is an element in this fictional text. Vlad's brother Robart, the stepfather and rapist of Nina, is also part of the secret network that is the lifeblood of Vlad's criminal business. The logic of the kin line for the family business is one that Benny puts to Nettie: 'I expect you'll go into your dad's business, yeh' (140). However, Nettie at that point in time ponders a career either as a ballerina or as a spy; both are future options for being-Nettie.

What the future might hold is a question raised by Nettie's great-aunt Laetitia, who presciently asks: 'And what of truth? What if you learned the truth?' A puzzled Nettie simply asks: 'What truth, Aunt?' (211). It is not until her friend Raisa translates the notebook that Nettie learns the truth and she can unwind the cocoon of illusion and confusion that has encased her 'until she stood like one naked, full of shame, exposed to the full truth' (308). Her tutor's words from the notebook offer a future of hope for the child: 'one day you would be free to enter the worlds as Nettie, not Nettie, the Robber Baron's Daughter' (308). This hope for Nettie is about learning to survive and live on beyond the terrible circumstances of her family. Nettie takes the performative and perlocutionary step towards not being the Robber Baron's daughter when she performs and narrates 'Swan Lake', naming the Swan Princess Nina and making it clear that the evil magician is her father. She finishes the performance with the swan, arms outstretched, pleading 'Save me, save me.' Looking straight into her father's eyes she pleads for the lives of the Swan Princesses: 'Please don't destroy these beautiful maidens' (320).

Nettie is the product of her parents and of the lifestyle gained through the blood of others, but she is also a living being, endowed with agency, yet she is uncertain about how she will live her life. Nina assures her that it will be through being a ballerina that she will be 'set free' (323). The ghosts, memories and secrets of her past are the curse of her scandalous origin. Like Hamlet, her 'curse' comes from the father and has made her world 'out of joint'. Nettie must also 'set it right'.[8] Nina too had to set right her world, but she chose a course of revenge, once she learnt of her sister's entrapment in the web of destruction created by Vlad. (The Mockingbirds also vow to make things right.) Nina wrote in her diary that *'life is nothing but choices. For every one thing you choose to do, there is another choice you could have made'* (278, emphasis original). These words seem resonant in relation to Hamlet. In choosing a course of revenge, Hamlet suffered the consequences. Nina too almost dies as a result of her choice of vengeance. But Nina is also the voice of reason who guides Nettie to choose a path that is right, anticipating a future for the young girl: 'you will have taken charge of your destiny, your own knowledge of right and wrong, good and bad' (312). Whether

Nettie succeeds is beyond the limits of the text, but readers are left with a sign that a new dawn awaits for both her and Nina: 'Nanny was waiting, and all three stepped out into the bright daylight, leaving Regent Mansion for ever' (324).

I began this chapter by drawing attention to the twin features of secret societies – their allure and danger. The fictions I have discussed engage with these elements as both motivation for, and consequence of, being a member of a secret society. They also demonstrate that for the young characters in these stories the allure and danger are integral to the ongoing and dynamic process of subject formation, of being and belonging, of longing to be. This act of anticipation of futurity is what is often assigned to the child or adolescent as someone who is moving away from childhood towards adulthood. The trajectory from past to future is also a moving-forward from present to future and is characterised by choice. Often agency is the attribute or drive ascribed to a young protagonist who attempts to *set things right*, to rephrase Shakespeare's words. Setting things 'right' may mean making a moral choice, which is what Nettie can be seen to have done when she uses language and performance to call into being the wickedness of her father through analogy of the evil magician, and, at the same time, she calls Nina, the Swan Princess, into being as a victim in need of saving. The courage required to undertake this perlocutionary and performative act is no less and no more than that required by Celeste's decision to leave Unity and make a new life for herself and her daughter, whose name embodies her desire for a future that is better than the past. These two texts demonstrate how secret societies that operate as fundamentalist communities or as crime families bind their members through blood lines and kinship relationships. Breaking away means breaking the trust that maintains the secrecy of the society as well as threatening the security that protects it.

The texts also illustrate Simmel's point that secret societies perform 'the double function of secrecy as a form of protection' (1906: 472). The protective character of the secret societies, discussed in this chapter, performs this double function through internal and external codes and actions. All the texts show how there is an inner protectiveness manifested by the code to preserve silence. Members must trust the motives of the society or its leader, whether for business interests, religious conviction, atonement or criminal actions, even when it may mean a break with moral imperatives. *Sister Wife* illustrates how internal protection is ostensibly enforced to ensure that external threat (or contamination) is averted, even when it means a loss of agency of its members. The secret societies in *The Chocolate War* and *The Robber Baron's Daughter* use psychological and physical threats to protect the secretiveness of their activities. These groups are excessive in every way – they have excessive power, and an excessive ability to terrorise without constraint. This excess is met with excessive submissiveness, or, indeed, an absence of power and individual agency by those who fall under the leaders' command. These two texts most vividly illustrate how in these kinds of secret societies danger permeates internally just as much as it does externally. Except for *The Mockingbirds*, with its commitment to internal organic growth through the changing of leaders and council members, the other texts have leaders who crave the allure of power and control. However, The Mockingbirds see themselves as arbiters seeking justice, but their punishment for rape is merely a withdrawal of personal prestige, and not one that demands punishment by law. In this way, their secret trial and treatment of the guilty is similar to how some secret or closed religious and secular organisations deal with sexual abuse, especially of children.

It is important to keep in mind that the above texts are works of fiction, not actual historical or contemporary phenomena. However, as J. M. Roberts argues, secret societies are themselves historical phenomena 'which embody both positive and mythological elements' (1974: 25). The mythological element is one that emerges from what people imagine to be the truth of a secret society, however distant this may be from its reality. Nevertheless, each of the texts I discussed in this chapter draws to some extent on what is known about secret societies or communities. After all, the purpose of a secret society is that it is secret, and unless there is documentary evidence that divulges its operations, we have to rely on witness reports, past members' accounts or novelistic invention in order to come to some understanding of secret societies. The next chapter asks: How do we gain an understanding of ourselves when we attempt to keep secrets from others, perhaps even lie to ourselves? Does self-deception offer its own allure and danger?

6
Our Secret Selves

Secrets are troubling not only because they demand that we conceal or reveal sensitive information but also because the keeping or telling of the secret can have an unpredictable or dangerous series of effects. In protecting ourselves from harmful, oppressive and frightening situations or encounters, we may seek to keep our fears and desires secret, disclosing them only in diaries, to a trusted friend, or locking them inside ourselves. Sometimes it is not only secrets that individuals harbour, but also lies that they tell themselves and believe. Bok argues that all self-deception 'must involve keeping something secret from oneself' (1989: 61). In examining how secrets and secrecy are very much part of our everyday lives, and, more significantly, shape our desires, our sense of self and our relationships, the fictional narratives discussed in this chapter include ideas of longing and belonging which were at the heart of secret societies discussed in the previous chapter. The texts also elucidate the complex interweaving of social and psychological relationships that arise from secrecy and deception. Like other texts discussed throughout this book, the focus texts in this chapter raise important questions about truth-telling as they position their readers in ethical or moral dilemmas analogous to those of the fictional characters.

Texts about secrets, lies and deception engage readers in a number of social and psychological issues that are relevant to the lives of many children and young adults. As previous chapters have argued, these texts attest to the frequent need to keep secrets and tell lies in conditions of familial, social or political conflict. The dilemmas experienced by the characters in these narratives confront readers with many of their own fears and desires, offering a potential space for reflection. These narratives also illuminate the self–other relations and the public treatment of those who are found to be liars. Given children's literature's implicit pedagogical and socialising function, books for younger readers invariably embody an ethical or moral outcome which often defuses the escalation of the problem, reaching a resolution through atonement, harmony and unity. Liberal humanist modes of representation emphasise the commonality of human nature and propose ways of being in the world. However, the following texts – *Liar*, *The Adoration of Jenna Fox*, *Skim*, *Why We Broke Up* and *Sunday Chutney* – offer alternative modes of representation and resist simple resolutions. Consequently, they raise questions about how we define subjectivity as they explore the limits of the Western myth of the autonomous, highly individuated subject and our ability to deal with difference, loss, trauma and dislocation in our lives.

Trauma, memory and secrets of the body

The two texts considered in this section – Justine Larbalestier's *Liar* (2009) and Mary E. Pearson's *The Adoration of Jenna Fox* (2009) – explore how a traumatic event shapes the subjectivity of the protagonists and their relations with family and friends. The nature of the traumatic event in these texts is kept secret, and in the case of Jenna Fox it is even kept secret from the traumatised subject. In writing about trauma narratives, Laurie Vickroy (2002: 11) says that 'traumatic experience can produce a sometimes indelible effect on the human psyche that can change the nature of an individual's memory, self recognition, and relational life'. In both *Liar* and *The Adoration of Jenna Fox*, remembering through the body provides the means by which Micah (*Liar*) and Jenna come to understand the traumatic component of their lives and how it impacts on their relations with others. While Jenna's trauma results from a near-fatal car accident, it is the subsequent trauma that her body endures in order to be re-engineered that compounds her ability to remember the past and its relationship to the present. Micah provides details of the traumatising effect on her body when she changes from a 17-year-old girl into a wolf – an involuntary transformation but one that is an inevitable part of her self-reported hybrid nature. However, Micah is a self-confessed liar and despite her convincing account and shifting admissions to telling the truth and telling lies, the wolf-self persona speaks to a deeper psychological and pathological side of her human psyche. Whether *Liar* is read as a shapeshifting novel or a story about a disturbed young woman, the implicit and explicit treatment in the text of mental health illness, marginalisation and race is characteristic of shapeshifting novels. McMahon-Coleman and Weaver argue that these physical, emotional and cultural conditions are often used as metaphors in shapeshifting texts (2012: 117). However, the authors also note that 'clinical lycanthropy has links with mental illness [...] as well as dissociative disorder, because they share elements such as disturbances to identity, consciousness, memory, and a shift in personality' (126). All these elements emerge in *Liar*.

Liar begins with a chapter entitled 'Promise': a promise to tell the truth. The first-person narrator, Micah, confesses that she is a liar, like her father, but that she is going to stop lying:

> I will tell you my story and I will tell it straight. No lies, no omissions. That's my promise.
> This time I truly mean it. (Larbalestier 2009: 3)

This statement invites the reader to respond in a way that accepts the veracity of the promise, or at least accept that the intention is pure. However, competent readers will also recognise that they are being positioned to take up this ideal response by an unreliable narrator: the disquieting combination of the confession by the narrator of being a liar ('My father is a liar and so am I') and that the promise is one that has been made in the past and failed ('This time I truly mean it'). The effect of this dual process of acceptance and suspicion of the narrator and of her story as truth or lies is central to the tension within the narrative. The story comprises three parts, each of which claims to offer a truer version of the truth than the previous one: Telling the Truth; Telling the True Truth; and The Actual Real Truth. These gradations of truth-telling provide further grounds for readers to suspect the veracity of Micah's accounts. But knowing how to distinguish the truth from the lies becomes a game that the text plays with the reader.

The story that Micah Wilkins tells about herself shifts between past and present, and the point at which time pivots – After or Before – is when Zachary Rubin goes missing and is later found brutally murdered, mutilated beyond recognition. Zach's murder, and Micah's relationship with him, her family and her schoolmates comprise the first part – Telling the Truth. As the narrator, Micah directly addresses the reader, confiding 'truths' that have been kept hidden for most of her life. We learn intimate details about Zach, and of how Micah and Zach loved to run together in Central Park, their passion for each other, the secrecy that they shared about their relationship. Micah also reveals that she has a younger brother, Jordan, whom she despises. Her relationship with her father is tense, and she hates to go upstate to the family home where 'the Greats' live – her grandmother and great-aunt Dorothy, along with her cousins, and the family dog Hilliard who was named after the deceased Great-Uncle Hilliard. She says that she must take the pill every day to control her periods as well as to stop hair growing over all of her body. She explains that she has seen countless doctors and specialists about this condition, which is hereditary ('the family illness'), but only the pill seems to help. She says that the family illness is a secret that is never revealed to anyone outside the family. We are positioned to accept these accounts and in doing so we also become witness to the lies that Micah tells the police and her peers and counsellors about Zach. However, these accounts of change to the body, the excessive cover of hair, female puberty/menstruation are also symptoms associated with female shapeshifters or werewolves (McMahon-Coleman and Weaver 2012: 44–5).

Micah confides to the reader through direct address that Zach is her boyfriend, but when the police question her about his murder she claims to not have known him at all, saying only, 'We were in some of the same classes' (46). She also denies being Zach's girlfriend to her classmates, who regard her with suspicion, knowing that she is a liar: she first passed as a boy, then as an hermaphrodite and then told them that her father was an arms dealer (40). In addition to the lies that she tells to the police and to Zach's other girlfriend Sarah, to whom she alternately confirms and denies her relationship with Zach, Micah also hints at other layers of the secrets she has: her love for running and climbing; her love of the sounds of nature where the Greats live and how urban sounds – traffic, music – hurt her ears, her brain; her ability to smell foxes and to track down their hiding places in Central Park; and the occasional wolf analogies she uses – 'like a wolf had moved into my throat' (9), how Zach 'liked the wild' in her (111), how she wanted to leap at the Principal and 'tear out his throat' (132) when he told the class about Zach's murder, and her enjoyment in eating steak. She explains her difference from the other students who are mostly white and rich – her parents struggle to make ends meet, and she describes herself as having 'nappy hair', flat chest and narrow hips. She says her father is black, her mother white. Her father's family – the Wilkins – live a reclusive, self-sufficient lifestyle on a 200-acre farm in upstate New York. When the students undertake DNA testing in their biology class, Micah fears seeing the results and refuses to share them with the others: 'I didn't want to see the proof of the family illness in black and white' (73). When Zach asks her why she tells lies all the time, she tells him: 'I was brought up my whole life on the belief that telling people the truth leads to disaster' (125).

Micah's stated commitment to not lie to the reader rings with the fervour of a *parrhesiastes*, who was known in early Greek society as a truth-teller who felt a moral obligation to always tell the truth (Foucault 2001). However, the comparison falls away when Micah tells lies to cover her secret about Zach and her mysterious family illness. Unlike *parrhesiastes* whose power as truth-tellers was tied up with their ethical character, Micah does not present as an ethical character despite her promise to tell the truth. The situation is further complicated in that evidence which could prove whether she is telling the truth or lying is not offered by a third person – either another (reliable) narrator, witness or focalising character. Consequently, Micah is in control of the story, the facts, the evidence, the lies, and readers are left to distinguish between their own internal and external perspectives on these matters. The second part, Telling the True Truth, begins with a confession – that Micah is a werewolf, but she swears that she didn't kill Zach.

In reading the accounts offered in part two, many of the so-called truths or partial truths recounted in the first part are revised, confessed as lies or expanded upon. Micah describes her 'wolf days' which occur three or four times a year in the summer. She says that she is a grey wolf, *Canis lupus*, which accounts for her long and skinny build and why she didn't want to share her DNA results. The Wilkins family have been wolves for a long time but not all of them are so (such as Micah's father). When 'The Change' comes most of the family remain either as a human (Grandmother) or remain a wolf (Great-Uncle Hilliard). Micah's earlier admission to being able to smell foxes is explained in fuller details displaying a deep knowledge of, and familiarity with, domestic and wild animals. She also explains that when she forgets to take the pill she may change into a wolf where she has to be locked into a three feet by six feet metal cage in her bedroom.

Micah compares being a wolf with being a human, citing the many benefits of a wolf life – 'cleaner, safer, happier', whereas her human life means her perceptions are dull, and her head 'is hammered with dark thoughts and feelings and confusion' (207). However, she admits that being a part-time wolf means she is not as competent as full-time wolves, and that being a wolf has its drawbacks, especially having to deal with ticks. She also says that when she is the wolf she doesn't remember much of the human, but when she is human all she can remember is the wolf (207). This wolf-self's lack of memory may also be construed as a perfect shield for not lying about whether or not she killed Zach. Lack of memory is also a characteristic of many werewolf characters who 'wake up after a shapeshifting event not knowing what has happened' (McMahon-Coleman and Weaver 2012: 123).

Part two is written convincingly with no withdrawals or revisions of information, and offers evidence in the form of subjective experience as a wolf to prove the veracity of her story. Leaving aside the truth or reality of the wolf life, the personalised accounts of a traumatic life provide a testimony of what is unspeakable, the secret that requires layers of secrets to cover it. Significantly, the inability to remember the human when she is a wolf can be interpreted as Micah's inability to revisit a traumatic past. This possibility accords with Vickroy's point that one of the lingering effects of trauma is that the past is not 'remembered in a conscious sense' (2002: 169). Micah reveals her palimpsest-like approach to keeping secrets and erasing memory: 'If you've got a big secret it's best to paper it over with lots of little ones' (Larbalestier 2009: 127).

Part three, The Actual Real Truth, is intended to surprise and shock the reader. Micah begins by explaining how difficult it is to be a liar, the need to 'keep track of your lies' (215), to keep things simple, and that the worst danger is when you begin to believe your own lies. This aspect of self-deception is one that Freud first argued was a result of a split ego, and which psychologists since have argued: 'a split self or even several selves are at work in self-deception to guard against anxiety-producing knowledge' (Bok 1989: 63). Micah explains how this split self or several selves operates, providing insight into the psychoanalytic analysis of the condition of becoming/being a pathological liar:

> You lose track of what's real and what's not. You start to feel as if you make the world with your words. Your lies get stranger and weirder and denser, get bigger than words, turn into worlds, become real.
>
> You feel powerful, invincible.
>
> [...]
>
> Once you start believing, you stop being compulsive and morph into pathological.
>
> It happens a lot after something terrible has happened. The brain cracks, can't accept the truth, and makes its own. Invents a bigger and better world that explains the bad thing, makes it possible to keep living.
>
> When the world you're seeing doesn't line up with the world that is – you can wind up doing things – *terrible* things – without knowing it. (217, emphasis original)

However, Micah claims that she has not gone 'over the edge' (218) and that is the reason why she is writing this story, which from now will be 'nothing but the truth. Truly' (218). Of course, this promise could be part of the self-deception that she has already described. She begins to confess to a number of lies that she has told in the previous chapters when she had promised that she was telling the truth, these include: the lies about having seen numerous doctors about her condition; that she has a brother named Jordan; that she hasn't changed into a wolf but has come close. But subsequently she discounts some of these 'truths' claiming that she did have a brother named Jordan who died from a terrible accident when he was ten and she was 12: 'We don't talk about it. / I can't think about it' (319); she also claims that she had changed into a wolf for four days during the time when Zach was killed, reportedly savaged by dogs. Her parents confront her with the fact that she had gone missing and they suspect she killed Zach when she was changed into a wolf. To prove her innocence and that she is not lying, she locates the 'white boy' that she said followed her and Zach at various times. She believes that the white boy is also a wolf, like her, and was the one who killed Zach. Of course, the white boy and Jordan could be scapegoats to whom Micah can transfer her own guilt and misdeeds.

Liar is possibly as much about lies and secrets as it is about traumatic memory or shapeshifting. Micah's accounts demonstrate how storytelling serves memory as much as it serves the telling of truths and lies. In remembering her past, Micah interweaves lies and possible truths, attempting to offer explanations and justifications for past actions and events. Her stories also enable forgotten or repressed aspects to be recovered, supplemented or reinvented. Much of Micah's accounts of trauma entail the pain that inflicts the mind and body. Her account of changing into a wolf when she finds refuge at her teacher's (Yayeko) home explores the limits of duress the body experiences:

> I'm itchy, I'm worse than itchy, it's like my skin is trying to tear itself from my flesh. Coarse hair has sprouted across my arms, my back, my everywhere. My head throbs, my eyes. Everything blurs. My muscles ache, my bones. My teeth shift, get bigger, move. My jaw is breaking [...] My hands and feet slip on the floor because they're not hands and feet anymore: paws, claws.
>
> I'm crouching, my backbone ripples, lengthens. There's howling. I think it's me. (361–2)

The pain of transformation is common to many shapeshifting texts.[1] However, Micah endures more than physical pain as her description of being imprisoned by her lies offers further testimony to the psychological suffering she experiences: 'I've been kept hostage by lies all my life. Imprisoned by them' (232). She follows this with a description of life behind bars, possibly a mental hospital, which could be interpreted either metaphorically or literally:

> Bars surround me. Prison guards bind my arms, bring me pills several times a day. They ask me – beg me – to tell them the truth. I am.
> Every single word.
> Truth.
> They don't believe in my wolves. (232)

By the close of the story, Micah admits to a lie of omission, the trial. Finally, she goads the reader: 'You were never fooled. You can read between the lines, pull away the werewolf bullshit, and see what's left' (370). And to confirm suspicion that she was guilty of killing Zach and has been placed behind bars, she further teases the reader: 'You don't think I wrote this from a cozy little apartment – you think it was composed from a cold, padded cell' (370).

Liar cleverly follows the pattern of a liar – the first part attempts to invoke readers' sympathy or interest; the second invites questions or arouses suspicion; and the final part attempts to alienate the reader with the possibility that Micah is a killer who used her knife to murder Zach, her teacher Yayeko and her daughter and mother. Her denials of such horrific acts carry no weight. As the focaliser and narrator Micah is not only the central figure of the narrative but she controls the point of view. We do not have access to how the deceived feel, except in the reported dialogues between Micah and others. In the following text, Jenna has a similar narrative function to Micah, but instead of being the deceiver she is the one who is deceived. Thus, she offers the perspective of what it is like to be lied to. However, unlike Micah who loses agency despite her manipulation of others, Jenna gains agency despite the attempts of others to manipulate her existence.

The Adoration of Jenna Fox begins with the words 'I used to be someone' (Pearson 2009: 1). This is a literal statement rather than a statement about past glory or lost celebrity status. Jenna Fox comes to the slow realisation that she has no memory of the person she once was; she also learns that she is recovering from a serious car accident that occurred a year ago. To help her remember this lost self, her mother encourages her to watch a box of stills and movies that her parents lovingly made of the first 16 years of her life before the accident. While her parents are eager for Jenna to remember and return to being their much adored daughter, Jenna finds the process difficult – some words, even simple words, are difficult to remember, and she has no memory of her family – her parents and her grandmother Lily. She has no capacity to feel emotions, and obediently follows the strict liquid diet she is told is necessary while she recovers. She dutifully watches the discs, but they initially provoke no trace of remembrance for her of Jenna Fox.

In this tale of memory, forgetting and remembering, loss becomes a central concept. For Jenna, it is her loss of memory and the experiences that come with being Jenna Fox. For her parents, it is the loss of the child they loved and adored. The discs Jenna is told to watch produce an almost daily chronicle of Jenna's growing up from *in utero*, through childhood and into adolescence. They are labelled and stored chronologically and Jenna is told by her mother to watch them in order. Only Lily tells her to watch them out of order, 'Skip straight to last year' (10). The box and its contexts represent an artefact of childhood where the past is seen through both still and moving images.

In her discussion of childhood, Elspeth Probyn draws on Foucault's ideas of event and phantasm as a way of thinking about how childhood can be understood differently from the trend of seeing childhood as a point of departure, a trajectory of *becoming*, becoming adolescent, becoming adult. As Probyn reasons, events are 'historical facts, scientific propositions, empirical observations, actual experiences, and attempts to render them concrete', while phantasmatic features of childhood are 'images that carry childhood into the realm of the pathologizable, images that float as memory (which are, of course, incorporated as fact, proposition, observation, and experience)' (1996: 96). Jenna's parents' insistence on her watching the discs can be understood as much as a way to help her remember her past as it is a record of nostalgia for them, the box serving as a memorialising container of Jenna's childhood. Each disc begins on Jenna's birthday. As she watches these films she tries to reconcile the young girl with golden hair with her 17-year-old self: 'Same blond hair. Same blue eyes. But the teeth are different. Three-year-old teeth are so small. My fingers. My hands. All much larger now. Almost a whole different person. And yet that is *me*. At least that is what they say' (9, emphasis original). Besides the obvious physical changes in growth, she detects something else that is different but can't name what it is: 'I scan the face. The face. She has something. Something I don't see in my own face, but I don't know what it is. Maybe just a word I have lost?' (8). It is not until she sees a later disc of herself as a ten-year-old that Jenna realises that the something about her face that had puzzled her is a scar, a thin, red line under her chin: a scar which she no longer has. She wonders if scars can completely disappear in seven years.

The accident has left other 'scars' or visible marks on the traumatised body. Jenna walks with a funny gait and her fingers are highly flexible but cannot interlace. These seemingly minor effects are nevertheless ones that serve to make Jenna feel her difference from others. However, when she finally convinces her parents that she wants to go back to school and meet other young people, she encounters a small group of students who are similarly 'scarred', either psychologically or physically. Her new school is an alternative school housed in a small run-down building with only a few students. The curriculum is self-guided with each of the students taking on the role of the 'collaborator-teacher' (62). The students include Ethan, Allys, Mitch, Dane and Gabriel – a collective that Dane calls sarcastically 'Freaks Unlimited' (63). Jenna soon learns the meaning behind the 'freaks' label: Allys has artificial legs and arms; Gabriel has an anxiety disorder; Dane is aggressive and unmanageable and his beautiful face looks empty; and Ethan nearly killed someone.

Jenna comes to learn that she used to live in Boston but now lives in a rambling old home somewhere in southern California with her mother (Claire) and her grandmother (Lily). The house is isolated somewhat and Jenna is generally confined to the house, often to her room to rest. These isolating features contribute to her sense of alienation as she gradually regains some memories, especially when she remembers Kara and Locke, her close friends from before the accident. Jenna struggles with her mother's control over her life and tries to become more agential and self-determining. Her diminished sense of self is exacerbated when she watches the active, happy, younger Jenna on the discs with the 'empty-life Jenna' (40) she feels she has become. While her parents seemingly want her to remember, they nevertheless attempt to control her capacity for remembering, knowing and feeling by not filling in the gaps about the past, and by avoiding her questions about aspects of her life. These strategies further exacerbate Jenna's already limited subjectivity and agency. When she meets her neighbour Clayton Bender, an environmental artist, who tells her of the newspaper report about her car accident, he also informs her that when he first met her he thought she had attitude as she gave him an honest opinion of his artwork, saying: 'You weren't afraid of anything' (55). However, Jenna's silent thoughts tell her otherwise: 'But I'm afraid of everything. Myself. Mother. Lily. Friends who haunt me in the night. Even going to school, which is something I asked for. If I have attitude, it is hiding somewhere deep, someplace I'm afraid I may never find' (55).

Her limp, fears, fragmented memory and lack of agency can be seen as symptomatic of the trauma Jenna has suffered, but as the story progresses we come to see how these traces of trauma originate from different pasts. Foucault says 'the body manifests the stigmata of past experience and also gives rise to desires, failings and errors' (1988: 3). One 'past experience' is Jenna's childhood. Agamben argues that we need to think of childhood not as something that proceeds chronologically, 'as an initial cause which separates in time a before self and an after self' (qtd in Probyn 1996: 101). Rather, he challenges us 'to risk oneself in a perfectly empty dimension' (11). For Jenna, the discs of her childhood are an 'empty dimension' as she cannot reconcile the 'before self' with the 'after self'. The discs' format means that she can play, pause, rewind, fast forward scenes offering multiple viewings and a position to reassess what she witnesses. The discs are also witness to her past life, comprising both events and phantasms. But as she becomes more aware of the gaps in her memory and life, and the desire to find answers to questions about her present life, she scrutinises the discs and notices that rather than delivering 'the truth' about Jenna Fox, they are constructions of a life that is performed, revised, captured and edited. They eventually prompt memories, but these are extended beyond the limits of what each disc can show, offering insight into her feelings that are not always apparent in the happy, lively, younger Jenna. One disc of Jenna aged 12 is of a holiday by the sea. Jenna 'smiles at the camera and says, "Come on, Mom, put it down and help me!" [...] the camera wobbles, and Claire's voice is loud. "In a minute. Let me get a little more first"' (55–6).

A second past experience, of which Jenna slowly learns, is the accident and its aftermath. The narrative interleaves between chapters an interior monologue often written as thought fragments. These texts carry traces of memory: about Jenna being urged to drive faster by Kara and Locke; her near-death experience; sounds of crying, praying, pleading; the anointing with holy water and Lily telling her, 'You can let go if you need to' (114). Jenna pieces together memory fragments with other information she gains from her new schoolmates and her own searches around her home and the secret files on her father's computer.

She learns from Ethan that the Federal Science Ethics Board controls the research that can be done, especially the use of Bio Gel, an artificially oxygenated, blue gel 'loaded with neurochips' (89) that enables an organ to be preserved for lengthy periods of time until it can be transplanted into someone who needs it. Lily had told Jenna that her father invented Bio Gel. When Jenna cuts her hand while trying to take the computer box labelled 'History of Jenna' she finds in a locked room of her home, she discovers that under the deep cut is a layer of blue gel. She also realises that she is now two inches shorter than she was a year ago. After she demands to know what has happened to her, Lily tells her that only 10 per cent of her brain was saved. Jenna learns that the three back-up files that her father has locked away contain the life histories and memories of not only herself but also her friends Kara and Locke. Furthermore Jenna discovers that her current state of being draws on these three sources and that the back-ups are intended to ensure that Jenna Fox will be immortal. It is only when she makes the decision to destroy all three back-ups that she hopes to achieve mortality like everyone else. This act of destruction is the point of Jenna gaining subjectivity. It is also the point at which she severs a life governed by her parents: a governmentality that began long before the accident. In her new *becoming*, Jenna opens herself to the limits that mortality places on bodies.

In dealing with trauma, memory and the body, *Liar* and *The Adoration of Jenna Fox* offer different perspectives on how secrets can impact on the lives of people in ways that damage or limit subjectivity, and cause conflicted relations with family and others. In the following texts – *Skim* by Mariko Tamaki and Jillian Tamaki (2008) and *Why We Broke Up* by Daniel Handler (2011) – the secrets of the heart take prominence and the discussion considers how both taboo and open romances can involve secrecy and deception.

The secret pain of being in and out of love

> The course of true love never did run smooth
> (Shakespeare 2003: 1.1.9)

Skim and *Why We Broke Up* illustrate the truth behind Lysander's consolatory words (above) to his lover Hermia in Shakespeare's *A Midsummer Night's Dream*. While it is difficult to know if one's love is ever 'true love', the problems that beset love, of which Lysander speaks, refer to the complexities involved in sexual interrelations. One of the difficulties with fiction about young adult lovers is that often readers are positioned to see the characters' desire as transitory, something that they will grow out of once they reach adulthood. This logic sees 'becoming' in developmental terms rather than accepting the intensity of feelings, excitements, pain and longing that the young protagonists experience as already a state of becoming part of something. As Elizabeth Grosz explains, using the Deleuzian notion of becoming: 'becomings then are not a broad general trajectory of development, but always concrete and specific, becoming-something, something momentary, provisional, something inherently unstable and changing' (1995: 184). In the following texts, this dynamic, changing state of becoming reveals how the course of love is not and cannot be smooth. It also shows that secrecy accompanies sexuality and desire.

Skim is what I term a graphic-diary, a hybrid form combining graphic novel and diary. The diarist is the fictional character, 14-year-old Kimberley Keiko Cameron (aka 'Skim'), and the illustrations are an integral part of the text, filling in the gaps left by the words and, at times, replacing words altogether. There are layers of secrets in this text that attempt to cover the deep secrecy of same-sex desire. Skim harbours a secret longing for her drama and English teacher Ms Archer and on one occasion the two share a taboo kiss. The other secret is revealed after the school volleyball player, John Reddear, commits suicide. This event occurs early in the text (Part 1: Fall) and triggers rumours about John's homosexuality. While the first secret remains between Skim and Ms Archer, the second one is revealed and spreads through the school after John's death. Up until news of his death, John apparently had to cover the truth of his sexuality and his love for another boy by dating Katie Matthews and performing his part of the ideal heterosexual couple. While John's sexuality is suspected there is no verifiable truth, only gossip and hearsay. By contrast, the reader is witness to the secret relationship between Skim and her teacher, and the intimate kiss they share is captured in a double-page illustration (Figure 6.1). While the readers are witness to this moment, the secret is too dangerous to be revealed to Skim's friends.

Skim enjoys Wicca, tarot cards, astrology and philosophy, pursuits that come under the umbrella of 'New Age', and which involve mysticism, secret teachings and practices, and esoterica. She maintains an altar with quasi-sacred objects and mystery ingredients. The form of the book manages to merge first-person female narration and incidental drawings, with a third-person illustration and comic-strip frame sequence. This overt third-person omniscient illustrator reveals the intimacies of Skim's life and secrets to the readers, but the perspective is necessarily partial and biased as it remains focused on tracking Skim.

Figure 6.1   Illustration from *Skim* by Mariko Tamaki. Illustrated by Jillian Tamaki

While Skim keeps the secret of her relationship with Ms Archer from others, readers have no knowledge as to whether this act of privacy is reciprocated by Ms Archer. Ms Archer leaves the school and we are positioned to know only as little as Skim does about her motivations for doing so. We can presume to know that the illicitness of their relationship is the motivation but we do not know if other people were responsible for this decision for her to leave.

Skim's secret and her successful attempts at keeping aspects of her life private contribute to a subjectivity which is only partially known by both readers and herself. She does not feel the need to reveal to others her secret desires and heartbreak and suffers in silence – drifting through the days at school, spending endless hours lying on the couch, preoccupied with thoughts of Ms Archer, despite her attempts to erase her from her mind: 'I am trying not to be obsessive. It is not good to only think about one ~~person~~ thing' (2008: 76). The illustrations convey her sense of inertia by depicting her lying on the couch feeding from a large box of popcorn.

In *Skim*, eyes are given special significance, and as Doane notes in her discussion of film, eyes are the 'most *readable* space of the body'

(1991: 47). Initially, Ms Archer tells Skim that she has 'the eyes of a fortune teller' (13), subsequently Skim notes, 'Ms Archer says she can't stop looking at my eyes' (31), and tells her that her eyes 'are very serious' (31). When Halloween arrives, Ms Archer dresses as a fortune teller, providing readers with a metonymic connection which precedes the taboo kiss. After the kiss, the seduction stops, and Ms Archer begins to distance herself from Skim, averting her gaze in class – 'She didn't really look at me' (70). When Skim hears that Ms Archer is leaving the school, she hides her eyes and her sorrow behind her cards – an image captured in a series of three frames from middle-distance to close-up, to extreme close-up (81). The close-up functions in a similar way to Doane's cinematic reading of the camera as Skim is the female subject that is gazed upon by the reader. Unlike the translucent veil that the *femme fatale* uses to lure the male, the cards serve as a mask, an opaque surface that resists any attempt to probe the depth that hides behind. In both instances, the trope of the veil/cards dismantles the surface/depth dichotomy and Skim is no longer the object of erotic desire, and thereby is not denied subjectivity.

While Ms Archer no longer looks at Skim, Skim feels that everyone else at school is looking at her. Skim argues with her friend Lisa who tells her to 'get out into the REAL WORLD every once in a while' (112). Secrecy becomes a burden weighing her down and isolating her from the social world. Bok notes that 'Secrecy guards [...] not merely isolated secrets about the self but access to the underlying experience *of* secrecy' (1989: 21). This access to the secrecy that envelopes Skim remains closed to others. In a self-reflexive moment, Lisa tells her at the close of the book that being in love changes you, adding: 'No one can put it into words' (141). Lisa's comment resonates with Skim, who is unable to speak of her love for Ms Archer not just because it is taboo, but because it is too complex to put into words. In this way, the diary with its images and minimal text breaks the silence by sharing the burden of her secret love. Her diary is a sort of public–private object. It is public in the way that when Skim writes in it there is a sense of audience – her words 'Dear Diary' suggest that the diary itself is the patient listener or receptor of her secrets, and as readers we also serve this function.

In *Skim*, subjectivity is predicated on the harbouring or disclosing of secrets. John's subjectivity is fractured and erased through his suicide and the ensuing gossip that it generates about his sexuality and double life. Skim harbours her secrets and finds silence the best way to cope with the shifting emotions that come with the blossoming and disappearance of love. Whether Skim wants to free herself from the desire that binds her to Ms Archer remains part of her silent misery and secret.

Skim and Ms Archer are in some respects star-crossed lovers. Skim's class is studying *Romeo and Juliet* with Ms Archer and the dark and cold autumn (Fall) that is captured by the black-and-white illustrations reflects the turmoil and misery that engulf the lives of the characters. The subtle play of Shakespearean signifiers creates the effect of a *mise en abyme* where the play *Romeo and Juliet* is simultaneously studied, lived and queered by Skim and her teacher, and by John and Katie. However, Skim is no Juliet and survives the painful emotional effects of lost love by discovering a new friendship with Katie, moving on from her friendship with Lisa, and remaining content with her secret.

Unlike John, who could not live his life with the boy he loved, Skim gradually moves towards social interaction and a renewed subjectivity. Her course of silence and withdrawal is not one that the 'Girls Celebrate Life Club' endorses. A group of do-gooders form the club as a way of helping Katie to overcome her depression following John's suicide and as a way to commemorate his life. They even have a movie night where the feature film is *Dead Poets Society*. The Girls Celebrate Life Club with its determined goodwill crusade embodies a survivalist ethic, which ironically works against its own rationale by perpetuating an at-risk subjectivity, especially for Katie, who in her misery slips and falls off a roof and breaks both her arms. Skim and Katie are resistant to the intended cathartic activities of the club. By putting pressure on Katie and Skim to participate in the club, the organisers fail to see how desire and femininity can be understood without recourse to phallogocentrism. They assume that Katie is heartbroken and construct her as a victim, and someone who lacks agency. The folly of trying to construct the female subject within a binary frame is subtly played out in the text in various ways across the public–private domains. This traversing of the public–private space also points to the paradoxical elements of secrets and subjectivity: both require and do not require public revelation. Just as there is never a point of fixed subjectivity, nor is there a point of total revelation. As Bok says: 'at the very moment of disclosure [...] yet further secrets remain to be unveiled' (1989: 36).

Notions of desire, especially those from a psychoanalytic perspective, have construed desire as a lack. While Skim struggles with a sense of lack in terms of the inaccessibility of the object of her desire, she also finds that the desire she experiences leads to her alliance with Katie. The same is true for Katie. Through their relationship they transform themselves, becoming something else, which is not based on one being the privileged object of desire, but on relating to each other in multiple ways – sharing confidences, laughing, and making observations about their schoolmates. The following text – *Why We Broke Up* by Daniel Handler – illustrates how the course of true love is not only bumpy but that 'breaking up' is as complex as any other stage in a relationship. By combining the 'Dear John letter' and the 'Return to Sender' scenario, the text reveals how desire is given both voice and visual representation by the female subject.

What makes *Why We Broke Up* an interesting text is the way it inverts traditional treatment of desire in film and literature, by silencing the male subject (Ed) and giving the female subject (Min) voice to express her intense and changing emotions: 'I'm telling you why we broke up, Ed. I'm writing it in this letter, the whole truth of why it happened. And the truth is that I goddamn loved you so much' (Handler 2011: 1). The artwork by Maira Kalman gives a visual representation of the love arte-facts that Min returns in a box to Ed. Each item is given a description of its changing significance and the part it played in their five-week relationship – 'October 5 until November 12' (1): the ticket for the first movie they saw together; an empty box of matches; a sports pennant; a seed pod; a bottle of perfume; a torn condom packet; a motel comb; and other items.

The letter and the contents of the box are also a confession of how much Min loved Ed, and how she constructs the truth of that relation-ship and the secrets that she and Ed had during that time. In explain-ing why she is breaking up with Ed, Min is also explaining how much he hurt her in not being aware of how his actions affected her. In this way, the letter and the artefacts are the means by which Min comes to understand herself. As Foucault explains: 'The confession is a ritual of discourse in which the speaking subject is also the subject of the state-ment' (1981: 61). So while Min is given the space to voice her concerns and openly confess her emotions, Ed remains the one whom she feels needs to hear her concerns and her reasons for why they broke up. For Foucault, this position of the one who receives the 'confession' is 'the authority', as a confession is 'also a ritual that unfolds within a power relationship' (61). Min performs her 'ritual' in a theatrical manner – by dumping outside Ed's front door a box containing numerous references and quotations from Min's favourite films, along with the props of their relationship: 'every last souvenir of the love we had, the prizes and the debris of our relationship, like the glitter in the gutter when the parade has passed, all the everything and whatnot kicked to the curb' (3).

Min wants to be a director and Ed's inability to see the movies in her head was one of the many reasons why they broke up (4). The repeated words – 'that is why we broke up' – after each item is explained serves as a mantra that fits with the ritual. However, the reason for the break-up is not always clear or rational to the outsider and speaks to the inner concerns and secrets Min has had locked inside her.

In her discussion of confession and its many different purposes, Bok says that 'confession may serve as a means for transforming one's life. It can bring new insight and a chance to re-create oneself' (1989: 76). This idea of transformation is similar to the Deleuzian notion of becoming discussed above and later in Chapter 7. For Min, her confession reaches into the layers of secrets, disguised emotions and unspoken disappointments. Bok says that confession can strengthen resolve (76). Min realises that while she was attracted to Ed and fell in love with him, she also lost something of herself in the process. This is captured in her recall of her time at the Beavers basketball competition where she likened herself to an actor miscast in a movie as she cheered for Ed and waved the pennant he gave her: 'my brain said, *Why are you watching this guy? Who is he? Why this guy and not other guys, any other one?* Because there was something wrong with the picture I was in [...] Like Deanie Francis in *Midnight Is Near* or Anthony Burn as Stonewall Jackson in *Not on My Watch*, wrong for the part, ill cast' (112, emphasis original). After the match, and the victory, she found herself without agency as she went along with Ed, the other players, their girlfriends and the team supporters to the victory party. She repeatedly says, 'I had no choice' (114–15); this was the part that was expected of the girlfriend of the co-captain.

Min's recall of the specifics of her relationship with Ed reveals how love is entangled with other emotions – melancholy, anger and joy. Min sees how her being 'in love' with Ed is a struggle with patriarchal values which encourage masculine notions of possession, ownership and sovereignty over the female. Ed is critical of her friendship with Al, even though Al is gay. Ed's need to 'own' Min troubles her. Yet, when Min discovers that Ed has been seeing his former girlfriend Annette after she and Ed had become lovers it is a betrayal that she cannot condone. When Min recalls in her letter how she confronted Ed about his two-timing he responds:

'Look, Min, I know you don't believe me, but this is hard. For me too. It's awful, it's weird, it's like I was two people and one of them was, yes, Min, *really* – really really happy with you. I did love you, I do. But then at night Annette would knock on my window and it was just like something else, like a secret *I* didn't even know about –' (332)

Min's perfect recall of the words that both she and Ed spoke is of course the fictionality of the genres that expose the secret lives of people – memoir, diary, epistolary, confession. As Bok explains in terms of Rousseau's *Confessions*, it is 'an extraordinary blend of laying bare, disguise, concealment, and invention, of flaunting the self in public while yet nourishing a sense of mystery' (1989: 74). A similar mix is formed in *Why We Broke Up*. In writing about their relationship, Min becomes like a character in one of the films she may one day direct. She is the first-person narrator, the focaliser and Foucault's speaking subject who is also the subject of the statement. She is also the props master – deciding which items she will include in the box. Ed is denied a perspective and readers come to know him through Min's words and the words she attributes to him.

The ritual – the letter, the box with its 'love souvenirs' – serves a healing function. The letter functions as a script which begins with Min recalling a French film, *The Sky Cries Too*, and likening herself to Aimée Rondelé, who 'plays an assassin and a dress designer, and she only smiles twice in the whole film' (4). The first time she smiles is when the 'kingpin who killed her father gets thrown off the building' and the second is 'when she finally has the envelope with the photographs and burns it unopened in the gorgeous ashtray and she knows it's over and lights a cigarette' (4). Min admits to thinking about the loud *thunk* that the box will make on Ed's doorstep and how this sound will make her smile. In the closing words to Ed, she tells how her forthcoming New Year celebration with Al will make her feel, and likens it to one of those films that show 'huddled happys at the large wooden table' (353). This feeling she says will come with the delivering of the box: 'Shutting the box with a wooden shuffle, exhaling like a truck pulling to a stop, thunking it to you with a Desperado gesture. I will feel that way soon, any sec now, friends or loved or content or whatnot. I can see it. I can see it smiling. I'm telling you, Ed, I'm telling Al now, I have a feeling.' She signs it 'L̶o̶v̶e̶, Min' (354). Her erasure of 'love' is similar to the female assassin's burning of the photographs. In writing her letter with flashbacks juxtaposed with 'voice-over' commentary, the rhythmic pattern of the refrain 'and that's why we broke up', the love souvenirs for the box, Min fulfils her desire to be a director. She has cast both Ed and herself as characters in the kind of off-beat films she so loves but for which Ed has no apparent appreciation.

The triangulated relationship that Leigh Gilmore develops in *Autobiographics* (1994: 121) between 'penitent/teller', 'listener' and 'tale' can be seen at work in these two texts. In *Liar*, Micah's desire to tell 'the reader' the truth and confess her lies positions the reader as the listener, in much the same way that Min expects Ed to be the silent listener to her tale of their relationship. In particular, the texts also demonstrate how the first-person narrator in these texts is not necessarily an authoritative self, but one who is adept at using strategies of disclosure, covering up, evasion, creativity and self-invention. The following text is a picture book that demonstrates how these same strategies may be self-deceiving but necessary.

The paradox of self-deception

The paradox of self-deception is that the lies we tell ourselves may bring short-term feelings of psychological well-being, and enable us to adapt to a situation, but do not change anything in the long run. David Nyberg says 'that we, all of us, crave to think well of ourselves to such an extent that we are willing to change reality when it doesn't fit our self-image', and that 'affirming self-worth must be at the core of human life' (1993: 87). Nyberg suggests that whenever we want to present ourselves as a certain kind of person – honest, reliable, intelligent, interesting – we create an appearance, cultivate a personality, develop a character that suits our purposes. In other words, we try to make ourselves into a person who we can imagine would be a better person, more successful, more loveable, more popular than the one we are. Nyberg notes that self-deception is something that most, if not all, people manage to do successfully, but asks: 'Is it possible for one willfully and intentionally to deceive oneself?' (1993: 89). Is it simply a matter of wishful thinking when we self-deceive or is it a case of refusing to change our perception even when evidence comes along?

Sunday Chutney, a picture book by Aaron Blabey, illustrates these paradoxical features of self-deception. Sunday says that she is 'a bit unusual' but offers the reason for being this way because of her father's job, which means that she travels and lives all over the world. The snapshots of a happy, but quirky-looking Sunday in places such as New York or outback Australia are overlaid onto a larger illustration of a dark and sombre-looking building with a small, solitary figure (Sunday) walking towards yet another new, large and formidable-looking school. Sunday confides the other side of her glamorous lifestyle: 'Trouble is, I'm always starting at new schools.' This pattern of contrasting emotions is a recurring feature throughout the text.

While Sunday readily admits that everyone thinks that 'the new kid is a bit weird' she counters the image of her insecurity with the statement – 'I don't care' – with an accompanying illustration of a jubilant, careful

Sunday dancing alone. In another scene, she insists that she enjoys her own company. The page splits the image: the first shows a smiling Sunday sitting alone at a long white table with a cup of tea, the second shows an extended table with the Mad Hatter and white rabbit joining her for tea and cakes. Sunday explains 'and I have an excellent imagination'. While the words and illustrations in this instance support the 'truth' of her statement, at other times they are at odds. For instance, she speculates that her 'future definitely lies in fashion design', but the image clearly indicates that this is not likely (Figure 6.2). Similarly, when she nominates soccer as another future career path, the illustration contradicts

... which is why I know my future definitely lies in fashion design.

Figure 6.2 Illustration from *Sunday Chutney* by Aaron Blabey

Or soccer.

Figure 6.3 Illustration from *Sunday Chutney* by Aaron Blabey

her claim by showing her kicking the ball into a team player's head and causing chaos on the field (Figure 6.3).

These instances of an imagined future could be easily explained as wishful thinking rather than genuine self-deception. Nyberg explains what he sees as the difference between the two: 'The self-deceiver resists stubbornly and ingeniously the implications of the evidence, while the wishful thinker will usually acknowledge, however reluctantly, the new evidence as counting against the belief' (1993: 89). Nyberg suggests that the idea of deceiving oneself is a threat to our sense of wholeness and implies that we have to think of ourselves as 'double selves' rather than as a psychological unity (90). *Sunday Chutney* plays with the 'double selves' (or Freud's 'split ego') showing Sunday creating two versions of herself as a means to adapt to situations – being the new kid at school/being carefree; being alone/having imaginary friends – and thereby reinterpreting situations in a way that is clearly at odds with the reality. While Sunday has the ability to reinterpret or recast difficult experiences and feelings, she is basically an optimist.

Sunday Chutney is a useful text for exploring different ways to understand our secret selves. Sunday's general exuberance for looking on the bright side, even when the evidence is clearly to the contrary, offers a different insight to how characters use self-deception to adapt to difficult situations. What becomes evident in this text is that Sunday appears aware of the mismatch between perception and reality. Moments of self-awareness are revealed when she says how she wishes things were different – 'But I really don't like my lazy eye'; 'I don't like the first lunchtime at a new school'; 'Sometimes I wish they [parents] didn't move so much.' The illustrations play a critical role as they offer external evidence to contradict her claims. For example, when Sunday says 'I'm really good now at making friends with girls,' the illustration shows how this truth statement may be untrue. The uncertain facial expressions on the three girls and Sunday's tentative wave in their direction suggest that the opposite may in fact be true.

At other times, the illustrations collude in the deception by showing Sunday enjoying the company of a bear and an elephant, and having a tea party with characters from *Alice in Wonderland*. These light moments show the positive value of self-deception that is necessary for Sunday to remain optimistic about what the future holds. Towards the conclusion she admits that 'if she could have one wish [pause represented by a new page] it would be to always have the same home'. The illustration shows a joyful Sunday surrounded by other smiling happy girls. This textual moment reveals that despite Sunday's claims that her imagination can summon up friends whenever needed, the deep truth is that she wants real friends. The final page, however, offers an alternative wish: 'Or maybe a monster truck. It depends.'

While I have taken a positive view of self-deception in the example of *Sunday Chutney*, it also needs to be noted that self-deception can represent what Falzon terms 'a *pathology* of thought, in which thought has come to be trapped in, and blinded by, its own categories' (1998: 32, emphasis original). As Falzon explains, when we interpret the world in a totalising way, we are not able to see or contemplate alternatives or evidence to the contrary. Self-deception in this sense is not paradoxical as we proceed completely in good faith, but at the cost of being trapped in a rigid, closed system of thought. *Sister Wife* with the blind adherence of the community to the law of the father, the Prophet, illustrates this pathological side of self-deception (see Chapter 5). *Liar* is another example.

In examining the secret selves of the characters in my selection of texts, I have considered the different ways that secrecy and self-deception are employed to protect, harm, adapt, and deceive both self and others. In *Liar* and *The Adoration of Jenna Fox*, trauma and its effects are seen as the justification for secrecy and lies and how forgetting can be a protective shield for not recalling a painful past. Because Micah has a history of lying, others treat her accounts of the truth with suspicion, and the narrative challenges readers to accept the veracity of her words. But as Jenna Fox discovers, being protected from the truth limits her sense of self and her ability to achieve self-determination. While the burden of secrecy that previous chapters have discussed can be relieved when the secret is shared with another, Skim demonstrates that sometimes choosing not to share is also an option that can enable the individual to work through their changing emotions. By contrast, Min finds that by laying the burden of her secret emotions at Ed's doorstep she is able to regain her sense of self and move on with her life. The diary and the letter are the confessional modes that Skim and Min use to recreate themselves. Sunday, however, finds that recreation is something that comes easily to her. Her optimistic personality enables her to reimagine a different self. Her self-deception persists despite the evidence. Rather than rely on another person to intercede on her behalf, Sunday is able to use self-deception to provide an alternative view of the world when the reality threatens to overwhelm. I'll leave the final word to Simmel, who also recognised the positive value of self-deception. He coined the term *Lebenslüge*, a 'vital lie', to explain the condition of the individual who needs to self-deceive 'in order to maintain his life and his potentialities' (1950: 310).

Part III
Tangled Webs

7
Mendacious Animals

This chapter begins the final section of the book, 'Tangled Webs'. While its reference to a proverbial saying may seem obvious – 'Oh what a tangled web we weave when first we practise to deceive'[1] – it is more commonplace today to speak of 'the web' as referring to the internet, specifically to the World Wide Web with its instant connectivity. Before the internet, there was the popular children's book *Charlotte's Web* by E. B. White (1952). In some ways the web that is spun by Charlotte (the spider) is a precursor to the now ubiquitous 'web' of cyberspace in that her weaving of words into the web served as 'posts' for others in the farmyard to read and spread to the wider community. In White's story, the web is the means by which Wilbur, the runt of the litter, is saved from the axe and becomes a farmyard celebrity. When Charlotte weaves the words – 'SOME PIG!', 'TERRIFIC', 'RADIANT' – she cleverly names the subject into being. Chapter 5 discussed the idea of 'being-called', and in White's text so too is Wilbur *being-called* by these words. Rod McGillis describes Charlotte's actions in a similar way: 'Charlotte gives Wilbur life by inscribing him on her web; or we might say she speaks him into life' (1996: 55). As McGillis notes, the web 'signifies both death and life', as its delicate pattern of connecting silky threads is designed to trap and kill prey, providing food for the spider's survival.

The web as a means of creation, escape, magic (and in the case of Wilbur, an identity makeover) reaches back to early myths and folktales of many cultures: Ariadne, Arachne, Sleeping Beauty, Ananse, Tsuchigumo and others. Spiders and their web-making skills have also helped save lives as recounted in the cultural stories of David, Muhammad and Yoritomo. In these stories, a spider weaves a web to conceal the hiding place of these men from their enemies. What distinguishes these instances of deception from other more familiar animal ploys such as camouflage and mimicry is that these actions are used in relation to the non-human's attempt to protect the safety of a human. In the continuous contest between predator and prey, these stories open out other ways of imagining the relationship that can and does exist when species meet. The tales also demonstrate the mendacious capacity of animals.

In exploring the idea of mendacious animals in this chapter I also examine how mendacity can be understood in ways that do not privilege humans. Mendacity (along with its synonyms, lying and deception) is a term most commonly used when referring to the behaviour of humans. One view that rejects any notion of mendacity in animals rests on the argument that animals do not have access to the signifying conventions of language, which has as its premise 'an explicit and unwarranted truth-claim' (Jay 2010: 40). However, Jay affirms that 'both the animal and vegetable kingdoms are replete with examples of deception and duplicity, which if not based on speech acts are still designed to produce the effect of a deliberate lie' (20). The argument that non-humans are capable of mendacity, or at least playful deception, is one that philosophers, post-humanists and non-anthropocentric researchers have been exploring for a number of decades: Deleuze and Guattari's (1988) writing on becoming-animal; Derrida's (2009, 2008a, 2003) questioning of Lacan's distinction between human and animal that rests on the symbolic and the imaginary; Haraway's (2008) exploration into what happens when species meet; the wide-ranging exploration of the question of the animal, language and species difference by Wolfe and others (2003); and Edelman and Seth's (2009) work on animal consciousness.

This chapter therefore considers the non-human as a living being that is capable of a range of responses and actions that may be considered mendacious among other things.[2] (The example of Orwell's *Animal Farm* (see Chapter 3) provides an exemplar of a fictional treatment of animal mendacity.) Before concentrating on specific texts in more detail, I want to briefly situate the topic within the larger cultural tradition of the animal story for children.

Stories for children featuring animals have promoted images that convey enduring attributes that can influence readers' attitudes towards both fictional and real creatures as being cute, wicked, loveable, cunning or possessing extraordinary powers. Literature's long history of animal stories has provided a seemingly endless source for popular cultural texts, with companies such as Disney and Pixar producing a constant flow of films that rework and reimagine animal characters. However, while literature and film for children are eager to exploit the animal-as-friend-or-foe dichotomy, there are many texts, as this chapter will demonstrate, where this anthropocentric bias is disrupted. By reading these texts from the perspective of a wide range of critical and cultural theories, we can begin to think about ways that texts and readers continue to separate humans from non-humans by relying on what Cary Wolfe terms 'the old saws of anthropocentrism (language, tool use, the inheritance of cultural behaviors, and so on)' (2003: xi). The scope is wide for mapping the question of the animal in all its various dimensions and literary and filmic representations. Therefore, in keeping with the theme of this section of the book, I consider how mendacity attributed to fictional animals has a basis of truth in real animal behaviour. Before rejecting this proposition out of hand, we need only think about how quick we are to draw an analogy between animals and humans, such as suggesting that someone is as clever as a fox (meaning good at using deceitful tactics), or as silent as a lamb (meaning submissive and powerless), or in the Australian vernacular calling someone a galah (meaning a foolish, silly person).[3] However, this kind of analogy is not confined to everyday discourse as literature and film reinforce the human–animal analogy in pervasive and persuasive ways.

In the absence of language: foxes, dingoes and dogs

Analogy occurs in language, and human–animal analogy, such as the ones mentioned above, uses 'humans as a benchmark' (Edelman and Seth 2009: 476). In novels that feature animals it is difficult to not privilege language, but in the case of picture books (especially ones without words) and films it is possible to some extent to move away from language and explore animal consciousness through visual representation. Edelman and Seth note that scientists assign 'primary consciousness' to animals as 'the ability to create a scene in the "remembered present" in the absence of language' (476). While research into consciousness without language is being undertaken in the sciences, writers of literature also experiment with ways to dismantle the Lacanian distinctions between the symbolic (language) and the imaginary (desire). When writers for children try to represent the thoughts or perspective of an animal they attempt to collapse this opposition between the symbolic and the imaginary. To imaginatively reconstruct animal experience or consciousness – *the remembered present in the absence of language* – may seem like an impossible goal. However, as the following discussion demonstrates, some texts give readers greater access to an imagined animal consciousness by defamilarising the animal-as-human analogy and shifting narrative authority by using focalisation to construct the point of view of another (the animal Other). Humour, illustration and animation also enable an alternative perspective and point of view to emerge.

Aesop immortalised the fox as a sly, mendacious animal that uses its 'natural' cunning to lure other 'dumb animals' into a trap. The Aesop fable 'The Fox and the Goat' tells of how a fox who is trapped in a well lures an unsuspecting goat into the well so that he can climb on to the back of the animal and use its long horns to escape. In Michael Hague's (1985) illustrated version of this fable, the fox is represented like a grinning pirate with a black patch over one eye, a waistcoat and trousers, and a full-length coat. With hands behind its back and sporting a wide mouth suggestive of a smile and its tongue sticking out of the corner, the fox is a humanised version of a victorious scoundrel. These anthropocentric narratives with the human benchmark continue the analogy of human foibles in the guise of animal characters, and say more about human nature than they do about animal nature. In the following texts – *Fog a Dox* by Bruce Pascoe (2012), *Fox* by Margaret Wild, illustrated by Ron Brooks (2000) and *Wombat Stew* by Marcia K. Vaughan, illustrated by Pamela Lofts (1984) – different attempts at representing animal consciousness are made by experimenting with authorial voice, humour and illustration for reconstructing the animal experience and point of view.

Fog a Dox is a story of how humans and animals can develop deep friendship, and communicate with one another in a way that is not based on hierarchical order or human language. It is a story where names describe the subject and their subjectivity. Albert Cutts is a tree feller and his companion Brim is a dog that gives birth to a litter of pups that are half dingo. But when Albert comes across some abandoned fox cubs he brings them to Brim to suckle. One of the pups – Fog – remains with Albert and Brim, and becomes more dog than fox, hence its hybrid name (Fog) and description as a 'dox'. Albert respects the animals that inhabit the remote forest environment that he shares with them. He is so attuned to their ways that he understands their embodied knowledge and capacity for deception: the lyrebird's tricks at 'imitating squeaking bush mice and rabbits' (8); the goshawk's ability 'to produce the illusion of having doubled in size' (19) as a mechanism of intimidation; and the sly fox cubs as 'creepers and hiders, using the bracken and grasses to camouflage their outlines, only leaping out when they felt sure they could catch their prey' (34). These examples of deception do not rely on language, but are nevertheless intended to produce the effect of a deliberate 'lie'. However, these few examples in the text confine mendacity to survival strategies of animals in relation to other animals. The main focus of the narrative is on animal–human relations and the potential for friendship. The human protagonist (Albert) privileges the notion of an animal subjectivity which enables a particular kind of intersubjective relationship with them. My examination of this notion of animal subjectivity is central to appreciating more generally the consciousness of animals, which constitutes what Barbara Smuts (1999: 118) terms 'the common ground' between animals and humans.

Albert knows that Brim can count, using what he calls her 'bone memories' to keep track of where her bones are hidden; she can also count foxes, and her own pups. In second-person address, Albert warns the reader: 'Don't laugh, dogs can count. Smart dogs, anyway' (11). This statement not only speaks with an authority that draws on situated local knowledge that comes from living and working with dogs, but also attributes a consciousness to animals whereby a *remembered present* is understood as 'bone memories'. While Brim may seem limited in her knowledge of the numeral system ('one fox, two fox, ah, ah, lotsa foxes': 11), and does not have a symbolic notation for representing numbers, her intuition and awareness of herself and her environment are significant for ensuring a reliable count and record of her food supplies.

Albert has a secret in that he knows words for animals from the 'old language', the language of his Aboriginal ancestors. The animals too 'knew the sound of their names, got used to Albert addressing them with respect' (13). This imaginative representation between human and animals is not an isolated instance, but runs throughout the novel and disrupts anthropocentricism by allowing a reciprocity of respect in the human–animal intersubjective relations. While Albert believes that animals have their own language, he also admits to 'talking with Brim' and the other animals. However, he delimits the relationship that can exist between humans and wild animals by saying that wild animals and humans can be 'deferential acquaintances, but never mates' (17). Albert believes that if a wild animal, like a dingo, lost its wildness, it would also lose its freedom to make decisions about its existence. This loss of freedom is essentially a loss of subjectivity. When Albert encounters Brim's dingo mate, he seems to understand the wild animal's interrogating specular hold on him as if the animal recalls knowledge of past encounters with humans:

> They'd only caught each other's eye a few times, but each time it felt to Albert like an interrogation. What sort of man are you? How do you treat your dogs? Do you keep chooks locked up at night? Would you get cranky if I fell in love with Brim or are you prejudiced against dingoes? That sort of look. (17)

The above passage begins with a third-person narration then shifts to an internal focalisation that enables Albert to interrogate the past as a reflective memory of humans' treatment of dingoes, but from the animal's point of view. Derrida (2008a: 96) notes that the encounter with animals allows humans to remember moments of weakness, of violence and suffering. In this instance, it is the animal's point of view that is privileged as it recalls and revisits past experiences with humans: humans' potential for harm, for denying animals food, and their prejudices. But the possibility of death is one that hangs over both human and animal in an isolated environment, and survival requires knowledge as well as good fortune. One day when Albert is cutting a large tree he gets his arm caught in the wedge that he had cut into the log he was trying to chop. Unable to move and in extreme pain, Albert tries speaking to Fog who has become his companion on these tree-cutting excursions. But human language fails to get the desired response and Fog stares 'in an anguish of incomprehension' (65). When Albert resorts to throwing sticks in the hope that Fog would get the idea of fetching the hammer so Albert could free his arm, Fog simply views this stick-throwing game as something that dogs did, not a dox. Fog understands species difference in a way that Albert does not. Finally, Albert comes to the realisation that Fog is a very good dox, 'but ya not too good at English are ya?' (66). From this point in the novel authority shifts away from the human to the animal.

As Albert slips in and out of consciousness, Fog struggles with trying to comprehend the situation. The narrator provides a note of authority in explaining that an animal knows instinctively when another animal is dying or suffering by hearing the rhythm of the heart, smelling the stress of the body (68), and this consciousness prompts Fog to action – that he must get help for Albert. This scene illustrates how Albert's linguistic authority to command an action from Fog fails, and it is the animal's pre-linguistic consciousness that 'creates a scene in the "remembered present"' (Edelman and Seth 2009: 476). Pascoe, as the author, uses his 'authority' to create a convincing chain of events whereby the reader is positioned to see Fog acting not as an anthropomorphised animal, but as an animal with its own reasoning and subjectivity. Unlike the more familiar owner–pet relationships, where the owner uses language as the principal means for ensuring that commands are carried out, this scene removes language from the relationship and enables readers to look beyond the possession of language as the distinction between humans and animals.

There is a minor parallel story of a young girl, Maria, who is seriously ill and the two stories converge at the Bush Nursing Centre. Fog is able to enlist Albert's cousin's help in transporting Albert to the Centre by horse. While animals intuitively sense when another animal is suffering, in this text the animals (including the horses who transport Albert and his cousin) also know when a human is suffering and sense the urgency of the situation. The dying child inverts the suffering or dying animal story. Maria has endured eight months indoors, watching nature shows and reading books, and yearns to be outdoors: 'to touch the animals, spy out the wild beasts, catch the elusive fish and smell the wild, wild wilderness of Tiger's river' (99). This inner call for the wild and her desire to be amongst real animals is a further shift from an anthropocentric viewpoint towards an animal-centric one. Maria's determination to experience joy instead of staying focused on suffering corresponds to anthropological accounts of animals who privilege joy over suffering (Smuts 1999: 110). When Maria is taken on an outing to Albert's home in the forest, the narrator offers readers an imagined empathy between the child and the animals:

> Fog and Brim were like bookends beside the frail little girl.
> 'I'm going to remember this forever,' Maria declared.
> And she did. (111)

This captured moment of time does not look backwards in regret, fear or anger, but forwards through a companionship between animal and human.

In the picture book *Fox*, we see how jealousy is often an unwelcome companion to friendship. The three protagonists are non-humans – Magpie, Dog (dingo) and Fox. Their names signify their animality. The frontispiece plays on readers' knowledge of the dingo or wild dog as a predator. Against a painted red background, a dingo appears to run with a black bird held in its mouth and it is easy to assume that the bird is at the mercy of its captor. But the opening text proves any such assumption wrong: 'Through the charred forest, over hot ash, runs Dog, with a bird clamped in his big, gentle mouth.' The juxtaposition of 'clamped' and 'gentle' alerts readers to take a view of Dog as a saviour, not as a predator. At first Magpie resists Dog's kindness, angered by the fact she will never fly again because of her burnt wing. But Dog perseveres and as he is blind in one eye, they come to an agreement: Dog will be Magpie's wings and she will be his missing eye. With Magpie on his back, the pair fly through the forest as one animal. A deep friendship forms as the seasons pass, but then fox 'with his haunted eyes and thick red coat' arrives on the scene, flickering through the trees 'like a tongue of fire'. The analogy warns of destruction of a different kind from the earlier bush fire.

The three animals co-exist in relative harmony for a period, but Magpie is always suspicious of Fox 'and can feel him watching, always watching her' (Figure 7.1). While Magpie remains suspicious of Fox, Dog is the ultimate humanist who accepts Fox unreservedly: 'He's all right. Let him be.' Three times Fox whispers temptation to Magpie, enticing her to leave Dog and go away with him: 'Do you remember what it is like to fly? Truly fly?' These enticements to enjoy an exhilaration of flight ultimately prove too difficult to refuse and Magpie takes off, riding on the back of the swift-footed Fox. This enticement to a memory of exhilaration is a further acknowledgement of animals' 'primary consciousness', and how the animal can create what Edelman and Seth term a scene in the 'remembered present'.

In 'remembering', Magpie is also deceived as Fox has no intention of remaining her friend. Rather, his motive is to remove her from Dog and destroy their friendship. His jealousy of their friendship and his desire that Magpie and Dog also endure loneliness is given voice after he reaches a destination that is far from where they began. Shaking 'Magpie off his back as he would a flea' he says: 'Now you and Dog will

Figure 7.1   Illustration from *Fox* by Margaret Wild. Illustrated by Ron Brooks

know what it is like to be truly alone.' Unlike other foxes, red foxes are social animals, but Fox in this story is different. And while difference is used in this text as an element that unites Dog and Magpie, it also marks Fox's inability to see himself accepted as part of the others' friendship. The relationship between Fox, Dog and Magpie is like the eternal love triangle in that it triggers jealousy and disharmony. However, the text attempts to disrupt readers' preconceptions of the differences between human and animal by providing an animal perspective on the triangulated relationship. Like *Fog a Dox*, *Fox* also offers readers the potential to look beyond the possession of language by focusing in this text on the relations between the animal characters, their desires and fears, and their individual capacity for kindness, mendacity and fickleness.

In the evolutionary struggle to survive, animals use acts of deception, such as mimicking other more dangerous animals, to fool their predators.[4] While Lacan concedes that animals are capable of using feigning behaviour (what he terms 'dancity', *dansité*) to put their pursuers off the scent by making false starts, he insists that 'the animal does not pretend to pretend' as to deceive 'would be tantamount to making itself the subject of the signifier' (1977: 338). However, Derrida argues against this point, noting that Lacan keeps the animal locked in the imaginary or presymbolic (*feigning without feigning feigning*) and is therefore 'deemed incapable of an authentic relationship to death' (2009: 171–2). Other forms of communication among animals can produce other kinds of non-linguistic deception when, for example, one animal wishes to deceive another about a food source (see Mitchell and Thompson 1986: chapter 1). Animal deception over food occurs in the Australian picture book *Wombat Stew*, which is a reworking of the old Stone Soup story. This light tale turns the table on the deceiver who becomes the deceived.

When dingo captures a wombat and boasts that he is going to make a wombat stew, one by one different passing animals advise the dingo to add a new ingredient: the platypus suggests 'big blops of billabong mud'; the emu recommends a few feathers; the blue-tongue lizard contributes one hundred flies; the echidna advises on the crunchy flavour of slugs and bugs; and finally the koala adds lots of gumnuts. But before the dingo lowers the wombat into the overflowing pot, the animals tell dingo that he couldn't put the wombat into the stew without first tasting it. On tasting the stew the dingo cries out: 'I'm poisoned [...] You've all tricked me!' The animals' mendacity serves an altruistic function because in deceiving dingo, wombat is saved (Figure 7.2).

One day, on the banks of a billabong,
a very clever dingo caught a wombat . . .

Figure 7.2 Illustration from *Wombat Stew* by Marcia K. Vaughan and Pamela Lofts

'The Machiavellian module': cane toads

While foxes and dingoes may be generally regarded as sly and cunning due to their predatory skills, and to the folklore that has contributed to this image, toads on the other hand are generally a minor player in children's literature, though there are some memorable toad characters. In Kenneth Grahame's *The Wind in the Willows* (1908), the wealthy Mr Toad of Toad Hall is a good-natured, smart, if not reckless and compulsive character that cannot resist indulging his obsessions and crazes (punting, houseboats, horse-drawn caravans and motoring). The toad's amphibian cousin, the frog, makes more appearances in fiction, often as a benign or set-upon character. The cane toad[5] on the other hand is rarely featured in stories, and Morris Gleitzman's satirical Toad series is an attempt to redress this absence.[6] *Toad Heaven* is the first book in this series (Figure 7.3).

Toad Heaven puts a different face on the despised cane toad through the sympathetic character of Limpy, a cane toad so named because of

Figure 7.3 Illustration from the cover of *Toad Heaven* by Morris Gleitzman. Illustration by Rod Clements

an accident with a truck. As a cane toad, Limpy is an unlikely romance hero. Nevertheless, he embodies noble virtues – courteous, imaginative, intelligent and caring. His quest is to save his family and relatives ('the rellies') from death and to deliver them to the safety of the national park where he believes they can live without fear of being killed by humans. He is unwavering in his quest despite Ancient Eric's dismissal of the plan: 'National parks are a myth. A fantasy for feeble minds. Think about it. If national parks existed, don't you think we'd already be living in one? Nature's given you a great gift, young man. A brain bigger than a leech's entire digestive system. Start using it' (18). Besides the threat of humans, Limpy's rival is Malcolm, a large cane toad with Machiavellian inclinations. Malcolm lies, cheats and deceives in order to achieve power as leader of the cane toads. His behaviour is similar to what Jay refers to as 'the Machiavellian module', an area of the subconscious that teaches both humans and animals to lie (2010: 21).

A crucial consideration in representation of the cane toads (and the other animals discussed above) relates to how point of view and focalisation encode non-human subjectivities and position readers. *Toad Heaven* privileges a cane-toad perspective on the precarious life they lead when their main predators are humans who use gardening tools (pitchforks, shovels), sporting equipment (baseball bats, tennis racquets, cricket bats), along with hammers and motor vehicles to kill them. Through focalisation readers are positioned to take a sympathetic position towards the toads and put aside temporarily their prejudices against (and knowledge of) this species. Readers are given access to the toads' thoughts, schemes and point of view, while a human perspective is almost absent except for a limited one from a young boy. While the story romanticises, in a comedic manner, the cane toad and its victimisation, it does raise the issue that Derrida, Haraway and others have explored, namely, the dilemma of killing and relationships of use between humans and non-humans. For Derrida (2003) there was the unanswered question – 'And say the animal responded?' – that was intended to disrupt the notion that humans respond, animals react, and was his challenge to Lacan's denial of the Symbolic to the animal. Derrida uses a trapping analogy to describe how Lacan saw the animal as always immobilised 'within the snare of the imaginary' (122). *Toad Heaven* provides an imaginative account of animal response and in so doing the figure of the cane toad is able to break through the distinction that Lacan makes between human and animal, that animals are capable of pretence (for mating, survival), but incapable of deception (because they lack speech).

Limpy and his rival Malcolm both employ deception to achieve their desired goals. Malcolm wants to be the leader of the cane toads but in order to achieve this goal he has to first get rid of Ancient Eric, the group's acknowledged leader. He successfully lures the driver of a four-wheel-drive vehicle over a rock under which Ancient Eric lives, with the impact flattening Ancient Eric. When the driver gets out of the car, Malcolm protects himself by pushing Limpy's sister, Charm, into his path. Presciently, Malcolm had announced his desire for self-preservation at all costs when he told Limpy 'a leader never risks his own life because he's too valuable a resource' (29). Charm reinforces his position by explaining further to Limpy: 'he has to keep himself safe so we can all benefit from his leadership' (29).

Malcolm convinces the other toads of his humility when he pretends to be the reluctant and unworthy successor to Ancient Eric. When everyone thinks that Limpy has died, Malcolm lies about his friendship with Limpy at his commemoration service: 'He was a close personal friend of mine' (49). Malcolm again lies when he tells the cane toads of the non-existent Sunset Estate and deliberately misleads them as he takes them on the long and dangerous journey out west. Malcolm promotes Sunset Estate as a Shangri-la where 'cane toads can live in peace and safety forever' (54). His real-estate spiel offers a tempting vision of plenty – 'forty-five percent more flying insects' (246) – and a promise of sound investment that the cane toads find irresistible: 'You'll love it. A real slice of cane toad paradise. And because you're all family, I'll be making your new homesites available at low, low discount prices, easy weekly repayments, flying insects accepted' (54–5). This kind of deception is one that Lacan and others would see as impossible for animals because they lack access to the order of the signifier and of Truth (Derrida 2003: 130).

Limpy's more altruistic goal to find a national park is another kind of toad heaven that proves just as elusive. Charm and Goliath join Limpy on the quest. The camaraderie is not only mythic in its construction, but reflects a cooperation that does in fact occur within and across species.[7] A similar kind of symbiotic animal cooperation for mutual benefit occurred between Magpie and Dog (*Fox*). Along their journey to the national park, the three cane toads need to be ever vigilant and resourceful to avoid being killed by humans. In one episode they find themselves on a boat in the Great Barrier Reef ('an underwater national park': 117) and to avoid detection are forced to pretend they are stuffed toad souvenirs, which some tourists readily purchase. There is an irony at play as the despised and ugly cane toads are transformed into desirable and 'cute' merchandise when humans believe them to be stuffed with sawdust. The three toads pose next to other genuine cane-toad souvenirs, mimicking their blank stare and frozen posture while holding in their hands a miniature baseball bat, tennis racquet and golf club – sporting items that are used as weapons by humans to kill cane toads. Only a young boy can see the way that the 'dead' cane toads holding sports equipment have been transformed into sporting trophies, and resists his mother's offer to buy Limpy: 'That's really cruel,' the boy says. 'Killing them just to make souvenirs. I'd only want a cane toad if I could have a live one for a pet' (121). Limpy's plan almost fails when the three of them are purchased by different tourists, but the intervention of the boy enables them to escape. While the boy sets the toads free, his desire to only possess the animals as pets, and not as souvenirs, also speaks of human dominance over animals. Despite its focalisation strategies, this fiction ultimately relies on humans as benchmarks in its portrayal of the cane toads as megalomaniacs, romantics and dupes in much the same way as fables. However, it nevertheless draws our attention to the animal Other and its precarious existence in relation to humans, a position that is strengthened by its attention to the characters' animality.

Deception and the question of animality

An underlying question that we could ask of the above animal stories is one that Steve Baker (2003: 147) asks in the context of the arts, namely, 'What is it to be animal?' Baker explores the continuing attraction of the animal for artists (and others) for their creative and other philosophical endeavours. Filmmakers, especially those making movies for the family market, repeatedly use animals as a vehicle for moral instruction or empathic awareness. Often the animal stands in for the child as a subject who appears powerless, and this imitation in the guise of an animal displaces the 'real' animal behind the animated figure. If Deleuze and Guattari are correct in their belief that 'becoming animal does not consist in playing animal or imitating animal' (1988: 238) then it might also be worth considering if the inverse also applies – becoming human does not consist in playing human or imitating human. Substituting human for animal in this theorising is to take the perspective of the Other and to consider if there is a shift in the power relation. The idea of deceit as acts – imitation, performance and disguise – that enable *becoming other* is central to the film *Lilo & Stitch* (2002). This film complicates the animality question that Baker asks as it also calls into question humanness, and posthumanism, in that the character that *becomes animal* is an electronic creation in the first instance.

The film opens with a council meeting being held at the Galaxy Defense Industries on the planet Turo where the lead scientist, Dr Jumba Jookiba, is being accused of illegal genetic experimentation. The scientists and the Grand Councilwoman are neither human nor animal but more a cartoon amalgam of human, animal and mythic creatures. For example, Mr Pleakley with his one eye and headshape and thin legs looks like a cross between Jiminy Cricket and Cyclops. Dr Jumba pleads that the so-called monster that appears before the council is a new species called 'Experiment 626' and lists its qualities which are a mix of comic-strip heroes, animal, high technology and supernatural beings – bulletproof, fireproof, and can think faster than a supercomputer, see in the dark and move objects many times his size. However, in proudly proclaiming that Experiment 626's only instinct is to 'destroy everything he touches', Dr Jumba unwittingly confirms the verdict of the council that the creation is a monster and must be either destroyed or exiled because it violates ethical and legal protocols. When Experiment 626 is given a chance to prove that he has some goodness inside him, he screeches an apparently horrifying statement – 'Meega, nala kweesta' – that shocks the council, thereby sealing his fate to be banished to a desert asteroid to live in exile. However, the plan does not work as Experiment 626 proves capable of subverting security and ends up crashing to Earth ('E-Arth') near where Lilo lives in Hawaii.

Lilo is also a wild creature, having just bitten another girl at school and disrupted the traditional dance rehearsal in the local community centre. Lilo is ostracised by the other girls for her uncontrollable behaviour, and chastised by her sister Nani who has sole guardianship of her since their parents' death. Lilo's behaviour casts doubt on Nani's ability to be a proper guardian, and the social worker (who is an ex-CIA agent and continues to look the part, but is ironically called Mr Bubbles) is ever-watchful of the situation. When Mr Bubbles interviews Lilo about her situation she lies and says that Nani disciplines her with bricks. This lie of child abuse worsens the situation and Nani is put on notice that unless things improve Lilo will be taken away. In trying to find a positive means for getting Lilo to behave, Nani agrees to her buying a dog from the local pound.

Dazed by the crash to earth, Experiment 626 gets run over by a truck and taken to the pound. There it wreaks havoc, intent on the destruction and terrorisation of the other animals. However, it sees a poster of a dog being held by a girl and morphs itself into a dog-like form. It manages to look like a hybrid dog-rabbit with a blue body, an angry, snarling face and large funnel-shaped ears. His deception brings rewards as Lilo wants only this dog, whom she names Stitch. Through naming, Stitch is transformed from monstrous Experiment 626 to a pet. However, the act of naming is also a marker of ownership: as creator of Experiment 626 Jumba attributed a scientific classification to his invention, and Lilo's naming marks her ownership of Stitch as her pet. However, Stitch is not without agency in this process and exploits the pretence of being a pet to his advantage. The pretend dog that Stitch becomes so that he can escape the pound is similar to the duck that becomes a dog in order to escape loneliness discussed in Chapter 1 (see *Wanted: The Perfect Pet* by Fiona Robertson). Stitch is in some ways an embodiment of Sony Corporation's first robotic pet dog, AIBO, developed in 1999. Ursula Heise (2003: 60) makes the point that electronically and genetically engineered animals in literature and film often appear alongside humans who also have undergone modification. In this film, humans are not genetically modified, but Lilo's behaviour improves and she develops an empathic awareness by the end of the film due to her relationship with Stitch.

Stitch is rejected from Turo because he is a genetically engineered life species which in the context of an animated film is a metafictive comment on the computer-generated creation of the film character before the viewer. Stitch's masquerade as a dog is not questioned by any human he encounters, although to the viewer the reality of a blue dog who has extraordinary powers of destruction would suggest this inability to see who Stitch is, or, more accurately, who he is not, speaks back to Derrida's argument that humans and philosophers continue to see the distinction between animals in terms of lack (no speech) and alterity. Stitch is doubly different according to human criteria: he is both a cyborg and an animal. In other words, his animality means he is not recognised. He becomes the monster that he was first called and it is only when his relationship with Lilo begins to break down, that Stitch begins to see himself as a creature that wants to belong. In order to satisfy his desire to belong Stitch has to resist his destructive programming and assimilate into the world of animals and humans on E-Arth. The Hawaiian term *o'hana* (family) is evoked by Lilo, and later Stitch, as a kind of truth-fulfilling mantra, binding them together – the statement 'family means nobody gets left behind' is repeated throughout the film. Stitch also becomes attached to Lilo's copy of *The Ugly Duckling*, and the image of the rejected, lost duckling provides an *imago* of himself, a mirror-image which sees identification with his double (see Lacan 1977: 4).

Stitch's attempts at transformation from monster to model citizen entails more imitation – such as performing like Elvis Presley, someone whom Lilo continues to admire and consider a model citizen. Lilo teaches Stitch how to *become* Elvis: dancing and hip swirling, playing a guitar and singing. All these performatives provide a further layer to the deception that cannot be seen. His invisibility as an animal but visibility as a human is made apparent in one scene when Stitch mimes the song lyrics 'you're the devil in disguise' (words that carry more than a grain of truth) during one of his Elvis performances, and is mobbed by a crowd of adoring female tourists and needs to be rescued by Lilo. All the time that Stitch attempts to be other than himself, Jumba and Pleakley also perform a series of deceptions in order to capture Stitch and return him to their planet. In a similar way, Jumba's and Pleakley's disguises and subterfuges are performed without any suspicion or detection by the human characters. The transformation of Stitch from a monster intent on destruction to an animal with feeling is complete when he is finally captured and about to be transported back to his planet. It is through a speech act that he is able to express his desire to stay: 'This is my family. I found it all on my own. It's little and broken, but still good.' This final acknowledgement of being results in the Grand Councilwoman declaring that Stitch can live out his life in exile on Earth and that his family is now under the official protection of the United Galactic Federation, a decision which serves both political and compassionate ends.

In the final scenes of the film a series of family snapshots fill a wall and the lyrics of an old Elvis Presley song, 'Burning Love', provide an uplifting musical accompaniment. The images show a transformed Stitch who is now sociable and clearly part of the domestic unit. Lilo is also transformed, no longer the wild girl but a happy, socially adjusted child. This shifting representation over the course of the film from the initial encounters with wildness to final domestication is a familiar scenario in children's films where the conclusion moves towards acceptance, tolerance and family. The recognition of the humans and 'animals' as a family collapses the idea of species difference. Furthermore, Stitch's use of language to communicate his desire to belong signifies a move into the Symbolic. There is also an acceptance within the story of other life-forms – the non-human and the cyborg – as Pleakley and Jumba become part of the extended family. This acceptance also works from the non-human perspective such as when the Grand Councilwoman modifies the law so that Stitch and Lilo can remain together as a family. This action demonstrates an ability to empathise with other living beings that disrupts the dominant perspective of human superiority over animals that currently exists in the Western world.

All the texts I have discussed in this chapter can be understood as attempts to provide a non-anthropocentric perspective whereby the animal or non-human is not regarded as an inferior species by insisting on the primacy of humans. By looking beyond language as something that separates humans and animals, the texts open up paths for considering how deception can be understood in these texts and in relation to real animal contexts in ways that are not dismissed as simply 'nature' at work. The narratives' explorations of animals' embodied knowledge, consciousness, subjectivity and mendacious capabilities imaginatively reconstruct animal experience and grant readers a greater access to the human in the animal. This complex defamiliarisation also alerts readers to how human–animal encounters have been historically framed in terms of cautionary tales about human morality and failing, or beasts to be tamed or killed. The specific strategies used to achieve this defamiliarisation include the shift in narrative authority from an anthropocentric point of view to a non-anthropocentric one that takes account of animal subjectivity and consciousness. To return to the web analogy that commenced this chapter, these stories show that while humans might create tangled webs of lies when they deceive others, for animals (at least for those discussed in these texts) there may be lessons to be learnt, but mendacity may also bring its own rewards.

8
Artful Deception

In an essay entitled 'The Fine Art', Joseph Conrad comments on people's capacity for deception as 'a sort of curious and inexplicable propensity to allow themselves to be led by the nose with their eyes open' (1945: 28). This view casts the reader as a dupe, a willing player who falls victim to the author's literary foils and deceptions. However, readers and reading are not easily reduced to such a simplistic equation. An essential element of the appeal of certain kinds of stories such as metafiction and tall tales is that a reader participates in the game of being led by the nose, but how successful this ruse is before the game is up depends more on the skill of the author than the gullibility of the reader. In the case of picture books, the illustrator too plays an important role in either assisting the reader in keeping their eyes wide open, alerting to clues and incongruities, or colluding with the author in the game of deception. Sanders makes the charge that scholarship on children's literature has a 'disdain' for 'comfortable fiction' and celebrates the 'discomfort provided by metafiction'; his basis for this claim is that children's literature scholarship embraces subversion and rejects didacticism (2009: 350). Sanders may have a point but generalisations like the liar paradox have a way of proving themselves wrong. My interest in this chapter is not to speculate on whether a text is subversive, didactic or uncomfortable, but *how* and *why* children's fiction performs an artful deception. This point returns to my comment made at the beginning of this book that fiction performs like a dancer of veils – revealing and concealing so as to tantalise readers, tricking them into seeing things in a certain light, and showing that even when eyes are wide open it is not possible to see a text stripped bare, as texts will always veil their nakedness (Derrida 1975).

Derrida's view on literature and secrecy is that literature withholds as much as it reveals, always leaving readers to ask questions of characters, events, motivations and meaning – What happened after ...? Why did ...? How is ...? Who said ...? Thus, readers come to literature with a sense of its secret 'that is at the same time kept and exposed, jealously sealed and opened like a purloined letter' (Derrida 2008b: 131). Kermode sees a dialogue between story and interpretation as a way of representing the 'capacity of narrative to submit to the desires of this or that mind without giving up secret potential' (1980: 86). Patricia Waugh provides a link between the ideas of Derrida and Kermode by considering the game that texts play with readers, specifically metafiction, as a form of fictional writing that 'self-consciously and systematically draws attention to its status as an artifact' (1984: 2). With these perspectives on fiction's ability to leave questions unanswered, keep hold of secrets and flaunt its fictionality, this chapter considers how texts work to deceive (manipulate) readers. It also considers how characters deceive other characters – leading them by the nose, disrupting expectations, concealing the truth and creating different realities. In focusing on the artistry of deception the concept of survival assumes different proportions as characters fight for their lives, wriggle out of difficult circumstances or are sacrificed. The discussion also includes how stories and lies told to a dying loved one may serve conflicting purposes.

Metafictional subterfuge

Waugh describes generally of metafiction its ability to establish and sustain 'the construction of a fictional illusion (as in traditional realism) and the laying bare of that illusion' (1984: 6). *The Name of this Book is Secret* by Pseudonymous Bosch (2008) and *A Pack of Lies* by Geraldine McCaughrean (1988) are fitting examples of metafiction that invite readers to participate in a playful deception of literary games.

The Name of this Book is Secret self-consciously foregrounds and exaggerates its own narrative manipulation. The 'author', Pseudonymous Bosch, forewarns the reader from the outset not to read this book: 'WARNING: DO NOT READ BEYOND THIS PAGE!', but knowing that readers cannot resist, subsequently praises them for being curious and brave. Curiosity is a quality of readers who seek to discover a text's secret and every book plays on that curiosity, beckoning readers to discover what lies between its covers. *The Name of this Book is Secret* is no different, despite its warning. Bosch explains that when books are read (like the box Pandora opens) they 'cause all kinds of problems': they can give you ideas, and provoke emotions, but warns that the main reason why this book is so dangerous is because it concerns a secret – 'A *big* secret' (2008: unpaged, emphasis original). Bosch is the master illusionist, assuming the right to make things appear true or real. Derrida says that literature has illusory qualities: '*in principle* the right to say everything and to hide everything' (2008b: 156, emphasis original). This *author*isation to perform literary tricks and illusions results in a playful textual game.

Bosch begins Chapter One with the title 'xxxxxxxxx', and proceeds to begin the story with a text composed of only the letter x in various combinations. The use of punctuation and conventional formatting of sentences and paragraphs maintains the illusion of a story in code. The following chapter, 'Chapter One and a Half', is given the title 'Apologia' with a footnote to explain what it means and does not mean: 'An apologia, if you're wondering, is not a variety of insect. Neither is it a type of cancerous tumour. It's an apology. In other words, it's not worth the paper it's written on' (3). The insertion of the footnote, and its cynical and humorous tone, is an early clue that this book is a game, a point that is underlined by the narratorial comment: 'Yes, this is a story *about* a secret. But it's also a *secret* story' (3, emphasis original). As the narrative progresses, readers find that this is true, except that it is a story that has multiple secrets.

The plot involves two children, Cassandra and Max-Ernest, who find a wooden box of crystal vials containing liquids, powders and other material, each with a different smell: the box is labelled, *A Symphony of Smells*.[1] The box proves to be the reason behind the near-death experiences the two characters later encounter. In their attempts to solve the mystery of a missing twin brother of a magician who has died mysteriously, the children need to become sleuths, decoding obscure riddles and using their (unappreciated) skills to solve the mystery and achieve a return to normal everyday life. The magician and his brother have synaesthesia – a confusion of the senses – and this fact makes a further connection to the *Symphony of Smells* box. The structure of the story is not unlike other quest stories or detective mysteries written for children, but by disturbing the surface of the narrative, readers can appreciate the artful deception of the text with its disingenuous narrator, numerous allusions, intertexts and moments of self-reflexivity.

Metafiction is concerned with literary convention, displaying its conventionality, and explicitly and overtly 'laying bare', as Waugh terms it, its own process of construction. I have already noted how the author of this fiction is disguised (Pseudonymous Bosch), which draws attention to its own secrecy in hiding the true identity of the author. The name of 'Bosch' could be a reference to the artist Hieronymus Bosch whose work is characterised by riddles. Furthermore, the names of other characters also appear to have allusive connections. Bosch steers readers away from making an association between the Cassandra in the story and the Cassandra of Greek mythology: 'Unlike the Cassandra of myth, the girl who figures in our story is not a prophet'; nevertheless, we are told that the reason for the character's name is because 'she resembles a prophet in that she is always predicting disaster' (8). This simultaneous instance of both disconnecting and connecting the two Cassandras performs a double function and in so doing creates an alternative fictional character: one which does not require readers to draw on their existing literary knowledge in order to recognise a hidden allusion which traditional literary convention sets up when trying to keep its secrets hidden.[2] We could also guess that Cassandra's friend Max-Ernest, who wants to be a stand-up comedian, is a veiled reference to the surrealist artist Max Ernst whose work exhibited a bizarre humour. However, an explanation of how Max-Ernest came to be named is told by way of an intercalation entitled 'A Short Story', which explains that his parents couldn't agree on a first name so they decided to 'split the difference' and named him with both their preferences. This narrative within a narrative may prove my hunch is wrong. Alternatively, it may be a deception intended to steer readers away from discovering its secret allusion. We are also told 'Max-Ernest was very fond of paradoxes, as he was of all kinds of riddles and puzzles and word games' (21), a characteristic which surrealists like Ernst also shared. As 'insiders', readers find ways to extract meaning and make connections within a text, even at the risk of causing the text to vanish into the interpretation (Kermode 1979: 10).

Another character that first 'pops up' (35)[3] and then doesn't reappear until nearly 50 pages later is Benjamin Blake, a fellow student of Cass and Max-Ernest whom they consider to be 'weird'. He also has synaesthesia. By having characters like Benjamin (and there are others) who pop up, the text deliberately plays with narrative convention by making it difficult to judge whether a character is a textual agent or just part of the text's idiosyncrasy. Benjamin is however essential to the plot as he is kidnapped by Ms Mauvais and Dr L, who are the Masters of the sinister spa known as the Midnight Sun. Benjamin's capture enables Cass and Max-Ernest to act bravely by rescuing him. However, Benjamin remains an enigma, denied any point of view, and given only some mumbled lines to utter. Yet, his character is a key to solving the mystery of the missing magician. Despite the text's metafictional moments and authorial denials, it nevertheless works to fulfil readers' expectations of narrative coherence.

While readers know that this text is a fiction, it is tempting to be led by the nose into a game of pretend with Bosch, who attempts through the convention of omniscient narration to tell a story that concerns a secret, and a dangerous secret at that. Bosch cautions from the beginning, and continues to do so throughout the book, that knowing the secret could be life threatening for both the readers and the characters. Therefore, a series of deceptions is put in place to make the text seem obscure, and to hide the secret. For instance, through direct address to the reader the text states that the real names have been substituted with fictional names and description: 'I can't tell you anything that would help you identify the people involved in this story if you were to meet them at your orthodontist's office' (4). Therefore, pseudonyms (just like the author's) are given: 'I'm going to give my characters names and faces. But remember these aren't their *real* names and faces. They're more like code names or cover identities, like a spy or a criminal would have' (4). This metafictional play attempts to reassure the reader that these characters are an invention, but that the story in which they play a role is true, and, more significantly, that the author ('I'm going to give my characters [...]') is constructing this text from his/her privileged, ontological position in the real world, thereby ironically flaunting the role of Author (Waugh 1984: 131). Bosch performs as an ironist, mocking the conventional notion of both an author and a children's book, declaring: 'endings are hard to write. You try wrapping up your story, showing how your characters have grown, sewing up any holes in your plot, and underlining your theme – all in a single chapter! No, really. Try. Because I'm not going to do it' (239). Bosch adds that he will give the reader some assistance in writing the ending: 'Oh, I won't leave you hanging entirely. There are levels of cruelty that even I am not capable of*.' A footnote pokes further fun:

> *When you take over this chapter, you should probably rewrite that last sentence to read, 'there are levels of cruelty *of which* even I am not capable.' Teachers don't like it when you end sentences with prepositions like *of* or *in*. Then again, you shouldn't be showing this book to your teacher anyway. (239)

This explanatory footnote is an instance of authorial intrusion whereby there is deliberate crossing of what Waugh sees as the 'ontological divide' between text and reader (1984: 131). However, Bosch is an invention that pretends to be the Real Author further complicating the status of authorship. Further flaunting of the Teller occurs as Bosch comments on both the content and the construction of the story, offering personal opinion, direct address to the reader, and by inserting breaks in the flow of the narrative: 'let's have a chapter break. I don't know about you, but I could sure use it' (208).

The metanarrative voice that carries throughout the story, like a voice-over technique in film, helps to give the text a ring of truth and an authoritative tone. When this *autho*rity gives lessons in grammar, provides explanations of obscure words and explains the difficulty of writing conclusions, it asserts the idea of the ontological presence of the Author, which Waugh describes as the 'lone Creative Figure busily inventing and constructing, producing the text from His position in the Real World' (1984: 130). Bosch's persistent interruptions of the third-person narrative with overt first-person or second-person intrusions help to remind the reader of the author's powers of invention.

Throughout the story, the 'author' is in control, taking on various roles as comic, teacher, cynic, guiding the narrative along its teleological path. Despite its recurrent warnings of danger ('Try to erase the image of Max-Ernest from your head as fast as you can – for your own safety': 20), and reluctance to reveal certain details ('I can't explain without putting Cass in a rather negative light': 30), the narrative toys with readers' expectations by refusing to deliver what Kermode considers to be the interest of readers: 'message and closure' (1980: 86). It does, however, fulfil the authorial statement of being a story *about* a secret and a *secret* story. Further deferral of closure is made when Chapter Thirty-Two offers readers a 'Do-it-yourself ending'. In order to maintain control (but deceptively under the guise of being helpful), the author organises some 'key incidents' according to the characters. Readers are invited to 'rearrange events as you see fit' (240), and to write their own version on two lined pages in a duplicate Chapter Thirty-Two entitled 'Your Version', with a footnote instruction to use black or blue ink only, and to attach extra pages as necessary (249). The delay of closure is enhanced by two more pages: the first page contains only the words 'THE END', followed by the words 'WELL, NOT REALLY' on the second page, and a final chapter entitled, 'Chapter Zero:[4] The Denouement'. By calling this chapter 'zero' Bosch explains it 'doesn't exist. It's a nothing chapter. The un-chapter. It simply doesn't count' (254). By refusing to call it 'the ending' and insisting on calling it 'the denouement', Bosch feigns a defiant stance against literary convention ('This chapter will make nothing clear; it will raise many questions; and it may even contain a surprise or two'). Rather, the assertion is that 'Denouement' sounds 'so sophisticated and French' (255). This self-conscious attempt to debunk convention and appear flippant draws attention to the text's construction as an artefact.

Kermode suggests that because readers 'have certain expectations of endings' (1979: 65), when texts fail to conform to these expectations they will accept something that will do, purely as a way of satisfying the desire for closure. The Denouement provides Cass and Max-Ernest with one more cryptic message to solve, and a letter which the author includes 'with one minor but necessary excision' (266). The deleted text, textually presented as 'xxxxx xxxx', is a final secret that the author withholds from the reader. The letter invites the two characters to become members of a secret society, the Terces Society, to fight against the ongoing evil of the Masters of the Midnight Sun. The invitation also forms the perfect segue to the next book in the Secret series.

From this discussion it will be obvious that one of the main characteristics of *The Name of this Book is Secret* is the manner of its telling. Bosch actively participates in the novel, sprinkling facts, opinion, witty comment and authorial asides from beginning to end. Footnotes are supplied to substantiate the 'truth' of the facts the author offers. But of course all the 'facts' are fictional, including the 'author', Pseudonymous Bosch. In purporting to disclose a terrible secret, a truth, the book paradoxically asserts the superiority of fiction as a mode of truth-telling. The book continually disguises a distinction between fact and fiction, truth and lies, by parodying the indicators of non-fiction or factual writing such as footnotes and appendices. These indicators purport to factuality, but in fact offer only tidbits of facts woven with authorial comment or debunking. Furthermore, Bosch is an ostentatiously intrusive storyteller. The next text – *A Pack of Lies* – similarly plays with *author*ity as it raises the question of who or what is an author. Just as a pack of cards can be assembled to form constructions that can easily collapse, or be manipulated through sleight of hand and other trickery, *A Pack of Lies* performs like a skilled card player leading readers to make false assumptions, or encouraging them to be watchful for deception.

Waugh says that philosophers, aestheticians and metafictional writers address themselves to two problems: 'first, the paradox concerning the identity of fictional characters; second, the status of literary-fictional discourse (the problem of referentiality)' (1984: 90). Geraldine McCaughrean's *A Pack of Lies* (1988) is a timeless example of metafiction that provokes thoughts about the two problems Waugh identifies.[5] It also invites readers to reflect on the relationship between fiction, truth and deception. Waugh's point that a fictional character 'both exists and does not exist' (91) is obvious to readers even when their immersion in the world of the story may make them temporarily forget that the character is a fictional construct. *A Pack of Lies* deliberately disrupts this logic through the character MCC Berkshire, a young man Ailsa meets in the library one day while doing her school project. MCC is unable to get a library ticket because he is not on the Electoral Roll and, on the threat of him being thrown out of the library for making a nuisance of himself, Ailsa suggests impetuously that he work for her mother at her Antiquary shop – a business that is struggling to survive since the death of Mr Povey, Ailsa's father.

A Pack of Lies requires readers to replay in their minds (or reread) some points they encountered along the narrative path based on the new knowledge that is presented in the conclusion. While MCC is a larger than life character, a compulsive reader and storyteller, it also turns out that he along with Ailsa and her mother are characters in the story that we read as *A Pack of Lies* written by a cricket-enthusiast and frustrated writer, Michael Charles Christie Berkshire, who in turn is another character created by Geraldine McCaughrean. This deceit is not revealed until the last chapter, but McCaughrean (and her creation Michael Charles Christie Berkshire) leaves clues for readers to detect the deception at play in the text. The initial clue appears to be when Ailsa first meets MCC, who hails from Reading, which he pronounces to rhyme with 'breeding' not 'bedding'. Given his love of reading and cricket his initials MCC are a clue that this young man, who wears only white cricket flannels with oval grass stains on both knees, is not what he seems and that his initials possibly come from his favourite cricket club – Marylebone Cricket Club. Ailsa's first instinct is that this man is a liar: '"You're a liar, sir," thought Ailsa. But nice, polite girls never say that kind of thing aloud. It is not in their upbringing' (6). A similar sentiment is offered at the conclusion when Michael Charles Christie Berkshire's mother goes up to his room and discovers the manuscript:

> She went to tidy the desk, and took a quick, incurious glance at the title of her son's latest little 'effort'. 'Oh, I don't think that's a very nice title, Michael,' she thought primly, crossly. And separating the one sheet from the rest, she tore up the title page of *A Pack of Lies* and dropped it into the wastepaper basket. (168)

Ailsa's mother is far more astute as she begins to suspect that MCC may be not what he seems, and that he possibly does and does not exist. It is left to readers to fill in the gaps that her words leave when she confronts MCC with her suspicions: 'It's just that you seem to know a lot more than is quite ... Look here, MCC. I don't know anything about you. I mean who are your people? Where's your family home? What's your *real* name?' (137, emphasis original). She cautions Ailsa repeatedly 'Just don't get too fond of him' (89). When MCC leaves the Poveys, Ailsa picks up the book that he has been reading and discovers that its title is *The Man who came from Reading*; the same title appears as chapter 1 of *A Pack of Lies*. She begins to read the words: 'He had on a green corduroy jacket worn bald in all the creases of elbow, armpit and round the button-holes [...] His white cricket flannels were colour-matched to his jacket by the long, oval grass stains on both knees' (162). This is the same description offered when MCC appears in the library at the beginning of the book (3). Ailsa comes to realise what her mother's words mean: 'If MCC doesn't exist, but we know his stories for true, there is only one explanation' (165). Michael Charles Christie Berkshire reassures himself in the final revelatory chapter that he made the right decision for his character to leave: 'I had to leave, though, didn't I? I couldn't stay forever' and explains that he had 'lost control' of his characters: 'You heard them: they were working it out! They got too real for me!' (167). His words resonate with Waugh's point that 'in fiction the description of an object brings that object into existence' (1984: 93), and by reverse logic, removing the 'object' means it no longer exists. Furthermore, the name 'MCC' is what Waugh would term an 'impossible name', an absurdity which flaunts the arbitrariness of naming characters altogether (93).

A metafictive clue offered early in the book is when Ailsa finds that the microfiche screen she is reading in the library has the following words, 'A Pack of Lies Oxford University Press 1988' but written 'upside down and inside out' (6). A further clue that this story is a fiction about a fiction can only be detected on rereading, after gaining knowledge of the deception. It appears when Mrs Povey first meets MCC and is undecided about whether or not she should take him on as an assistant in her shop, she is sympathetic to young people desperate to get work, and muses: '"He was so very *willing* ... Such a good-looking boy, too," she added vaguely' (8). Of course, this is a conceit that the implied author Michael Charles Christie Berkshire has included about himself, which is later exposed as a lie by McCaughrean's narrator who describes the 'real' MCC in this unflattering manner:

> He caught sight of himself in the mirror, his eyes shrunken to piggy little smudges by the grotesque thickness of the glasses. His sparse, mousy hair was stuck to his pallid head with the sweat of concentration. That drawn, sickly face in the mirror was like the glimpse of an

old enemy across the room at a party – someone he had spent years trying to avoid. (166)

The title *A Pack of Lies* is metafictionally self-reflexive. It also can be understood as signalling the disruptions of the multiple realities that the text constructs. The charge that the text is a pack of lies is a familiar one made of fiction – the text too involves itself in this debate with characters arguing whether the stories that MCC tells are lies or entertaining stories. When Mrs Povey accuses MCC of telling lies to her customers in order to sell them items, he responds indignantly, as the following interchange shows:

> '*Lies*, madam?'
> 'Well, er ... yes, actually ... Lies.'
> 'Not *lies*, madam,' he declared, magnificently unrepentant. '*Fiction*. That's the thing to give 'em. That's the thing everyone wants. *Fiction, madam!*' (24)

Ailsa too comes to understand the difference between telling stories and telling lies when she comes to this realisation about MCC: 'He didn't tell lies at all! His stories were all true, Mother!' (164). Ailsa's statement returns us to the question of the truth-status of fiction but more specifically for this chapter it also asks us to think about the truth of what is taken to be 'reality' within the ontological world of the text and how texts (and their characters) artfully deceive readers into believing their version of the truth.

Aesthetics and deception

> 'I seen a man so short he had to get up on a box to look over a grain of sand.' (Hurston 2005: unpaged)

In his book *On the Comic and Laughter*, Propp asks the question: 'Why, and under what conditions, can *a lie cause laughter?*' (2009: 88, emphasis original). Propp suggests that in answering this question we need to consider that there are two different types of comic deceit – when the liar presents a lie as truth; and when the liar does not mean to deceive but to amuse. The tall tale is characteristic of the second type as the epigraph above exemplifies. In both instances, the reason for the comic deceit rests with the 'conditions under which stupidity and lack of logic can create a comic effect' (Propp 2009: 88). As the preceding chapters have shown, not all deceits are comical. Some deceptions are quite literally deadly serious, as was the case in Naidoo's *The Other Side of Truth* (see Chapter 2) when Sade and Femi needed to lie in order to stay alive. I discussed in Chapter 6 how perpetual liars such as Micah (*Liar*) use excuses as a way of extenuating or removing blame for an action, usually of their own making. A similar kind of liar was evident in Chapter 7 in the character of Malcolm the Machiavellian toad (*Toad Heaven*) who persistently tells lies to achieve his own selfish goals. The following discussion considers tellers of tall tales and other liars, and how successful deception requires skill and manipulation. While some forms of deception may serve an ulterior purpose to mask an action from moral or instrumental considerations, others serve a different purpose.

Tall tales are a form of lying that depends on exaggeration and humour. They also necessitate some contextual knowledge. The readers (or listeners) are usually aware that what is being told is not the truth and therefore they do not suspend their disbelief but nevertheless become willing participants. Tall tales illustrate Wittgenstein's language games[6] in that the tales mobilise the imagination to challenge ontological worlds both inside and outside the text. Tall tales also use a particular range of language, style or discourse that is mostly ordinary, mimetic of everyday speech, rather than heightened poetic or literary language. Nevertheless, tall tales participate in linguistic game-playing through puns, hyperbole and analogy; these linguistic games enable deception to emerge as part of what Metcalf sees as 'the humor of extravagance and excess' (1990: 130). The excerpt that began this section is taken from *Lies and Other Tall Tales* collected by Zora Neale Hurston. It creates its humour of excess by drawing an implicit analogy between diminutive human size and a grain of sand. In print versions of tall tales, illustrations provide a further aesthetic dimension, giving visual representation to the extravagance or incongruity of the story. The illustration in Figure 8.1, from the short story 'Land of Contrasts' by Australian raconteur Ron Edwards, gives a literal interpretation of the narrator's words explaining that in Jindabyne (New South Wales)[7] it gets so cold that men's words can freeze as they speak and they have to be stored in an esky (ice box) and taken home to thaw out on the stove in order to hear what they have been talking about.

Tall tales are often a form of benign mendacity as they are generally harmless. In their expressive use of language, tall tales rely on oral storytelling techniques to embellish their claims or assertions of the truth. In her discussion of Pippi Longstocking books, Metcalf suggests

Figure 8.1 Illustration from *Lies, Flies and Strange Big Fish: Tales from the Bush* chosen by Bill Scott. Illustrated by Craig Smith

that the comic expressions of these tall tales can be attributed to Pippi's ability to perform and tell her story:

> This is especially true when she is carried away – as she frequently is – by an unrestrained abandonment of commonsense and by the pure delight of telling a story. Apropos to walking in a gutter full of water, Pippi contends that 'In America the gutters are so full of children, that there is no room for the water. They stay there the year around.' (Metcalf 1990: 131)

This example demonstrates how incongruity is stretched to the limits of any credibility. Pippi's disregard for adhering to the facts and her tendency to blur the lines between truth and lies are appealing features of her character. Whereas children may be punished for telling lies, Pippi 'merrily straddles the grey zones between fact and illusion, and goes unpunished' (Metcalf 1990: 132).

Children's early mastery of communicative discourse is evident in their social interactions and their use of rhetorical features, which are carried over into their games, where they learn how to bluff and deceive. From around the age of six, many children are not only aware that other people have different perspectives on the world but they also come to understand that others may be telling lies and thus 'gain sensitivity to the clues that give away deception' (Jay 2010: 43). This ability to grasp deception is vividly portrayed in Lauren Child's *I Will Not Ever Never Eat a Tomato* (2000). After devising a renaming game to entice his young sister Lola to eat vegetables – calling carrots 'orange twiglets from Jupiter', saying that green peas are 'green drops from Greenland' and potato mash is 'cloud fluff from the pointiest peak of Mount Fuji' – Charlie is surprised when Lola asks for a tomato (her most hated form of vegetable). When he questions her choice, Lola replies: '*moonsquirters* are my favourite'. By participating in his language game, Lola shows that she has reached linguistic maturity in her ability to use metaphor. The picture book also participates in the game of deception at another level through its collaged illustrations, which lend a veracity to the fantasy element of Charlie's subterfuge: for example, a green creature joins Lola in eating carrots ('orange twiglets from Jupiter'). The illustrations therefore are collusive in the semantic play at work in the text.

The picture book *Baloney (Henry P.)* by Jon Scieszka and Lane Smith (2001) participates in a language game which works at a different level of deception. The title signals to readers that this story is nonsense or at least that Henry P. is full of nonsense. However, as the ending reveals, neither is quite true. The story is typical of children's inventive excuses for not doing such things as their homework. In this case, Henry P. appears to be particularly adept in coming up with excuses for being late for school. When asked by his teacher why he is late for class, warning him that he will have 'Permanent lifelong Detention ... unless you have one very very good and very believable excuse', Henry P. is able to deliver on both counts. He tells a long story of mishap beginning when he misplaced his 'trusty zimulis' (which the illustration reveals is a pencil). But from then on one disaster follows another – whereby he finds his *zimulis* on his deski but someone then puts his *deski* on a *torakku*, that takes him away from *szkola* forcing him to abandon the *torakku* where he finds himself at a *razzo* launch pad and travels to a different planet where he encounters aliens who attack him with a *blazza*, and so on, until finally he arrives safely at *szkola*, but is seven minutes late. The story demonstrates that Henry P. is a gifted storyteller who is skilled at embellishing stories with imagination and inventive language. By the end of his account, the teacher informs him that the day's assignment is to compose a tall tale, something Henry P. is keen to do if only he can find his *zimulis*, which he seems to have misplaced.

The Afterword provides both a statement of authenticity and a lie. It asserts that 'this transmission was received directly from deep space' and after decoding the signals 'it became clear that this was a story about a lifeform similar to many Earthlings'. However, this purported authorial assertion is followed by another purported fact which is in fact true: 'Even more amazing was that the discovery that the story is written in a combination of many different Earth languages including Latvian, Swahili, Finnish, Esperanto, and Inuktitut. Who knows why.' This 'even more amazing' fact implies that truth is stranger than fiction suggesting the former statement is possibly stretching the truth. But the *real truth* that follows is one that is out of the hands of the 'Author' who apparently has no knowledge why these languages were included in the transmission ('Who knows why'), and by implication has no control over the content of the story.

The story that Henry P. tells may be a tall tale but the illustrations (and the Afterword) frame it as science fiction – Henry P. and his teacher are drawn as strange-looking, green aliens; the endpapers capture a sense of deep space with their black sky and multiple planets and stars; and Henry's unfolding story shows him travelling to different planets. The endmatter too lends support to the text's sci-fi status with

©2001

printed in large font above the publisher's details. While 2001 is the actual publication date of *Baloney (Henry P.)* it is also an intertextual reference to the science-fiction film *2001: A Space Odyssey*,[8] and is a fitting reference to reflect Henry P.'s reported intergalactic adventure. This blurring of genres is a subtle ploy to deflect readers' suspicion that the story could be a tall tale, which is effective only if readers recognise the aesthetic features of the text as being science fiction (or conversely as being a tall tale). The seemingly invented words may be understood as part of an alien language, which is true for all readers unless they are multilingual. But the illustrations, which work semiotically (as well as aesthetically) to assist readers in decoding Henry's strange words, also rely on readers' knowledge of pictorial codes.

Lie detection

Barnes's (1994) study of children and deception argues that children learn how to lie as part of the wider task of learning how to handle language with increasing skill and confidence. And learning to lie is part of the wider process of learning to deceive. Children learn a variety of deceptive techniques which become increasingly adapted to their audience. For example, they learn to simulate expression that they do not feel either in a natural manner or with exaggeration; they may learn to feign a 'poker face', to pretend to not know something when they do. In fiction, especially picture books with their visual cues, characters adopt similar deceptive strategies.

The Cow that Laid an Egg (2006) by Andy Cutbill and Russell Ayto plays a trick on readers by disrupting their expectations of the truth. Marjorie the cow is down in the dumps because she doesn't feel special – she can't do things the other cows can do like riding bicycles, and doing handstands. The reader knows that cows can't do these things so is an insider to the fact that this is not a true story. However, the chickens hatch a cunning plan to help Marjorie feel good about herself. They plant an egg under Marjorie so that when she wakes in the morning she believes she has laid an egg. An egg-laying cow is a big news item and it is not long before Marjorie becomes famous and feels very special. However, the other cows become jealous and suspicious and so challenge her to prove that she laid the egg. Poor Marjorie sits on the egg for days waiting for it to hatch. Finally, there is a *tap tap tap* sound and the egg cracks open and out pops a 'small brown feathery bundle'. Not only is this a surprise for the reader (and the cows) but the next page adds veracity to Marjorie's incubation when the baby opens its mouth wide and loudly cries: '**MOOOOOOOO!**' Marjorie pronounces her baby 'a cow' and promptly names it Daisy.

Naming the baby 'Daisy' exemplifies the performative and perlocutionary nature of language; however, it also exemplifies how downtrodden Marjorie is able to exercise a degree of linguistic agency, resignifying a chicken as a cow which in turn signifies a break between the natural order and the truth. These multiple functions in naming, in this specific instance in the text, combine to make the final grand deception. Whether we read this story as a tall tale or a fanciful one, the ending provides both in-text and extra-textual deception: the baby's cow-like cry and Marjorie's naming it Daisy constitute an effective response to the other cows' accusations that Marjorie is a fraud and a liar. Prior to this point, readers are encouraged to take a sympathetic view of Marjorie, one that aligns with the well-intentioned chickens who plant the egg. Within the ontological world of the text, the cows who read about Marjorie in the local newspaper 'Moos of the World' are unable to accept the reported 'truth' about Marjorie laying an egg, despite their own ability to ride bicycles and perform handstands. Extra-textually, of course, all these truth claims are false. But the story cleverly dispenses with common sense and truth, and highlights the arbitrary nature of language.

The picture book *Uncle David* by Libby Gleeson and Armin Greder (1992) is about the 'truth' that characters believe, or want their audience to believe, is the true 'reality'. *Uncle David* also draws on a familiar 'character' in fairy stories, that of the giant. However, this is not a fairy story. Rather, it offers at first reading what seems to be a child's perception of a very tall person. The illustrations reinforce the idea of a child's view of the world by using perspective in an artistic way to add veracity to the child's account of his Uncle David, who he announces from the beginning 'is a giant'. However, readers are positioned to view this statement as hyperbole given that Ned 'is the smallest in our group'. The use of the first-person plural pronoun in this observation suggests it is an insider, perhaps another child, who reveals this comparison. Ned gives several facts about Uncle David to support his claim:

'He puts me on his shoulders and I can touch the ceiling.'
'He can even lie on the floor in the dining room with one hand in the lounge room and one hand in the hallway.'
'Uncle David's boots are bigger than mine and Mum's and Dad's all piled on top of each other.'

These truth-claims are somewhat enhanced when the teacher is shown reading the story of 'Jack and the Beanstalk' to the children. The fairy story highlights for the children the possibility of giants, and when the children tell their parents about David's uncle, the illustrations of different giants support the children's stories – one holding a group of children in the palm of his hand, one with his hands on the ceiling, and a third lies with his head at the front door of a house and his feet out the back door. The parents decide to take action to dispel these untruths by taking the children to meet Uncle David. When they arrive at Uncle David's home, they find it is a gothic mansion, and when

Figure 8.2 Illustration from *Uncle David* by Libby Gleeson and Armin Greder

Ned leads them up the long, wide staircase a smiling gigantic Uncle David greets them at the door (Figure 8.2). The illustration positions readers at a low angle, which emphasises Uncle David's height and supports Ned's assertion that he is a giant.

The children investigate Uncle David's bedroom, kitchen and dining room and discover further proof that Ned is telling the truth. However, the next day, Jessie announces: 'My Aunty Meg is a witch.' This ending opens up the possibility that there is another truth to be discovered. While the ending is perhaps intended to show that children love to make up stories and will always try to outdo one other, it also acknowledges the fact that giants and witches are not simply characters in fairy tales.

Barnes notes that children, like adults, 'look for compatibility between what is said and how it is said when deciding whether a speaker is being sincere or is lying' (1994: 118). As these texts have shown, illustrations encourage readers to look for compatibility or incompatibility between what words say and what illustrations show, often in subtle ways. Illustrations assist young readers in detecting lies; and conversely, attempt to deceive them in accepting lies as the truth. Barnes's point highlights how a good liar needs to be a good performer, someone who, like Pippi Longstocking, can perform, as well as tell, a convincing lie.

The following discussion considers practised liars, or at least characters that are artful dodgers of the truth.

Artful dodgers

In naming this section 'artful dodgers' I'm participating in a performative utterance, or, perhaps more specifically, I'm making an interpellative call, which is similar to calling someone 'Liar'. The Introduction to this book began with the children's chant – 'Liar, liar, pants on fire.' In the picture book of the same name by Miriam Cohen (2008), young children detect that the new boy, Alex, is a liar as he repeatedly tells lies about things which the other children believe not to be true. Hence, in Althusserian terms, they 'hail' him by calling – 'Liar, liar, pants on fire!' According to Althusser (1971), in being hailed, the subject is thereby constituted in the act of naming. In *Excitable Speech*, Butler revises Althusser's notion of interpellation by considering it as a citation utterance that relies on context and convention in order to be effective (1997: 33). The rhyme 'Liar, Liar' did not originate with the children in Cohen's picture book, but like children in the real world, they cite the convention of this particular form of hailing. In the picture-book example, Alex does not refuse the name that he is called, but he nevertheless modifies his behaviour by becoming silent and withdrawn. The other children marginalise him until their teacher intervenes, offering an alternative view: 'Maybe Alex isn't really lying. Maybe he's just trying to get you to notice him. Try to be friends with Alex. Remember, it isn't easy to be new.'

The teacher's words are intended to show the children that their name-calling may be missing the mark in that Alex may not be a liar but lonely. In this instance, her authority helps to reinstate Alex into the kindergarten community. In another instance, also cited in the Introduction to this book, Hilaire Belloc's 'Matilda' (who told lies and was burned to death) was repeatedly subjected to interpellative calls of 'Little Liar!' with the result that her cries of 'Fire' were not met with a response of assistance. However, the passers-by in Belloc's story engage in a speech act, but do not take action: they do not try to put the fire out and save Matilda. As a cautionary tale, 'Matilda' issues a dire warning of the consequences of lying.

Similarities can be drawn between the story of Matilda and Aesop's fable 'The Boy who Cried Wolf', which carries the message that nobody will believe a liar even when they are telling the truth. A contemporary version of Aesop's story is the Australian picture book *The Cocky who*

Cried Dingo (2010) by Yvonne Morrison and Heath McKenzie. Cocky (cockatoo) is a mischief-maker who likes to 'play naughty tricks'. Every evening as the birds are settling into sleep, Cocky calls out with a shriek: '"Trouble!" he hollered. "Oh help me, by jingo! I'm trapped in the jaws of a big hairy dingo!"' After falling for his ruse a couple of times, the other birds ignore his call when a dingo really does attack him. However, Cocky does not meet the same fate as Matilda, as he manages to escape. His only loss is that his once proud yellow crest has been snipped short. In following the line of argument that Butler posits with respect to interpellation, Cocky refuses to be 'called' a liar, and while he repents and says that 'Never again will I tell such a lie' this does not stop him from inventing further deceptions to play out on the other birds, as the final illustration clearly reveals (Figure 8.3).

Inveterate liars like Cocky (and Matilda) serve a similar pedagogical function as those icons of the truth noted in the Introduction to this book. However, these lessons on moral integrity, while worthy, are also hypocritical as societies are built upon linguistic fabrication and domination, and upon the silencing of others whose stories, lies or truths might challenge accepted orthodoxies. This point has been demonstrated in other chapters that discuss political allegory and raise the question of ethics of deliberate fictiveness, mass deception and myth-making in governance 'for the good of the people'.[9] There is another view of the inveterate or pathological liar which the next text considers.

Figure 8.3   Illustration from *The Cocky who Cried Dingo* by Yvonne Morrison and Heath McKenzie

The overt message may be that a good story never hurt anyone, it may even make life appear more interesting than one where story, myth and fiction are banned – a Plato's Republic. However, as I consider in the following discussion of *Big Fish*, storytelling or 'lying' is construed as an art, a fabrication of ingenuity, but it nevertheless carries a weight of changing significance – indicative of the uneasy tension between a father who knows only the truth of story, and a son who has tired of story and wants only the truth.

The film *Big Fish* (2003), based on the novel by Daniel Wallace, begins with a voice-over that proudly asserts the story's artful deception and the inseparable relationship between truth and lies: 'This is a Southern story, full of lies and fabrication, but truer for their inclusion.' Emily Dickinson wrote, 'Tell all the Truth but tell it slant —',[10] and in *Big Fish* Edward enjoys telling stories *slant*. Edward is a storyteller, or an inveterate liar, depending on one's perspective. He enjoys being the centre of attention, and delights in retelling the story of the big fish, a story which Edward tells on the wedding night of his son Will. The story is of how a young Edward caught the elusive big catfish by using his gold wedding ring as a lure. The fish snatches the ring and snaps through the fishing line. Edward is determined to get his wedding ring back – 'the symbol of fidelity to my wife, soon to be the mother of my child'. After three days and nights he manages to catch the fish, retrieve his ring and then sets the fish free. He decided to let the big fish go because he realised that he and the fish 'were part of the same equation': both were about to become parents.[11]

The adult Will feels distant from his father and is annoyed by his inability to separate truth from fiction. Will explains in voice-over: 'In telling the story of my father's life, it's impossible to separate fact from fiction, the man from the myth. The best I can do is to tell it the way he told me.' In telling his father's birth story, Will describes how when his grandmother was in labour and about to push, suddenly the baby literally pops out and rockets at a great speed into the unprepared hands of the doctor. The baby is slippery like a fish and shoots out of the doctor's hands and causes chaos as nurses and doctors try to catch hold of the newborn, which appears with a giggling smile on its face as it speeds down the corridor of the hospital.

Big Fish focuses on the father–son relationship and Will's need to hear the truth from a father who is incapable of knowing what the truth is. However, as Will seeks answers to his questions, he needs to revisit the stories and the people in those stories that his father has told him since he was a boy. As Edward moves closer to death, Will tries to reason with him, explaining that he needs to know the truth about him as he will soon become a father himself and he doesn't want his child going through his whole life never understanding him, like he has with Edward. The following dialogue illustrates the different ways in which the two characters think about the truth:

[Will]:   'I have no idea who you are because you have never told me a single fact.'

[Edward]:   'I've told you a thousand facts. That's all I do, Will. I tell stories.'

[Will]:   'You tell lies Dad. You tell amusing lies.'

Will is after a truth that is scientific, verifiable. Edward sees truth in much the same way as literary theorists argue with respect to literature, that it offers a different kind of truth, one that may contain numerous facts, but mostly probabilities. Edward's stories are 'amusing lies', but they conform to fiction's ability to engage the emotions by providing its own internal logic, embellishments, and not having to worry itself with matters such as historical accuracy, or truth. The ancients going back to Plato pondered whether fictions were lies, inventions or entertainments, and whether poetry corrupted or improved one's outlook. One of the arguments Plato had against poetry was that it incites emotions, which cause people to think and act irrationally;[12] a position to which Will would probably subscribe. By contrast, Edward knows about the emotional pull of a good story, and uses this to full effect in all his encounters – both fictional and real. Will believes that truth about his father can only be known through rational, ordered thought, and that Edward's constant storytelling impedes his quest to gain this knowledge. The story positions its audience to see that Will's quest is not necessarily the most desirable one. Will's need for facts proves to be unsatisfying as the following interchange between Will and the doctor illustrates. The scene begins after Edward has been taken to hospital following a stroke:

[Will]:   'How would you describe him?'

[Dr Bennett]: (*reading the chart*) 'Five-eleven. One-eighty. Regulated hypertension.
              How would his son describe him?'

Dr Bennett asks Will if his father ever told him the story about the day he (Will) was born. When Will replies that he has heard the story of the uncatchable fish a thousand times, the doctor tells 'the real story': a prosaic tale which explains that it was a perfect delivery, but his father was unable to be present because he was away on business. After the story, the doctor asks: 'Not very exciting, is it? I suppose if I had to choose between the true version and an elaborate one involving a fish and a wedding ring, I might choose the fancy version. But that's just me.'

By the close of the film, Will has become the storyteller, telling his father a final story about how he dies back in the water morphing into the giant catfish that swims away. The film interleaves fantasy and realism with Will's story providing the excitement of a final adventure – leaving the hospital in a wheelchair, travelling to the lake, and slowly immersing a peaceful Edward into the water with all his friends (and story characters) standing on the shore to bid him a final farewell. The alternating scene-cuts between interior and exterior settings contrast the factual account of a father dying in a hospital bed with the imaginative story his son tells him.

Big Fish exemplifies what Krajewski (1992: 44) says about truth: 'truth might be relative, relative to ways of determining it, and contingent upon the circumstances of its appearance'. He says that one of the contingencies rhetoricians ponder concerns the question: 'What does the situation call for?' (44). *Big Fish* clearly shows that sometimes a situation might call for a story, full of lies and fabrication, or a truth told slant. This is the decision that Will comes to as his father dies. He casts away (perhaps temporarily) the frustration of living with a father who could not separate truth from fiction to give his father a final story of death and rebirth that both completes and perpetuates the mythic story cycle that Edward loves to tell. The following text, *A Beautiful Lie* by Irfan Master (2011), also entertains the same question – What does the situation call for? – and invites readers to consider what they would do in the same circumstance.

A Beautiful Lie is one of a number of films and novels in which a character tries to hide the harsh reality of a situation from another by using imagination and deception. A predecessor to this children's novel is the film *Life is Beautiful* (1997), directed by and starring Roberto Benigni. The film is a story of a Jewish Italian book keeper (Guido) who attempts to shield his young son (Giosuè) from the horrors of their internment in a Nazi concentration camp. Guido hides the truth of the situation from his four-year-old son by convincing him that the camp is a complicated game in which Giosuè must perform the task Guido gives him, earning him points. The goal is to reach a thousand points, which will earn the winning team a tank. Guido warns Giosuè that he will lose points in the following ways:

> Whoever's scared loses points.
> You'll lose your points for three things.
> One, if you cry.
> Two, if you want to see your mommy.
> Three, if you're hungry and you want a snack.

Guido is so convincing in this game of deception that young Giosuè is never suspicious and is an eager participant. Even until the end, Guido mocks a serious goose-stepping march as soldiers lead him to the gas chamber. His final task for Giosuè is to hide in the tank. Fortunately, this proves to be a safe refuge for the boy who is discovered in the tank when the American soldiers liberate the camp.

A Beautiful Lie is also a game of deception, but in this text it is the child who feels the need to conceal the truth from the father. Both texts use imagination to cover an unbearable truth, to make life bearable for a loved one by denying the unspeakable into existence. The unspeakable in *A Beautiful Lie* – the partition of India – is one that 13-year-old Bilal must ensure is never spoken to his dying father, Bapuji. Unlike the other texts in this chapter, *A Beautiful Lie* appraises readers of the need for Bilal's deception and while the narrative keeps some secrets by withholding information, the focus is more on how and why secrets are kept and revealed amongst the characters. Thus, readers come to appreciate (but not necessarily condone) the nature and extent of the characters' artful deception. The narrative has a straightforward plot (there are no metafictive elements) and the authorial perspective places readers in the position of sympathetic witness. However, the text also urges readers to consider whether the deception is justified. It does this by locating the narrative within a context of political turmoil.

The story takes place in Anaar Gully in northern India in 1947 prior to the Partition of India and the dissolution of the British Indian Empire and the end of the British Raj. The unrest that is occurring in other parts of India is also simmering in Bilal's market town. Doctorji informs Bapuji that his father has probably only one or two months to live and tells him: 'Now you must continue as normal. Keep him in good spirits by going about your usual routine' (Master 2011: 10). However, it is difficult to continue as normal at a time when his father and the India his father loves are coming to an end. Bapuji is an educated man who loves books, he has a wall of books in his small mud hut which acts as a partition, dividing the internal space between his room and his son's. There is an analogous relationship between the internal domestic partition and the external partition of India into two dominions. Although he is ill and confined to bed, Bapuji retains a keen interest in India's current state of affairs and asks Bilal of news of the discussions presumably over the Indian Independence Plan: 'What's the news today, son? Have those vultures come to a decision yet?' (16). His disgust with the idea of a partition is undisguised: 'Harpies, the lot of them. They just don't understand, do they? The soul of India can't be decided by a few men gathered around a map clucking like chickens about who deserves the largest pile of feed' (16). He speaks of 'Mother India' and connotes a united figure embracing her children regardless of their religious affiliations – Muslim, Hindu, Sikh. Like the line[13] which will divide India, Bilal also has to decide if he will cross another metaphorical line – the one that separates truth from deception.

Bilal makes a vow to hide the truth of what was to come for India so that his father 'would die thinking that India was as he remembered it and always will be' (19). The lie that Bilal decides to tell requires a master plan of deception, which he undertakes with the help of his friends Chota (who is Hindu), Manjeet (who is Sikh) and Saleem (who is Muslim like Bilal). The boys' pact resembles the united India of Bapuji's dreams. The boys work out a plan whereby they will intercept any visitor to Bapuji by keeping a close watch on the house during the day when they are supposed to be at school. As Chota 'was never in school anyway' (23) he is chosen as the look-out, stationing himself on a rooftop which gives him a clear view of the house. Whenever he sees someone approaching the house, he is to jump down from the roof and throw a pebble through the classroom window to alert the other boys.

Throughout the story readers are positioned to see the deception of Bilal and his friends from Bilal's perspective. His father's perspective remains limited and therefore readers are unable to assess the epistemic reliability of Bilal's motivations and beliefs. However, the narrative discloses the moral tension between revelation and concealment through Bilal's internal struggles over truth and lies. Although Bilal makes a vow to keep the truth from his father, he continues throughout the rest of his life to struggle with this burden of telling a lie. The tension between lies and truth is discernible when Bilal argues with his older brother Bhai, who angrily rejects Bilal's decision: 'But it's a lie, Bilal. You're lying to him. It's all a lie!' (191). The two brothers are also on different sides of an invisible line that the political situation creates. However, like the line that will soon divide India, the demarcation is not simple, as Bilal intimates in his retaliation to Bhai's objection to his lying: 'So it's a lie. But if we're talking about the truth – if *you're* the truth – then I prefer the lie' (192, emphasis original). Bilal's struggles with his deception come to a head when he visits another village with Doctorji. During this visit, Bilal continues the tradition that his father had begun by reading a story to the children of the village. On this occasion, Bilal becomes angry with himself and expresses to Doctorji his desire to be different, to not be a dreamer like his father, but a realist, someone who is guided by logic, not by ideas and emotion. Ironically, because of his similarity to his father he and Doctorji are able to escape after the village men imprison them, believing they are spies. Their saviour is a young girl to whom Bilal had loaned his father's book of stories. Before they leave, Bilal tells the girl, 'pretend this never happened' (154), once again realising that deception is often necessary for survival.

The intertwined relationship between artful deception and politics is played out in the text, and in both instances survival is contingent upon deception and lies. Balil deceives his father and others through his invented stories and lies. He tells his father lies to protect him from knowing the reality of the current situation in India and its political future, and tells lies to prevent friends from visiting his father and revealing the truth about India. His father's books and stories over the years have trained Bilal in the knowledge that India needs its storytellers – despite their potential for subversion. As a self-appointed storyteller, Bilal is simultaneously vulnerable and powerful. He risks his relationship with his brother and others, yet has the power of censorship and invention. Bilal is tied up with the politics of his country whether he intends to or not, and by his own narrating of events through a mock newspaper he writes for his father, he shapes the perpetuation of an imagined India. However, he is aware of the ambiguity of self: as loyal son and artful dodger of the truth.

In the last moments of his father's life there is a renewed urgency to the dilemma with which Bilal struggles: *'Tell him. Tell him now before it's too late.* All the webs I had spun in my mind were unraveling. Each knot was coming undone. *Tell him! Tell him! [...] I'm a liar!*' (273, emphasis original). But on the stroke of midnight the cheering sounds of an independent India are heard in their room. Bilal cries 'India is free' – acknowledging to himself that *'This is forever my burden. Forever.'*

Bapuji whispers his final words to his son, 'You are my India' (274, emphasis original). The significance of his father's final words is not immediately apparent to Bilal. However, readers may detect a clue that Bapuji's words allude to something outside of his hopes for India's future.

Revelation comes retrospectively through the epilogue. In closing the story, the future and past come together, providing a perspective on the burden of deception and the liberating power of the truth. Bilal returns to his village 60 years later as a Chief Justice, a man who has spent his career as – *'A defender of the truth'* (283, emphasis original). On his return Bilal feels compelled to confess to everyone about the lie he has carried with him for many years. After the crowd disperses, a young man remains and hands Bilal a letter which his grandfather Doctorji had saved for many years. The letter addressed to Bilal from his father was written on 14 August 1947 – the day when the Islamic Republic of Pakistan was born at the stroke of midnight, and the day before the official announcement of India's independence from British colonial rule. The letter explains that Doctorji had told Bapuji about his son's deception to which Bapuji says *'when I found out, I cried, not in misery but in joy of knowing I had a son like you'* (288, emphasis original). While Bapuji may not have condoned Bilal's deception, he was able to appreciate why his son took on such a burden. In the closing scene, Bilal hands Doctorji's grandson the crumpled sheet of paper that contains the story of his lie, saying: 'It no longer belongs to me' (289). This gesture suggests that he has finally been set free by the truth. While this scene implicitly carries religious overtones of confession and absolution, the handing over of the written story to Doctorji's grandson is also a reminder of the 'sins' of the past and the psychological weight of lies.

A character being set free by the truth is a familiar closing message in many children's books. Others, however, such as *Big Fish* and *The Cow that Laid an Egg* speak of the liberating potential of storytelling, of artful deception. As this final section of this book has shown, deception is not an aberration of the human condition, but an essential element of both human and animal behaviour. In exploring the deception that characters have undertaken, the texts show how the aesthetic treatment of deception can cause us laughter by seeing how life is full of incongruity and moral paradoxes, and how texts engage in playful linguistic games, perhaps lead readers by the nose. Texts also teach readers how to detect deception, and to view the world slant by replacing common sense with nonsense. They also assist readers to discover allusion, to detect unreliability, to challenge notions of authority by questioning the status of untrustworthy 'authors' who claim to be telling the truth, to give credence to a child's perspective in the face of sensible adult knowledge of the world, and to see that deception does not always come from a dark place of evil, but can emerge from a desire to protect another from harm. However, it must also be noted that even when the motive to deceive is altruistic, there is always the question: what gives someone the right to decide what another will or will not know?

Conclusion

In discussing secrets, lies and children's fiction, there have been several recurring elements which support my argument that survival often underlies the reason for secrecy and deception. While telling lies is arguably part of enculturation that children learn from a young age, throughout this book I have tried to show that to dismiss or condone lying and deception as 'natural' or to condemn all lying as morally reprehensible simplifies and obscures other factors which account for why we often choose to lie or deceive rather than tell the truth. In choosing between truth or lies, disclosure or concealment, characters in the texts I have discussed variously find themselves in situations which call for them to act in a certain way either by adapting their behaviour, transforming themselves, or becoming compliant or resistant. When choosing to become an active subject with the power to resist domination, characters are often faced with moral dilemmas that may test their ability to remain a moral subject.

For some, Truth is solid and knowable. For others, truth is as slippery as Edward's big fish, and just as difficult to grasp. No doubt every reader of this book could give a description of what truth is, but as many of the texts I have discussed show, truth is not always knowable, describable or, in some cases, desirable. We could argue that there is not one truth, but multiple truths, and that truth is a guide to moral conduct. Those who do not tell the truth are labelled liars, deceivers, artful dodgers or storytellers, and we are wary of ever believing them even when they cry out the truth – 'Wolf!', 'Fire!', 'Dingo!'

We call liars names, we warn them of the dire consequences that await them and we shun their company. Other liars we tolerate, perhaps even seek out, because their stories are amusing lies: they take us into impossible worlds where we put aside any concern for the truth or a search for certitude. We dismiss literal adherence to the facts as boring, and welcome the imaginative and the playful. Liars, it would seem, carry a stacked deck; they are the mavericks of wily words, allusive and elusive in their rhetoric, and cunning in how they play their cards – using bluff, banter and distraction to win the game. The language games that literature plays show how linguistic structures and symbols shape a perception of the world in a particular way. These texts show how using exclusionary negative metaphors to name others can result in marginalisation, scapegoating and discrimination. Conversely, by re-signifying or using positive language, metaphors and symbols, literature can encourage compassion and inclusion. There is another kind of liar that we have encountered in this book, and that is the liar who needs to protect either self or other. In these instances, the truth could harm; it could be dangerous or lethal to speak. In circumstances of oppression, unspeakable trauma or a dying loved one, truth is swept under the cover of deception. However, truth refuses to be silent, nagging consciences to set it free. And then there are secrets.

Secrets fall between truth and lies, occupying a kind of limbo. In keeping a secret, one may find comfort in knowing that this fact, emotion or desire is private. In sharing and receiving a secret, a different kind of feeling and responsibility is experienced. In disclosing a secret, there are consequences – a loss of trust, or a sense of relief. In not speaking some secrets, we may worry that we are not telling the truth and that silence is a form of deception. This charge is one that has been levelled at fiction – a pack of lies! But as this book has argued, the case that fiction is lies is lost on the grounds that fiction by its very nature does not purport to tell 'the truth'. Fiction may contain facts, truths and lies, but these are woven into the fabric of story. Story is something we want to hear, and we continue to tell, read and write stories because, like Kipling's elephant, we have an insatiable curiosity. This same curiosity feeds our desire to know secrets, to find the truth, to use deception, cunning and whatever other means we can muster to reveal a lie, to save our lives, to shield a loved one, to entertain a willing audience and to be liked.

Children's literature invites readers, both young and old, to understand that life is full of paradoxes and predicaments, that people are not simply good or bad, that darkness and light are necessary partners in life. Texts draw readers in with their magic, which has been honed by a crafting of words and illustration: a magic which withholds secrets, yet entices readers to discover them, to track clues and solve the puzzles of its fictional gameplaying. By sharing stories of lies, deception and secrets, fiction introduces children to diverse ways of being in a pluralistic world, or a world that feigns pluralism but may in fact be rigid, rule-bound and singular in outlook. Fiction teaches its readers to consider how difficult situations can be managed, the consequences of poor choices, the rewards or penalties that come with actions that may be variously moral or immoral, how comic deceit may break down boundaries and the fact that not all adults have children's best interests at heart.

Children's literature introduces readers to the grey zones of life – where matters are not black or white, but a mixture of both, and a mix that is continually changing as contexts and situations change. Often fiction uses allegory to tell of a situation or a context in which what needs to be said cannot be said directly for some reason. Allegory is indirect, like Emily Dickinson's truth told 'slant'. Other literary devices – metaphor, simile and allusion – are also helpful in presenting the truth in a different way. When the truth cannot be told directly, allegory provides the 'veil of words', the veil that mediates the truth. As chapters in this book have shown, lifting a veil does not necessarily reveal the truth. Rather, the veil serves to draw our attention to its surface, to consider what it conceals.

The world that children inhabit with adults is always changing, and this has always been so. Uncertainty is a necessary condition of life, and secrets, lies and truth are an indispensable part of life. We may seek truths, and there are those truths that require agreement in order for the world to function. But as the ethicist Margaret Somerville argues, these are '"temporal truths" – always open to challenge, of course, and to change' (2006: 82). Somerville takes a pragmatic view of truth, suggesting that there can be 'equally valid but different versions of the truth about something, rather than one person or body having the full and exclusive truth and others having no access to it' (83). This view aligns with many of the texts discussed in this book where certain groups, individuals, governments and secret societies consider that they have 'a full and exclusive truth'. Texts shine a light on the different versions of the truth that exist, illuminating conflicts, resolutions and dominant beliefs. Fiction also reveals secrets and lies and in doing so opens up worlds for readers to explore, at least temporarily.

Notes

Introduction: The Burden of Truth

1. This poem is attributed to William Blake (1810) but I have not been able to verify this.
2. See, for example, Stephens (1992).
3. For example, in Homer, Odysseus encounters Calypso ('the veiled one') who detains the Greek hero on her island for a number of years.
4. Another account says that Phryne removed her own garments.
5. I thank Rod McGillis for this insight.

1 Unveiling the Truth

1. Some of the Arabic terms for veil include: kimar, niqab, burqa. For an extensive list of descriptions see El Guindi (1999: 6–9).
2. While this chapter's focus is on the veil and femininity, El Guindi notes that men in Arab society also veil. For a detailed discussion of the veil and masculinity in Arab society see El Guindi (1999: ch. 7).
3. On her official website, Randa Abdel-Fattah explains that she has used her writing as a medium for expressing her views on the occupation of Palestine, Australian Muslims and the misunderstood status of women in Islam. *Does My Head Look Big in This?* was an attempt to invite readers into the world of average Australian Muslim teenage girls to see beyond the stereotypes and to show that a Muslim girl experiences 'the same dramas and challenges of adolescence as her non-Muslim peers', www.randaabdelfattah.com/faqs. asp, accessed 25 January 2012.
4. See Foucault (2000). Foucault later changed the phrase 'regimes of truth' to 'games of truth'.
5. The film *Persepolis* (2007) was based on the books by Marjane Satrapi, who also wrote and co-directed the film. Although the film won several international awards and nominations, it also met with opposition. When Nabil Karoui, director of Nessma TV, screened the animated film, the broadcast led to protests in Tunisia because it contained a scene depicting God, which some consider to be forbidden by Islam (see www.iewy. com/40569-tunisia-persepolis-trial-a-setback-for-free-expression.html, accessed 25 January 2012). On 3 May 2012, a Tunis court found Karoui guilty of 'spreading information which can disturb public order' (see www. amnesty.org/en/news/tunisia-persepolis-trial-verdict-signals-erosion-free-speech-2012-05-03, accessed 27 December 2012).
6. *Ralph* was a former monthly Australian men's magazine which published photographs of scantily clad female models and celebrities.
7. See Foucault (1997).

8. Another picture book, *The Pesky Rat* (Child 2002), is a story with a similar theme; in this case, a rat wants to be a pet with a name. For a discussion of this picture book see Allan (2012: 77–8).
9. A similar kind of civilising strategy was employed by colonial settlers and missionaries to make over naked indigenous bodies in an image of (colonial) self-perpetuation. Jenkins (2003) takes up this discussion of nudity in South African children's books.
10. The American edition of *When You Reach Me* (2009) published by Yearling (Random House) does not have the dotted lines along the street map.
11. A 'wrinkle in time' refers to how the children in L'Engle's book are able to travel through time by means of a tesseract, a fifth-dimensional phenomenon explained as being similar to folding the fabric of space and time.

2 Lies of Necessity

1. See Kant (1949: 346–50) 'On a supposed right to lie from altruistic motives' for a full discussion of his position.
2. Afghan girls continue to be discriminated against in terms of education and for many it remains a fraught and dangerous endeavour. In June 2012, 400 girls from six girls' schools in the Takhar province were poisoned after drinking from a school well that had been deliberately contaminated. Other attacks include burning down of buildings or throwing acid in girls' faces (*Sydney Morning Herald*, 9–10 June 2012, World 17). A more recent attack (October 2012) was made on 15-year-old Malala Yousafzai, an outspoken defender of Afghan girls' right to an education, who was shot by Taliban gunmen (and two other girls were also wounded) while travelling on a bus.
3. According to the Qur'an, pomegranates grow in the gardens of paradise.
4. This text differs from other graphic novels in that it does not present its images as a series of panels but utilises 'hyperframes' (Groensteen 2007: 30) of entire pages, often presenting each full-page hyperframe in a series of incremental temporal moves across a slowly changing or static space. These hyperframes highlight the movement of characters and serve as points of focalisation. The effectiveness of these focalising strategies is that the backgrounds (streets or interiors of buildings) are neutral, allowing the subjective experience of the character/s to be perceived by readers. Key pivotal events in the narrative that are viewed as a number of sequences are: Part 1, *Chapter 1: The Thief* introduces the *mise-en-scène* – Paris and the train station, and the main character, Hugo, who moves through the station's open and hidden spaces, climbing through a grate to reach secret corridors and a spying place behind the giant clocks; *Chapter 9: The Key* is one of a number of chase scenes. In this one Isabelle chases after Hugo through the busy train station and collides with a commuter, revealing the special key that is needed for the automaton on the chain around her neck. *Chapter 12: The Message* is the point when the automaton is restored to working order and draws the iconic image – of the man in the moon with a rocket in his eye – from Méliès's famous film. Part 2, *Chapter 9: The Ghost in the Station* is an extended sequence that shows Hugo being pursued through the station – its secret and public spaces – by the Station Inspector before he falls and is taken by the Inspector and placed in a metal cell in the Inspector's office.

5. The puzzle behind the name is revealed by Selznick to have a more prosaic origin: 'I remembered a toy I loved as a kid called "Hugo, the Man of a Thousand Faces," and I thought the name Hugo sounded kind of French. The only other French word I could think of was *cabaret*, and I thought that *Cabret* might sound like a real French name. *Voilà* ... Hugo Cabret was born' (2011: 13). However, Selznick's evolution of Cabret from cabaret does not discount McGillis's linguistic moves through Prof. Alcofrisbas to Alcofrisbas Nasier to Rabelais to carnival as Selznick's invention of the character Alcofrisbas draws on a similar character devised by Méliès. Whether or not Selznick makes the association between the anagram and Rabelais and carnival is not revealed in his commentary in the book, the cover blurb for which claims is 'for fans of all ages'. Nevertheless, this example of an authorial explanation of the genesis of key names points to how a text is never finished but always in process as new sources of knowledge and understanding will continue to emerge.

6. Bankruptcy and a gradual disaffection of the public for his films caused the real Méliès to become disillusioned. He burned the costumes and sets he had used in his films, and was eventually forced to sell many of his films to a company that melted the stock and turned them into celluloid heels for shoes: a cruel irony for a man who fled his parents' shoemaking industry to pursue a more creative life through filmmaking.

7. Selznick says that he first saw *A Trip to the Moon* when he was a young boy. The film prompted him to want to write 'a story about a kid who meets Méliès', but it wasn't until years later when he discovered a book about the history of automata, *Edison's Eve* by Gaby Wood, that the story began to take shape (2011: 12).

8. Some facts are: René Clair was the director of the film *The Million* (Selznick 2007: 202), and Isabelle's comment that Harold Lloyd starred in *Safety Last* is true (173).

9. In the film, an uncanny resemblance is achieved with make-up in transforming the actor Ben Kingsley into Méliès.

10. The skilful movement from pages of text to series of charcoal illustrations achieves a similar storytelling quality and momentum as the silent black-and-white movies that the story is about. The dual semiotic paths of the book lead readers on a linear trajectory towards closure with what appear as intermezzo pages that take time out for readers to pause over the early sketches for Méliès's film sets and scenes (Selznick 2007: 284–97) and stills from his early films (498–505). These primary visual sources (and there are others throughout the book) create a different visual modality from the charcoal illustrations, extending the semiotic duality of the text.

11. By the early twentieth century, a time when Georges Méliès produced his successful films, especially *A Trip to the Moon* (*Le Voyage dans la Lune*, 1902), automata had become antique collectibles. An automaton, like the one that is described in *The Invention of Hugo Cabret*, was built c. 1800 and could draw four different drawings and write three poems. When it was restored, the identity of its maker was finally revealed when it signed his name: 'Henri Maillardet'. In Selznick's book the name appears as Georges Méliès. Selznick acknowledges that when he visited the Franklin Institute in Philadelphia he was shown the workings of this nineteenth-century automaton which

the museum received in 1928 after it was damaged by fire (Selznick 2007: 528). Similar circumstances are incorporated into Selznick's fictional text (see 127–30).

12. These questions are similar to what Derrida says readers constantly demand of fiction to supply, but which it will reveal and conceal depending on the reader's own interpretive ability.

13. This is most likely referring to the 1925 film version. (Selznick's story is set in 1931.)

14. Georges Méliès was highly regarded as an exponent of early forms of phantasmagoria in his stop trick films, which included the frequent appearance of ghosts, rear projections and 'the substitution trick, which made it possible for things to appear and disappear on screen, as if by magic' (Selznick 2007: 355). The silent, experimental, black-and-white films that Méliès made have faded into the memory of film history; the stop tricks replaced by more sophisticated computer imaging technologies.

15. McGillis's point has a parallel in Samuel Beckett's *Endgame* which uses 'Winding up' towards the end of the play when Hamm observes Clov holding an alarm clock and asks, 'What are you doing?' Clov's response, 'Winding up' (1958: 72). This response is ambiguous in a similar way to Selznick's text as it could mean he is starting or finishing, beginning, or beginning to end. 'Winding up' could also be seen in Beckett's context as a game in which the two characters engage throughout the play – winding up each other.

3   The Scapegoat

1. The origin of the scapegoat comes from Leviticus 16, where the process is prescribed by law. The story is that Aaron is told to lay both his hands upon the head of a live goat and confess all the sins, transgressions and so forth of the people of Israel and put them upon the head of the goat and to send the goat away into the wilderness. The goat bears all their sins and is exiled to live in a solitary land.

2. The Dreyfus Affair has been the subject of films and books, including an early series of short films by Georges Méliès (*L'Affaire Dreyfus*, 1899). Méliès is the subject of *The Invention of Hugo Cabret* (see Chapter 2). At the time of writing, Roman Polanski is to direct a political thriller about the Dreyfus Affair entitled 'D'. Polanski notes: 'I have long wanted to make a film about the Dreyfus Affair, treating it not as a costume drama but as a spy story. In this way one can show its absolute relevance to what is happening in today's world – the age-old spectacle of the witch-hunt of a minority group, security paranoia, secret military tribunals, out-of-control intelligence agencies, governmental cover-ups and a rabid press' (http://latimesblogs.latimes.com/movies/2012/05/roman-polanski-dreyfus-affair-robert-harris-new-film.html, accessed 30 December 2012).

3. For a detailed discussion of Girard's discussion of sources of scapegoating, refer to Fleming (2004: ch. 2).

4. For additional discussion of *Dancing the Boom Cha Cha Boogie* see Bradford and Huang (2007) and Dudek (2006).

5. The CIA initially funded Louis de Rochemont who in turn hired Halas & Batchelor, an animation firm in London that had made propaganda films for the British government. For a detailed account of the CIA's involvement and their association with Louis de Rochemont see Leab (2007).
6. For the source of the quotation see www.lrb.co.uk/v29/n13/j-hoberman/short-cuts, accessed 2 January 2013. Also, refer to Leab (2007) for full details of the CIA's involvement in the film.

4 Secrets of State

1. Disinformation is a neologism to stand for the spreading of false information to hurt adversaries. Disinformation is often employed by the media and governments to try to influence public opinion against opposition parties or individuals on both the domestic and international fronts.
2. These questions were discussed in Chapter 1.
3. The same scenario can be offered for some secular state religions or quasi-religious groups which draw on secrecy, ritual and hierarchy to maintain the 'aura of sacredness' (Bok 1989: 172).
4. In his article for *Vanity Fair*, James Wolcott draws the comparison between mass entertainment and politics: 'The old punditocracy, grounded in facts, credentials, and rationale debate, has been overpowered by a new breed of political entertainer, who deals in raw emotion [...] they aren't trying to change the way people think [...] they don't want their audiences to think at all', www.vanityfair.com/politics/features/2011/02/wolcott-201102, accessed 16 March 2012.
5. 'Tribute' is another Roman reference. Various ancient states gave a tribute (or contribution) often 'in kind' as a sign of respect, submission or allegiance.
6. While my discussion focuses on the first book in the trilogy, Vivienne Muller writes of the three books and makes the following observation regarding the ways the texts, with their collapsing of the virtual and the real, could be seen as inviting readers 'to treat the virtual and the real as equivalents and to forgo our capacity to make moral distinctions about the truth or significance of what we see' (2012: 61).
7. 'Ethics of care' is a term used by Noddings (1984).
8. For example, *The White Mountains* by John Christopher (1967), and Robert Cormier's *I Am the Cheese* (1977).
9. Gadzheva (2008: 63) notes that face-recognition surveillance was used at the NFL Super Bowl in 2001 and at the Fédération Internationale de Football Association (FIFA) World Cup in Germany in 2006. The latter served to combat black-market sales and ticket forgeries.
10. Gadzheva explains that the term 'ambient intelligence' is adopted by the European Commission Information Society Technologies Advisory Group, whereas the United States uses 'ubiquitous computing', and Japan adopts the term 'ubiquitous network society'. She notes that ubiquitous computing, or ambient intelligent space, is the third wave of the information technology revolution of the twenty-first century (2008: 61).
11. This alternative meaning is significant in *The Other Side of Truth* (see Chapter 2) and *Web of Lies* (see Chapter 3) by Beverley Naidoo.

12. Treasure Island is an artificial island in San Francisco Bay. Robert Louis Stevenson lived in San Francisco for a short time in the late nineteenth century and the island was named after his book. There is an interesting connection in that the island is used as a covert detention centre in *Little Brother* and has been used as a stage location for films about computing hacking and rebellion such as *The Matrix* and *The Caine Mutiny*.
13. Extraordinary rendition is a practice which was accelerated during the presidency of George W. Bush. President Obama suspended extraordinary rendition in 2009, but the practice was subsequently resumed.
14. Waterboarding is a form of torture that has been used since World War II. The account of waterboarding that Marcus suffers in *Little Brother* accords with other reports of this technique.
15. 'In cryptography, a public key is a value provided by some designated authority as an encryption key that, combined with a private key derived from the public key, can be used to effectively encrypt messages and digital signatures. The use of combined public and private keys is known as *asymmetric* cryptography. A system for using public keys is called a public key infrastructure (PKI).' Source: http://searchsecurity.techtarget.com/definition/public-key, accessed 5 April 2012.
16. John Carroll argues that Joseph Conrad's *Heart of Darkness*, written in 1899, speaks to many of the issues which led the way to the 9/11 events. This is a story that Carroll contends has been retold in various fictions – *The Waste Land*, *The Third Man*, *Apocalypse Now*, *Blade Runner* and most particularly in the film *Fight Club* 'which ends with American skyscrapers being blown up, the modern metropolis disintegrating in terror' (2002: 33).
17. A comparison can be made with the totalitarianism in *Animal Farm* (see Chapter 3).

5 Secret Societies

1. Recent examples include the Moonshadow Ninja series by Simon Higgins, and Tom Dolby's Secret Society series, currently *Secret Society* (2009) and its sequel *Trust* (2011). Moonshadow has been trained by a secret brotherhood, the elite Grey Light order, to fight against fanatical warlords who are bent on bringing Japan into chaos. Current titles include: *Eye of the Beast* (2008), *The Work of Silver Wolf* (2009) and *The Twilight War* (2011). Dolby's *Secret Society* concerns the secret society in an elite New York school. The HarperTeen website includes a fast-paced video promotion of Dolby's *Secret Society* with the ominous warning that 'secret society: once you get in you can never get out', www.harperteen.com/contests/secretsociety/. The site also has a quiz 'Take the Crux Ansata Quiz', which invites participants to see if they can find the answers to 'the nagging (and dangerous) questions' with which the books' characters Nick, Phoebe, Lauren and Patch struggle. There is also an opportunity to enter 'the Secret Society sweepstakes' to win a free signed copy of the book by the author and an exclusive ankh tattoo, and 'learn what it's like to gain endless privileges at the expense of personal freedom. Get Initiated!'

2. In Australian Aboriginal cultures 'secrecy' is often separated into two dominant groups based on gender: 'men's secret business' and 'women's secret business'. 'Secret' or 'secret sacred' is used to designate either men's or women's religious knowledge, objects, and activities that are not shared with the rest of their society. Clare Bradford notes that many stories are 'sacred texts, some of which may be told to general audiences while others are restricted to initiated people, along lines determined by kinship and association with particular tracts of country. Some secret/sacred stories are also subject to rules concerning gender, so that they can be performed and heard only within a gathering of men or of women' (2003: 203).

3. Polgyny is a common marriage arrangement in some parts of the world. However, it is illegal in the United States and many other Western countries. The practice in Unity of assigning young girls with older men is similar to the members of the Fundamentalist Church of Jesus Christ of Latter-Day Saints. Currently, breakaway Mormon fundamentalist communities exist in parts of western United States, Canada and Mexico. Polygamists are difficult to prosecute, because, as in Unity, marriages are conducted secretly in the communities, and couples do not seek an official marriage licence.

4. In 2013 an 'online hacktivist group' Anonymous recovered and posted a video of male students talking about a rape of a drunken 16-year-old girl at a party in Steubenville, Ohio. At the time of writing two male students await trial on the alleged rape. The intervention by Anonymous is similar to The Mockingbirds but in this real-life instance the posts went viral through social media and brought the incident to the attention of a global community.

5. Jamila Gavin's book is also published under the title *See No Evil* by Farrar, Straus and Giroux (2009).

6. The book's attribution of Eastern European names (Vlad) to the Robber Baron and a woman of Bulgarian descent (Miss Kovachev) could be seen as drawing on stereotype. However, there is a recorded trend of 'Russian mafia groups trafficking women from the former Soviet states' (Tailby 2001: 5).

7. People trafficking has been defined in a second Protocol to the United Nations Convention, namely the Protocol to Prevent, Suppress and Punish Trafficking in Persons, Especially Women and Children (the Trafficking Protocol), as: 'The recruitment, transportation, transfer, harbouring or receipt of persons, by means of the threat or use of force or other forms of coercion, of abduction, of fraud, of deception, of the abuse of power or of a position of vulnerability or of the giving or receiving of payments or benefits to achieve the consent of a person having control over another person, for the purpose of exploitation. Exploitation shall include, at a minimum, the exploitation of the prostitution of others or other forms of sexual exploitation, forced labour or services, slavery or practices similar to slavery, servitude or the removal of organs' (Article 3).

8. These quotations refer to the following lines from *Hamlet*:

> The time is out of joint. O cursed spite,
> That ever I was born to set it right.
> (Shakespeare 1982: I.v.196–7)

6 Our Secret Selves

1. See McMahon-Coleman and Weaver (2012: 120–2) for a description of the pain of transformation that shapeshifting characters endure in other texts.

7 Mendacious Animals

1. This proverbial saying comes from Sir Walter Scott's *Marmion* (1808) Canto VI, Stanza 17:

> 'Yet Clare's sharp questions must I shun;
> Must separate Constance from the nun –
> O, what a tangled web we weave,
> When first we practise to deceive!
> A Palmer too! No wonder why
> I felt rebuked beneath his eye'

2. For a full discussion of the historical and philosophical perspectives on non-human deception see Mitchell and Thompson (1986).
3. Galahs are pink- and grey-coloured parrots. When flocks of galahs gather they are noisy, with the birds' constant calling. Hence the term 'galah session' when people talk or gossip for a long time.
4. 'Batesian mimicry is named after Henry Walter Bates, a British scientist who studied mimicry in Amazonian butterflies during the mid-to-late nineteenth century. Batesian mimicry refers to two or more species that are similar in appearance, but only one of which is armed with spines, stingers, or toxic chemistry, while its apparent double lacks these traits. The second species has no defense other than resembling the unpalatable species and is afforded protection from certain predators by its resemblance to the unpalatable species, which the predator associates with a certain appearance and a bad experience.' Source: 'The Arts of Deception: Mimicry and Camouflage' by Rhett Butler, http://rainforests.mongabay.com/0306.htm, accessed 11 August 2012. See also an account of Bates and his research on deceptive imitation in Darwin (1936: 666).
5. Cane toads are large heavily built amphibians with dry warty skin. The natural range of cane toads extends from the southern United States to tropical South America. They were deliberately introduced from Hawaii to Australia in 1935, to control scarab beetles that were pests of sugar cane. The cane toad is tough and adaptable as well as being poisonous throughout its life cycle. Cane toads are considered a pest in Australia because they: poison pets and injure humans with their toxins; poison many native animals whose diet includes frogs, tadpoles and frogs' eggs; eat large numbers of honey bees, creating a management problem for bee-keepers; prey on native fauna; compete for food with vertebrate insectivores such as small skinks; and may carry diseases that can be transmitted to native frogs and fishes. Source: Australian Museum: http://australianmuseum.net.au/Cane-Toad.
6. At the time of writing there are four books in the series: *Toad Rage*, *Toad Away*, *Toad Surprise* and *Toad Heaven*.

7. Jay offers the example of the deer who alerts the herd to the presence of a wolf rather than running away to save its own life (2010: 24).

8 Artful Deception

1. The 'symphony of smells' is a borrowed phrase from James Joyce's novelistic fragment entitled 'Giacomo Joyce'. For an interesting account of how Joyce uses this phrase in his text see Delville (1998: 24–38).
2. For example, in Rowling's *Harry Potter*, Hagrid's pet, the three-headed dog named Fluffy, is an undisclosed allusion to Cerberus, the three-headed beast who guards Hades in Greek mythology. However, the narrator playfully notes that Fluffy was purchased from a 'Greek chappie'.
3. Frank Kermode (1979: 110) remarks that in *Ulysses* Joyce notes the mystery of the Man in the Macintosh when the character Bloom asks 'Where the deuce did he pop out of?' Kermode uses this citation to explain the puzzlement that readers experience when they try to solve or understand a textual inconsistency or irrelevance.
4. Despite the author's insistence that this is a nothing chapter, it could nevertheless be a reference to another book entitled *Chapter Zero* by Carol Schumacher: a mathematics book, which invites readers to write their own proofs. Schumacher offers 'proof sketches' and helpful technique tips to help readers develop their proof-writing skills. The author of *The Name of this Book is Secret* uses a similar technique.
5. For additional discussions of *A Pack of Lies* see Nelson (2006) and Jones (1999).
6. For an accessible discussion of language games see chapter 3 in *Wittgenstein: Key Concepts* (2010) edited by Kelly Dean Jolley.
7. Jindabyne is a town in south-east New South Wales (Australia) near the Snowy Mountains.
8. *2001: A Space Odyssey* (1968) was a popular film produced and directed by Stanley Kubrick. The screenplay was co-written by Kubrick and sci-fi writer Arthur C. Clarke.
9. See Chapter 3 'The Scapegoat' and Chapter 4 'Secrets of State'.
10. The full poem (1129) by Emily Dickinson (https://en.wikisource.org/wiki/Tell_all_the_Truth_but_tell_it_slant_%E2%80%94, accessed 13 December 2012):

> Tell all the Truth but tell it slant —
> Success in Circuit lies
> Too bright for our infirm Delight
> The Truth's superb surprise
>
> As Lightning to the Children eased
> With explanation kind
> The Truth must dazzle gradually
> Or every man be blind —

11. A parallel can be drawn with *Kojuro and the Bears* when Kojuro realises that he and the bears that he hunted were all part of the wheel of life (see Chapter 3).

12. See Plato's *The Republic*. Full text available at: http://classics.mit.edu/Plato/republic.2.i.html, accessed 12 December 2012.
13. The partition of India was announced on 17 August 1947 as a boundary demarcation line (the Radcliffe Line) between India and Pakistan. The line was so named after Sir Cyril Radcliffe, who was chairman of the Boundary Commission. The 1947 partition resulted in extreme violence and one of the largest migrations in history. The first Indo-Pakistani war broke out in late 1947. For full details see Chester (2009).

Bibliography

Primary

Abdel-Fattah, Randa (2005) *Does My Head Look Big in This?* Sydney: Pan Macmillan Australia.

Aesop's Fables (1985) Illustrated by Michael Hague. London: Methuen.

Allen, Jonathan (1996) *Fowl Play*. London: Orion Children's Books.

Andersen, Hans Christian (1993) *The Emperor's New Clothes* (1837). Illustrated by David Mackintosh. Nundah, Qld: Jam Roll Press.

Belloc, Hilaire (2002) *Cautionary Tales for Children* (1907). Rediscovered and illustrated by Edward Gorey. New York: Harcourt.

Blabey, Aaron (2008) *Sunday Chutney*. Camberwell, Vic: Penguin/Viking.

Bosch, Pseudonymous (2008) *The Name of this Book is Secret*. Crows Nest, NSW: Allen & Unwin.

Breslin, Theresa (2010) *Prisoner of the Inquisition*. London: Random House.

Child, Lauren (2000) *I Will Not Ever Never Eat a Tomato*. London: Orchard Books.

—— (2002) *The Pesky Rat*. London: Orchard Books.

Christopher, John (1967) *The White Mountains*. London: Simon & Schuster.

Cohen, Miriam (2008) *Liar, Liar, Pants on Fire!* (1985). New York: Star Bright Books.

Collins, Suzanne (2008) *The Hunger Games*. London: Scholastic Children's Books.

—— (2009) *Catching Fire*. London: Scholastic Children's Books.

—— (2010) *Mockingjay*. London: Scholastic Children's Books.

Cormier, Robert (1974) *The Chocolate War*. London: Collins.

—— (1977) *I Am the Cheese*. London: Gollancz.

Cutbill, Andy (2006) *The Cow that Laid an Egg*. Illustrated by Russell Ayto. London: HarperCollins Children's Books.

Doctorow, Cory (2008) *Little Brother*. London: HarperVoyager.

Edwards, Ron (2000) 'Land of Contrasts'. In *Lies, Flies and Strange Big Fish: Tall Tales from the Bush*, chosen by Bill Scott, illustrated by Craig Smith. St Leonards, NSW: Allen & Unwin, pp. 26–30.

Fowles, John (1969) *The French Lieutenant's Woman*. London: Jonathan Cape.

French, Jackie (1997) *The Book of Unicorns*. Pymble, NSW: HarperCollins.

Gavin, Jamila (2008) *The Robber Baron's Daughter*. London: Egmont.

Gleeson, Libby and Greder, Armin (1992) *Uncle David*. Melbourne: Ashton Scholastic.

Gleitzman, Morris (2001) *Toad Heaven*. Camberwell, Vic: Puffin.

Golding, William (1954) *Lord of the Flies*. London: Faber and Faber.

Grahame, Kenneth (1908) *The Wind in the Willows*. London: Methuen.

Gregory, Philippa (2012) *The Changeling*. London: Simon & Schuster.

Handler, Daniel (2011) *Why We Broke Up*. Art by Maira Kalman. New York: Little, Brown.

Heffernan, John and McLean, Andrew (2001) *My Dog*. Gosford, NSW: Scholastic Australia.

Hrdlitschka, Shelley (2008) *Sister Wife*. Victoria, BC: Orca Book Publishers.

Hurston, Zora Neale (collector) (2005) *Lies and Other Tall Tales*, adapted and illustrated by Christopher Myers. New York: HarperCollins.

Larbalestier, Justine (2009) *Liar*. New York: Bloomsbury.

L'Engle, Madeleine (1962) *A Wrinkle in Time*. New York: Ariel Books.

Lowry, Lois (1989) *Number the Stars*. New York: Laurel Leaf.

Master, Irfan (2011) *A Beautiful Lie*. London: Bloomsbury.

McCaughrean, Geraldine (1988) *A Pack of Lies*. Oxford University Press.

Morimoto, Junko (1986) *Kojuro and the Bears*. Adapted by Helen Smith. Sydney: Collins.

Morrison, Yvonne and McKenzie, Heath (2010) *The Cocky who Cried Dingo*. Praharn, Vic: Little Hare Books.

Naidoo, Beverley (2000) *The Other Side of Truth*. London: Penguin.

—— (2004) *Web of Lies*. London: Penguin.

Oliver, Narelle (2005) *Dancing the Boom Cha Cha Boogie*. Malvern, SA: Omnibus Books.

Orwell, George (1949) *Nineteen Eighty-Four*. London: Secker & Warburg.

—— (1987) *Animal Farm: A Fairy Story* (1945). London: Penguin.

Pascoe, Bruce (2012) *Fog a Dox*. Broome, WA: Magabala Books.

Pearson, Mary E. (2009) *The Adoration of Jenna Fox*. Crows Nest, NSW: Allen & Unwin.

Potter, Beatrix (1902) *The Tale of Peter Rabbit*. London: Frederick Warne.

Rees, Celia (2000) *Witch Child*. London: Bloomsbury Children's Publishing.

Robertson, Fiona (2009) *Wanted: The Perfect Pet*. Camberwell, Vic: Penguin.

Satrapi, Marjane (2003) *Persepolis: The Story of a Childhood*. New York: Pantheon.

—— (2004) *Persepolis 2: The Story of a Return*. New York: Pantheon.

Scieszka, Jon and Smith, Lane (1989) *The True Story of the 3 Little Pigs!* London: Penguin.

—— (2001) *Baloney (Henry P.)*. New York: Puffin Books.

Selznick, Brian (2007) *The Invention of Hugo Cabret*. New York: Scholastic Press.

Shakespeare, William (1982) *Hamlet*. Arden Shakespeare, Second Series, ed. Harold Jenkins. London: Methuen.

—— (2003) *Shakespeare's A Midsummer Night's Dream*. Illustrated by Arthur Rackham. New York: Dover.

Simmons, Kristen (2012) *Article 5*. Milsons Point, NSW: Pier 9.

Somerville, Margaret (2006) *The Ethical Imagination: Journeys of the Human Spirit*. Melbourne University Press.

Sophocles (2007) *Dramas of Sophocles*, trans. Sir George Young. Rockville, MD: Wildside Press.

Speare, Elizabeth George (1958) *The Witch of Blackbird Pond*. Boston: Houghton Mifflin.

Stead, Rebecca (2009) *When You Reach Me*. Melbourne: Text Publishing. First published (2009) New York: Yearling (Random House).

Tamaki, Mariko and Tamaki, Jillian (2008) *Skim*. London: Walker Books.

Ure, Jean (1992) *Come Lucky April*. London: Methuen.

Vaughan, Marcia K. (1984) *Wombat Stew*. Illustrated by Pamela Lofts. Sydney: Scholastic Australia.

White, E. B. (1952) *Charlotte's Web*. Harmondsworth: Penguin.

Whitney, Daisy (2010) *The Mockingbirds*. New York: Little, Brown.

Wild, Margaret (2000) *Fox*. Illustrated by Ron Brooks. St Leonards, NSW: Allen & Unwin.
Wilson, Jacqueline (2002) *Secrets*. London: Corgi Yearling.
Winter, Jeanette (2009) *Nasreen's Secret School: A True Story from Afghanistan*. New York: Beach Lane Books.
Wiseman, Eva (2012) *The Last Song*. Toronto: Tundra Books.

Filmography

Animal Farm (1954) Dir. John Halas and Joy Batchelor. Halas and Batchelor Cartoon Films.
Animal Farm (1999) Dir. John Stephenson. Animal Farm Productions Ltd.
Big Fish (2003) Dir. Tim Burton. Columbia Pictures.
Hugo (2011) Dir. Martin Scorcese. Paramount Pictures.
Life is Beautiful (1997) Dir. Roberto Benigni. Cecchi Gori Group Tiger Cinematografica.
Lilo & Stitch (2002) Dir. Dean DeBlois and Chris Sanders. Disney.
Persepolis (2007) Written and Dir. Marjane Satrapi and Vincent Paronnaud.

Secondary

Agamben, Giorgio (1993) *The Coming Community*, trans. Michael Hardt. Minneapolis: University of Minnesota Press.
Allan, Cherie (2012) *Playing with Picturebooks: Postmodernism and the Postmodernesque*. Basingstoke and New York: Palgrave Macmillan.
Althusser, Louis (1971) Ideology and Ideological State Apparatuses. In *Lenin and Philosophy and Other Essays*, trans. Ben Brewster. London: New Left Books, pp. 123–73.
Alvarez, Alex (2010) *Genocidal Crimes*. New York: Routledge.
Austin, J. L. (1999) Truth. In Simon Blackburn and Keith Simmons (eds) *Truth*. Oxford University Press, pp. 149–61.
Awan, Muhammad Safeer (2007) From Witch-hunts and Communist-hunts to Terrorist-hunts: Placing Arthur Miller's *The Crucible* in the Post-September 11 Power Politics. *Pakistan Journal of American Studies* 25(1/2), pp. 1–22.
Baker, Steve (2003) Sloughing the Human. In C. Wolfe (ed.) *Zoontologies: The Question of the Animal*. Minneapolis: University of Minnesota Press, pp. 147–64.
Barnes, J. A. (1994) *A Pack of Lies: Towards a Sociology of Lying*. Cambridge University Press.
Barthes, Roland (1957) *Mythologies*. London: Jonathan Cape.
Bearman, Josh (2009) *Books, Movies, Magic: The Rediscovered Genius of the Automaton*, http://therumpus.net/2009/09/books-movies-magic-the-rediscovered-genius-of-the-automaton/, accessed 5 January 2012.
Beckett, Samuel (1958) *Endgame and Act without Words*. New York: Grove Press.
Benjamin, Walter (1968) The Work of Art in the Age of Mechanical Reproduction. In Hannah Arendt (ed.) *Illuminations*. New York: Schocken Books, pp. 217–52.
Blackburn, Simon and Simmons, Keith (eds) (1999) *Truth*. Oxford University Press.
Bok, Sissela (1989) *Secrets: On the Ethics of Concealment and Revelation*. New York: Vintage Books.

—— (1999) *Lying: Moral Choice in Public and Private Life*, 2nd edn. New York: Vintage Books.

Bradbury, Malcolm (1987) Introduction. *Animal Farm: A Fairy Story by George Orwell*. London: Penguin, pp. v–xvi.

Bradford, Clare (2003) 'Oh How Different!': Regimes of Knowledge in Aboriginal Texts for Children. *The Lion and the Unicorn* 27(2), pp. 199–217.

Bradford, Clare and Huang, Hui-Ling (2007) Exclusion and Inclusion: Multiculturalism in Contemporary Taiwanese and Australian Picturebooks. *Bookbird* 45(3), pp. 5–13.

Bradford, Clare, Mallan, Kerry, Stephens, John and McCallum, Robyn (2008) *New World Orders in Contemporary Children's Literature: Utopian Transformations*. Basingstoke and New York: Palgrave Macmillan.

Butler, Judith (1997) *Excitable Speech: A Politics of the Performative*. New York: Routledge.

Cadden, Mike (2000) The Irony of Narration in the Young Adult Novel. *Children's Literature Association Quarterly* 25(3), pp. 146–54.

Carroll, John (2002) *Terror: A Meditation on the Meaning of September 11*. Melbourne: Scribe Publications.

Chester, Lucy P. (2009) *Borders and Conflict in South Asia: The Radcliffe Boundary Commission and the Partition of Punjab*. Manchester University Press.

Clark, Kenneth (1956) *The Nude: A Study of Ideal Art*. Harmondsworth: Penguin.

Coetzee, J. M. et al. (1999) *The Lives of Animals*, ed. Amy Gutmann. Princeton University Press.

Conrad, Joseph (1946) The Fine Art (1905). In *The Mirror of the Sea: Memories and Impressions*. Dent Collected Edition. London: Dent, pp. 23–35.

Cover, Rob (2003) The Naked Subject: Nudity, Context and Sexualisation in Contemporary Culture. *Body & Society* 9(53), pp. 53–72.

Culler, Jonathan (2007) *The Literary in Theory*. Stanford University Press.

Darwin, Charles (1936) *The Descent of Man*. London: Watts.

Deleuze, Gilles and Guattari, Félix (1988) *A Thousand Plateaus: Capitalism and Schizophrenia*, trans. Brian Massumi. Minneapolis: University of Minnesota Press.

Delville, Michel (1998) *The American Prose Poem: Poetic Form and Boundaries of Genre*. Gainesville: University Press of Florida.

Derrida, Jacques (1975) The Purveyor of Truth. *Yale French Studies* 52, pp. 31–113.

—— (2003) And Say the Animal Responded? In C. Wolfe (ed.) *Zoontologies: The Question of the Animal*. Minneapolis: University of Minnesota Press, pp. 121–46.

—— (2008a) *The Animal that Therefore I Am*, ed. Marie-Louise Mallet, trans. David Wills. New York: Fordham University Press.

—— (2008b) *Literature in Secret* (1995), trans. David Wills. University of Chicago Press.

—— (2009) *The Beast and the Sovereign: The Seminars of Jacques Derrida*, vol. 1, trans. Geoffrey Bennington. University of Chicago Press.

Doane, Mary Ann (1991) *Femmes Fatales: Feminism, Film Theory, Psychoanalysis*. New York: Routledge.

Douglas, K. (2006) Cyber-Commemoration: Life Writing, Trauma and Memorialisation. Life Writing Symposium, 13–15 June. Flinders University. Archived at Flinders University: dspace.flinders.edu.au.

Dudek, Debra (2006) Of Murmels and Snigs: Detention-centre Narratives in Australian Literature for Children and Young Adults. *Overland* 185, pp. 38–42 [online], accessed 20 April 2013.

—— (2011) Disturbing Thoughts: Representations of Compassion in Two Picture Books Entitled *The Island. Jeunesse: Young People, Texts, Cultures* 3(2), pp. 11–29.

Eagleton, Terry (1983) *Literary Theory: An Introduction*. Minneapolis: University of Minnesota Press.

Edelman, David B. and Seth, Anil K. (2009) Animal Consciousness: A Synthetic Approach. *Trends in Neuroscience* 32(9), pp. 476–84.

Egoff, Sheila A. (1981) *Thursday's Child: Trends and Patterns in Contemporary Children's Literature*. Chicago: American Library Association.

El Guindi, Fadwa (1999) *Veil: Modesty, Privacy and Resistance*. Oxford: Berg.

Erickson, Bonnie H. (1981) Secret Societies and Social Structure. *Social Forces* 60(1), pp. 188–210.

Falzon, Christopher (1998) *Foucault and Social Dialogue*. London: Routledge.

Faulkner, Christopher (2011) Musical Automata, La Règle du jeu, and the Cinema. *South Central Review* 28(3), pp. 6–25.

Fish, Stanley (1980) *Is There a Text in this Class? The Authority of Interpretive Communities*. Cambridge, MA: Harvard University Press.

Fleming, Chris (2004) *René Girard: Violence and Mimesis*. Cambridge: Polity Press.

Foucault, Michel (1975) *Discipline and Punish: The Birth of the Prison*, trans. A. M. Sheridan Smith. Harmondsworth: Penguin.

—— (1978) *The History of Sexuality*, vol. 1, trans. R. Hurley. Harmondsworth: Penguin.

—— (1980) *Power/Knowledge: Selected Interviews and Other Writings, 1972–77*, ed. and trans. C. Gordon. New York: Pantheon Press.

—— (1981) Questions of Method: An Interview with Michel Foucault, trans. C. Gordon. *Ideology and Consciousness* 7, pp. 51–62.

—— (1982) Sexuality and Solitude. In D. Rieff (ed.) *Humanities in Review*, vol. 1. Cambridge University Press, pp. 3–21.

—— (1983) The Subject and Power, Afterword. In Hubert Dreyfus and Paul Rabinow, *Michel Foucault: Beyond Structuralism and Hermeneutics*, 2nd edn. University of Chicago Press.

—— (1984) Nietzsche, Genealogy, History, trans. D. Bouchard and S. Simon. In Paul Rabinow (ed.) *The Foucault Reader*. New York: Pantheon.

—— (1988) The Ethic of Care for the Self as a Practice of Freedom. In J. Bernauer and D. Rasmussen (eds) *The Final Foucault*, trans. J. D. Gauthier. Cambridge, MA: MIT Press, pp. 1–20.

—— (1996) Truth and Power. In Lawrence Cahoone (ed.) *From Modernism to Postmodernism: An Anthology*. Malden, MA: Blackwell, pp. 379–81.

—— (1997) What is Enlightenment? In Foucault, *Ethics: Subjectivity and Truth: The Essential Works of Michel Foucault 1954–1984*, vol. 1, ed. P. Rabinow, trans. R. Hurley and others. Harmondsworth: Penguin, pp. 303–19.

—— (2000) Truth and Power (1977). In Foucault, *Power*, ed. J. D. Faubion, trans. R. Hurley. New York: New Press, pp. 111–33.

—— (2001) *Fearless Speech*, ed. Joseph Pearson. Los Angeles: Semiotext(e).

Gadzheva, Maya (2008) Privacy in the Age of Transparency: The New Vulnerability of the Individual. *Social Science Computer Review* 26(1), pp. 60–74.

Gill, Jo (2006) Introduction. In Gill (ed.) *Modern Confessional Writing: New Critical Essays*. London: Routledge, pp. 1–10.

Gilmore, Leigh (1994) *Autobiographics: A Feminist Theory of Women's Self-Representation*. Ithaca and London: Cornell University Press.

Girard, René (1965) *Deceit, Desire, and the Novel*, trans. Yvonne Freccero. Baltimore: Johns Hopkins University Press.

—— (1977) *Violence and the Sacred*, trans. Patrick Gregory. Baltimore: Johns Hopkins University Press.

—— (1978) *Things Hidden Since the Foundation of the World*, with Jean-Michel Oughourlian and Guy Lefort, trans. Stephen Bann and Michael Metteer. Stanford University Press.

—— (1986) *The Scapegoat*, trans. Yvonne Freccero. Baltimore: Johns Hopkins University Press.

Groensteen, Thierry (2007) *The System of Comics*. Jackson: University of Mississippi Press.

Grosz, Elizabeth (1995) *Space, Time, and Perversion*. St Leonards, NSW: Allen & Unwin.

Halberstam, Judith (2005) *In a Queer Place and Time: Transgender Bodies, Subcultural Lives*. New York University Press.

Haraway, Donna J. (2008) *When Species Meet*. Minneapolis: University of Minnesota Press.

Harris, Sam (2010) *The Moral Landscape: How Science Can Determine Human Values*. London: Bantam Press.

Harvey, David (1990) *The Condition of Postmodernity*. Oxford: Blackwell.

Heise, Ursula K. (2003) From Extinction to Electronics: Dead Frogs, Live Dinosaurs, and Electric Sheep. In C. Wolfe (ed.) *Zoontologies: The Question of the Animal*. Minneapolis: University of Minnesota Press, pp. 59–82.

Hirsch, E. D. Jr (1967) *Validity and Interpretation*. New Haven: Yale University Press.

—— (1984) Meaning and Significance Reinterpreted. *Critical Inquiry* 11(2), pp. 202–25.

Jameson, Fredric (1971) *Marxism and Form*. Princeton University Press.

Jay, Martin (2010) *The Virtues of Mendacity: On Lying and Politics*. Charlottesville: University of Virginia Press.

Jenkins, Elwyn (2003) Nudity, Clothing and Cultural Identity in Some South African Children's Books. *English in Africa* 30(1), pp. 87–101.

Jolley, Kelly Dean (ed.) (2010) *Wittgenstein: Key Concepts*. Durham: Acumen Publishing.

Jones, Dudley (1999) Only Make-Believe? Lies, Fictions, and Metafictions in Geraldine McCaughrean's *A Pack of Lies* and Philip Pullman's *Clockwork*. *The Lion and the Unicorn* 23(1), pp. 86–96.

Kant, Immanuel (1949) On a Supposed Right to Lie from Altruistic Motives (1797). In *Critique of Practical Reason and Other Writings in Moral Philosophy*, ed. and trans. Lewis White Beck. University of Chicago Press, pp. 346–50.

Kearney, Richard (1995) Myths and Scapegoats: The Case of René Girard. *Theory, Culture & Society* 12, pp. 1–14.

Kermode, Frank (1979) *The Genesis of Secrecy: On the Interpretation of Narrative*. Cambridge, MA: Harvard University Press.

—— (1980) Secrets and Narrative Sequence. *Critical Inquiry* 7(1), pp. 83–101.

Krajewski, Bruce (1992) *Traveling with Hermes: Hermeneutics and Rhetoric*. Amherst: University of Massachusetts Press.

Lacan, Jacques (1977) *Écrits: A Selection*, trans. Alan Sheridan. New York: Routledge.

Lamarque, Peter and Olsen, Stein Haugom (1994) *Truth, Fiction and Literature*. Oxford University Press.

Lampert, Jo (2012) Sh-h-h-h: Representations of Perpetrators of Sexual Child Abuse in Children's Picturebooks. *Sex Education* 12(2), pp. 177–85.

Latham, Don (2002) Childhood Under Siege: Lois Lowry's *Number the Stars* and *The Giver*. *The Lion and the Unicorn* 26(1), pp. 1–15.

Leab, Daniel J. (2007) *Orwell Subverted: The CIA and the Filming of Animal Farm*. University Park: Pennsylvania State University Press.

Maestripieri, Dario (2007) *Machiavellian Intelligence: How Rhesus Macaques and Humans Have Conquered the World*. University of Chicago Press.

Mallan, Kerry (2002) Picturing the Male: Representations of Masculinity in Picture Books. In John Stephens (ed.) *Ways of Being Male: Representing Masculinities in Children's Literature and Film*. London: Routledge, pp. 15–37.

Marx, Gary T. and Muschert, Glenn W. (2009) Simmel on Secrecy: A Legacy and Inheritance for the Sociology of Information. In Cécile Rol and Christian Papilloud (eds) *Soziologie als Möglichkeit: 100 Jahre Georg Simmels Untersuchungen über die Formen der Vergesellschaftung* [The Possibility of Sociology: 100 Years of Georg Simmel's Investigations into the Forms of Social Organization]. Wiesbaden, Germany: VS Verlag für Sozialwissenschaften, pp. 217–33

McGillis, Roderick (1996) *The Nimble Reader: Literary Theory and Children's Literature*. New York: Twayne.

—— (2008) Fantasy as Epanalepsis: 'An Anticipation of Retrospection'. *Papers: Explorations into Children's Literature* 18(2), pp. 7–14.

McMahon-Coleman, Kimberley and Weaver, Roslyn (2012) *Werewolves and Other Shapeshifters in Popular Culture*. Jefferson: McFarland.

Metcalf, Eva-Maria (1990) Tall Tale and Spectacle in Pippi Longstocking. *Children's Literature Association Quarterly* 15(3), pp. 130–5.

Metcalfe, Daniel J. (2009) Editorial: The Nature of Government Secrecy. *Government Information Quarterly* 26, pp. 305–10.

Mitchell, Robert W. and Thompson, Nicholas S. (eds) (1986) *Deception: Perspectives on Human and Nonhuman Deceit*. Albany: State University of New York Press.

Modood, Tariq (2008) Multiculturalism after 7/7: A Scapegoat or a Hope for the Future? *RUSI Journal* 153(2), pp. 14–17.

Muller, Vivienne (2012) Virtually Real: Suzanne Collins's The Hunger Games Trilogy. *International Research in Children's Literature* 5(1), pp. 51–63.

Neal, Lynda (1992) *The Female Nude: Art, Obscenity and Sexuality*. London: Routledge.

Nelson, Claudia (2006) Writing the Reader: The Literary Child in and beyond the Book. *Children's Literature Association Quarterly* 31(3), pp. 222–36.

Nietzsche, Friedrich (1954) *The Portable Nietzsche*, trans. and ed. Walter Kaufmann. New York: Viking Press.

Noddings, Nel (1984) *Caring: A Feminine Approach to Ethics and Moral Education*. Berkeley: University of California Press.

Nodelman, Perry (2002) Making Boys Appear: The Masculinity of Children's Fiction. In John Stephens (ed.) *Ways of Being Male: Representing Masculinities in Children's Literature and Film*. London: Routledge, pp. 1–14.

Nyberg, David (1993) *The Varnished Truth: Truth Telling and Deceiving in Ordinary Life*. University of Chicago Press.

O'Farrell, Clare (2005) *Michel Foucault*. London: Sage.

Pagès, Alain (ed.) (1996) *Émile Zola: The Dreyfus Affair: J'accuse and Other Writings*, trans. Eleanor Levieux. New Haven: Yale University Press.

Pók, Attila (1999) Atonement and Sacrifice: Scapegoats in Modern Eastern and Central Europe. *East European Quarterly* 32(4), pp. 531–48.

Probyn, Elspeth (1996) *Outside Belongings*. New York: Routledge.

Propp, Vladimir (2009) *On the Comic and Laughter*, ed. and trans. Jean-Patrick Debbèche and Paul Perron. University of Toronto Press.

Rashkin, Esther (2008) *Unspeakable Secrets and the Psychoanalysis of Culture*. Albany: State University of New York.

Reynolds, Kimberley (2007) *Radical Children's Literature: Future Visions and Aesthetic Transformations in Juvenile Fiction*. Basingstoke and New York: Palgrave Macmillan.

Ricoeur, Paul (1981) Narrative Time. In W. J. T. Mitchell (ed.) *On Narrative*. University of Chicago Press, pp. 165–86.

—— (1985) *Time and Narrative*, vol. 2, trans. K. McLaughlin and D. Pellauer. University of Chicago Press.

Roberts, J. M. (1974) *The Mythology of the Secret Societies*. Frogmore, St Albans: Paladin.

Sanders, Joe Sutliff (2009) The Critical Reader in Children's Metafiction. *The Lion and the Unicorn* 33(3), pp. 349–61.

Sarland, Charles (1999) The Impossibility of Innocence: Ideology, Politics, and Children's Literature. In Peter Hunt (ed.) *Understanding Children's Literature*. London: Routledge, pp. 39–55.

Scholes, Robert (1981) Language, Narrative, and Anti-Narrative. In W. J. T. Mitchell (ed.) *On Narrative*. University of Chicago Press, pp. 200–8.

Schumacher, Carol (2000) *Chapter Zero: Fundamental Notions of Abstract Mathematics*. Boston: Addison-Wesley.

Scott, Carole (1994) Clothed in Nature or Nature Clothed: Dress as Metaphor in the Illustrations of Beatrix Potter and C. M. Barker. *Children's Literature* 22, pp. 70–89.

Selznick, Brian (2011) *The Hugo Movie Companion*. New York: Scholastic Press.

Sim, Stuart (2004) *Fundamentalist World: The New Dark Age of Dogma*. Cambridge: Icon Books.

Simmel, Georg (1906) The Sociology of Secrecy and of Secret Societies. *American Journal of Sociology* 11, pp. 441–98.

—— (1950) *The Sociology of Georg Simmel*, ed. Kurt H. Wolff. New York: Free Press.

Smith, David Livingstone (2004) *Why We Lie: The Evolutionary Roots of Deception and the Unconscious Mind*. New York: St Martin's Press.

Smuts, Barbara (1999) Reflections. In J. M. Coetzee et al., *The Lives of Animals*, ed. Amy Gutmann. Princeton University Press, pp. 107–20.

Smyth, John Vignaux (2002) *The Habit of Lying: Sacrificial Studies in Literature, Philosophy, and Fashion Theory*. Durham, NC: Duke University Press.

Somerville, Margaret (2006) *The Ethical Imagination: Journeys of the Human Spirit*. Melbourne University Press.

Stephens, John (1992) *Language and Ideology in Children's Fiction*. Harlow: Longman.

Stewart, Susan Louise (2011) 'Be Afraid or Fried': Cults and Young Adult Apocalyptic Narratives. *Children's Literature Association Quarterly* 36(3), pp. 318–35.

Strawson, P. F. (1999) Truth. In Simon Blackburn and Keith Simmons (eds) *Truth*. Oxford University Press, pp. 162–82.

Tailby, Rebecca (2001) Organised Crime and People Smuggling/Human Trafficking to Australia. *Trends and Issues in Crime and Criminal Justice* 208, pp. 1–6.

'Tunisia: "Persepolis" Trial a Setback for Free Expression', www.iewy.com/40569-tunisia-persepolis-trial-a-setback-for-free-expression.html, accessed 25 January 2012.

United Nations (2000) Convention against Transnational Organised Crime, A/55/383, Incorporating the Protocol Against the Smuggling of Migrants by Land, Sea and Air, and the Protocol to Prevent, Suppress and Punish Trafficking in Persons, Especially Women and Children.

Vickroy, Laurie (2002) *Trauma and Survival in Contemporary Fiction*. Charlottesville and London: University of Virginia Press.

Waugh, Patricia (1984) *Metafiction: The Theory and Practice of Self-Conscious Fiction*. London: Routledge.

Weckham, George (1970) Primitive Secret Societies as Religious Organisations. *Numen* 17(2), pp. 83–94.

Weems, Mason L. (1833) *The Life of George Washington; with Curious Anecdotes, Equally Honourable to Himself, and Exemplary to his Young Countrymen*. Philadelphia: Joseph Allen.

Whitlock, Gillian (2007) *Soft Weapons: Autobiography in Transit*. University of Chicago Press.

Wolcott, James (2011) That's Political Entertainment! *Vanity Fair*, February, www.vanityfair.com/politics/features/2011/02/wolcott-201102, accessed 16 March 2012.

Wolfe, Cary (ed.) (2003) *Zoontologies: The Question of the Animal*. Minneapolis: University of Minnesota Press.

Wood, D. (ed.) (1991) *On Paul Ricoeur: Narrative and Interpretation*. London: Routledge.

Yahav, Rivka and Sharlin, Shlomo A. (2007) Blame and Family Conflict: Symptomatic Children as Scapegoats. *Child and Family Social Work* 7, pp. 91–8.

Zakayo, Ole Mapelu (2011) Rendition and Extradition in Kenya. *Evolution Africa*, http://evolutionafrica.com/rendition-and-extradition-in-kenya/, accessed 26 February 2012.

Žižek, Slavoj (2009) *Violence*. London: Profile Books.

Index

Printed and bound by
CPI Group (UK) Ltd, Croydon, CR0 4YY